"THRILLING."
Newark Star-Ledger

"Springs energetically from the gate,
creating tension and pace . . .
GRIPPANDO DEMONSTRATES EXPERTISE
in police and legal procedures."
Publishers Weekly

"PLOT TWISTS KEEP THE PAGES TURNING."
Des Moines Register

"Good characters and a twist . . .
A GREAT BEACH WEEKEND BOOK."
Toronto Globe and Mail

Acclaim for
UNDER COVER OF DARKNESS

"Another riveting tale of
suspense from Grippando."
Library Journal

"An intriguing mystery . . . a shocking and utterly
unpredictable ending . . . engrossing on several
levels . . . the perfect beach read."
January Magazine

"Grippando writes well, and has created an
interesting character in Gus Wheatley."
Cleveland Plain Dealer

"A smart, straightforward, and—yes, the
pun is unavoidable—gripping thriller."
Booklist

"Better than any John Grisham novel . . . well
written and gripping . . . A must for summer
reading with twists and turns galore."
Barnes & Noble *Guide to New Fiction*

"A real gripper from the eerie opening to the
catastrophic denouement."
BookPage.com

"I've always liked Grippando's intrigues . . .
There's humor bubbling along with the suspense."
Poisoned Pen

FOUND MONEY

"Readers will want to applaud . . .
Number this intelligent, cleverly
constructed thriller among the best."
Booklist

"Thrilling . . . filled with terrifying images of
money's dark side. Grippando has done it again."
Library Journal

"A wild ride . . . A cautionary tale of greed, family
secrets and the dangers of getting what you wish
for . . . The final revelation is a kicker."
Publishers Weekly

THE ABDUCTION

"Truly dirty politics and crime . . . Hits a nerve . . .
As timely as today's headlines."
San Francisco Chronicle

"Breathless."
Philadelphia Inquirer

THE INFORMANT

"Grippando writes with the authenticity of an insider . . . A thoroughly convincing edge-of-your-seat thriller."
John Douglas, former chief of the FBI's Investigative Support Unit and *New York Times* bestselling author of *Mind Hunter: Inside the FBI's Elite Serial Crime Unit*

"Spectacular effects . . . entertaining . . . Grippando has done his homework on FBI forensics, criminal profiling and the internal protocol for backstabbing . . . Plenty of blood is spilled on the rug."
New York Times Book Review

THE PARDON

"A gritty mystery that . . . rings true to the emotional realities of contemporary life. Readers will turn the pages of *The Pardon* faster than a bailiff can swear in a witness."
People

"A gripping mélange of courtroom drama and psychotic manipulation . . . possesses gritty veracity, genuine characters that elicit sympathy, and superb plotting and pacing . . . A bona fide blockbuster."
Boston Herald

JAMES GRIPPANDO

UNDER COVER OF DARKNESS

AVON BOOKS

An Imprint of HarperCollinsPublishers

"My Mommy Comes Back" by Hap Palmer and Martha Cheney, copyright HapPal Music, Box 323, Topanga, CA

"Fire," Music and lyrics by Arthur Brown and Vincent Crane

This is a work of fiction. Names, characters, places, and incidents are products of the author's imagination or are used fictitiously and are not to be construed as real. Any resemblance to actual events, locales, organizations, or persons, living or dead, is entirely coincidental.

AVON BOOKS
An Imprint of HarperCollins*Publishers*
10 East 53rd Street
New York, New York 10022-5299

Copyright © 2000 by James Grippando
ISBN: 0-06-109747-0
www.avonbooks.com

First Avon Books paperback printing: May 2001
First HarperCollins hardcover printing: July 2000

Avon Trademark Reg. U.S. Pat. Off. and in Other Countries, Marca Registrada, Hecho en U.S.A.
HarperCollins® is a trademark of HarperCollins Publishers Inc.

Printed in the U.S.A.

10 9 8 7 6 5 4 3 2 1

This one's for Tiffany. *Surprise!*

UNDER COVER
OF DARKNESS

Prologue

The noose was prepared with exceptional care. Too large a knot, poorly placed, could gouge chunks of flesh from the face and neck. Too much line with a drop too far could mean decapitation.

A rope around the neck left little room for error.

He tied the loop in a simple slip knot, rather than the classic noose. The classic version was for swift executions, where the long knot of coiled rope would snap against the back of the head, knocking the victim unconscious like a blow from a blackjack. The cervical vertebrae would crack. Bone fragments would crush the spinal cord, bringing on paralysis and, in theory, a painless death. In theory. For centuries witnesses have said it was never truly painless. They've told of grimacing faces, bodies thrashing violently at the end of the rope, lungs wheezing in futile gasps for air. It was merely a reflex, some contended, like the proverbial headless chicken scampering around the barnyard. Others insisted the pain was real, even in a "clean hanging."

This afternoon the old debate was irrelevant. This wasn't supposed to be a clean one. That wasn't his plan.

The yellow synthetic rope was eight feet long and three-quarters of an inch thick. He'd stolen it from a construction site about a mile from his house. Cutting it was almost like sawing through steel cable. Rope this strong could pull five or six water skiers at a time or yank tree stumps from the ground, roots and all.

It could surely suspend the weight of a fifteen-year-old boy.

He climbed the stepladder with the rope in hand, nearly tripping on the frayed cuff of his pants leg. The baggy jeans and cotton turtleneck sweatshirt were a daily uniform. He was by far the smartest in his sophomore class, yet his grades were average, and he looked like almost every other boy at school. Thin and gangly. Feet so big he was shaped like an L. Scattered pimples marked the onset of puberty. A few precious facial hairs formed a semblance of a mustache.

He peered out the foggy garage window. A thermometer mounted on the window frame said forty-nine degrees—warm for the dead of winter, but somehow the garage seemed colder than the outdoors. His gaze drifted up toward the rafters, fixing on a steel pulley bolted to the pine. Gently, he tossed up the rope and looped it around the pulley. Two four-foot lengths dangled from above, draped like pigtails over his simple apparatus. The noose was at one end. The other end was frayed and unknotted. He gave it a tug. The pulley creaked, and the noose rose slowly. All was in working order.

He drew a deep breath and placed the noose around his neck.

The surroundings immediately assaulted his senses; he was suddenly aware of everything around him, as if the rope were talismanic. The rain tapped rhythmically on the old roof and garage door. A fluorescent light hummed near the workbench along the wall. Oil stains from his father's junky old Buick dotted the cracked cement floor. The stepladder had raised him less than two feet above the floor, but it seemed much higher. He was reminded of the bungee jumpers he'd seen on one of those thrill-seeker shows on television, their ankles tethered by a long elastic band, their eyes burning with excitement as they dove off some bridge and into the canyon.

Let 'em try this, he thought.

He unfurled the cotton turtleneck and flattened the collar all the way up to his chin. The protective fabric had to be tucked beneath the noose all the way around, so that no part of the rope touched the soft skin of his neck. Bruises were inevitable, but he had learned to prevent rope burns.

He cinched up the slip knot, drawing it tightly around his neck. His feet instantly felt lighter, though they were still planted firmly on the stepladder. With each swallow the rope pressed against the Adam's apple. He licked his lips and grasped the unknotted end of the rope with both hands. Slowly, he pulled.

The pulley creaked. The slack disappeared. The noose gripped his neck and tilted his head back. His heels left the platform. He was standing on his tiptoes.

Another pull.

He heard himself groan. His vision blurred. His groaning turned to wheezing. He pulled again, and again, hand over fist. His toes instinctively reached for the floor, but safety was out of reach. He was in midair, hanging by the neck.

We have liftoff!

His grip tightened. His legs were kicking. The limbs were at war: The feet wanted back to earth, but the hands wouldn't release the rope.

The noose was working perfectly. Arterial flow continued in the head and neck, bringing more blood from the heart. The veins, however, were completely compressed, leaving the blood no escape, building pressure on the brain. His head pounded with congestion, like the worst sinus headache imaginable. The eyes bulged. His face flushed red. He could taste blood in his mouth as small bleeding sites erupted in the moist, soft mucosa of the lips and mouth.

Then he felt it—the bizarre physiological result of muscle sphincters that spasm and relax uncontrollably. It was one of three known ways to achieve erection, even climax. Sleep. Sex. And hangings.

His eyes closed. All went black. The death grip was broken. The pulley squealed as the loosened rope raced around its wheel. His limp body plummeted to the floor, toppling the ladder.

Instinctively, he rose to his knees and untied the noose. He coughed twice, gasping for air. His chest swelled and his skinny shoulders heaved involuntarily. Gradually, the blackness improved to fuzzy vision. He regained his focus.

"Hey! What the hell is goin' on out there?"

It was his father yelling from inside the house. He always yelled. It seemed like the last time they'd actually had a normal conversation in the same room together was sometime before his mother died, before her teenage son found her limp body twirling from the rafters in the attic of their old house.

"Nothing." His voice squeaked; it wasn't from puberty.

"Break something and you'll get your ass beat!"

His old man was spoiling the revelry, so he blocked him out of his mind as he rose to a hunched-over position with his hands on his knees, catching his breath. The feeling was better than any runner's high, any rush of endorphins. Had he been with a buddy he would have skinned a high-five. But his friends would never have understood. Better to let them believe the bruises on his neck really were hickeys. For the time being, this was an experience unto himself.

He gathered up the rope and untied the knot. He had used it before. He would use it again. Practice makes perfect, his mother used to say. He was definitely approaching perfection. Someday, he would be the one to show others the way. Because *he* had been there. Many times.

And he knew the way back.

Part One

FOURTEEN YEARS LATER

One

The rain was a sign of good luck and happiness.

Andrea Henning had heard that old wives' tale at least thirty times today. She wondered if Mr. Gallup had ever conducted a poll to find out if couples who married on sunny days actually had higher divorce rates than those who waded through puddles on their way to the altar. Not that it really mattered. Rain on this wedding had been a virtual certainty. It was, after all, late winter in Seattle.

Andie—no one called her "Andrea"—wasn't bothered by the weather or any of the things a bride typically worried about. Maybe it was her training as an FBI agent, or maybe it was her innate common sense. Whenever something couldn't be controlled, Andie just dealt with it, and it usually worked out. Her crash diet had been a disaster, but the dress still fit perfectly. The best man was an idiot, yet he'd somehow remembered the marriage license. And the old candlelit church had never looked better. Bouquets of white roses with lace and pink ribbons adorned each pew. A long white runner stretched down the center aisle from the vestibule to the altar. The crowd was spread evenly, left side and right, soothed by a gentle harp as the last of four bridesmaids walked down the aisle. Rain or not, it was the wedding her mother had always told her to dream of.

Andie moved into the open double doorway in the rear

of the church. The wedding consultant helped with the satin train behind her.

In front, the silver-haired minister waited at the altar, flanked on his right by bridesmaids dressed in red velvet dresses. To his left stood three young groomsmen and Andie's handsome husband-to-be. Rick looked nervous, even from a distance. His steely blue eyes glistened. They were almost glazed—probably from all the drinking his friends had inflicted on him last night. The rented tuxedo seemed a little tight for his chest and shoulders, but maybe he was just taking deep breaths. He would have been far more at ease in blue jeans. So would have Andie.

The sound of the harp faded away. The guests fell silent. All heads swiveled toward the back of the church.

Andie took her father's arm. Though a half foot shorter than her, he was a pillar of strength—normally. At the moment she could feel his hands trembling.

"Ready?" he asked.

She didn't reply. The time had come.

The pipe organ blared. Andie cringed. She had explicitly instructed the organist *not* to play the traditional "Here Comes the Bride." Her meddlesome mother had struck again.

Together, Andie and her father started down the aisle.

A camera flashed in her face. Then another. It was like staring into a strobe light. At this rate, she'd not only be filing a married couple's tax return this year, but she'd also have to mark yes in that little box that asks "Are you blind?" Andie focused on the burning candles on the altar as she continued down the aisle.

Friends and relatives beamed as she passed. They made her feel beautiful, though all of her life she'd been told she was beautiful. She resembled neither of her adoptive parents, of course. She had the prominent cheekbones and raven black hair of the American Indian mother she never knew. The deep green eyes were presumably from an Anglo father. The result was striking, an exotic ancestral mix.

Halfway down the aisle, Andie slowed the pace. Her nervous father was walking way too fast. His hand was sweating in hers. She squeezed it, then released. Finally, they stopped before the minister, standing side by side. The loud organ ceased abruptly.

Butterflies fluttered in her stomach. The minister raised his hands, then lowered them, instructing the crowd to sit. A quiet shuffle filled the church as two hundred guests lowered themselves into oak pews. When all was quiet, the minister raised his voice and asked, "Who gives this bride?"

The question echoed against Gothic stone arches.

Her father swallowed hard. "Her mother and I do."

Andie could barely recognize the shaky voice. He lifted her veil and kissed her on the cheek. "I love you," she whispered.

He couldn't speak. He turned and walked to the front pew, taking the seat beside his wife.

Andie climbed the two marble steps. The groom reached for her hand. She turned away, however, and faced the guests. She drew a deep breath, then spoke with self-assurance. "I know this is unorthodox. But before we get started, I want to thank some people."

The guests seemed confused. Her parents looked at one another. Nobody moved.

Andie continued, "First, I want to thank my parents. Mom, Dad. I love you both very much. I want to thank Reverend Jenkins, who has known me since I was a gangly teenager and who has been looking forward to this day probably more than anyone. I also want to thank each and every one of you for coming today. It means so much to have your friendship, your support." Her voice trailed off. She averted her eyes, then drew a deep breath and looked squarely at the clock in the back of the church. "But most of all," she said, her voice shaking, "I want to thank Linda, my lovely sister and maid of honor." She glared to her right.

"For sleeping with the groom last night."

The crowd gasped. Andie whirled and hit the groom squarely in the chest with her bouquet. Anger and embarrassment rushed through her veins. She hiked her long white wedding dress and ran for the side exit.

"You son of a bitch!" her father cried, charging toward the groom. The best man jumped forward to restrain the old man but knocked him flat in an accident that looked like a sucker punch.

"My back!" He was groaning, sprawled on the tile floor. The best man towered over him, Mike Tyson versus Red Buttons.

"He pasted her father!" someone shouted.

It was like the cheap shot heard 'round the world, as a dozen other men leaped from their pews, some to help the fallen father of the bride, others to take up the attack. Rick's buddies came to the defense. Shouting led to shoving, and in a matter of seconds a black-and-white pile of thrashing men in tuxedos was rolling toward the altar. A shrill scream rose above the uproar as the horrified maid of honor raced for the exit.

"Get her!" shouted the flower girl.

The crowd scattered. Women screamed. Fists were flying. A groomsman was suddenly airborne, slamming into the lectern.

"People, please!" shouted Reverend Jenkins. "Not in the house of the Lord!"

Andie didn't stop running. She burst through the exit and headed down the hall. It sounded like a soccer stadium riot behind her. She hoped no one would follow. She needed to be alone. She ducked into an empty office and quickly locked the door.

She was out of breath, shoulders heaving. Part of her felt like crying, but she fought back the emotions. He wasn't worth crying over. He wasn't worth marrying.

A tear ran down her cheek. She quickly brushed it away. Just one tear. That much she would allow. As she leaned against the wall, her shoulder blade inadvertently hit the light switch behind her and cut off the light. The room went black. She smiled weakly, recalling her grandpa's dying words.

"Turn out the lights, the party's over," she repeated softly.

The thin smile faded, and she was alone in the darkness.

Two

Sundays were Gus Wheatley's favorite workday. Monday to Friday was always a nonstop chain of conference calls and meetings in and out of the law firm. Saturdays too brought only interruptions. Ambitious young lawyers would drop by his corner office to impress the managing partner, just to let him know they weren't spending the weekend on the tennis court. Sunday was his one day to crank up the stereo and clear his desk.

For a workaholic, Gus was an impressive physical specimen, due largely to the typical overdo-it fashion in which he had heeded a doctor's warnings about his family's history of heart disease. He usually jogged or cycled before sunrise. Conference calls were often handled on the treadmill in the small fitness room adjacent to his office. He rarely drank at business dinners or cocktail parties, preferring always to keep his mind sharp. His confident good looks commanded attention in any setting. At forty-one, he was the youngest lawyer ever to serve as managing partner of Preston & Coolidge, Seattle's premier law firm. He'd spent his entire legal career there, having passed up a Supreme Court clerkship after graduation from Stanford Law. For some, a year at the nation's highest court would have been the ultimate experience. For Gus, drafting appellate opinions was simply too academic. From his first day of law school his goal had been to head up one of the nation's leading law firms. Preston & Coolidge allowed him to live his dream. Night and day. Seven days a week.

The firm technically had a five-member executive committee, but no one disputed that it was Gus who really ran things, the benign dictator who controlled the fate of two hundred attorneys. Gus loved the control, though it took the skill of a consummate politician to build consensus among partners whose egos could barely fit inside the building. It took passion to run a law firm and still find time to schmooze new clients and even practice a little law. He did have help, of course. Two of the firm's best secretaries kept his life in order. Also at his disposal were two gofers, loyal young men who did everything from picking up clients at the airport to shining their boss's shoes. For more substantive matters, an international lawyer, Martha Goldstein, was his anointed managerial assistant. That was a rather unimpressive title for such a coveted position, as it was widely assumed that Gus was grooming Martha to replace him. It would be years before that would happen. In the meantime, she had the brains and charisma to impress clients when Gus couldn't be there, and she was handling an increasing number of intrafirm administrative matters Gus hated to deal with. It might have been borderline sexism, but it was still a fact that older male partners screamed less about their annual bonus when it was presented by an attractive thirty-six-year-old woman.

Gus tapped his pencil on the accounting summaries before him, keeping time with the music blaring from his stereo. Only Sinatra could add pizzazz to his obligatory review of the firm's eleven million dollars in monthly billings. The speakers on his rosewood credenza were beginning to rattle. Too much "New York, New York." He leaned back and lowered the volume.

"Care to order out for Chinese?"

The woman's voice in the doorway caught him by surprise. It was Martha.

He checked his Rolex, not realizing it was dinnertime. "Yeah, sure," he said with a smile. "Wanna bill it to your client or mine?"

She knew he was kidding. Martha had just lost a major international bank as a client after sending out a bill that included "laundry service" charges that one of her associates had slipped onto the statement. It wasn't for money laundering. He'd actually sent his shirts to the hotel cleaners and billed the client.

"Not funny, Gus."

The desk phone rang. He hit the speaker button. "Hello."

"Mr. Wheatley?" the woman replied.

"Yes."

"This is Mrs. Volpe at the Youth Center."

"Who?"

"I'm the instructor in the tumbling class for six- to eight-year-olds. Your daughter participates every Sunday afternoon."

"Oh, right," he said, knowing absolutely nothing about it. "Morgan loves that tumbling."

"Actually, she's still quite timid about it. That's not why I'm calling, though. She told me not to bother you at work, but she's been waiting on a ride home for over two hours. It's almost six o'clock. Everyone's gone. We're ready to close up."

"Thank you for calling, but Morgan's mother takes care of the car rides."

"Yes, she usually does. But no one has seen your wife all day. We can't reach her by phone."

Gus glanced at Martha, who could overhear the conversation on the speaker. She whispered, "Just send a cab."

His eyes brightened, as if Martha were a genius. "Mrs. Volpe, if you can wait just a few more minutes, I'll send a taxi right over."

There was a pause on the line. "I'm sorry, sir. But the only people who can pick up children under the age of twelve from the youth center are parents or designated chaperones whose photographs and signatures are on file with the front office. We don't send children home with strangers."

"Oh. Of course." He ran a hand through his hair, thinking. "Are you sure you can't reach my wife?"

"I've been trying for two hours."

"All right," he said with exasperation. "I'll try to find her. One of us will be there as soon as we can." He hung up, then quickly punched out his wife's cell phone number. After four rings he got the recorded message announcing that the customer was unavailable.

"Damn it, Beth. Turn your stupid phone on." He looked at Martha, obviously annoyed. "I'll take a rain check on dinner. Looks like I have to go play chauffeur."

"Where's Beth?"

"Who the hell knows."

"She do this often? Just forget to pick up the kid?"

He crossed the room and grabbed his overcoat from the hook behind the door. "It's always some damn thing with her."

"Sounds like she could use a good smack on the back of the legs."

Gus shot a look.

Martha said, "Just a figure of speech. I heard one of my British clients say that the other day."

"Hopefully not about his wife."

"Lighten up. I wasn't being literal."

"Yeah, okay. I'll see you tomorrow."

He headed down the hall. An electronic access card allowed him through the metal gate that secured the firm's dramatic three-story lobby on weekends. He punched the button on the panel to call for the elevator. It would take a minute or two for a car to reach the forty-ninth floor. While waiting, he was thinking about Martha's comment. A crack like that was pretty awkward, given the state of his marriage. His fifteen years with Beth had had its share of rumors and allegations. It just wasn't anything to joke about. Or maybe he was just more sensitive lately, more aware of how unsettled his own feelings still were.

At times it seemed a miracle he stayed married to Beth.

Three

Gus and his daughter sat up watching *The Lion King* video. It was way past her Sunday night bedtime, but Gus thought he'd take her mind off her worries with extended television privileges. It didn't work.

"When's Mommy coming home?" She must have asked that question every fifteen minutes. Gus had come up with just about every excuse he could think of. Traffic. Running late. By ten o'clock he was out of explanations. He put Morgan to bed, which was an ordeal. He read to her, sat with her, and finally crawled in bed with her. Anything to ease her mind. She was clearly sensing his own anxieties.

Finally, she was asleep.

He sank into the leather recliner and channel-surfed with the TV remote, stopping on the local news. The usual review of weekend crime sent his mind adrift until the broadcast shifted to a late-breaking live report of a fatal traffic accident on I–5. A tangled mess of metal appeared on the screen, the remnants of two cars and a dump truck. He leaned forward, then relaxed. The victims were male, no women involved in the crash.

He chided himself for getting his pulse up. Of course it wasn't Beth. Her car was still in the garage.

That, however, was part of his confusion.

He knew she had dropped off Morgan at the youth center at two o'clock. Morgan had confirmed that much. Gus had gone over it with his daughter several times, but she just couldn't remember if Mommy had said she would be back at four, or if she had said Daddy would pick her up. He racked his brain, trying to recall if Beth had told him she was going somewhere and had asked him to pick up Morgan. Maybe he'd just forgotten about it. That had to be it. Over the past few months they'd become the world's worst communicators. She'd probably mumbled something to him three days ago on his way out the door. Typical Beth.

Gus rose from his chair and went to the kitchen. The breakfast nook in their hillside mansion was built like a hexagonal glass jewel box, its floor-to-ceiling windows taking in a two-hundred-seventy-degree vista. The night view was his favorite. It was the only one he really knew. He was always gone before dawn, home after dusk. The Wheatleys lived north of downtown in the more upscale section of Magnolia, where new dream homes and magnificent century-old estates offered both city and water views. Glass and stone office towers lit up the skyline to the southeast. Tonight, as on many nights, the tops of the tallest buildings were cut off by low-hanging clouds. His own office sat right at the cloud line, a perpetually lighted cubicle in the sky. To the west was Puget Sound, the huge north-south finger of water that separated the port city of Seattle from the Kitsap and Olympic peninsulas. It took some imagination, but if you thought of northwest Washington as a big right-hand mitten, it was the thumb-like peninsulas and Olympic Mountains to the west that kept the Pacific Ocean from ravaging Puget Sound and Seattle to the east. The Sound was dark now, only some shipping lights visible. A few more twinkling signs of life dotted Bainbridge Island. Gus focused on the faintest light in the distance, somewhere in the night.

Where the hell is Beth? he wondered.

*　*　*

Monday morning was anything but routine. Gus had been up all night. At six a.m. he felt the programmed urge to make the usual spate of calls to his East Coast clients, all of whom were three hours ahead of him. The urge, however, was not compelling. It came as somewhat of a surprise, an affront to the priorities of a man consumed by his profession. But his heart and mind were elsewhere. Morgan would be awake in thirty minutes. She'd want to know where Mommy was.

He wanted to know where her mommy was.

Gus poured himself a cup of black coffee and sat alone at the kitchen table. The *Wall Street Journal, New York Times* and *Seattle Post-Intelligencer* lay rolled up and unread on the counter. The rain pattered lightly against the kitchen window. The sun had not yet risen. A thick predawn fog robbed him of any view out the window, no moon, no stars, no downtown city lights. It was still early, but he needed some answers before his daughter woke. Since Morgan's birth Beth had kept a list of phone numbers taped to the refrigerator, people to call in case of emergencies. He dialed the top number and braced himself for a battle.

The fourth ring was followed by a raspy "Hello."

"Carla, it's Gus. Sorry to wake you."

She didn't reply. For a second Gus thought she might hang up. Carla was his younger sister, but that was secondary. First and foremost, she was his wife's best friend. Growing up, they had never been close. Marrying Beth and effectively coming between her and her best friend had only made things worse. Whenever Beth had a complaint about Gus, Carla was on her side. Sometimes it seemed as though Carla was even leading the charge. Through it all, however, they had managed a level of civility. A low level.

"It's twenty after six," she said, groaning. "What do you want?"

"I'm a little concerned about Beth."

Her voice took on urgency. "What did you do to her?"

The accusatory tone angered him. God only knew what Beth had been telling Carla. "I didn't do *anything* to her. Can you please just answer a simple question for me? When's the last time you talked to Beth?"

"We went out for brunch yesterday. Why?"

"Did she say she was going anywhere—going away?"

"You mean, like a vacation?"

"Anything at all. In town, out of town. It doesn't matter."

"The only thing she mentioned was that she had to take Morgan over to the youth center at two. Why are you asking me all this?"

He sighed, then said, "Beth dropped Morgan off, but she never picked her up. I had to get Morgan myself. Beth never came home last night. I don't know where she is."

"She's not here with me, if that's what you're implying."

"I wasn't implying anything. I'm just trying to locate my wife. Do you have any idea where she might be?"

"No. But I can speculate."

"Go right ahead."

"Has it occurred to you that perhaps Beth has finally seen the light and found the courage to leave you?"

She sounded so smug, he wanted to tell her to go to hell. But he knew Carla's theory wasn't out of the question. "If that was the case, don't you think she could have found a better way to do it than to leave her six-year-old daughter stranded at the youth center with no ride home? Does a reasonably intelligent woman do something like that?"

"If she's confused enough, maybe she does. Beth was very unhappy. You have no idea how unhappy she was."

"That doesn't explain everything. I've been through her closet, her drawers. All her clothes are still there. Her shoes. Her photo albums and collectibles. Nothing seems to be missing. It just doesn't look like she was planning an escape. Even her car is still in the garage."

"She doesn't have to drive to leave you."

"I've been making phone calls since four A.M. I've checked with every cab company in the city. None of them picked up Beth from our house yesterday. I've called every hotel between here and White Pass. No Beth Wheatley. I even called highway patrol to see if there were any accidents."

"Did you try Sea-Tac?"

"The airlines won't give out passenger information."

"There you go. She could be flying the friendly skies as we speak."

"I don't think so."

"Why not?"

"Come on, Carla. I know what's going on here. I've suspected for months."

"Suspected what?"

"She's seeing someone, isn't she?"

"Another man? No way. You've soured her on the species for life."

"Carla, be straight with me. If she spent the night with another man, that's between her and me. But if that's not the case, then something scary is going on, and I need to call the police so they can start looking for her. So tell me, and you'd better tell me the truth. Things haven't been good between me and Beth lately. But this is Morgan's mother we're talking about. Your niece."

"I honestly don't know what to tell you."

"Stop covering for her." He was louder than he'd intended. He drew a deep breath, but he still spoke harshly. "This is serious. Does a woman leave her husband without a suitcase? Without a purse, a wallet, her driver's license? Without so much as a fifty-dollar withdrawal from our bank account? Don't make me drag in law enforcement if you know this boils down to another lover. But if we can agree she might be in trouble, it's time to call the cops. Which is it, Carla?"

There was a pause on the line, as if she were trying to put aside the lifetime of anger she'd built up against her brother. Finally, she answered in a shaky voice. "I think you'd better call the police."

The response chilled him. He didn't say thank you. He didn't say good-bye. He just hung up the phone and dialed the police.

Four

The Meany Science, Math and Arts Academy let out at three-thirty. Five hundred middle-school students burst through the exits like escaped prisoners. Some headed for the playground until their ride arrived. Others went straight for the long line of yellow buses. Noisy groups of kids who lived close enough to walk home were escorted off the school yard by volunteer patrollers. Benny Martinez and his two sidekicks walked alone.

Benny was big for a sixth-grader, confident to the point of cockiness, a natural leader. As to whether he'd devote his talents to good use or gang life, the verdict was still out.

He walked slowly down the sidewalk and away from the school, passing the crowded buses. He wore a flashy blue and gray NFL Seattle Seahawks athletic jacket. Once outside the school property, he clipped a chain dog leash to his oversized blue jeans, just for effect. Although his parents wouldn't allow the skinhead haircut that was a gang trademark, his hair was cropped as short as his scissors could possibly cut it.

"Come on, Benny," his buddy said. His voice shook with nervousness. He was clearly in a hurry.

"Be cool." Benny clutched his knapsack, which concealed a stolen football. Experience had taught him never to run when carrying stolen goods. Some twenty percent of his classmates had been suspended at some time during the school year. Benny had yet to be tagged for anything. Fools, all of them. Coolness was key.

He smiled at the patrolwoman on the corner as he and his two buddies crossed the street. His friends looked as if they were about to wet their pants. Benny muttered beneath his breath, "Run and I'll kill you both."

His friends slowed their pace. Past poundings from Benny had taught them to do exactly as he said.

Benny seemed to glide across the street, not anxious in the least. His friends tagged along on either side of him, with Benny a half step ahead. They walked as a unit for several blocks until Benny signaled halt. They'd reached the entrance to Washington Park Arboretum, a two-hundred-acre woodland northeast of downtown. A light breeze from Union Bay stirred the towering fir trees before them. The sun was just a fuzzy amber ball behind a patchy blanket of clouds. Benny unzipped his knapsack and removed the leather football. Only now did he allow himself a smile.

"Go long," he said.

His friends sprinted into the park. Benny waved, telling them to keep going. He heaved the football with all his strength. Wind-aided, it nearly made it to his friends. They wrestled with each other and rolled in the grass to gain control of the bouncing ball. Benny ran to catch up with them. His friend pitched it back to him, rugby-style. The threesome ran along the asphalt bicycle path, pitching the ball back and forth among them. The winding trail took them up and over a hill, deep into a lush green meadow. The impressive Japanese tea garden loomed ahead. The boys were more focused on the ball than the sights. The long run had them breathless, but no one wanted to be the sissy who stopped the game. Benny pitched a high one. His friend got a hand on it but missed. The ball rolled down the hill into a heavily wooded area.

"Idiot!" shouted Benny.

"Me? You threw it!"

They stood at the edge of the bike trail. The hillside dropped off at a steep forty-degree angle. The longpole pines were nearly thirty feet tall, the Douglas firs even taller. Yet the ravine was so deep that some of the treetops were at the boys' eye level. They could hear running water splashing against the rocks somewhere below, but the evergreens were too thick to actually see the creek.

Benny glared at this friend. "Go get it."

"No way."

Benny shoved him off the ledge. He rolled about thirty feet down the hillside before grabbing hold of a tree. Loose gravel continued down the hill. He looked up in fear, about ready to cry. Benny didn't flinch. "Get the ball," he said.

The other boy spoke up. "Just forget it. It was stolen anyway."

"You afraid?" asked Benny.

"No. Are you?"

Benny's eyes narrowed. "If you get there before I do, you can keep the ball."

His pal smiled at the challenge. Quickly but carefully they started sliding on their butts down the side of the hill. It was grassy at the top, making it easier to control the descent. But the mud near the bottom made the slide even faster. Too fast. They were bouncing, then tumbling out of control. Low-hanging branches slapped their faces. Mud was flying everywhere, into their shoes and up their shirts. The farther the descent, the darker it got. The sound of the creek grew louder, until finally they landed with a thud at the foot of the hill.

Benny groaned. His friend groaned louder. They were only a few feet apart, but there was barely enough light for them to see one another.

"Benny?"

He shook his head, getting his bearings. "Yeah?"

"What the heck is that?"

"What?"

His friend pointed. "That. Up there, behind you."

Benny turned. His eyes were slowly adjusting to the dimness. Something was in the tree, a good twenty feet overhead. He stared, trying to focus. Finally, he could see it. Turning. Twisting. His eyes widened. There was no mistaking it.

A body was hanging at the end of a rope.

The boys looked at each other, then screamed in unison as they ran the other way along the side of the creek.

For a special agent in the FBI, it was hard to define a "typical" Monday. The Monday after a wedding like Andie's definitely was not typical.

Andie had been in the FBI for three years, all in the Seattle field office. The bureau wasn't exactly a lifelong dream of hers. It was more of a safe landing for a self-assured thrill seeker who might well have courted the other side of the law had Mr. and Mrs. Henning not adopted her at the age of nine and channeled her energy in the right direction. She was a Junior Olympic mogul skier till her knee gave out and a certified scuba diver by the time she was sixteen. She went away to college at the University of California, Santa Barbara, thinking she would build a life near the beach. To everyone's surprise she chose a rather serious major, psychology. Her grades were good enough to get her into law school, and, yet another surprise, she went. But it wasn't until her final year that real inspiration struck. At a recruitment panel on alternative careers, she was mesmerized by a woman who had just returned from an investigation of a terrorist bombing. That had settled it. She would join the FBI.

The decision had thrilled her father, himself a cop who had introduced her to guns at an early age. During her training at the academy, she had become only the twentieth woman in bureau history to make the "Possible Club," a ninety-eight-percent-male honorary fraternity for agents who shoot perfect scores on one of the toughest firearms courses in law enforcement. Despite the distinction, she'd spent her first six months doing routine background checks on prospective federal employees. It was a career dead end reserved for marginal agents, or for someone like Andie, who simply looked young for her age and wasn't taken seriously. Fortunately, one of the supervisory special agents spotted her talent: "Unmatched drive and a healthy spirit of adventure," he had written in her evaluation, "tempered by serious brainpower and exceptional technical skills." He got her assigned to the bank-robbery squad, where she'd made a name for herself over the next eighteen months. At twenty-seven she still looked young. No one, however, had trouble taking her seriously anymore.

At least not before the wedding.

Andie struggled to keep smiling throughout the day. It wasn't easy. Nobody said a word about the wedding, though a group of secretaries at the watercooler had giggled after she'd passed. Everyone knew about it, of course. Some of them had been there. One of them was sporting a black eye to prove it.

"See ya mañana," said Andie on her way to the elevator. The receptionist waved and buzzed her through the electronically secured door.

It was early, around four-thirty. Thanks to the canceled honeymoon, her calendar was completely clear, making it a stretch to fill her day with anything meaningful. She didn't feel like going straight home, another night alone. Nights were awfully long this time of year, even without a heartache. She headed a few blocks south from the federal building toward historic Pioneer Square, the old downtown business district where quaint cobblestone streets and nineteenth-century brick buildings were home to trendy galleries, boutiques, and restaurants. Andie stopped at

J&M Cafe, a popular saloon that boasted the most impressive wooden bar this side of San Francisco. It was her favorite place for nachos, the perfect sinful ending to the rabbit food diet she'd endured for the bikini she wouldn't wear on the Hawaiian honeymoon she'd never take.

The bar was crowded and noisy, as usual, but she felt alone. A steady stream of patrons brushed against her back as they squeezed past on the way to the rest rooms. Halfway through her mound of gooey tortilla chips, she sensed someone standing close behind her. She glanced over her shoulder.

A handsome black man was staring at the empty stool beside her. "Excuse me," he said, still looking at the stool. "But is this woman taken?"

Andie raised an eyebrow. *"That* has to be the lamest pickup line I have ever heard."

"Thank you." He pulled up the stool and extended his hand. "Bond's the name. B.J. Bond."

She shook his hand. "What's the B.J. stand for?"

"Bond James."

"So your full name would be . . . ?"

"Bond James Bond."

They lost it simultaneously, sharing a laugh as they let the charade go.

"Isaac," she said playfully, "nice to know I can count on your goofball sense of humor to lift my spirits."

He grinned widely, then caught the server's eye and ordered a cup of American coffee. Isaac Underwood was the assistant special agent in charge of the FBI's Seattle field office, or ASAC, the number two man in an office of a hundred and sixteen agents. He had been Andie's immediate supervisor for eighteen months before the promotion.

He settled into the stool and reached for a fully loaded nacho. "Pretty decadent dinner," he said with his mouth full.

"Like they say, we didn't work our way to the top of the food chain to eat tofu."

"Amen to that." The server brought his coffee. Isaac reached for the sugar. "So, kiddo. You doing okay?"

"Yeah," she said, adding a quick nod for emphasis. "I am."

His expression turned serious. "Andie, if there's anything you need. Time off. Even a transfer."

She raised a hand, halting him. "I'm okay. Really."

He sipped his coffee. "If it's any consolation, I always thought that guy was a bit of a prick."

"Now you tell me."

"You didn't notice?"

"He wasn't always that way. We were inseparable all through law school. Even talked about opening up a firm together. When I ditched the idea of practicing law and joined the FBI instead, I think he had it in his mind that the bureau would eat me alive, that I'd quit before long. He definitely didn't think it would last three years."

"Plenty of people change their minds about marrying cops. Most of them just cancel the engagement."

Andie lowered her eyes. "In hindsight, I think he tried. We had a huge fight last week. From the day we got engaged, we always talked about raising a family. All of a sudden he tells me no kids so long as my job description includes bullet dodging."

"Sounds like *you* should have canceled."

"I know. My mother talked me into going through with it. She had me convinced we could work it out, that Rick was just bluffing. I guess he wasn't bluffing. Just wish he hadn't picked such a sleazy way to keep us both from making a terrible mistake. And now I really wish I hadn't turned it into a circus."

"I'm sorry, Andie."

"Thanks. But don't be. I just want to get back to normal as soon as possible."

"I'm glad you see it that way. Because I've got an assignment for you."

"Isaac, how sweet. You arranged to have a bank robbed just to take my mind off my personal problems."

"Not exactly." He smiled, then was serious again. "Victoria Santos is coming over from Quantico tomorrow morning."

Andie didn't know Santos, but she certainly knew of her. Santos had taught the course on criminal psychology to Andie's class of cadets at the academy. More to her credit, she was a legend among criminal profilers in the FBI's elite Investigative Support Unit.

"What for?" asked Andie.

Isaac glanced at the crowd of customers hovering around them. "Let's talk about this outside, all right?"

They paid the bill, poured their coffee into paper go-cups, and stepped outside. The busy city street crackled with the sound of rush hour on wet pavement. A damp chill cut through their overcoats. The sun had set only minutes ago, but the temperature had dropped precipitously. Andie sipped her hot coffee. Isaac kept talking as they walked together down the wide, tree-lined sidewalk.

"Local police have asked the FBI for assistance," he said. "They have some homicides that may be related. Possibly a serial killer at work."

"How many victims so far?"

"Two that they're pretty sure of. A third was found today."

"What makes them think they're related?"

"The first two took place in different parts of the town, about a week apart. But they were virtually identical."

"You mean the similarities are in the killer's m.o. or in the victims' characteristics?"

"Both. From the victimology standpoint, it's like one was a carbon copy of the other. Both white males. Both fifty-one years old. Same color hair and eyes. Both divorced. They even drove the same kind of vehicle. Ford pickups."

"How did they die?"

"Basically strangulation. But there was a lot of evidence of overkill. Multiple stab wounds, blunt trauma. Even some burns."

"So we've got a serial killer who hates middle-aged white men?"

"Not exclusively. The third victim is a white female in her mid-thirties. Some kids found her body this afternoon."

"Why do the police think her murder is connected to the men's?"

"She was strangled, for one thing. And like the others, her body showed significant signs of overkill. But the cops aren't sure there's a connection. That's why they called in the FBI. I'm not even sure the geniuses back at Quantico think it's a serial killer just yet. I presume that's why they're sending Santos from ISU as opposed to a profiler from CASKU."

Andie nodded, though she wasn't entirely familiar with the FBI's division of labor between the Investigative Support Unit, which had pioneered criminal profiling, and the Child Abduction and Serial Killer Unit, which was a more recent creation.

They stopped at the corner near Andie's car. "What do you want me to do?" she asked.

"I want you to be the local coordinator. Team up with Santos. Help get her whatever she needs while she's out here."

Andie hesitated, surprised. "You know there's nothing I'd rather do than work side by side with Victoria Santos. But there are at least fifteen other agents in the office who'd kill for this assignment."

"You're the only one with a degree in psychology. These days that's virtually a prerequisite for any agent who hopes to get a foothold with the ISU. Why waste this assignment on someone who has no chance of breaking in?"

"Isaac, I really do appreciate this. But let me be straight

with you. I don't want it if your decision is based on sympathy for what happened to me on Saturday."

"This isn't charity. It's just good timing. You're qualified. This is what you've always wanted to do. And you're available. Frankly, now that you've canceled your honeymoon, you're the only agent in Seattle with a completely clear calendar for the next two weeks."

"I guess Rick did me a favor."

"Maybe he did both of us a favor."

For a split second she thought maybe he was talking on a personal rather than professional level. Before she could even sort out her thoughts, he had popped open his briefcase and was handing her a file.

"Here's a copy of the materials we sent to Santos. Police reports, autopsy protocols, crime-scene photos—everything she wanted from the first two homicides. Look it over tonight."

The traffic light changed, allowing pedestrians to cross. Isaac stepped off the curb. Andie tucked the file under her arm and remained at the corner by her car.

"Beyond that," he said, "just be in my office at eight A.M. sharp. And prepare to work your ass off."

A cold rain started to fall. Andie popped her umbrella. "Need a ride to your car?"

"Nah. I'm just a half block away." He turned.

"Isaac," she said, stopping him. "Thank you."

The rain was falling harder. He gave her a mock salute and dashed across the street. Andie watched from the curb. Halfway across, he slipped on the wet pavement, then raised a fist triumphantly as he regained his balance with hardly a break in stride.

B.J. Bond, she thought, smiling as she headed for her car.

Five

The police weren't the help Gus had hoped they would be. To them, a thirty-five-year-old woman in a rocky marriage who was missing less than twenty-four hours seemed a more likely candidate for an extramarital affair than foul play. They did let him fill out a missing-persons report. Beyond that, Gus was pretty much on his own.

He canceled his Monday appointments and spent the morning and most of the afternoon trying to reconstruct Beth's weekend. He called the credit card companies to see where she had charged things, then visited those stores and restaurants. It was privately embarrassing, but his most recent photograph of Beth was almost a year old; things had gotten that bad between them. Even so, one of the assistant managers at Nordstrom's department store recognized her. She hadn't seen Beth in weeks. No one else could even place her.

Around three o'clock he got an emergency call from one of those ever so considerate clients who just wouldn't take "family crisis" for an answer. Two minutes turned into ten, ten into thirty-five. Gus finally had to fake a dead battery in his cell phone to shake free. He spent the balance of the afternoon at home making phone calls. Beth kept an address directory on their computer. He scrolled down the list alphabetically, calling each entry, asking if they'd seen her.

The process became mechanical after a while, and he lost track of time. He was phoning the P's when the doorbell rang.

Gus answered it. Carla was standing in the doorway with a covered dish.

"I brought Morgan dinner."

Before he could even invite her inside, she was heading for the kitchen. Gus followed. "Okay if I eat some, too?"

The ribbing didn't break the ice. He said, "Actually, Morgan's having dinner over at a friend's house. I've been making phone calls all day. I didn't want her around."

"Business never stops for you, does it?"

"It wasn't business. I've been trying to find Beth."

"Oh," she said sheepishly. Her combativeness dropped a notch. "Actually, so have I."

"Any luck?"

She laid her casserole on the counter and removed her gloves. "No. But that doesn't mean anything. It hasn't been that long."

Gus looked away, then back. "Can I ask you something kind of personal?"

"It depends."

"Just forget for a minute that you're my sister. Put on your hat as Beth's best friend."

"Okay."

"Lately, I can't really say I've seen the two of you together all that much. Sometimes best friends can be like sisters. Sometimes it's just a label. Were you and Beth close?"

She made a face, as if the question were complicated. "We were at one time."

"But not lately?"

"We've been closer. There was no big blowout or anything. It's like I told you this morning. Beth has been really unhappy the last few months. She was pretty unapproachable."

Gus nodded. "That's what I'm finding out. I've been going down her address book, calling all her friends. I haven't talked to anyone who's seen her or even talked to her on the phone in the past two months."

"Maybe she was too embarrassed. Abused women often blame themselves."

He turned away, exasperated. "I never laid a hand on Beth. I don't know why she said that. Other than to hurt me."

"Gus Wheatley a victim? I don't think so. From what I saw of Beth lately, she was more likely to hurt herself than to hurt you."

Their eyes locked, as if a light had just gone off. Each could tell exactly what the other was thinking. Gus said, "You don't think—"

"God, I hope not."

The phone rang. Gus grabbed it on the second ring. "Hello. Yes, this is he." He started to pace, listening intently. The eyes widened with concern, borderline panic.

"I can be there in twenty minutes," he said finally and hung up.

Carla seemed on the verge of explosion. "*What?*" she asked with urgency.

"Police found a body in Washington Park Arboretum. Looks to be a woman in her mid-thirties."

She raised a hand to her mouth in horror. "Is it—"

"Don't know. They want me to come down for an ID." He swallowed hard, his voice cracking. "They think it could be Beth."

Like most FBI agents, Andie didn't often go to the medical examiner's office. Barring some connection to the federal government or some congressionally legislated federal offense, dead bodies were basically a matter of state and local jurisdiction. Locals frequently did call upon the FBI for assistance in certain areas of expertise. The FBI crime lab, for one. Criminal profiling, for another. Andie didn't need to be reminded, however, that the locals still ran the investigation, even after the FBI answered the call for assistance.

Fortunately, Andie had wasted no time reviewing the case files Isaac Underwood had given her. She was completely up to speed when he telephoned after dinner to tell her she needed to get down to the medical examiner's office right away.

The King County Medical Examiner's office was housed in the basement of the Harbor View Medical Center. Andie arrived a little after seven. One of the office attendants took her straight to the main examination room. A detective from the Seattle police department met her outside the door. He was a heavyset man with thinning brown hair and a broad, flat nose, like an ex-boxer.

"Andie Henning," she said, introducing herself.

He seemed taken aback, as if the "Andie" he was expecting was Andy a man. "Dick Kessler," he said as they shook hands. His tone was uninspired, like the beige and white office in which they stood.

"Isaac Underwood sends his regards." He didn't, really, but Andie could see from the immediate smile on Kessler's face that the mere mention of her boss's name was a sure ice breaker. Isaac had an excellent relationship with the Seattle police department; he had started his law enforcement career there.

"Good ol' Isaac," he said with a nostalgic smile. "What a kick it used to be watching that guy on the witness stand. Did you know he still holds the department record for the most cocky criminal defense lawyers chewed up and spit out?"

"That doesn't surprise me."

"Is he coming?"

"He sent me. Said he got a call saying you were doing an ID tonight on the latest body—the woman you thought might be connected to a serial killer. I was hoping I could talk you into putting it off until tomorrow morning, when our ISU profiler arrives from Quantico. She'll be on a jet tonight."

Kessler shook his head. "Can't put it off. Wouldn't be fair to the family. Assuming we have the right family."

"Who's coming down to make the ID?"

"Gus Wheatley. Big-shot lawyer downtown."

"I've heard of him. What's his relation to the victim?"

"He reported his wife missing this morning. Honestly, we didn't do much with it. Not until this body was discovered."

"What makes you think it's her?"

"Not much so far. Unidentified white female. Mid-thirties. Brown hair. About a hundred twenty pounds. Could be her."

"No driver's license or other identification on the body, I presume."

"No."

"Clothing match?"

"Uh-uh. Body was found nude."

"No other distinguishing physical characteristics?"

"We'll need Mr. Wheatley's help with that. It's hard for us to say at this point. Birds and critters have already eaten away a good bit of the flesh. She's a little taller than the height Mr. Wheatley reported for his wife, but the body could be somewhat elongated from hanging at the end of the rope."

The door opened to the examination room. Dr. Rudolf Fitzsimmons, chief pathologist, stood in the open doorway. He had very blond hair, almost as white as his lab coat. The skin too was pasty. Andie had seen more color in cadavers. Too much time down here in the basement, she surmised. He invited them in with a wave of his arm.

"All set," he said. "Would you like a preview?"

Kessler stepped aside, allowing Andie to enter first.

She was immediately struck by the cold and the lights. Autopsy rooms were like walking into Antarctica, bright and frigid. The body lay in the center of the room atop a stainless steel examining table. One leg, most of the torso, and the left side of the face were covered with white cloth, which didn't strike Andie as standard procedure.

Dr. Fitzsimmons explained, "I've covered the more gruesome wounds for Mr. Wheatley's benefit. No need to show a man which parts of his wife are now nourishing the wildlife at Washington Park."

Andie asked, "Do we have to bring the poor man right into the autopsy room to make the identification? It's hard enough to see a loved one pulled out of a drawer in the morgue."

"Ordinarily, I wouldn't do this," said Kessler. "But I don't want to lose any more time in this case. I've asked Dr. Fitzsimmons to be prepared to proceed with the autopsy just as soon as Mr. Wheatley makes the identification."

"If we could just wait twelve hours," said Andie, "I think we would all benefit from Agent Santos's examination of the body before autopsy."

Kessler paused, thinking. "Well, perhaps we could postpone some of the more invasive procedures. But I would at least like Dr. Fitzsimmons to proceed far enough to rule out suicide. If we're going to explore the possibility of a serial killer, we might as well know if this woman was in fact the victim of a homicide."

"I can answer that question right now," said the doctor.

Kessler looked at him curiously. "How?"

"Look here." He shined a spotlight on the side of the victim's neck. Both Andie and the detective walked toward the head of the table for a closer look. "See the narrow bruise around the neck?" asked the doctor. "It's a straight line all the way around, matching the pressure of the rope. Those markings indicate strangulation by ligature. With a hanging, you typically have a very well-defined inverted V-shaped bruise. Think of the way the noose fits around the neck."

Kessler said, "But she was found hanging in a tree. Why no inverted-V bruise?"

"Bruising requires blood flow," said Andie.

"That's exactly right." The doctor seemed impressed.

Andie leaned over, inspecting the neck. "Doctor, are you saying she was dead before her body was strung up?"

"Yes. Strangled, to be precise."

"So we're not talking suicide?" said Kessler.

Dr. Fitzsimmons shook his head. "More likely homicide."

Kessler nodded. "Committed by someone who wanted it to look like suicide."

"Possibly."

Andie rose, chilled by her thoughts. "Or by someone who delights in displaying his kill."

Gus's Mercedes cut across Seattle in record time. The attendant greeted him at the door and took him down the hall that led to the autopsy room. Gus had been expecting to go to the morgue and have his wife rolled out of a drawer, like on television. Lately, nothing had been going according to his expectations.

"Please wait here," said the attendant as they reached the waiting room.

Gus sat alone on one of two Naugahyde chairs that shared a vintage seventies smoked-glass coffee table. The lighting was bad fluorescent, the kind that bothered the eyes. Gus had never practiced criminal law, but suddenly he had an appreciation for the stakes, the drama. He felt as though someone in the next room literally had life-or-death power over him. Yet it wasn't as if the medical examiner had a juror's prerogative to change the outcome. Either it was Beth or it wasn't.

He'd know in a minute.

His mind flooded with fond thoughts for his wife. The romantic dinners in San Francisco while he was in law school. The weekend hikes around Mt. Rainier when they'd first moved to Seattle. Their honeymoon in Hawaii, cut short by a phone call from Gus's supervising partner. The birth of their daughter, which had come two weeks early, while Gus was in Hong Kong on yet another business trip that Beth had begged him not to take. They'd loved each other once, though he couldn't put his finger on the exact sad moment when she'd realized that he loved his job more.

"Mr. Wheatley?"

He rose eagerly.

"I'm Andie Henning, FBI."

He stepped forward and shook her hand. "What's the FBI doing here?"

"I'd like you to come inside and make the identification, if you can. I should warn you. The body is not in perfect condition. We've prepared it so that when Dr. Fitzsimmons pulls back the sheet, you'll see only the right side of the head and face. I think that should be enough."

Gus felt a lump in his throat. "Okay. Let's do it."

Andie led him inside. Gus felt a definite chill on his face and hands, but the change in room temperature barely fazed him. He entered slowly, one step at a time, eyes fixed ahead on the stainless steel table in the center of the room. Beneath the bright lights, a clean white sheet covered the body. It seemed to rise for one breast but not for the other. Likewise with the feet. His hands shook. That must have been what Agent Henning had meant when she'd said the body wasn't perfect.

He stopped beside the autopsy table. Andie was to his right. Detective Kessler stood on the other side, beside Dr. Fitzsimmons.

"Are you ready, Mr. Wheatley?" asked Andie.

He blinked nervously, then nodded.

Dr. Fitzsimmons pulled back the sheet, exposing the head.

Gus's eyes filled with tears. He could barely speak. "It's not Beth," he said, then quickly turned away.

Six

Andie watched from behind as Gus headed for the door. The transformation had been sudden and remarkable. One moment a bundle of nerves bouncing off the walls; the next, a beaten man sinking through the floor. For friends and relatives, accounting for a missing loved one was always the same painful roller coaster.

It certainly put a screwed-up wedding in perspective.

"Mr. Wheatley?" she said as Gus opened the door.

He stopped in the doorway. "Yes?"

"Would you mind waiting in the lobby for a few minutes? Detective Kessler and I will be right with you."

He hesitated. "I'd really just like to pick up my daughter and go home."

"Just five minutes. Promise."

Gus nodded, then left the room.

Detective Kessler looked at her quizzically from across the table. "Just let the guy go. I can do the paperwork later."

"This isn't about paperwork. I have some things I'd like to ask him about his wife."

"Now? Why?"

"I don't want to speak out of turn," said Andie. "Agent Santos is the expert, and she'll give us her views tomorrow. But just look at what you've got so far. Three homicide

42

victims. All strangled, with evidence of overkill. The first two are like a pair—almost identical. The third is a woman in her mid-thirties."

She glanced at the body before her. "If you look at the state of decomposition, I think we all suspected this wasn't Beth Wheatley. As I'm sure Dr. Fitzsimmons will attest, it's not easy to pinpoint the time of death on a body that has been exposed to animals and the elements. But if I had to guess, I'd say this woman was dead before Beth Wheatley disappeared on Sunday."

"Probably a fair assumption," said the doctor.

"So?" asked Kessler.

Andie continued. "We may be dealing with—I don't know what you'd call them. Bookend homicides. The first two are men who match each other, like bookends. The third is a woman who has nothing in common with the men, other than the strangulation and overkill. But she does happen to bear a physical resemblance to Beth Wheatley, who disappeared yesterday."

"You're thinking Beth Wheatley is this woman's bookend, as you call it?"

"I'm saying it's possible. That's why we need to find out more about Mrs. Wheatley. Her daily routine, her lifestyle. As much as we can learn. Once we have a better understanding of who Beth Wheatley is," she said, glancing at the body, "I think we'll have a much easier time figuring out who *this* is."

Kessler scratched his head, mulling it over. "Sounds like the kind of thing an FBI agent would come up with."

"What do you mean by that?"

"Nothing. If you want to ask Wheatley some questions, be my guest. But excuse me if I don't jump in with both feet."

His cynicism was annoying, but as she started toward the door she could think only of the beleaguered man in the waiting room. She stopped for a moment and looked

Kessler in the eye. "You know, Dick, I hope you're right. I hope my bookend theory is full of shit. Because if it's not, this is one hell of a good news, bad news scenario."

Kessler got her drift. "Good news, Mr. Wheatley. That's not your wife stretched out on the table."

"But the bad news is, it probably will be." She opened the door, and they entered the waiting room.

She decided to interview him right where he was, in the waiting room. It was private enough and would feel less like an interrogation. Andie was big on not making victims feel like suspects.

Gus remained seated on the couch. Andie and Kessler pulled up chairs, facing him. Andie spared him the "bookend" theory. His nightmare was bad enough already. No need to subject him to police speculation about a serial killer who likes his victims in matching pairs.

"Mr. Wheatley," she said softly. "I'd like to get some information from you about your wife. Not the height, weight and hair-color things. Some personal things."

"How personal?"

"Nothing embarrassing. If I get too nosy, you don't have to answer. Let's start general. Does your wife work outside the home?"

"No."

"What is her daily routine like?"

Gus shrugged awkwardly. "I guess it depends on the day."

"Let's take them one at a time. Monday."

"She takes our daughter to school in the morning."

"What else?"

"She picks her up."

She smiled, trying to put him at ease. "Quite a gap there. How does she fill her day?"

"On Mondays, you mean?"

"Let's not get hung up on specific days here. I want to

make this easy for you. Pick any day of the week you like. Just tell me what kinds of things she does with her time."

"I checked with the credit card companies to piece together this last weekend, just to see where she'd charged things. But I can't say as a general matter I know every little thing she does on a typical day."

"Well, does your wife belong to any kind of clubs or organizations?"

"I think she's in . . . something. No, that was before Morgan was born."

Andie glanced at Kessler, then back at Gus. "How about lunches? Does she have a favorite restaurant?"

"I'd imagine she does." He paused, as if drawing a blank. "But I can't say she ever mentioned it. Maybe if I went back to the credit card statement I could figure it out."

"What about food shopping? Where does she go to buy groceries?"

Gus said nothing.

"Does she belong to a gym?"

"*Yes*," he said emphatically, pleased to have hit one.

"Which one?"

His enthusiasm faded. "I'll have to check."

Andie hesitated before asking the next question. The silence seemed to make him uncomfortable. Kessler leaned forward, arching an eyebrow. "Mr. Wheatley, are you and your wife *happily* married?"

"What does that have to do with anything?"

"You seem to know very little about the woman who sleeps beside you."

"Is that what this inquisition is all about? You still think this has something to do with a marital quarrel?"

Kessler gave an assessing look. "I'm not ruling anything out."

"Well, you'd better rule it out. Or you're going to piss away valuable time."

"Please," said Andie, "don't get angry."

"I have every right to be angry. So what if I don't know every little detail about my wife's daily routine? That doesn't mean I don't care what happens to her."

"You're absolutely right," she said.

"Then why are you putting me through this?"

Andie started to say something, then stopped. It was premature to tell him his wife might be a bookend homicide, and this inquiry was going nowhere. "I'm sorry, Mr. Wheatley. It's late, and you've been through an awful lot for one night. Go home to your daughter. I'm sure she needs all the support you can give her."

"And then some," he said, seemingly overwhelmed.

Kessler pressed on, as if Gus's lousy answers had suddenly fueled his interest. "Mr. Wheatley, is there someone else who could answer these questions for us?"

"Probably my sister, Carla. She was Beth's best friend before we got married. My biggest enemy after we got married."

"What do you mean by that?"

"Nothing. I'm exaggerating. Let's just say Carla's always been a lot closer to Beth than she ever was to me."

"Anyone else?"

"My daughter, of course. But she's only six. I'd rather keep her out of this."

Andie said, "We'll handle her appropriately when and if the time comes."

"Your wife's mother and father live anywhere nearby?" asked Kessler.

"They're both deceased."

"You have a housekeeper?"

"We have a woman who comes in twice a week, Mondays and Thursdays. She just does her work and leaves."

"What's her name?"

"Uh, jeez. Ramona something. I don't know her last name."

"What about a nanny?"

"We had one till recently. Michelle Burgette."

"What happened?"

"Beth let her go when Morgan started first grade. Didn't need a live-in anymore."

"You know where she is now?"

"No idea."

Kessler raised an eyebrow. "She raises your kid for six years, then that's it? Cold turkey, no contact?"

"Look, I don't know. Maybe they've talked on the phone. For all I know, she's even come by to visit. Beth would have taken care of all that."

Kessler jotted down a note to himself. "You mind if I talk to any of these people, Mr. Wheatley?"

"Why would I mind?"

"You tell me," he said, eyes narrowing. He was clearly trying to intimidate.

Gus rose, speaking with controlled anger. "I don't really like the way I'm being interrogated here."

"I don't really like the answers I'm getting."

Andie stepped between them. "Ohhh-kay, boys. Let's call it a night."

Gus glared, then looked away. He shook Andie's hand. "Thank you," he said, looking only at her. "*You've* been nice. Please call me as soon as you hear anything."

"We will," she said, seeing him out. As the door shut behind him, she faced Kessler and said, "Are you always so confrontational?"

"Only when the subject is evasive."

"I didn't think he was being evasive."

"I see it all the time. These smartass attorneys who think the only safe thing to tell a cop is either 'I don't know' or 'He went that-a-way.' You can't get a straight answer out of a guy like that."

"He wasn't playing games. Didn't you see the embarrassment in his eyes? The pain in his expression?"

"Give me a break. I'm not the world's greatest husband.

I bet I even work longer hours than he does. But even I know where my wife buys groceries."

"Is that so?" she said, toying with him. "Where?"

His mouth opened, but the words stumbled out. "The grocery store."

"Nice try, Detective."

"No, give me a second. I know this."

She checked her watch, waiting. "Tell you what. E-mail me. I really have to get home. Got a long day tomorrow." She started for the door.

"Safeway!"

Andie stopped. "What?"

"That's where my wife buys the groceries."

She smiled thinly. "That's very impressive, Dick. But to truly be a better man than Gus Wheatley, you have to put your knowledge to use."

"What do you mean?"

"Now that you know where the store is, why don't *you* go buy the groceries?" She gave a friendly wink, then headed out the door.

The disguise was simple but effective. A brown wig and mustache. Eyeglasses with a tortoiseshell frame. Tinted contact lenses turned his blue eyes brown. A bulky winter coat with padding underneath made him look a good thirty pounds heavier, well over his normal one-eighty-five. The leather gloves were completely inconspicuous. By 11:00 P.M. the temperature had dropped below freezing, and a cold wind was blowing off the Sound. Only a fool wouldn't bundle up.

The Quicksilver Copy Center was open twenty-four hours a day. It was located next to a pizza place in a strip mall. Any time of day you could find half a dozen bleary-eyed souls standing at the Xerox machines, and tonight was no exception. As an all-purpose business center it also offered everything from mail boxes and conference rooms to fax machines and computers by-the-hour. It was the computers that interested him—specifically, anonymous Internet access that could never be traced back to him.

The bell on the door tinkled as he entered, but no one looked up. He approached the counter and stopped. The clerk, a college-aged woman, was on the telephone. He made no faces, showed no sign of impatience. He simply waited. He would do nothing to make his visit memorable to her or anyone else.

Finally, the clerk said good night to her boyfriend and hung up the phone.

"Can I help you, sir?"

"I need a computer." He offered a twenty-dollar bill, his gloves still on.

She took the money, made change from the register. "Pod number three is open. Thank you for using Quicksilver."

He scooped the change from the countertop and walked away. Each computer was separated by shoulder-high office dividers, one customer per cubicle. That was all the privacy he needed.

He sat at the terminal and removed his leather gloves. As an animal skin, leather could leave behind distinctive patterns not unlike fingerprints. He wore flesh-tone rubber gloves beneath the leather, no prints of any kind. His fingers danced across the keyboard as he logged onto the Internet.

He went to the mail center, from which he could send e-mail. He typed in the address, which he had memorized. He did not identify the sender; it would read only "Quicksilver Copy Center." There was space to type a message, but that too he left blank.

He pulled a diskette from his coat pocket and loaded into the b: drive. He uploaded it to the computer and attached it as a file to his blank message. The file contained everything he needed to communicate. It had no words on it. Only pictures. Pictures he had taken.

A picture was worth a thousand screams.

He smirked to himself as he hit the SEND button, firing off his bloody missive.

Seven

Gus was home by ten o'clock. He paid the baby-sitter, sent her off in a taxi, and checked on Morgan. She was asleep in her room, which was a relief. He wasn't prepared to answer any more questions about Mommy.

He hadn't slept much in the last two days, but he wasn't sleepy. He went to the kitchen to fix a sandwich. Sliced ham and baby Swiss were in the refrigerator. He rolled it like a hotdog and stuffed it into a baguette, slathering on some Dijon mustard. Almost as an afterthought, he glanced at the label on the package, just to see where Beth had bought it. Boar's Head was all it said. Could have come from anywhere. He still didn't know where she shopped.

He pulled up a stool and sat at the counter, alone with his thoughts. Detective Kessler had definitely ticked him off, but maybe he was right. Beth's disappearance didn't automatically add up to foul play. Ego had him jumping to conclusions. It was perversely self-centered, but what man didn't think his wife was more likely to be abducted than to find a worthy replacement? Perhaps he had put too much stock into the fact that she'd left without her car, her clothes, even her purse and credit cards. For all he knew, she'd been stockpiling cash for months. She could have bought a whole new wardrobe, rented a red convertible, and driven to Acapulco. *Adios, Gus.*

The question was, would she come back? Of course she would. She was just making him squirm. This was payback time for all those times he had left her alone with absolutely no idea when he'd be back. Funny, but he could map the decline of his marriage through all those business trips. As a first-year associate he used to schedule his meetings on a Friday or a Monday so Beth could fly out with him, and they'd spend the weekend in places like Malibu or Monterey. That stopped when Beth tired of hopping on airplanes just to watch her husband work by the swimming pool. Then he started traveling alone, but he would call home every night before bed. That was nice for a while, but it too faded. The more senior he got, the more business he crammed into each trip. Client dinners could last hours. It got to the point that he'd go away for days and be lucky to squeeze in a call from the airport to let her know he was on his way home. Even that became unworkable. Somewhere along the way he just gave up and left it to his secretary to leave a message telling her where he was. He was comfortable with that. It was his secretary, after all, who had picked out the gifts for birthdays and anniversaries, who sent Beth flowers whenever he had to cancel their plans. Beth got a lot of flowers.

A noise from down the hall caught his attention. He was suddenly alert, listening. He heard it again, more clearly this time.

"Mommy." It was coming from Morgan's room.

His pulse quickened. *Was she back?*

"Mommmmmeeee." The cry was desperate.

Now what do I do? He slid off the stool and started down the hall. The calls grew louder, separated by brief, pathetic pauses. "Mom. Mommy!"

Gus drew a deep breath and opened the door. A crack of light from the hallway cut across the bedroom. Morgan was sitting up against the headboard. She was wearing pink Minnie Mouse pajamas. It was amazing how skinny and fragile a kid could look in those clingy cotton pajamas. He went and sat at the edge of the bed.

"It's okay. Daddy's here."

Her voice quaked. "Where's Mommy?"

"She's not here, sweetheart."

"Where is she?"

"She's . . ." Gus had no clue, but he had sense enough not to scare her. "Mommy had something she had to take care of."

"When is she coming back?"

"Soon. I think. It should be soon."

"Can we call her?"

"No. Not tonight."

"Tomorrow?"

"We'll see."

She was plainly skeptical. In the dim shadow of a Winnie the Pooh night light, Gus felt grilled. Just ten seconds of punishing silence had given him a whole new insight into the shrewdness of an only child who spent more time around adults than other children. Six years of training from a no-nonsense nanny who'd seen every trick in the book hadn't hurt either.

Morgan asked, "Where did she go?"

"That's her secret. She didn't say."

"Why didn't she take me with her?"

His throat tightened. "It's just something she had to do by herself, sweetheart. That's all. Sometimes parents have to do things by themselves."

She didn't look satisfied. Gus moved closer, urging her toward the pillow. "Let's go back to sleep now."

She leaned back obediently. Gus sensed the stiffness in her body, the unresolved fears. He stroked her forehead gently. "Just close your eyes and go to sleep."

Her eyes closed, but the lids quivered. He wondered what she was thinking. She sure asked smart questions. She could probably handle a witness better than half the so-called trial lawyers at his law firm. One question in particular stuck in his brain. The one Morgan had struggled to ask. The one Gus had found most difficult to answer.

If Beth had just decided to leave him—if she'd really wanted to get his attention—why *didn't* she take Morgan with her?

He remained at her side and watched her fall asleep, searching for an answer that didn't seem to be there.

Andie went straight home from the morgue, thinking. Gus hadn't really given them sufficient details to test her "bookend" homicide theory. Still, she didn't buy Kessler's idea that Gus was being intentionally evasive. For whatever reason, he and his wife had simply become strangers while living under the same roof.

Somehow, that seemed almost as sad as her disappearance.

Andie was in bed by eleven-thirty, but the night would be a restless one. She was definitely nervous about meeting Victoria Santos at the airport. She set two alarms just to make sure she didn't oversleep. Assuming she ever fell asleep. Her eyes were wide open, staring at the ceiling. The bed felt different these days. Although Rick had never officially moved in, they'd spent nearly every night together for several months before the wedding. It didn't matter that she owned one of those expensive coil mattresses on which you could drop a bowling ball and not disturb your mate. When you're used to sleeping with someone, you know when you're alone.

By midnight her thoughts had turned from Rick to Gus, then to Gus's wife. It was certainly possible that something horrible had happened to her. But she couldn't dismiss another possibility. She knew the pain of *almost* marrying a man who didn't truly love her. She could only imagine what a woman might do after a wasted decade of living with her mistake. Sure, Andie had experienced more than her share of lonely Saturday nights. But nothing was worse than feeling alone when you weren't.

The alarm buzzed but she woke unrested, unable to distinguish her dreams from the things she had lain awake worrying about. She was dressed and ready to go by the time Tuesday's early edition of the *Seattle Post-Intelligencer* landed on the doorstep. She stepped right over it on her way out the door, but the blazing headline practically reached out and tripped her: SERIAL KILLER LEAVES THIRD VICTIM. Beneath it in smaller typeset: *May Be Killing in Pairs.*

Andie tore open the paper and devoured the lead article. She finished with a two-word summary of her own, uttered aloud. "Oh, shit."

Victoria Santos was scheduled to arrive at Sea-Tac airport in thirty-five minutes, so she jumped in the car and then dialed Isaac Underwood at home on her cellular phone. She knew he was an early riser, probably staring at the paper and choking on his corn flakes right about now.

"Isaac, hey it's Andie. Seen this morning's *P-I* yet?"

"Just did. Not one of your better moves, Andie."

"Isaac, I swear. I don't know how it hit the papers. All that stuff about bookends—I just came up with that last night. I haven't told anyone but Kessler. I would never leak without prior approval from a supervisor."

"I believe you. The problem is, it looks like you did an end run on an ISU profiler. That isn't going to sit well with Victoria Santos. Yesterday she had a clean slate. Now you've got her boxed inside a theory she may think is silly."

"What should I do?"

"First, don't freak. Second, check the mirror every now and then. If you find your face turning blue, remind yourself: breathe."

"I'm serious. I'm meeting Santos in less than an hour."

"You want me to talk to her?"

"No. It's my mess. I'll fix it."

"That's what I thought you'd say. I know you're short on time, but it would help if you could get a handle on how this leaked."

"I'll call Kessler."

"Good. But be careful with him."

"How do you mean?"

"I get along fine with him, but not everybody does. Back in my days with the department, people used to say he's perfectly balanced. Got a chip on *both* shoulders."

"Now you tell me."

"Hey, if anybody can dust off his shoulders, it's you."

"Thanks, boss," she said, then hung up. Morning traffic on the interstate was getting heavier by the minute. With one eye on the road, she dug Kessler's business card out of her purse and dialed him at home. His wife answered and said he was in the shower.

"Can you get him, please? This is extremely important."

Andie cut off a van as she veered toward the airport exit. Finally, Kessler came to the phone. "He-low," he said, a bit like a bumpkin.

"Dick, I don't mean to level any accusations, but how did the sum and substance of our conversation last night in the autopsy room make it into this morning's newspaper?"

"I called them."

"Without telling me?"

"I'm a firm believer in using the media to help solve crimes. Victoria Santos is, too. I've heard her lectures."

"I don't argue with the concept," said Andie. "But floating an untested theory might just put ideas in some whacko's head and make it come true. Hell, even you didn't buy the theory when I first suggested it."

"The more I thought about it, the more sense it made."

"We should have at least run it by Agent Santos."

"It's too damn late for that now. FBI politics is your problem, not mine."

"That's true," said Andie. "I was just hoping we all could get off to a little better start than this."

"Should have thought of that before you started making smartass remarks about who does the grocery shopping in my family."

"Come on, Dick. Let's not get petty, all right?"

"I'm not being petty. I'm actually doing you a favor. This press leak gives you the perfect opportunity to find out right from the get-go whether the rumors are true."

"What rumors?"

"From what I hear, Santos has one trait that overshadows even her brilliance."

"Her patience?" Andie said hopefully.

"Her ego. Best of luck, kid. Call me when her royal majesty is ready to meet."

Andie tossed the phone onto the passenger seat and checked herself in the rearview mirror. "Breathe," she said as she approached the airport.

Eight

Morgan was dressed in her plaid jumper and knee socks, ready for school, asleep on the couch in Gus's office. Gus had gotten her up much earlier than usual, dressed her in her elementary school uniform, and taken her to work with him. She'd been out cold since they'd arrived downtown more than two hours ago, before dawn. He'd managed not to wake her as he held her in the elevator and carried her to the couch. She didn't have to be at school till nine, but he had to be at the office before seven. He arrived on time, sleepy kid in tow.

At eight-fifteen the eyes blinked open, and she began to stir. Gus looked up from the paperwork spread across his desk. He had never watched Morgan wake before, at least not the whole adorable process. It was such a contrast to the adult world of buzzing jolts from alarm clocks. He thought of those time-released films of flowers in bloom. She yawned like a bear cub shaking off hibernation, fending off the sunlight streaming through the east window of the big corner office.

She slid off the couch and went straight to the window, struck by the view from the forty-ninth floor. "Wow. This is like the Space Needle."

Her nose was pressed against the glass as she gazed toward snow-capped Mt. Rainier. Gus smiled wanly, then shrank inside. Six years old, and Morgan had never been to her father's office.

"No wonder you live here." The window fogged as she spoke into it.

"This is just an office, sweetheart. Daddy doesn't live here."

"Mommy says you do."

The words cut to the core. No point debating it.

Morgan stepped away from the window. The colorful collection of carved wooden horses on the end table had caught her attention. She took one. Gus jumped up before she could grab the others. "Those aren't toys, honey."

"They look like toys."

"That's because they were, once. But now they're antiques. Expensive antiques." He took the carved thoroughbred and put it back on the table by the others.

"Are you going to take me to school today?"

"Sort of."

A young man appeared in the open doorway. "Ready, Mr. Wheatley?"

Morgan glanced up, as if to ask, "Who's that?"

Gus got down on one knee so they could speak eye to eye. "Morgan, this is Jeremy. He's very nice. He works in the mail room. He's going to take Daddy's car and drive you to school."

"Why don't you take me?"

"I can't. Not today."

"Why can't Mommy take me?"

"It's like I said last night. Mommy is taking some time away."

She frowned. "Will she pick me up?"

"I don't know. We'll see."

Morgan lowered her head in silence. Gus wasn't sure if he should say something, maybe give her a hug. He rose and gave Jeremy the car keys. "She goes to Bertschi."

"To what?"

Jeremy wasn't the kind of kid who'd know the way to a grade school with a five-figure annual tuition. Gus quickly sketched a map on his legal pad. "It's on Tenth Avenue. Easy to find. Drive carefully. And be sure she rides in the backseat."

"No problem."

Morgan was still visibly upset. With one finger Gus lifted her chin from her chest. "Hey, no long faces, okay? I promise, if your mother doesn't pick you up this afternoon, I'll pick you up myself. Is that a deal?"

She clutched her nylon book bag, saying nothing.

He gave her a kiss on the cheek. "Can Daddy have a hug?"

Her arms never left her side. He hugged her anyway, but she didn't hug back. He rose, somewhat embarrassed in front of Jeremy. "You better get going. She has to be there by nine."

Jeremy guided Morgan to the door. Gus watched as they passed the secretarial pod outside his office and started down the hall. Instinct told him to act normal around Morgan until he heard from the police, not to say anything that might scare her. Problem was, he had very little sense of what was "normal" between him and Morgan.

He closed the door and started back toward his desk. He stopped in mid-step. The end table caught his attention, his collection of antique horses. One of them was missing. The one Morgan had been playing with.

He checked first under the table. Nothing. He searched the couch where she'd been sitting, shoving his hand between all the seat cushions. A couple of pens emerged, a lost nickel. But no carved horse.

He glanced out the window, focusing on the waist-high palm prints Morgan had left on the glass. An unsettling feeling slowly washed over him, but the conclusion was inescapable.

His own daughter had just shoplifted.

* * *

Andie entered the main terminal through the American Airlines entrance. The sun had yet to rise, but the airport was bustling. The hour before dawn was like yin and yang at SEA-TAC. Half the people were full of energy, hurrying toward flights that marked the start of their day. The other half were like zombies, arriving from some faraway place after a long night of travel. Andie was somewhere between the extremes, excited about her new assignment yet sickened by the shaky start. She hadn't decided exactly what to tell Victoria Santos about the press leak, but she had to think of something fast. Throughout the terminal, it seemed like every fifty feet there was another newsstand blasting the premature headlines about a serial killer. She tucked a copy of the *Seattle Post-Intelligencer* under her arm and moved with the crowd toward the baggage carousels.

At the turnstile she stopped short. Just ahead was Victoria Santos.

She was dressed comfortably for the long flight, slacks and a sweater, but Andie recognized her instantly. Santos was a bit of an FBI legend, especially among female agents. Years ago she had made a name for herself with the Child Abduction and Serial Killer Unit. It was her profiling and hard work that had cracked the famous "tongue murder" case, a nationwide string of bizarre murders that were connected only by the killer's gruesome signature—the extraction of each victim's tongue. It was the first of many success stories. She was well established as a supervisory special agent by the time Andie had met her for the first and only time, at a training course Santos taught at the academy.

She was slightly taller than Andie, with eyes every bit as intense as Andie had remembered. Up until a month ago, her long, dark hair had been one of her more striking features. Rumor had it that she'd cut it to shoulder length on her forty-fifth birthday, that she hadn't gone to some expensive hair stylist, just grabbed the scissors from her desk drawer and whacked it off.

It was no secret that criminal profilers had one of the highest burnout rates in the bureau. Some said Victoria was approaching the point in her career where she'd crawled inside the head of too many psychopaths, that she'd looked into the eyes of too many lifeless victims. Others thought she was still steaming over the inexplicable decision to derail her promotion to unit chief at CASKU by transferring her to the Investigative Support Unit. Her supporters said she was extremely aggressive. Her detractors said she was extremely aggressive. Bureau politics being what they were, you didn't have to be the highest-ranking woman in a predominantly male unit to get stabbed in the back.

"Ms. Santos?" Andie extended her hand. "I'm Agent Henning. It's a pleasure to meet you. Actually, it's an honor."

Andie cringed at the "honor" bit, concerned that she was sounding like a kiss-ass.

"I hope you're not too honored to call me Victoria," she said as they shook hands.

"Okay, Victoria."

They exchanged smiles, but Victoria looked understandably tired. She'd just flown coast to coast on the red-eye, having left her home in Virginia some time after midnight. Andie glanced at the two bags at her side.

"I see you already got your luggage."

"Yeah. Let's get out of here."

Andie and Victoria reached for the same suitcase at the same instant. They knocked heads. Andie backed away, startled. The rolled-up copy of the *Post-Intelligencer* slid from under her arm and fell to the floor. The page-one story was right at their feet. Victoria rubbed her forehead where Andie had butted her. She did a double-take at the catchy headline, then picked up the paper and gave it a quick read.

"A serial killer slaying in pairs? Where did *this* come from?"

Andie cringed as she replied. "It's a theory."

"Who's theory?"

"Mine," she said, shrinking.

"What's it doing in the newspaper?"

"The local police leaked it."

She glowered. "I'd better read this," she said as she snapped open the newspaper.

"I think so, too," Andie said.

Victoria walked as she read. Andie followed behind, toting her bags. Andie said not a word all the way to the car, just trying to gauge Victoria's reaction to the article. Victoria opened the passenger door and got in. Andie tossed the bags in the backseat, got behind the wheel, and drove out of the garage.

Victoria folded the newspaper and laid it on the dashboard.

Andie was bracing herself for a shakedown, but Victoria simply popped open her briefcase and buried her nose in a notepad as Andie maneuvered out of the airport. For ten minutes, Andie endured the silent treatment. Finally, she couldn't take it anymore. "Excuse me, but aren't you going to say anything?"

Victoria glanced up from her notes. "I'm not going to chew you out, Andie. What's done is done. But if you're looking for me to say everything's okay, it's not."

"I wasn't trying to upstage you or impress you. I wasn't trying to impress anyone. It was just a theory."

"And I'm not saying your theory is necessarily a bad one. The real damage is that once *any* theory hits the press and gets ingrained in the heads of the local police, it's hard to get them to come off it. Makes my job a lot harder than it needs to be."

"But I wasn't the one who leaked it. It was a detective named Kessler."

"That's no excuse. It's your job as coordinator to gain the respect of the locals. If you have their respect, nine times out of ten they'll listen to you if you ask them to keep something out of the press."

Andie felt a pang in her gut, realizing she'd never expressly asked Kessler to keep the theory out of the papers. "You're right. For that I apologize."

Again, there was only silence.

Andie said, "I don't mean to be pushy, but it would make me feel a lot better if you were to say something. Like 'Apology accepted.'"

Andie kept her eyes on the road, waiting for a reply. Finally, she glanced over and caught Victoria's eye. It wasn't the disapproving glare Andie had expected. Quite the opposite. It was as if Victoria had warmed to her fight.

"Apology accepted," Victoria said. "And don't worry about it. Happens to all of us."

Andie was only half-relieved. "Somehow I don't think anything like this ever happened to *you*."

"Actually, it did."

"Serious?"

"Long time ago. My first year in Quantico. We had a geographically transient serial killer. The only lead was an anonymous newspaper informant who had an uncanny ability to predict each murder, time, place, victim. My unit chief was convinced the informant was himself the killer. I wasn't. I went over his head, straight to the assistant director of the Criminal Division. Laid my reputation on the line."

"How did your unit chief feel about that?"

"About the way you'd expect. He was madder than hell."

"How did you smooth things out?"

"Sometimes, things have a way of smoothing themselves out."

"How do you mean?"

"It's simple, really. Now that your theory is printed in

black and white all over Seattle, you just have to hope for one thing."

"What?"

"That you're right."

Andie started to smile, then realized that Victoria wasn't kidding. She cranked up the heater and merged into rush hour on the crowded interstate.

Nine

Gus went back to work after Morgan left, but he couldn't focus on the documents spread across the leather desktop. At eleven A.M. he and three of his department heads were scheduled to pitch their services to a Japanese manufacturer seeking Seattle counsel. "Beauty pageants" lawyers call them, where every major law firm in the city trots out its finest lawyers to win the hearts and wallets of major corporations. The analogy had its limits. In Gus's experience, not a single contestant had ever vowed to feed starving children or promote world peace, and *never* did the runners-up smile and congratulate the winner.

This morning his thoughts were entirely on Beth, swinging from one troubling extreme to the other. One minute he was sure she was safe but had left him. The next, he imagined she was dead. The shoplifting incident had only confused him further. Morgan probably sensed something was wrong and was acting out for attention. Or perhaps it was a symptom of long-standing psychological problems of which Gus had been unaware till now. Maybe even Beth had blamed herself, saw herself as a failure, and in a moment of weakness had run away in despair. Whatever the answer, Gus needed to prepare himself better to deal with Morgan. He could call on professionals for guidance, but it was never his practice to consult anyone cold. Surely there were articles on the Internet about the psychological effects on children who had lost a parent. He pulled up his chair and switched on the computer.

The screen brightened and prompted a message. "Your password is about to expire. Please enter a new code."

For security reasons, the firm required its attorneys to change passwords every ninety days. Gus tried to conjure up a new four-digit number. He usually used dates. The date he was graduated from Stanford. The day he was elected managing partner. This morning, however, he was feeling a little sentimental. He started to type in his wedding anniversary. He entered the month—09—then drew a blank on the exact day. It was either the fourteenth or fifteenth of September. He wasn't sure. It was definitely a Saturday.

Of course it was a Saturday, you idiot.

A reprieve came with a knock on the door. It opened before he could say "come in," which meant it was either the president of the United States or Martha.

"Need a friend?" It wasn't the chief executive.

"Come on in."

Martha had the look of a concerned friend, entering quietly and closing the door behind her. She sat on the edge of the couch, anxious. "Any word on Beth?"

"Just a waiting game now. Police don't really seem to know anything. I'm just trying to stay focused."

"I think that's wise. I wouldn't read too much into what the papers say."

"Papers? What do you mean?"

"You haven't seen this morning's *P-I*?"

"No. I've been so busy, I didn't even have time to check. Is there something about Beth?"

"I'm sorry. Don't be alarmed."

"What is it?" he said with urgency.

"They don't mention her by name. It's just a story about a possible serial killer who is killing his victims in matching pairs. Two men were the first victims. Now they found a woman. They don't come out and say it, but from the physical description, it sounds like Beth."

"I was at the morgue last night. They asked me to view a woman's body. It wasn't Beth."

"It must be the unidentified woman they mention in the article."

"And now they think what? That Beth is her match?"

"Her bookend is the term they use."

He was suddenly alarmed. "Now that you mention it, there was a slight physical resemblance."

"I'm not trying to scare you, Gus. The police don't come out and say anything about Beth directly. That was my inference. All the article says is that they have two male victims, both strangled, both a lot like each other, very similar crime scenes. Now they have a female victim, also strangled. What they don't have is a second female victim. Only fears that the killer might strike another woman who resembles her."

"Who *might* be Beth." Gus snatched up the phone and buzzed his secretary, calling for a copy of today's paper. In a matter of seconds she entered, dropped it on his desk, and left without a peep. Gus devoured the lead story in silence. Finally, he lowered the paper and looked at Martha.

"I can't believe this. I was just with the FBI last night. They never said a word to me about a serial killer."

"That's probably because they don't think Beth is a bookend."

"How can you read this article and say that?"

"Because I don't think Beth is a bookend either."

"So you think all this talk of a serial killer is what— premature speculation?"

"I didn't say that. There may be a serial killer in Seattle. He may be killing in pairs. I just don't think Beth is one of his victims."

"And on what crackerjack investigative expertise do you base that opinion?"

She hesitated, then answered. "I'm sorry. But if anyone was to ask me, I'd say Beth probably left you."

He leaned forward. "Have you talked to her?"

"No."

"Do you know something I don't know?"

"Just call it gut instinct."

"Instinct?" His voice had a dubious tone.

"More than that, really. It's an opinion based on observation. You and Beth have a history that can't be ignored. It wasn't that long ago that she accused you of abuse."

"That was over five years ago."

"Whatever. A woman doesn't make false accusations without some agenda. With Beth I think it was a classic case of a wife crying out for her husband's attention."

Gus moved nervously in his chair. Their marriage counselor had said the same thing. The accusations weren't malicious. They were an act of desperation. "What's your point?"

"Obviously, she couldn't make you listen. So she finally left you."

"That's so simplistic."

"Maybe. But I'm one of those people who tends to think the simplest answer is often the right answer. Sure, it's wise to consider all the possibilities. Based on what I've heard this morning at the watercooler, people have already written Beth off as victim number four of this serial killer. But for me, it's clear. Beth is fine. Wherever she decided to go."

"She wouldn't just leave without Morgan."

"Maybe she'll come back for her."

"Are you trying to make me feel better or worse?"

"I'm not trying to make you anything. I just want you to know all the facts." She looked him in the eye, her tone softening. "I never told you this before. I never told anyone this before. The last time I saw Beth was at the firm holiday party. I'll never forget the way she looked at me. Death rays all night."

"For what?"

"For being the other woman."

"Other woman?" he scoffed. "Hold on there, Martha. This may come as news to you, but as far as I'm aware, you and I have never had sex."

"There are other levels of marital infidelity."

"What are you talking about?"

"Intimacy. It's not just a physical thing. It's a matter of who you make time to talk to every day. Who you call first to share good news. Who you turn to for advice, who helps you solve your problems. True, we've never seen each other naked. But on every other level, I understand you better than your own wife. In every room but the bedroom, I'm the woman you would rather be with. Two people don't have to jump in the sack to be soul mates."

He smiled awkwardly. "Martha, I like you. I like you a lot. But we're a far cry from soul mates."

She looked sad for a split second, then angry.

"Come on," he said. "We're *not* soul mates."

"Fine. If labels make you uncomfortable, drop it. But you don't have to insult me by acting like it's the most ridiculous thing you've ever heard."

"Oh, please. Don't get thin-skinned on me now."

She checked her watch, rising. "I better go. Before you really say something you regret."

"What's that supposed to mean?"

"I've always stood by you. When Beth accused you of abuse, the executive committee was primed to dump you from the partnership before the story hit the papers and tarnished the firm's image. Some people saw it as an opportunity for a change in firm leadership. They saw you as vulnerable."

"What does that have to do with anything?"

"Quite possibly nothing. But if it turns out Beth finally did walk out on you, don't be surprised if the rumbling starts all over again."

"People will think what they want to think."

She leaned forward, her palms resting on the edge of his desk as she looked him straight in the eye. "All I'm saying is be careful. Now more than ever, you can't afford to lose friends."

She turned and headed out, letting the door close behind her.

Gus took a deep breath. He'd seen her angry before, furious in fact. This was different. He wasn't quite sure how to handle it. All he knew was that he didn't need another problem to solve.

He faced his computer. The cursor was blinking on the screen, still asking him to enter a new password—still waiting on his wedding anniversary date. He searched his memory, but the date didn't come. In his mind he heard Martha, his self-proclaimed soul mate, expounding on her own brand of marital infidelity. A tightness gripped his chest. For all his marital problems, the one thing he'd clung to was that he had never cheated on Beth. He never would. For the moment, however, he felt as though he had.

He stared blankly at the screen, trying to remember the anniversary. It was hopeless. In a flurry of frustration he entered a new four-digit password.

It was the date Beth had disappeared.

Andie drove Victoria straight from the airport to the downtown police station. She had been invited by the locals, so it was only logical that the FBI would meet on their turf.

They entered through the main entrance on Ninth Street. Andie shook the rain from her umbrella onto the green tile floor. A pair of detectives hurried in right behind them, their trench coats soaked from the cold morning drizzle. Cops in blue uniforms crisscrossed the lobby. A half dozen suspects were handcuffed and waiting on a bench along the far wall. The oldest one was an aging relic of the sixties with long, stringy gray hair. He had dried vomit on his shoes and an annoying determination to sing Sonny and Cher's "I Got You Babe" to the female officer who had dragged him in for disorderly conduct. Amazingly, his screeching voice was nearly drowned out by the general noise and commotion echoing off the high ceilings. With a quick check of her watch, Andie realized the station was buzzing with the early morning change of the guard. It was easy to tell who was coming and who was going. There was no face more telling than that of a cop coming off the midnight-to-eight shift.

Victoria went straight to the duty officer to announce their arrival. Andie's beeper chirped. She recognized the number. Gus had given her his private line last night.

"We're a few minutes early," she said to Victoria. "I'd like to return this call."

"Sure. Go ahead."

"Thanks." She went down the hall to a pay phone and dialed. She pressed the receiver tightly to her ear and put a finger to the other, blocking out the noise from the lobby.

"Gus?" she said into the phone. "It's Andie Henning. You paged me?"

"Why did I have to read about this serial killer in the newspaper?"

Her heart sank. All morning long she'd been worried about Victoria's reaction. That paled in comparison to the way Gus's voice made her feel. "I'm sorry this happened."

"Sorry it leaked? Or sorry my wife is dead?"

"No one said your wife is dead. The bookend theory is just that—a theory."

"Why didn't you tell me last night?"

"Because it's very preliminary."

"Not too preliminary to make front-page news."

"Believe me, I was just as surprised as you were to read about this in the paper."

"Excuse me?"

"I never intended that theory to hit the newspapers."

He scoffed. "That's reassuring. Sounds like you've really got things under control."

"It's—" Andie struggled. At this point, it seemed the more she told him, the deeper she dug her hole. "I wish I had time to explain. But I don't right now."

"Explain this much for me, will you please? I'm still curious as to why the FBI even has a hand in this. I'm not a criminal lawyer, but homicide isn't normally a federal crime. Do you think Beth was kidnapped and taken across state lines? Is that why the FBI is involved?"

"No. The FBI is involved only to support local law enforcement."

"What does that mean?"

"You really want to know?"

"My wife is missing. I have a right to know."

Andie couldn't argue. A few details might help put him at ease. She glanced back toward the lobby. Victoria was waiting. "I have to make this fast," she said into the phone. "One of our agents from the Investigative Support Unit arrived this morning. She and I will meet with the local homicide detectives."

"To do what?"

"First off, we'll try to determine whether we even have a serial killer."

"Then what?"

"If we think we do, we'll probably take steps toward organizing a multi-jurisdictional task force."

"Led by the FBI?"

"Not exactly. It can get complicated, the more agencies that are involved. The best way to sum up the arrangement is to say things generally don't work the way you see them on television. The FBI doesn't conduct the investigation. That's the job of local law enforcement. We help organize things and make sure the locals get the services they need—crime analysis, formulation of investigative strategies, technical and forensic resource coordination, use of

the FBI Evidence Response Teams or FBI laboratory services. Our experts will also review the evidence to construct a psychological profile of who the killer might be. It
helps police sharpen their investigation, helps them zero in
on certain types of people. It basically gives them somebody to look for when they don't know who they should be
looking for."

"So, who are you looking for?"

"There's no profile yet. That takes a little time."

"These profiles—you can tell a lot about the killer from
them, right?"

"They get fairly detailed, yes." She glanced again toward the lobby. Victoria was pacing. "I'm sorry, Gus. I really have to go."

"Wait, wait. There's one thing I'm particularly interested in."

"What?"

"In this profiling stuff, is there any way to know if the
killer keeps his victims alive? For a while, I mean."

"I told you. We don't have a profile yet."

"I'm *asking* you." His voice was loud, desperate. "I need
some information. Just something to go on, okay? If there
is a serial killer, and he does have Beth . . . how much time
have we got?"

"I wish I could answer. There's just no way to say for
sure."

"There must be a rough estimate you can give me."

"Guessing wouldn't be productive."

"Then damn it, give me the facts. You have three victims
so far. How long was it from the time the victims disappeared until the estimated time of death?"

"We don't know on the woman. We don't even have an
ID yet, so we can't say how long she was missing before
she died."

"What about the men?"

She hesitated, fearful of the inference Gus might draw. "The crime scene was the death scene."

"Talk English, please."

"Both men were murdered in their own homes. The killer didn't transport the victims before killing them. As far as we can tell, he killed them exactly where he engaged them. They were ambushed."

"So, you're saying . . . what?"

"Nothing for sure."

"You're saying it's too late for Beth, aren't you?"

"It's important we act fast. That's true in any case."

"You've written her off for dead."

"That's not true."

"I hear it in your voice. You're already thinking about the next victim. Beth's a statistic."

"No," she said sharply. "If you knew the kind of people who do this work, you would never say that. You'd know they don't forget the victims. Not ever."

"So Beth *is* a victim."

"I didn't say that."

"In your own mind, she is. You just said so."

"You're twisting my words. Stop acting like a lawyer."

"How else should I act?"

"Like the intelligent, rational man I'm sure you are. Please, Gus. I'm on your side."

"Okay. You want me to act rational, I'll be rational. Just tell me one more thing."

"What?"

"How is my six-year-old daughter supposed to act?"

Andie was silent.

"Be sure to call me when your multi-jurisdictional task force figures that one out."

The line clicked, which was just as well. Andie couldn't think of anything to say.

Ten

The first meeting of task force leaders took place in a windowless office in the Seattle Police Department. The long, rectangular table was too large for the room, making it impossible to move unless someone stood up to let the other pass. A droopy brown plant stood in the corner. A detailed map of King County stretched on one wall. Blue push pins marked the spot of two homicides. A red pin marked the spot where the third body had been recovered, as the actual site of her murder was unknown. Three bulging case files were arranged neatly on the table like an imposing centerpiece.

Andie sat beside Victoria Santos, their backs to the map. On the other side were Detective Kessler and his direct supervisors, both sergeants in the homicide division. Behind them, seated against the wall, were the patrol officers who had been first on the scene at each of the three homicides, as well as the ID technicians who had been dispatched to each crime scene. Also in the room were homicide detectives from the King County Sheriff's office, a pathologist from the medical examiner's office, and a rep from the Washington state troopers. They weren't likely to contribute much to the construction of the profile at this early stage, but involving certain key people from the get-go was an effective way to build inter-agency cooperation.

Lieutenant Ethan Wile of Seattle P.D. entered the room at precisely nine a.m., the oldest man in the room but easily the most handsome. It was Wile who had personally contacted the FBI and pushed for the creation of a multi-jurisdictional task force.

"Good morning." He was speaking to the group, but his eyes were on Victoria. She smiled back. It was the first time Andie had seen her smile that way, with sparkling eyes that bespoke true affection, possibly an old romance. The age gap between Victoria and Wile was like the one between Andie and Isaac, though Andie wasn't exactly sure why that thought had popped to mind.

It was no surprise Victoria had come to know Wile. The FBI's criminal profilers generally covered certain geographic regions, and the Pacific Northwest seemed to draw more than its share of serial killers. Maybe it was the mysterious rain and fog that drew them, an eerie shroud for the victims of their unspeakable violence. Maybe it was the challenge of a worthy adversary, a well-trained police force that had understood the psychopathology of serial murderers since Ted Bundy moved from a spot on the Washington governor's 1972 reelection campaign to the FBI's Ten Most Wanted list. Whatever the reason, travel to Seattle had earned Victoria enough frequent-flyer miles for a trip to the moon.

Wile said, "I can't stay for the whole meeting, but let me highlight some of the things that prompted my call to the FBI."

"Please," said Victoria.

"We've got three victims. All strangled. All three received multiple stab wounds, but the medical examiner puts all invasive wounds as postmortem. In each case the victim appears to have died from strangulation before the killer ever unsheathed his knife."

"So you have serious overkill."

"Not just overkill, but a killer who degrades his victims.

All were left in demeaning positions. The latest unidenti-fied woman was found hanging naked from a tree in a pub-lic park. The men were found at home, but they were also nude and positioned on the floor in such a way that their bloody body was the first thing you'd see when you walked in the door. And they both had foreign objects in-serted in their rectums."

Kessler scoffed. "Foreign objects? Are you trying to say the knives were made in China?"

Wile glanced at Andie as if she were his daughter. "Yes, there were knives."

Victoria said, "You don't have to soft-pedal things in front of Agent Henning. She looks young, but she's seen a lot worse than you'd imagine."

Andie wasn't sure if she was supposed to thank Victoria for coming to her defense, or perhaps belch and spit on the floor to show she was one of the boys.

Victoria asked, "Were you able to tell if the killer had brought his own knives with him to the crime scene, or if he just grabbed whatever was available?"

"He didn't bring any knives. He took them from the kitchen."

"Interesting." She made another notation, as if that was significant. "Go on."

"Speaking of the crime scenes, we have similarities there, too. It's bizarre, because with the men, you have a scene where, at first blush, it looks like a madman cut loose, repeatedly stabbing his victims long after they were dead. But in every other respect the place is completely sanitized. Not a single fingerprint."

Victoria made a note in the margin that Andie read as "staging." She underlined it twice. "Go on."

Wile continued, "The most compelling common thread is that the rope used in all three strangulations was the same. Triple-braided yellow synthetic. Three-quarter inch. Like water ski rope."

"Have any of the newspapers mentioned what kind of rope was involved?"

"No. Fortunately, we've kept that quiet. That's the main reason we think all three are victims of the same killer. Too close for coincidence. And a copycat wouldn't know what kind of rope to use."

Victoria quickly reviewed her notes, then flipped the page on her legal pad. "What about *dis*similarities?" she asked. "I don't mean the obvious things, like the sex and age of the victims. Any subtleties you've focused on?"

"One thing in the autopsy report caught my eye," said Wile.

"What's that?"

"The throats were crushed to varying degrees. Even though he used the same rope, different pressure was applied for different lengths of time."

"And why does that surprise you?"

"In a case like this with signs of overkill, I'd expect the guy to lose his cool and hold the rope as tight as he can, for as long as he can. That would be a fairly constant level of pressure for a fairly constant length of time. But that's not what he did."

"Timing and opportunity could explain that. He could have stalked the woman for ten days, stalked the man for ten minutes. He could have been drunk or on drugs. All these things affect a killer's strength."

Andie spoke up. "Or maybe he simply applies whatever amount of pressure is necessary to strangle each particular victim."

Wile answered, "But that's not consistent with a killer who engages in overkill. He's not going to stop when the job is done. He's going to stop only after his rage subsides."

"Or when his victim stops suffering," said Andie.

Victoria glanced at her approvingly. "What are you saying, Andie?"

Butterflies churned. It was the first time a supervisory special agent had actually offered Andie the floor. "You start with the fact that strangulation is a method of homicide that shows a lot of personal anger. A person kills in that way to inflict suffering. That's especially true here, where the guy brings his own rope to the crime scene. If you're going to bring a weapon, why not bring a gun? Only one reason: you want your victim to suffer."

Victoria said, "You're saying his signature is torture, then. He wants to inflict pain."

"Yes."

Kessler asked, "Then why all the stabbing? If he's into torture, why mutilate a dead body?"

"Possibly to confuse us," said Victoria. She flipped back to the notation she'd made about "staging" on the previous page of her notepad. "I obviously need to study this before coming up with a profile, but from what I've heard so far, we have a mixed bag."

"Signs of both an organized and disorganized killer," said Wile.

There were some blank faces. Victoria said, "Those are very important terms Lieutenant Wile just used—organized and disorganized. For criminal profilers, that's the fundamental way of separating two very different types of personalities who commit multiple murders. Organized killers are better planners who carefully select and control their victims. They're generally more intelligent and possess good verbal and social skills. Think of the smooth-talking con man who lures his victims into his car or apartment. The disorganized killer is the opposite. He's often delusional, and the crime scene reflects his confusion and lack of preparation. Think of the social misfit who talks to his shadow and drinks blood out of coffee cups."

"Why do you say the profile is mixed here?" asked Kessler.

"Lots of reasons. The killer brings his own murder

weapon, which is organized. But he leaves the rope at the scene, and also uses knives from the kitchen, which is disorganized. The bodies show no sign of defensive wounds, suggesting the victims were at all times completely under the killer's control. That's organized. But then the bodies are mutilated after death. That's disorganized. The killer makes no attempt to hide and dispose of the body. Again, disorganized. But there is no sign of forced entry, which suggests he may have used a ruse or a con to get inside. Not a single witness saw or heard anything suspicious. And he doesn't leave a single fingerprint at the crime scene. All organized."

"What about the way he left the woman?" asked Kessler. "Taking her from the murder site and hanging her in the tree. What does that say?"

"In this context, it makes me even more inclined to say we don't really have a disorganized killer, or even a psychological hybrid."

"Why is that?"

She glanced again at her notation. "It's quite possible that the disorganized aspects of these crime scenes are completely staged. I see a highly organized killer who is simply trying to throw us off the track by deliberately exhibiting some disorganized traits. I see an experienced killer whose fantasy about killing is so well developed that he not only plans the crime to the last detail, but he also stages his crime scene. The fact that he displayed his latest victim by hanging her from a tree in a public park tells me he's growing more bold, more confident. He's taunting police, probably reveling in the media coverage. He thinks he's too good, too smart to be caught. Which means one thing for certain. He *will* kill again."

The room was eerily silent. Andie cringed inside, thinking of Gus Wheatley's wife, wondering if he had *already* killed again. Finally, Wile spoke up. "Sounds like we're up against some homicidal egomaniac who thinks he can pull off the perfect crime."

"Fortunately, there's no such thing," said Victoria. "Even if he weren't taunting us with clues left behind at the crime scene, a killer would always reveal himself through post-crime behavior. That's why it's so important to focus on what he's doing now—after the kill."

Kessler grumbled. "How the hell are we supposed to know what to look for?"

Her look hardened, the eyes narrowed. It was as if she were already entering the mind of a serial killer. "That's exactly what I can help you with."

Eleven

Gus skipped the beauty pageant. It surprised his partners. Gus was never one to miss an opportunity to land a new client. The mention of a serial killer had changed everything. It was time to find his wife.

Agent Henning's explanation for the newspaper article had left him angry and dismayed. She didn't know how the newspaper had gotten hold of her theory. *Right*. He knew a BS excuse when he heard one. Either she wasn't being honest, or she had no control over the investigation. Either way, someone had to take action.

Publicity was key. Get Beth's picture out, get people looking for her. He and the law firm's publicity director spent several hours making personal calls to media contacts. He did a phone interview with the *Times* and the *Post-Intelligencer*. The local television stations wanted an interview at his home. Gus did it right after lunch, well in time for the piece to air on the evening news.

The last interview finished just after two o'clock. The reporters thanked him, wished him luck. The crews packed up their lights, microphones, tangle of wires, and bulky equipment. Gus showed them to the door. The vans pulled away. The door echoed when it closed. After the flurry of activity he felt like the widower after the last guest has left from the post-funeral gathering.

Alone in the empty house.

He needed something to do. Usually, that meant work. But not this time. He phoned the office, told Jeremy he didn't need him to pick up Morgan, and drove straight to the Bertschi School north of Capitol Hill.

He knew where Bertschi was in the sense that he knew the street address. He had never actually been there before. Beth had checked out the school before Morgan enrolled last September. Gus was out of town for the first biannual parent-teacher conference. He missed the holiday party in December, too.

As he turned on to Tenth Avenue, he could see the line of cars forming at the curved private drive that led to the main entrance. Jaguars, BMWs, Range Rovers. It looked a lot like his law firm's parking garage. He pulled behind the last car and waited his turn, inching forward at less than walking pace. At this rate it would take a good twenty minutes to reach Morgan. Maybe more. Bertschi was a small private school, averaging fourteen students per class, but a hundred seventy-five students meant a line of a hundred-seventy-five cars every afternoon. Many of them had obviously arrived long before Gus had. Apparently the trick was to get there before school actually let out. He was beginning to understand what Beth did with all her "free" time.

He found some light jazz on the radio and tried to relax. A sudden anal-retentive impulse had him reaching for his phone to check his voice mail, but he was in no mood for the rest of the world's problems. Finally, he reached the entrance. He was one of the last. In fact, he was the very last. Morgan stood outside the front entrance. Her skinny legs were covered by warm red knee socks, sticking out like toothpicks below her bulky winter coat. She didn't look happy. Two adults stood at her side. Gus rolled down the window as one of the supervisors came to his car.

"Hi, I'm here for my daughter."

"And you are . . . ?"

"Gus Wheatley. Morgan's father."

"Beth always picks her up." She checked her watch. "Usually a lot earlier than this."

"I know, I know. Beth couldn't make it. So I came. If you could just bring Morgan over here, we'll be on our way."

"I'm not sure I can do that, sir."

"Why not?"

"You're the last car, and Morgan's the only student left. But when you pulled up, I asked her if this was her ride. She said she doesn't know you."

Gus rolled his eyes. "Okay, I'm late. She's mad." He pulled his driver's license from his wallet and showed her. "See, I'm Gus Wheatley."

She checked the photo and handed it back. "Wait right here."

She went back to the school entrance, took Morgan by the hand and brought her to the curb. She crouched beside Morgan and pointed at Gus through the open passenger-side window. "Morgan, is this man your father?"

She pursed her lips, then answered reluctantly. "Yes."

Gus popped the automatic door locks. The woman opened the rear passenger door and buckled Morgan in the backseat, obviously having seen enough 600 series Mercedes to know they came with dual air bags in front. As the rear door closed, the woman reappeared at the open window, looking at Gus. "Come by and see us some time, Mr. Wheatley. We here at Bertschi encourage parent involvement."

He smiled sheepishly and pulled away. Beth had once mentioned that Morgan's teachers thought she was smart enough to skip a grade. He was beginning to wish for a way to skip elementary school altogether.

At the stop sign, he glanced in the rearview mirror. Morgan was pouting.

"Sorry I'm so late, sweetheart. I'm new at this."

"I thought you said Mommy was going to pick me up."

"I said Mommy would come if she was back in time. She's not back yet."

"When is she coming back?"

"I don't know. Soon, I hope."

Morgan peered out the window. Gus knew he was going to have to tell her something soon. This very instant, however, didn't feel like the right time. "Hey, how about some ice cream?"

"Mommy doesn't let me have ice cream before dinner."

"I won't tell if you won't."

She shrugged, seemingly indifferent. "Okay."

With a little coaxing from Gus, Morgan navigated the way to her favorite ice cream parlor. It was a quaint place with old-fashioned wire chairs and marble-top tables. The walls were exposed red brick, warmed by some orchids and green plants hanging from timbers in the vaulted ceiling. Gus and Morgan were the only customers. Most people didn't flock for ice cream when it was forty degrees outside, but for Morgan it was never too cold. An assortment of flavors was arranged in big tubs behind the glass display. Rows of pizza-sized cookies were on the top shelf. Morgan ordered a "create-your-own" sundae: one scoop of bubble gum sorbet, two scoops of rocky road ice cream, topped with crushed Reese's Pieces and pineapple sauce. Gus suddenly lost his urge for anything sweet. He ordered coffee. They sat in a corner booth near an old, broken jukebox that was just for show. Morgan was totally absorbed in her treat, careful not to spill a drop from the overflowing bowl.

"How was school today?" he asked.

"Okay."

She was scooping the ice cream at a steady clip. The bizarre combination of flavors alone was enough to land her in the hospital. Speed would only hasten the belly ache. "Slow down a little," he said. She ignored him. "Morgan, did you hear what I said?"

She scooped even faster. He was angry for a split second, then concerned. She seemed more hungry than defiant. "Morgan, did you eat lunch today?"

She shrugged.

"Does that mean you don't remember, you don't care, or you don't think so?"

She shrugged again, still dipping into her ice cream.

"Are you worried about something, sweetheart?"

She stopped eating, speaking into her sundae. "Aren't you?"

He knew what she meant, but he didn't want this to be their talk about Beth. Not yet. "Actually, I am a little worried. About you."

"I'm okay."

He looked away, then back. "Morgan, I'm going to ask you a question. I promise you, I won't get angry, no matter how you answer it. So long as your answer is the truth. Is that a deal?"

She nodded. Melted ice cream was dripping from her chin. Gus reached across and wiped it away with the napkin. "Do you remember that little wooden horse in my office? The one I said was not a toy?"

"Yes."

"Did you take it?"

She froze, saying nothing.

"Just tell me the truth. I won't get mad. Did you take it?"

She lowered her eyes. Her head moved almost imperceptibly, but it was definitely a nod.

"Why did you take it?"

She shrugged again. "I don't know."

"You know that's wrong, don't you? Did anyone ever tell you that it's wrong to take things without permission?"

Another shrug.

"I'm confused again, Morgan. Are you saying you don't know it's wrong to steal things?"

She just sat there. Gus studied her expression. She seemed troubled, as if she were hiding something. "Morgan, did anyone ever tell you it was *okay* to steal?"

Her shrug was slower this time, more exaggerated. More ambiguous.

"Is that a yes?"

"No one really told me that. I just . . ."

"You just what?"

She lowered her chin to the tabletop. Her eyes locked on the half-empty ice cream dish before her. "I saw Mommy do it."

He winced, incredulous. "You saw your mother steal something?"

She nodded.

"Where?"

"At Nordstrom's."

That was Beth's favorite department store. "Are you sure?"

"Mmm-hmm."

"Tell me what happened."

"She just . . . put some clothes in her bag."

"Mommy put clothes in her shopping bag?"

"Yeah. And then we walked out."

"You didn't stop at the cash register to pay for it?"

She shook her head.

"Are you sure about that?"

Her voice was flat, but the answer was firm. "I'm sure. It happened lots of times."

"What do you mean lots of times? More than twice?"

She nodded.

"More than three times?"

Again, she nodded.

"More than five times?"

Morgan was still. Slowly, she nodded.

Gus leaned back in his chair, flabbergasted. Then it hit him, and the shock gave way to pity. He suddenly understood. Morgan was angry, that was all. She was afraid her mommy had left her, and now she was making up bad stories about her.

"Morgan, are you mad at Mommy for something?"

She shrugged. Gus had seen enough of her shrugs to know which ones meant yes, which ones meant no. This was definitely a yes.

"You shouldn't be mad at Mommy. But it's normal to be a little worried. I'm a little worried, too."

"You are?"

He nodded. "In fact, I've already asked some people to help look for your mother."

"Did something bad happen to her?"

"We don't know that. There are certain things I have to do, just to be extra careful."

"What kind of things?"

He paused, afraid it might overwhelm her to talk about the FBI and the media. "Remember last year, when your class took a field trip to the zoo and you got lost for a little while?"

"Yeah."

"Your teacher got really nervous, because you were gone, and she didn't know where you were. She had the other kids looking for you, the other teachers, the zookeepers. I think the chimpanzees were even looking for you."

She smiled a little. "Not the chimps."

"All right, maybe not the chimps. But a lot of people were worried and looking for you. And the whole time you were just standing and watching the polar bears."

"You think that's where Mommy is?"

"No. But it could be something that simple. She could

be just fine. So promise me you won't get scared if you see people looking for Mommy, wondering where she is. We're all just being very careful."

She stopped eating her ice cream. She was staring down at the table.

"Morgan? You promise?"

She was silent. After a few seconds he noticed a slight movement, a very faint shrug of the shoulders. He decided not to push.

"Come on, sweetheart. Let's go home."

Twelve

The personal phone calls were beginning to take their toll. It seemed everyone had been content to leave her alone for a few days to recover from Saturday's marital disaster. By Tuesday, however, the comfort cushion was over. The whole world suddenly seemed to think it was time to check on Andie. Friends called. Her father called. Her mother called. Several times.

"Mom, really. I'm okay." Her voice was strained. She had one eye on all the work piled up on her desk.

"You're sure?"

"Yes, I'm sure. Honestly, I've been so busy I haven't even had time to think about Rick."

Her mother paused, as if something other than Andie's well-being were on her mind.

"What is it, Mom?"

"Why did you go through with the ceremony, Andie?"

"What?"

"If you knew he had cheated on you, you should have just canceled. It would have saved a lot of embarrassment."

"Rick deserved it."

"It's not him I'm talking about. It was embarrassing for the whole family."

"Gee, Mom. Sorry I ruined your day."

"Don't be that way. Your sister made a terrible mistake and immediately apologized."

"Linda couldn't wait to jump out of bed with Rick to come tell me she'd fucked him."

"Andie!"

"It's the truth. That's the real reason she knocked on my door in the middle of the night to give me her so-called apology. She hates me. She always has. What did you think, forcing me to name her as my maid of honor would suddenly make her love her adopted sister?"

"You should have shown more consideration for your guests."

"I was angry."

"It was cruel."

"Cruel? Can't you just let me have my moment and move on? Maybe it's not the way you would have handled the situation. But for me it brought closure. That's just my personality. I need to get even."

"That's not a very Christian attitude."

The mention of Christian values was an all too familiar and infuriating tactic. All her life, whenever she had misbehaved, her mother had found a subtle way of attributing it to the fact that she was half Native American, an adopted child.

There was a knock on the door. It opened a foot, and Victoria poked her head in. "There's a break in the case."

Andie cupped her hand at the receiver, trying not to let Victoria know it was her mother. "I gotta go," she muttered into the phone.

"We're not done," her mother answered.

"Let me put you on hold." With a push of the button she cut off her mother's protest, then waved Victoria in.

"We got a message from someone who may be the killer."

Andie did a double-take. "What kind of message?"

"E-mail from a copy center in Seattle. One of those temporary office places where you can rent a computer for an hour and send all the e-mail you want over the Internet."

"He sent an e-mail?"

"Photographs, actually. They appear to be our Jane Doe, alive. From the looks of things, however, I wouldn't guess she was alive for very long after the little photo session. Looks very weak, obviously been beaten. The neck was badly bruised, too, which suggests some ligature strangulation."

"You sure she was alive?"

"No question. One look at those eyes, and you know she's looking right at her killer."

Andie fell silent. "How'd you get the photos?"

"Minneapolis field office sent them to me."

"He e-mailed the FBI in Minneapolis?"

"No. He sent it to the Torture Victims' Institute, which is in Minneapolis. They contacted the local FBI."

Andie asked, "There's an institute for torture victims?"

"Quite an impressive organization, actually. Some very skilled psychotherapists. Victims of political torture all over the world go there for treatment and counseling."

"So maybe he's insinuating there's some political agenda attached to his killings."

"No political agenda," said Victoria. "His message is more straightforward."

"Which would be what?"

"You said it at the meeting. We're dealing with a sadist. And his agenda is torture. Period."

Andie was suddenly flummoxed. Victoria sensed her discomfort. "Not sure how you should feel, are you?"

Andie shook her head.

"That's the thing about profiling. Once you figure out what kind of monster you're dealing with, there's no rejoicing in being right. Not till he's caught."

Andie said nothing.

"I'm having hard copies of the photos reproduced. You

need to get them distributed to the task force as soon as they're ready. You'll also need to coordinate with the Minneapolis field office on their follow-up with the institute. I don't think an airplane trip is necessary, but make sure the personnel records are thoroughly reviewed, with an eye in particular for disgruntled former employees. Certainly if the institute has received any messages like this in the past, you'll want to check that out. And there's also an International Center for Victims of Torture. It's in Denmark. Touch base there, see if this jerk sent them anything."

"Right."

Victoria stepped out of Andie's office and closed the door behind her. Andie went back to the phone. The hold line was blinking. Her mother was waiting, primed to hash out a problem that now seemed more trivial than ever.

Andie punched the button and deliberately disconnected.

In the solitude of his bedroom, he held a pendant in his hand. His newest acquisition was already his favorite. The long braided chain weaved in and out between his fingers like golden rope. He held it higher, toward the light, allowing it full extension. No bigger than a dime, the heart-shaped pendant dangled at the end of the strand. It was a gold frame of diamonds, hollow in the middle. The fluorescent desk lamp made it sparkle. With his eyes narrowed, it looked curiously like the noose at the end of a rope. *That* was what he loved about it.

The so-called experts would have called it a trophy—a keepsake taken from the victim. That was one of those terms he had picked up from the multitude of books written by former criminal profilers. He'd read them all and knew their secrets. It amused him the way those authors denied they were making it possible for future serial killers to avoid apprehension. Sociopaths are psychologically compelled to engage in certain conduct, the experts argued, so publication of those traits couldn't possibly prompt a serial killer to change his behavior and make himself more difficult to catch. They were overlooking one crucial fact. Their assumptions were based on the assholes who got caught.

He turned the chain in his hand, let it twist slowly. Spinning round and round, it reminded him of those afternoons in his garage as a curious teenager. His own body suspended by the neck, hanging for as long as it took to lose consciousness, then falling to the ground with the release of the rope. For added effect he had taken to twisting the cord like a kid on a tire swing. He could spin as fast or as slow as he wanted, depending on how tightly he wound it. Just an added rush for the average fifteen-year-old boy hanging by the neck with an erection to be proud of.

Carefully, almost lovingly, he lowered the gold chain back into the box. It coiled into a felt-lined compartment, next to a pair of earrings. A pearl necklace. A wristwatch. A ring. Each piece brought back its own memory. The ring, however, was a sea of mixed emotions.

It had belonged to someone special.

He closed the lid on the jewelry box and stepped toward the bed. On bended knee he pulled a large manila envelope from between the mattress and the box spring. He emptied it on the bedspread, spilling a collection of Polaroid snapshots. Mostly young women, a few men. Some naked, some clothed. Frightened faces mixed in with peaceful expressions. It all depended on whether it was before or after.

He stared down at them and a heat rose from within him. It was cool in the room, but he was beginning to perspire. Such were his powers of concentration. He was focused on the details of each deadly pose. The position of the hands. The tilt of the head. The display of the victim. This wasn't simple reminiscing. He regarded these photos not as windows to the past but as blueprints—for the future. It all had to be perfect.

He left the photos neatly arranged on the bed beside him and crawled beneath the covers. Naked and somewhat aroused, he checked the clock on the nightstand. Not quite four P.M. Just enough time to revel in his fantasy. Then to work.

He rolled onto his back and closed his eyes.

Thirteen

Andie didn't normally fret over what people thought about her, but Victoria was different. Competition for a spot with the elite ISU was almost prohibitive. A good word from Victoria could go a long way. A bad word would slam the door.

In truth, Andie wanted more than just one woman's approval. Certain colleagues in the office refused to let her wedding disaster die quietly. Just today some jerk had left a doctored photocopy of the FBI shield in her in-box with the FBI motto—Fidelity, Bravery, and Integrity—changed to *In*fidelity, etc. Though it was the groom who had slept with the maid of honor, the joke was on the bride who had announced it at the ceremony. A bang-up job as profile coordinator might silence the morons at the watercooler.

Victoria had seemed mildly impressed by Andie's torture analysis at the task force meeting, which was borne out by the photographs from Minneapolis. But without so much as a word to Andie, she had spent the rest of the day studying the files alone in a small, windowless office that was the perfect home-away-from-home for a special agent from the ISU. The Investigative Support Unit was quite literally buried beneath the earth back at the FBI Academy in Quantico, two stories below the gun vault.

By four o'clock Andie figured it was time to get a read

on Victoria's thinking. That was a dangerous prospect, considering the amount of time Victoria spent thinking like a serial killer. Undaunted, Andie walked down the hall and knocked on the door.

It opened. Victoria was blurry-eyed behind her reading glasses. "Yes?"

"Sorry to interrupt," said Andie. "But have you got a minute?"

Victoria seemed distracted but stepped aside and let her in. Crime-scene photographs were spread across the table, like pieces of a gruesome puzzle. Andie wasn't a total neophyte, but it unsettled her to stare into the bulging eyes of a strangulation victim.

Victoria returned to her seat, facing the photographs. Andie pulled up a chair. "This will just take a minute."

"It's okay," said Victoria. "I needed a break anyway."

"I've had something on my mind since the task force meeting."

"Was there something we didn't cover?"

Andie felt baited. It was as if Victoria knew why she had come. "Actually, yes."

"Your bookend theory?"

"That's the one."

Victoria smiled thinly. "I was wondering how long it would take for you to come talk to me about it."

"I'm not pushing it. I'm just curious, that's all. It did make front-page news this morning. But in the whole three-hour meeting, you hardly mentioned it."

"Everyone in that room had read this morning's paper. A serious discussion about it would have galvanized their thinking. It's like I told you in the car. If it's a bogus theory, we don't want to give our task force a full head of steam heading in the wrong direction."

"Why are you so sure it's bogus?"

"I didn't say it was."

"Do you think it has any merit? Possibly, I mean?"

"Would it make you feel better if I said I did?"

"Maybe."

Victoria raised an eyebrow. Andie said, "Okay, yes, it would. And that's not because I'm some kind of egomaniac. It's just that your little speech in the car this morning left me twisting in the wind."

"How do you mean?"

"You said it was okay that my theory leaked to the press, so long as I was right."

"That's right."

"Well, I don't think it's fair to hoist the blade up the guillotine and then give me no indication as to whether *you* think I was right or wrong."

Victoria nodded and said, "That's a fair complaint."

Andie wasn't sure if she was agreeing with her or simply acknowledging her right to gripe. "So, what do you think about the bookend theory?"

"It has definite appeal, if you focus on the first two victims. Both white males, fifty-one years old. Same hair and eye color. Divorced, middle-class. From a victimology standpoint, the only apparent difference is that one drove a 1989 Ford pickup and the other's was a '93. And, of course, the similarities don't end with the choice of victim. Both were strangled and stabbed exactly eleven times after death, mutilated and degraded the same way, left on display in their own living rooms. And here's something I just picked out of the police reports. In both cases the television was on when the cops arrived. Tuned to the same damn station. KOMO, channel 4."

"So you understand where I'm coming from," said Andie.

"Of course. But there are dissimilarities, too. Until we construct a more complete profile of the killer, it's hard to know if these differences are meaningful psychological indicators or just cosmetic changes in m.o."

"But like you say, the more you review these three cases, the more viable the bookend theory becomes."

"I didn't say that. I said the two men were remarkably similar."

"Jane Doe was also strangled."

"Yes. And unlike the men, she was photographed alive, and the pictures were sent to the Torture Victims' Institute."

"But it was the same kind of rope in all three cases. Doesn't that make you think that victim number four will look a lot like her, maybe even have her picture sent to Minneapolis?"

"Not enough to put it in the newspaper."

Andie withdrew, deflated.

Victoria shifted gears quickly, as if not to let *all* the air out. "By the way, what did you make of the busted eardrum?"

"The what?"

She glanced at her notepad. "I was just reading the final autopsy report on our Jane Doe, hot off the press. Didn't you pick up on that?"

"I guess I didn't focus on her ears."

"Says she had a ruptured right eardrum. Strangulation obviously creates pressure in the head, but I've never heard of it causing an eardrum to burst. Interestingly, we don't have any kind of ear trauma in the two male victims."

"You're saying what? My bookend theory is out the window because victim number three had a busted eardrum?"

"Right now the flaw in your theory isn't as subtle as that. The various similarities and simple fact that the same rope was used in three confirmed homicides tells us we probably have a serial killer. But it's hard to label our serial killer a so-called 'bookend killer' when we have only one set of bookends. There's no way to be certain there will be a match for Jane Doe."

"That's being a little conservative, don't you think?"

"You want to send this city into a panic? Thanks to this

morning's newspaper, every thirty-something brunette in Seattle is probably looking over her shoulder."

"Maybe that's not a bad thing."

"Or maybe it's a terrible thing. Maybe we've just lulled every blonde and redhead in King County into a false sense of security."

She suddenly understood Victoria's reluctance to embrace her theory—at least publicly. "Maybe it is premature to give our killer a name. But let's look down the road. Say the killer next strikes a woman who matches Jane Doe as closely as the two male victims matched each other? Or, let's say Beth Wheatley is already victim number four, and Jane Doe isn't just another thirty-something brunette. What if it turns out she's also the wealthy mother of a six-year-old daughter and was estranged from her high-powered husband—just like Mrs. Wheatley?"

"Not to be difficult, but I don't take anything at face value. I would probably check Mrs. Wheatley's ears."

"And if there's a busted eardrum?"

Victoria glanced at the photos on the table, then back at Andie. "Then I'd have to say we're dealing with one scary son of a bitch."

Andie's voice filled with trepidation. "And I would have to say you're right."

Gus didn't really want his daughter to see it. In fact, he hadn't even told Morgan he was going to be on the evening news. Carla had. Gus hadn't explicitly told her not to tell Morgan, but he'd expected his sister to have more sense. The fact that he'd tried to keep it a secret only seemed to make Morgan more determined to watch.

She was parked on the leather couch a good fifteen minutes before the five o'clock local news. He wasn't about to let her watch, even if she was more mature than most six-year-olds. He did take a few minutes to explain why the reporters had come by the house, what he had told them. He kept reminding her of the zoo story. It was a safe image, her mommy off by herself watching the polar bears. He wished it were that simple.

"Please, can't I watch?" she asked.

"I don't think that's such a good idea."

"But I want to see Mommy's picture."

"I'll videotape it for you, okay? And then we can talk about whether you can see it."

"Why?"

"Morgan, there's no debate." He spoke in his stern discipline voice that told her he meant business. She pouted but followed him obediently to her room.

"You promise you'll let me see the tape? Please?"

"I promise to think about it," he said, then closed the door.

It was exactly five o'clock when Gus returned to the room.

"Good evening," said the newscaster. "Tonight's top story . . ."

It wasn't Beth. He felt let down, though no one had told him it would be the *lead* story. Still, he couldn't help but feel that his was the important story, far more important than the latest flap over political campaign fund-raising.

He plugged a tape into the VCR, as he promised he would. He felt cold as he waited, doubtful he would let Morgan watch the recording any time soon, dead positive he could never have prepared her for the live broadcast. He wondered if *he* was prepared.

Finally, the news turned local. "In other news, the wife of a prominent Seattle attorney is reported missing . . ."

Gus went numb at the sight of Beth's photograph on the screen. It was worse than he had anticipated, seeing his wife on television with the dramatic graphic MISSING displayed alongside her.

The young anchorwoman said, "More on this story from investigative reporter Vince Daniels."

Gus was taken aback. He had never talked to a Vince Daniels. It had been a woman who had come by the house to interview him. The story was taking an unexpected tack.

The screen flashed to a stocky reporter standing live outside the state courthouse. He had a microphone in one hand, papers in the other.

"Judy, this is not the first time alleged acts of violence have touched the Wheatley family. In court documents obtained exclusively by *Action News*, Beth Wheatley filed this domestic-violence complaint against her husband, Gus Wheatley, the managing partner of Seattle's most respected law firm. The report was filed five years ago, at a time when insiders tell us the couple was contemplating divorce. Although the Wheatleys did reconcile, in this explosive report Mrs. Wheatley alleges a pattern of spouse abuse that lasted over a year. Abuse that didn't end, she says, until he physically struck her."

"Vince, is there any indication that police are investigating a possible connection between the abuse and Mrs. Wheatley's disappearance?"

"So far police aren't talking. But we will be watching this story very closely."

A stunned Gus grabbed the remote control and switched off the television. He was already shaking as a voice startled him from behind.

"That's why you didn't want me to watch." It was Morgan.

He hadn't heard her sneak out of her room, but it was too late to scold her and tell her to go back. "Morgan—"

"Did you hit Mommy? Did you make her go away?"

"Morgan, no."

He saw hatred in her eyes, then fear. She ran from the room. Gus hurried after her. "Morgan, please."

She only ran faster, straight to her room. The door slammed in Gus's face. He tried the knob. It was locked.

"Morgan, let me explain." He knocked and tried the knob again.

"Go away!" she shouted.

He wanted to tell her it wasn't true—that he had never hit Beth, that she had withdrawn the complaint. Crucial details that a sensationalist newsman hadn't bothered to report.

"Morgan?"

"Just go away!"

He pressed his ear to the door. His mind whirled, then stopped, as though he'd hit a stone wall at full speed and was crushed beneath the fallen rubble.

Inside, he could hear Morgan crying.

Fourteen

Even the rain looked cold. Tiny droplets sprinkled the windshield, where they huddled together on the brink of freezing until the intermittent wipers cleared them.

A light rain had been falling all day, classic winter weather in the Pacific Northwest. In any given year, dozens of American cities got more precipitation than Seattle—Miami, Atlanta, even New York City. But it seemed nowhere did the rain come down so continuously, so steadily for hours, days or even weeks on end.

Colleen Easterbrook adjusted her wipers. The rain was falling harder. The wet road ahead glistened beneath the long reach of her headlights. She had left the Red Lion airport hotel at nine-thirty, after an exhausting ten-hour shift. As assistant manager she was used to overtime, hardly able to remember the last time she'd worked an eight-hour day. Today had been the usual stressor. Five bus loads of rowdy Rotarians all trying to check in simultaneously. It was always some group coming or going. Her interstate commute was a welcome daily ritual, almost like therapy. That precious time alone in her car was her only chance to unwind.

The radio shifted from pop to news on the half hour. She was about to change stations, but the lead story caught her attention. More mention of a possible serial killer from the baritone newscaster. Her finger froze on the button as she listened.

"Unidentified police sources say the killer may be striking pairs of victims in rapid succession, killing one and then another who bears a stunning resemblance to the first."

She switched it off. She'd read the same story in this morning's newspaper with only passing interest. "Bookends" was what the paper had called it. The first two were men, neither of whom struck a chord with her. The third was an unidentified white woman. She was a brunette, in her mid-thirties, roughly five feet five inches tall. Like her. And probably like twenty thousand other women in the metropolitan area. Back at the bustling hotel, the vague resemblance she bore to some unidentified victim had barely caught her attention. With a quick dismissal she'd moved on to the Arts section and checked out the latest movies. Driving alone at night, however, was a different story. The thought of a missing bookend and a potential fourth victim gave her serious pause. The similarities seemed closer to home. Too close.

Traffic slowed beneath the overpass. A string of blinking red taillights dotted all five lanes ahead. Probably a fender bender. Her Mustang slowed to a crawl. Nearly every night for the past two years she'd driven past this exit. Tonight was the first time she'd encountered a traffic jam. It was a chilling coincidence. She was suddenly reminded that the Green River Killer—Seattle's worst serial killer—had dumped one of his victims not far from here. More than a decade had passed, but that unforgettable television newscast was still ingrained in her memory—the police pulling that poor woman's naked body from the grassy field, her lifeless left arm dangling from beneath the blanket.

She glanced at the radio. It was off, but she could still hear the newscaster talking about the bookend killer. Another thought interrupted: the Green River Killer had never been caught. Forty-nine probable victims, and he was possibly still going strong.

Her car came to a complete stop. She was trapped at the exit. She checked her fuel gauge. Less than an eighth of a tank. Not enough to sit through a long traffic jam. Her mind flashed with fears of running out of gas somewhere down the road. The doors were locked, but that would hardly keep a madman from running through the rain, smashing her window, grabbing her around the throat, and dragging her into a ditch. The need to keep moving soon overwhelmed her. At the first opening she turned into the far right lane, the only one moving. She weaved recklessly through the jam, cutting off cars and eliciting angry horn blasts. She passed the wreckage on the highway and broke into the clear with a final, quick lane change. One last rubber-necker had to swerve his van to the shoulder to avert a collision. She glanced in her rearview mirror. He was flipping her the bird. She drew a deep breath, surprised at herself. She was normally the most courteous driver on the road.

Damn, what the hell's gotten into you?

It was just nerves, she told herself. She switched the radio on and found some music. Traffic thinned over the next few miles. She was speeding without realizing it, pushing past seventy. Her exit came quickly. As she steered down the ramp, she considered a stop for gas at the station on the corner, then decided to keep going. She had enough to get home. She'd fill the tank in the morning, during daylight. Blessed daylight.

She was eager to get home, but she didn't speed. The traffic lights were synchronized. If she went too fast, she'd hit red lights. She held exactly at the limit and sailed right through each intersection.

Her house was on Carter Street, third from the end. Every house on the block was built in the 1950s and looked just about the same. Gabled roofs, clapboard siding. Some neighbors had distinguished their yards with impressive gardens of shrubs, rocks and flowers. Colleen barely found time to mow the lawn. As she pulled into the driveway, she wished she had taken the time to install that low-voltage landscape lighting that was so popular in her neighborhood. Her house was too dark. She hadn't even left a porch light on. Not a smart way to live with a serial killer on the prowl.

She opened her car door and headed up the rain-slick walk. Her house key was firmly in her grasp as she cut briskly through the chilly night air. Instinctively, she checked over her shoulder a couple of times, then climbed the stairs. It was crazy to think that with all the women in the Puget Sound area, she might be the killer's next victim. Why would a serial killer target an attractive, thirty-five-year-old woman who lived alone, came home every night at exactly the same time without an escort, and had no dog or alarm in her dark house?

Why *wouldn't* he?

Her hand shook as she inserted the key. The tumblers clicked. The lock disengaged. She pushed the door open and hurried inside. Her heart was racing. She didn't even take time to flip on the light before she threw the lock and hooked the chain back on the door. It was all in her mind, surely, but she'd felt she was being chased. She leaned against the door, relieved to be safely inside.

A floorboard creaked in the middle of the room. She turned, startled. She saw nothing in the darkness. She waited, listening. She heard nothing, but she was afraid to switch on the light. Slowly, her hand reached for the wall switch. She flipped it. The foyer lit up. Her eyes filled with fear. Standing right before her was a man in a black body suit, his face covered by a ski mask. His arms extended outward, like an eagle about to pounce on its prey.

She was about to scream, but the man moved too quickly. A swift blow silenced her. His arms came together in a lightning-quick motion, palms open, slamming against her ears in a simultaneous blast to either side of the head. It took only an instant, but he seemed to move in slow motion. The stunning blow, the pop in her ears. It was louder and more violent in the left ear, the blow from his right hand. The deafening explosion knocked her nearly unconscious. She fell to the floor. Her vision was blurred. Her sense of balance was gone. She looked up, helpless. The man's mouth was moving, as if he were speaking, maybe even shouting. But she heard not a word. She heard absolutely nothing. Her hearing had been destroyed.

Her eardrums were ruptured.

In another quick motion she was pinned flat on her stomach, her attacker's knee squarely in her back. The pain in her ears worsened, leaving her too disoriented to resist. Her arms lay helpless at her side until he grabbed her by the wrists and cuffed her hands behind her back. Her body stiffened. She tried to scream but couldn't. She was unable to fight, yet she was strangely aware of everything that was happening to her. A nylon rope slipped over her head. A tightness gripped her throat. Her larynx was crushed, robbing her of speech. Her eardrums were shattered, so she couldn't hear.

Yet somewhere deep in her mind was the piercing sound of her futile screams.

Part Two

Gus had been up most of the night trying to decide the best way to tell Morgan the truth. He didn't want to corner her in her room and ambush her into conversation. He'd wait patiently at the breakfast table until she came out. But she didn't come.

The doorbell rang around eight-thirty. It was Carla. She was Morgan's ride to school.

"I can take her," said Gus.

She gave her brother a knowing look. "She wants me. She called twenty minutes ago and said she didn't want to ride with you."

Gus shrank inside. No need to explain to Carla. She'd undoubtedly watched the news last night and probably believed every word of it.

Morgan walked straight from her bedroom to the front door, dressed and ready for school. She didn't even look at her father as she passed him.

"Morgan?" he called.

She stopped halfway down the steps, but she didn't turn around.

"Have a good day, sweetheart. Daddy loves you."

Her head turned slightly, but not enough to meet his eyes. Carla led her by the hand to the car.

Gus watched them pull away, then locked up the house

113

and got in his car. He hadn't planned on going into the office, but Bonnie, his secretary, had called to tell him she had organized a support group at the office. Nothing formal. Just some secretaries and staff who wanted to help. The meeting was in the main conference room at nine. Gus misjudged the commuting time, so he arrived a few minutes late, dressed in coat and tie. He wasn't trying to impress anyone with the power look, but he figured any change in appearance—such as dress—would only feed rumors that he was losing his grip on the emotional slide. He didn't need that.

His secretary met him at the elevator. "Gus, thank God you're here."

She was out of breath, as usual, undoubtedly having run from door to door, gathering people for the meeting. "The Road Runner" was her nickname because she was always in a hurry. Guinness Book of Records didn't know it, but the land-speed record had actually been set by the amazing Bonnie DeVreeze in the hallowed halls of Preston & Coolidge.

"What's wrong?"

She caught her breath, leading him down the hall. "Everyone's waiting."

They stopped outside the conference room. Muffled conversations hummed behind the closed door. "How many are there?"

"Close to a hundred."

"Wow."

She smiled. "Yeah. Wow."

"What should I say to them?"

"Just thank them. They really want to help."

"That's very nice. But I'm not sure what they can do."

"I had the copy center print up flyers and posters. Thousands of them. We can pass them out here and get volunteers to post them in grocery stores, malls, all over."

He was once again grateful that at least *one* of them was organized. "Thank you."

"You're welcome."

He started for the door, then stopped. "About that news-cast last night. The abuse allegations—"

She cut him off. "Isn't it enough that all these people showed up to help you? Doesn't that tell you anything?"

For the first time in days he felt good inside. "It tells me a lot. Thank you."

He gave her a hug and headed inside.

The seventh floor of the Federal Building buzzed with the usual level of morning energy. It wasn't the chaotic kind of bustle that filled big-city police stations. A quiet dignity permeated the halls of an FBI field office, a sense of im-portance and efficiency. Still, there was the occasional out-burst, like the jubilant group at the watercooler celebrating last night's drug bust in Port Angeles. Normally, Andie would have gone over to get the details, but today she just closed her office door and tuned it all out.

Earlier that morning Victoria Santos had called her at home. Andie wasn't exactly sure how she'd found out about Gus Wheatley's appearance on the nightly news. Perhaps she and Isaac had spoken. Whoever the source, Victoria wasn't happy. In her eyes, Gus's contacting the media without even telling Andie showed a complete breakdown of trust and communication. It was Andie's job to get it back.

Andie didn't want to be knee-jerk. She needed to talk to Gus, but she had to get her facts straight first. One thing was clear about last night's television broadcast, with its emphasis on the old abuse allegations over Beth's recent disappearance: Gus hadn't steered the story in that direc-tion. That left the question: who had?

She feared he would think it was her. Gus had told her about the abuse the other night at the medical examiner's office. The possibility that the FBI had leaked that infor-mation to the media must have crossed Gus's mind, especially after the serial killer leak to the newspapers. She wanted to assure him it wasn't the FBI, and she wanted to go even further and say it wasn't law enforcement, period. Problem was, she wasn't sure.

She picked up the phone and dialed Seattle homicide.

"Hey," said Detective Kessler, "I was wondering when I'd hear from you."

"You saw last night's newscast?"

"Sure did."

"What did you think?"

"Didn't surprise me."

She paused. "Is that because you had something to do with it?"

"You mean, all that abuse talk?"

"You know what I mean."

"Not me, sweetheart."

"You were pretty fixated on the alleged abuse when we interviewed Mr. Wheatley. Are you saying you've let it go?"

"I never let anything go till I have my killer."

"Does that mean Gus Wheatley is a suspect in your eyes?"

"I wouldn't say that."

"Look, I don't need to tell you that if Gus Wheatley is a suspect, that changes everything about the way we have to deal with him. So I'd like to know: Are you or are you not exploring a possible connection between the abuse and Beth's disappearance?"

"Depends on what you mean by exploring."

"I don't have time to play word games with you."

"No games. No suspects. Let's say it's just a theory at this point."

She closed her eyes, frustrated. "I think you're getting sidetracked."

"I think you're overstepping your role. I don't need the FBI to play Sherlock Holmes. So far all we asked for was a psychological profile of the killer from one of your experts."

"And I can tell you that when Victoria Santos completes her profile, those abuse allegations aren't likely to fit anywhere in the FBI's thinking."

"Maybe they should."

"Dick, listen—"

"No, you listen. Are you going to tell me that an FBI profile has never been wrong?"

Andie was silent.

"I didn't think so," he said. "I thank you for your call. If I need anything more from you, I'll be in touch."

The line clicked before she could respond. She slammed down the receiver and fell back in her chair. *Idiot.*

Gus was encouraged when he left the staff meeting. The show of support was heartening. At least he wasn't totally alone.

Before he made it through the lobby, however, he was called to an emergency meeting of the executive committee. He assumed they wanted to ask how much time he would take off and what the firm could do to help. It was a nice gesture, prompted no doubt by the outpouring of support from the staff. His high-ranking partners were never to be outdone, even if it meant having to extend an act of kindness.

He headed to the north conference room to meet the committee. It was an interesting choice of venue, the only conference room with a round table. No one could sit at the head, Gus's usual position.

"Hope I haven't kept you all waiting," said Gus as he entered.

In unison they mumbled something to the effect of "no problem." Martha was seated on the far side of the table, her back to the window. Beside her was the chairman of the litigation department, and next to him was the chairman of the corporate department. Buster Ullman was standing at the window, taking in the view. He was the firm's administrative partner, the whip cracker and keeper of the purse. He tracked each lawyer's "productivity," making sure they billed the requisite hours, sent out their invoices on time, and collected the hours they billed. A phone call from Ullman was like an audit letter from the IRS.

Upon Gus's arrival, the entire five-member executive committee was present.

"Have a seat," said Ullman. The tone was serious. Gus pulled up one of the empty chairs opposite Martha.

Ullman remained standing. "I assume you know why we called this meeting."

"You want to help find my wife?"

He coughed. "Well, we do hope the police are making progress on that. But the immediate focus of this committee has to be those things that are within our power and control."

"Meaning?"

"Meaning we have to deal with the potential public and client relations problems caused by that newscast last night."

Anger churned inside—though he wasn't totally shocked. "My wife is missing, and you want to talk public relations?"

"Please don't put it that way."

"What way?"

Ullman stepped closer. "This is a personal tragedy for you. We're all very sorry. But somebody has to make sure this personal tragedy doesn't turn into a firm crisis."

Gus glanced at the others at the table, fixing last on Martha. "Is that the way you all feel? My personal life is a liability to the law firm?"

They were silent. Ullman said, "This can't come as a total surprise to you, Gus. We went through this same discussion five years ago. An allegation of spouse abuse against the managing partner of this law firm can have serious ramifications. Clients could fire us. Female recruits could fall off. Bad press follows. And so forth."

"None of those things happened the last time."

"No. But until last night no one knew that Beth had actually filed a formal complaint."

Gus felt like lashing out, but he thought before he spoke, measuring his words. "After all this time, don't you find it peculiar that Action News somehow got wind of that complaint?"

"Peculiar? I don't follow you."

"When this whole thing started five years ago, I was upfront about it. None of it was true, but for some reason Beth had accused me of abuse. I brought it to the attention of this committee just in case it became public."

"You said she had told a girlfriend that you had hit her. You didn't tell us she had filed a formal complaint."

"She withdrew the complaint the day after she filed it. Because it simply wasn't true. We put it behind us, never really talked about it again. Very few people knew it had ever been filed. In fact, I could probably name those people on one hand. Maybe even one *finger*." He was looking right at Martha.

She glared in return. "You're out of line, Gus."

"Am I?"

Ullman intervened. "Well, let's not make this personal. All we're saying is that we are truly sorry about your personal situation. But this law firm can't stop operating because of it."

"It hasn't stopped. I've been away for three days."

"And you will undoubtedly be away longer."

"I'm sure I will."

"Good. I'd hoped you would be reasonable about this."

"Reasonable about what?"

"About the appointment of an interim managing partner. Someone to take over in your absence."

Gus smelled a political coup, with his own blood on the rug. He knew that under the partnership agreement it would take four votes to replace him. He needed his own vote and one other. He glanced at Martha. She looked away. After that "soul mate" fiasco yesterday morning it was clear he didn't have her vote.

Ullman said, "I nominate Martha Goldstein to serve as interim managing partner."

Gus did a double-take. Boy, did he *not* have her vote.

"Second," said another.

"All in favor?" said Ullman.

It was unanimous. Gus stewed in silence.

Ullman said, "Try to be objective, Gus. Surely you can see the wisdom of putting a woman at the helm when the existing managing partner is getting bad press about wife-beating allegations."

He rose slowly and quietly. "This firm can have whoever it wants at the helm." He glared at each of his partners around the table, then finally at Martha. "And in this case, you deserve what you're getting."

He turned and left the room, slamming the door on the way out.

Sixteen

Andie allowed herself a mid-morning refill. She needed the caffeine, but it was definitely a trade-off. Coffee never used to bother her stomach, but the one-two punch of a serial killer investigation on the heels of her own death at the altar had apparently changed her constitution.

The phone rang as she settled into her desk chair. She started, spilling a full hot cup across the papers on her desk. She was just about to phone Gus, and she had the strangest feeling it was him beating her to the punch. *Not too jittery this morning, are we?*

The phone kept ringing. She frantically soaked up the hot coffee with a too small napkin and grabbed the phone with the other hand. "Henning," she answered.

"Is this Agent Henning of the FBI?"

It was a woman's voice. Andie lifted a coffee-soaked memo by the corner, pitching it in the trash like a dead animal. "Yes, it is."

"You don't know me, but I'd like to talk to you about the disappearance of Beth Wheatley."

She snapped to attention. "I'm listening."

"I don't know how important this will be to your investigation, but it's important for me to get a few things out in the open."

"What kind of things?"

The line crackled with her sigh. "Let's not do this on the phone. If I'm going to put my trust in someone, I prefer to do it in person."

"That's fine. We can use my office. Or I can meet you somewhere."

"How about Waterfront Park? Say around twelve-thirty?"

"Sure." She made a note in her coffee-soaked appointment calendar. "You know, I assumed from your tone that you were calling anonymously, so I didn't ask who you were. But since we're meeting face to face, you want to give me your name?"

"Only if you'll agree not to tell anyone we talked."

"Why is that of concern to you?"

"You'll understand when we meet."

"All right. I'll do my best to accommodate you."

"What does that mean?"

"It means that if all goes well, I won't reveal your name unless a court orders me to."

"I guess that's good enough."

"So what is your name?"

She paused. "I'll tell you when we meet. Wouldn't want you doing any homework on me beforehand. It doesn't do anyone any good to come into a meeting like this with preconceived notions."

This was a strange one. "Okay. How will I recognize you?"

"Just wait by the entrance to Pier 57. I know what you look like."

It was a little creepy, the way she had said that. "Okay. See you at half-past."

"See ya."

Andie disconnected with her finger, then quickly dialed Isaac Underwood. She got his voice mail. "Isaac, it's Henning. Got a source on the Wheatley case that wants to meet around lunchtime. Just the two of us. I need backup to watch us." Out of the corner of her eye, she caught a glimpse of the Jane Doe autopsy photo atop the files on her credenza.

"Just in case," she added.

Gus went through a thousand flyers in a single morning. He tacked them up on walls and billboards at bus stops, gas stations, grocery stores—anywhere someone might see them. Momentum and a blank mind kept him going. When he finished, one thought crept up on him: What if she had just walked out on him? That didn't seem likely. Not after last night's newscast. It was only logical that she would have called and at least put Morgan's mind to rest that her mommy was safe, no need to worry. Which meant the converse was true: there *was* reason to worry.

It was precisely that kind of worry that had driven him to the gun shop. Gus was no stranger to firearms. One of his clients was an avid skeet shooter, and Gus had discovered he was a natural on their first of many weekend outings. He had owned a pistol for home protection some years ago, until Morgan proved to be an overly curious toddler. Now seemed like a good time to replace the old 9mm Smith & Wesson. Hopefully, Beth would be home before the waiting period for handgun purchases elapsed. If not—if she was the victim of foul play—Gus and his daughter weren't going to be next. At least not without a fight.

As to Morgan, he had other worries as well. In the late morning he called Carla to see if they had talked all about him on the way to school. Despite her denials, Gus suspected that if the well hadn't already been poisoned, it was now bubbling over with toxins.

His flyer-posting campaign had started downtown and worked north, so he stopped for lunch in north Seattle near the University of Washington. An eclectic mix of bookstores, newsstands, pubs, shops, and inexpensive eateries lined University Way Northeast, the "Ave" as it was called locally. Gus stopped at Shultzy's Sausage, THE BEST OF THE WURST, according to the sign outside.

He ate his steamed bratwurst in silence, unfazed by the noisy students and business people at nearby tables. He hardly noticed the vagrant at the counter finishing off the last few bites of a hotdog some overstuffed patron had left behind. His worries were getting the better of him, making him irrational. He was kidding himself about the gun. If Agent Henning was right—if Beth was the victim of a serial killer—Gus would be no match for a psychopath who killed for sheer enjoyment. He had no specific reason to think he would come after him or Morgan, but there was no assurance that he wouldn't. If he was serious about protection, it was time to act serious.

He pulled his directory from his briefcase and scrolled through his client list. Gus could have called a dozen corporate executives who knew everything there was to know about private security. He settled on Marcus Mueller, a bona fide corporate mogul who hadn't gone anywhere without a bodyguard since fellow Seattle gazillionaire Bill Gates got hit in the face with a cream pie in Belgium. According to his secretary, Marcus was lunching with his wife at the Seattle Yacht Club. Yachting season didn't start until the first Saturday in May, but the salmon steaks in the clubhouse were flavorful year round.

If it had been anyone else but Marcus, Gus might not have interrupted a husband-wife lunch date. But it was likely a business lunch. Mrs. Mueller called the shots in that family. It was her father who had started the company that her husband now ran. And he ran it well. That was the reason Gus wasn't terribly worried about the firm's appointment of Martha Goldstein as "interim" managing partner. As long as he had Mueller—whose company accounted for nearly twenty percent of the firm's billings—Gus could wrestle back his control. It was just a matter of forging new alliances with all those partners he kept busy.

Gus reached him on his cell phone. His timing was good. Leslie was in the restroom, so he had Marcus all to himself.

"Marcus, I need a favor."

"Oh?"

It was a cautious "oh," a little surprising from a man who had promised never to forget the lawyer who had saved his corporate ass from a criminal antitrust indictment. Gus said, "It's a safety matter. I'm a little concerned about my daughter, Morgan."

"What happened?"

"It's just . . ." Gus hesitated on the details. It wasn't good for business to let a major client know how screwed up your personal life was. "You heard about Beth, I imagine?"

"Yes. I, uh, saw the newscast."

Gus wondered which one he'd seen—with or without the abuse allegations. He didn't probe. "With all that's going on, I think it might be smart to have someone looking after Morgan. A bodyguard, I mean."

"I understand. I'm very concerned for Beth."

"We all are. If anything were to happen to Morgan— well, I don't even want to think about it."

"If you're that scared, can't you send her out of town to stay with relatives?"

"I don't think sending her away is the best thing. It's good for her to be around her friends at school. I'd like to keep things as normal as possible."

"Putting a bodyguard on her is hardly going to make her feel normal."

"We don't have to tell her he's a bodyguard. We can call him a driver or male nanny, whatever."

He chuckled. "Most of the guys I'd recommend are built more like the rock of Gibraltar than Fran Drescher."

"I'm not looking for the bouncer type. I'm thinking more along the lines of a private investigator."

"You're a wealthy man, but I hate to see anyone spend more than he has to. A good P.I. will cost more than just a bodyguard, and he probably won't give Morgan any better protection."

"I need more than just protection."

"What kind of skills you looking for?"

"I want to take some initiative here. I need someone who can help me find Beth."

"Hold on a second, Gus."

Gus had shared enough meals with the Muellers to know what was going on. Leslie was returning to the table, an event as auspicious as the Queen of Heart's return to that garden in Wonderland: "Off with your head" if you didn't drop everything, bow, and pay homage.

"Who's that on the phone?" Gus heard Leslie ask.

"Gus."

"Gus Wheatley?" she asked pointedly.

The shushing came as crackling over the line. Marcus was clearly sensitive to his wife's tone. "He wants help."

"You are *not* going to do that wife beater any favors. Tell him what we've decided."

"I can't tell him now. He sounds terrible."

"Tell him."

Gus could hear the embarrassment in Marcus's voice. "Gus, can I call you back?"

"I heard what Leslie said. What is it you need to tell me?"

"It's purely business."

"What kind of business?"

"I really don't want to do this on the phone."

"What," Gus scoffed, "are you firing me?"

His voice dropped, deadly serious. "For the time being, I think it's best if we severed our relationship."

Gus gripped the phone. "Over a stupid newscast? Come on."

"It's more than that."

"Then you must know something I don't know."

"Apparently I must."

"What are you saying?"

The hesitation in his voice was palpable. Leslie was undoubtedly tightening the screws with one of her deadly glares. "Gus, I really can't discuss it."

"Does this have to do with the management change at the firm?"

"Let's not get into law firm politics."

"It's just an interim appointment. Until this passes. It's not permanent."

"Yes. And that's exactly the way you should view our separation. A temporary thing."

Gus went cold. His client's hollow tone made it painfully clear that neither change was temporary.

"Gus, I truly wish you the best of luck."

"Yeah. Thanks for nothing."

He switched off his cell phone. A flash of anger made him want to call Martha Goldstein, yell at her, ask her what the hell was going on. He caught himself fidgeting with his wedding ring, however, and the impulse instantly evaporated. It was a nervous habit of his. Whenever he got stressed, he would pull the platinum band on and off. It was off now. He checked the inscription inside, though he had it memorized.

It made him smile. Beth's sense of humor used to make him smile all the time. Back then. Now, however, it was a sad smile. Sadder than ever.

PUT ME BACK ON, it read.

He slid the ring back on, grabbed his briefcase full of flyers, and headed for his car.

Seventeen

Waterfront Park was on the eastern edge of downtown, hugging Elliott Bay. It was Seattle's version of a soothing boardwalk, with elevated walkways that offered grand vistas of Puget Sound. On sunny summer weekends it was a prime spot for watching the water show put on by the city's fireboats, as geysers of sea water shot into the air at the rate of 22,000 gallons a minute. Grassy areas attracted picnickers and shirtless Frisbee fanatics. On a cloudy winter day, however, it was just another shade of gray, its concrete walkways blending with the fog that shrouded land and sea.

Andie arrived a few minutes early, walking briskly in the cold mist. The moisture gathered on her trench coat, not quite enough to warrant an umbrella. A group of hardy tourists tried their luck with the twenty-five-cent telescopes at the pier's edge. Occasionally the fog would break, perhaps offering them a glimpse of a tugboat or timber-laden barge cutting across the sound. Altogether, Andie saw no more than a half dozen pedestrians in the area, with no way of knowing which if any was the woman who had called her. She had mentioned the entrance to Pier 57, but Andie wasn't sure of the exact meeting spot. She stopped at the plaque commemorating the beginning of the Alaska Gold Rush in 1897. It seemed appropriate enough, as she herself was hoping to hit pay dirt.

"Agent Henning?"

She turned at the sound of the woman's voice. It was like looking in a smoky mirror. An attractive young woman wearing a drizzle-soaked trench coat. Perhaps she was a little older than Andie.

She stepped forward and extended her hand. "I'm Martha Goldstein."

"Nice to meet you." Her tone conveyed no recognition.

"I'm a partner at Preston and Coolidge. Gus Wheatley's law firm."

"I see. I presume that's why you don't want to use your name?"

"Exactly."

"You could have told me that on the phone. You were so cagey about your identity, it made me a little suspicious."

"Sorry. When you asked for my name, I freaked a little. Believe me, I'm having second thoughts even as I stand here."

"You shouldn't. Not if you're going to tell me the truth."

"Oh, everything I have to say is gospel truth."

"Tell me. You think you know something about Beth Wheatley's disappearance?"

Martha looked away, as if struggling. "Let me say this. I don't know Beth very well, but I've known Gus for a very long time. Over six years."

"How well do you know him?"

"Well enough to know he isn't a serial killer, like the one described in Tuesday's newspaper."

"So it wasn't the *P-I* story that prompted you to call me."

"No." Her eyes met Andie's. "It was the allegation that Gus abused his wife."

"What about it?"

"I saw the television newscast implying there might be a connection between the abuse and Beth's disappearance."

"Do you think there's a connection?"

"All I know is that Gus was acting strange the day Beth disappeared."

"How so?"

"He and I were in the office together. He had to cancel dinner with me because Beth didn't pick up their daughter from some place. He got really mad. He said something like, 'She deserves a good smack across the back of the legs.'"

"Kind of an odd expression."

"Yes. That's why I distinctly remember him saying it."

"Are you suggesting he's still abusing her?"

"I just want to be up-front and cooperative. If the police suspect that the abuse might somehow have led to Beth's disappearance, I want my name totally in the clear."

"I don't understand. Why wouldn't it be in the clear?"

She sighed nervously. "Gus and I have a . . . how should I put it? A history."

"Oh?"

"To be perfectly frank, he pursued me for years. I kept our relationship professional, but he always wanted more. He was so obvious at times that rumors started. They were just rumors. Nothing physical was going on between us. I liked Gus, but I always made it clear that so long as he was married, nothing could happen. Now that his wife has suspiciously disappeared, I don't want the fact that he was so hopelessly in love with me to implicate me in any way."

"Hopelessly in love?" Andie sounded more doubtful than intended.

"Yes," she said defensively. "Gus Wheatley was in love with me."

"I see. And why would that implicate you in his wife's disappearance?"

"I didn't say it *would*. I was just afraid it might give someone the wrong idea."

"Who?"

"I'm not stupid. I know how these homicide investigations work. The police make their list of suspects and go through them one by one, process of elimination. As a woman who was rumored to be Gus's mistress, I was bound to end up on somebody's list. So I figured I might as well come forward. Even though I knew it would be a double-edged sword."

"How do you mean?"

"Well, I would be clearing myself. But I might be implicating Gus. That's not easy for me to do. Gus is someone I'm very fond of."

"Implicate him how?"

She sighed yet again, ever the reluctant witness. "For a long time Gus felt trapped in his marriage. A few years ago he tried to leave Beth. For me. That's when she accused him of abuse. He had no choice but to go back to her. She wasn't going to let him go. Not without ruining his good name and reputation."

"How do you know that?"

"I know."

"Did he tell you?"

"It was *obvious*."

"So, you're saying what? Beth refused to let him go, so he finally got rid of her?"

"That's for you to decide. I would never say that."

Andie gave her a hard look. Martha didn't flinch, her expression deadly serious. The mist was turning to rain, falling harder. Andie popped her umbrella. "Do you want to go inside, talk more?"

Martha checked her watch. "I have to get back to work. I've told you pretty much everything I can think of."

"Yeah, I've probably heard enough anyway. Let me give you my card, though. If something else comes to mind, call me anytime."

She took it and tucked it in her coat pocket. "You're going to look into this, then?"

She sounded more eager than curious. Andie offered a

pat answer. "We take all credible leads seriously."

They shook hands. Martha took one step away, then stopped. "You understand why I came here, I hope. I just want to air out the facts. I'm not trying to hurt Gus."

"I understand."

"Gus is a friend of mine."

Andie looked her in the eye but said nothing.

"A good friend." She smiled awkwardly, waiting for a reply. Andie was silent. Martha turned and walked away, her heels clicking on the wet sidewalk.

Some friend, thought Andie as she watched her fade into the fog.

Eighteen

Gus spent the balance of Wednesday afternoon posting more flyers. He made a special point of hitting restaurants Beth used to visit, her workout gym, her grocery store, her favorite shops. All those details came from Carla. She had called him on his cell phone, just to make it clear that she would be picking up Morgan from school. Morgan wanted it that way.

Gus didn't argue. He knew he had to talk with his daughter, and staying busy all day was perhaps a way of postponing further rejection. He wasn't sure what to tell her yet. He would deny ever abusing her mother, of course. But that wouldn't go far enough. He needed answers to the questions she would naturally ask. Was Mommy coming back? When? Where had she been all week? Was she safe? By nature, Gus hated any meeting or conversation in which he didn't have all the answers figured out beforehand. He knew he was going to have to get past that if he was going to be a single parent, whether it be for the short term or the long run.

His biggest fear was that he'd say the wrong thing, only make it worse. That seemed like the kind of problem a professional could help him work out. On the quick, he found a respected child psychiatrist who agreed to squeeze him in at the end of the day. He drove halfway to Bellevue, only to find that in rush-hour traffic he was never going to make it by six-thirty. A total waste of time. He called ahead and canceled, turned the car around, and went home.

By then it was eight o'clock. Carla met him at the door. She had picked Morgan up at Bertschi, spent the rest of the day with her, fed her dinner, and—to his dismay—already put her to bed.

"Poor little darling was wiped out," said Carla. "I don't think she's sleeping well."

"Thanks for looking after her," he said as he tossed his leather jacket on the kitchen table. "With all that's going on, I can really use all the help I can get."

"Glad to do it. Morgan's like a daughter to me."

That was hardly an overstatement. With no living grandparents, Morgan had grown very fond of her Aunt Carla. Somewhere, there had to be a softer side to her. The side that wasn't totally beaten down by an abusive old boyfriend who had truly done far worse things to Carla than had ever been made up about Gus and Beth. Knowing how Carla had suffered at the hands of a manipulative brute made Gus more understanding, more forgiving of a sister who had tried to convince his own wife that no man could be trusted. It took Beth's disappearance to make him finally realize how little he'd done over the years to convince Carla he *could* be trusted.

"Listen, Gus. I just wanted to say, I know you haven't been to work all week. You're out there looking for Beth. Doing whatever you can." She lowered her head and dug her hands in her jeans pockets, struggling for words. "Anyway, I was pretty ugly to you right after Beth was missing. I'm sorry about that."

"Forget it."

"No, really. You've surprised me."

He looked askance, sort of a backhanded compliment. But he would take whatever he could get. "I think that's the nicest thing you've ever said to me, Carla."

"Could be the only nice thing."

It was funny in a way, but neither one laughed. It was pathetic, too, but they just shared the moment, the simple pleasure of brother and sister having a somewhat normal conversation.

"There's brisket in the oven if you're hungry. Morgan didn't eat much of it."

"Thanks." He glanced down the hall, then back at Carla. "I was hoping to talk to her tonight. Didn't want to let this fester too long."

"She's out. Wait till morning."

"Yeah. Probably a good idea."

Carla grabbed her coat. "Well, good night. Call me if you need anything."

"I will." He followed her to the door, opened it.

She stopped at the threshold. "When you talk to Morgan, do me a favor."

"What?"

"Be the new Gus."

He gave a subtle nod. She walked to her car and pulled away. He watched her all the way, looking away only when the glowing orange taillights were completely out of sight.

He drove well below the speed limit. Used his blinker when turning. Was courteous to other drivers, avoiding any possibility of collision. His cargo was too precious to take risks. Lifeless, but precious.

Odor was not an issue. The windowless van was filled with flowers, literally dozens of beautiful, fragrant bouquets. He'd purchased them in bulk at wholesale, most of them on the verge of dying, so they were cheap enough. If he were stopped for any reason—a traffic ticket, a broken taillight—he was just a delivery boy for some mom-and-pop florist shop. Only a trained canine could sniff out the stench of death from beneath the bed of blossoms.

He had wanted to dispose of the body last night, but it

hadn't worked out. It wasn't until he had driven all the way to the dump site that he developed a keen suspicion that police were staking out the public park he had selected. It wasn't anything obvious, just a sixth sense that more patrol cars were in the area than usual. He trusted his instincts on such things. Just to be safe, he had decided to hold the body till tonight and dump it well outside Seattle.

It was over an hour's drive, but he didn't mind it. He often took long drives. It was curious, in a way. He'd read a book by a former FBI profiler who said geographically transient serial killers often took long drives. Only after reading it did he develop the urge. The power of suggestion. Or maybe he really did fit the profile.

No way.

The road turned more desolate as the van headed west, mile after mile. Somewhere above the thick blanket of clouds was a beaming full moon, but the misty night was black, especially this far into the wilderness. It would have been easy to get lost had he not known the way. The dilapidated old barn at the base of the hill marked his turn. He steered off the highway and onto a gravel road. The talisman hanging from the rearview mirror swung sharply with the turn, nearly hitting him in the face.

It was a gold ring on a long chain.

Muddy water splashed up from a puddle and onto the windshield. He switched on the wipers and cleared the mess away. The van slowed to a crawl. He switched off the headlights. Just ahead was the park entrance. He hit one last pothole. The van rocked. Flowers fell behind him. The gold ring and chain slipped off the rearview mirror. He tried to catch it in midair but missed. It fell to the floor, rolling like a lost penny. He hit the brakes in a panic, slammed the van into Park. He was on his knees searching for the ring, groping beneath the seat.

"Damn it—*shit!*"

It was futile in the darkness, but he didn't dare switch on

a light this close to the dump site. Blindly, he reached beneath the passenger seat, searching frantically. A pen and a coin he tossed aside furiously. Then he stopped. And smiled. He had it. Relieved, he clutched the ring tightly. He drew a deep breath, as if drawing on its power. To him it was more than just a piece of jewelry. The engraving inside said it all: IN APPRECIATION — T.V.I.

It was his father's ring—commemorating his many years of service at the Torture Victims' Institute.

He slipped the ring into his pocket and zipped it closed, now ready for the task at hand.

Nineteen

A shrill scream woke him.

Gus jackknifed in bed. The master bedroom was quiet and dimly lit. Another rainy night had turned into a gray Thursday morning. He had tossed and turned most of the night, wondering if the police were doing enough to find Beth, wondering if Morgan would ever trust him again. By dawn he had finally reached a deep sleep. The sudden noise had him awake but disoriented. His heart pumped with adrenaline. He couldn't remember what he was dreaming, or if he had been dreaming at all, but he was sure he must have dreamed the scream.

Until he heard it again. Louder. He jumped out of bed. It was no dream. It had come from Morgan's room.

"Morgan!" He sprinted down the hall to her room. The door was open a crack. It slammed against the wall as he burst inside.

He stopped cold. Morgan was kneeling atop the mattress, hunched over her pillow. Crimson droplets stained the pink pillow case. She looked up with terror in her eyes. Her mouth was bloodied.

"Oh, my God!" He rushed to the bed and held her.

"My toot'," she mumbled.

He pried her mouth open. One of her incisors was dangling by the roots, horribly twisted. She had apparently worked it free in her sleep. It was painful just to look at it, yet he was somewhat relieved. In his sprint of panic down the hall, he had feared much more than the loss of a baby tooth.

"It hurts!"

"I know it does, sweetheart." He touched it gently, testing the exposed root.

"Ow!"

"Sorry. It doesn't seem ready to come out yet. At least not the rest of the way out."

"Take it out!"

He raised his hand to her mouth, then pulled away tentatively. The gum was red and raw, ripe for infection. "I don't want to make it worse."

"Get Mommy. I want Mommy to do it."

He wasn't sure what to say. "Let's go see your dentist."

"I hate the dentist."

"So do I. But she's the best person to do this."

She started to cry. "Mommy's the best person. Mommy wiggled my other teeth out."

"Mommy's not here."

"Call her. Tell her she needs to come home."

The piercing eyes made him shiver. He saw total distrust, as if she knew he had the power to bring her mommy home but for some reason he wouldn't. She'd nearly ripped a tooth from her mouth to force his hand. It was a savvy six-year-old's power play: either call Mommy home, or prove it wasn't you who made her go away.

"Let's go see the dentist, okay?" He held her tight, brushing the hair from her face. "Then you and I should have a talk."

The alarm sounded, and then the phone rang. It was a double-whammy, like rolling out of bed and stepping on a land mine. Andie oriented herself, cut off the screaming alarm and answered the phone.

"Hello."

"Henning. Dick Kessler here. Got another body."

Andie was suddenly wide awake. She jotted down the information. "I'll see you there," she said, then hung up. In less than five minutes she was out the door and on the road, headed for Lakewood Park.

The town of Issaquah was southeast of Seattle and beautiful Lake Washington. It was an area more rural than suburban Bellevue to the north, though everything in the region had built up since she was a little girl exploring with her father. Still, parts of town had remained much the way Andie had remembered it, nestled in a valley between Squak, Tiger and Cougar mountains, a quaint shopping attraction with wooden boardwalks, plenty of colorful flowers in planters, and old clapboard-style homes that had been turned into stores. Memories came back as she cruised past the general store and continued to the park just outside the village.

Andie couldn't remember the last time she'd visited this area, but she'd never forget the first. She was ten years old, living at the time well south of Seattle outside Tacoma. She and her father had driven up to Issaquah for a town festival. On the way home, Andie wanted to navigate. Her father checked the glove compartment for road maps, and Andie saw his handgun. As a cop, he always carried it with him. Andie had forever wanted to shoot it, but under her mother's rule she had a three-year wait: no guns till the thirteenth birthday. Andie prevailed on him all the way home, promising never to tell Mom if he would just let her fire off a few rounds. Finally he gave in. They got off the highway and drove a short while to a wide-open spot in the White River Valley. Her dad set up some soda cans on a tree stump. He stood behind her, holding her small hands in his as she closed one eye and took careful aim. Her hand shook slightly as she squeezed the trigger. She missed the first one, then hit the next three. She was squealing with delight when a stranger startled them from behind. He was an old man with long gray hair and a weathered face. Two dark feathers protruded from his brimmed felt hat.

"Who is that, Dad?" she whispered nervously.

"He's an Indian."

The man spoke, his face expressionless. "You can't shoot here. This is reservation land."

"But I'm part Indian."

Her father took her by the hand. "Let's go, Andie. That doesn't matter."

She loved her parents, two hardworking white middle-class people who truly loved their half-Indian adopted daughter. To this day, however, those words stuck with her. Maybe it was the tone in her father's voice. Maybe it was the way he had scowled at the old Muckleshoot Indian. But those three words—"That doesn't matter"—seemed to sum up her past. Out of respect for her adoptive parents, she had never bucked their wishes and sought out her birth mother's Indian heritage. That void in her own life had affected her in many ways. Ironically, it may well have fueled her fascination for this kind of police work—victimology and criminal profiling. There, *everything* mattered. Every little detail about a person's life mattered so completely.

She steered onto the side road, that thought in mind. Details. Intimate details, from the number of fillings in her teeth to the legs that had needed shaving. The scrapings beneath the fingernails. The search for semen in her pubic hair. The contents of her stomach. It made Andie feel guilty in a way. She, a perfect stranger, was about to learn more than anyone had ever known about a young woman in Lakewood Park.

Victim number four.

Twenty

Andie parked in the lot and walked toward the squad car and two deputy sheriffs who were posted at the gated entrance. It wasn't much of a gate, just a long metal pole that ran parallel to the ground and swung on a hinge. It kept vehicles out after dark, but vagrants on foot could simply duck under it and come and go as they pleased. Yellow police tape was strung across the entrance. Just inside the park, rows of police officers walked three feet apart, combing the grounds for clues, like a farmer plowing the field. Andie pulled her trench coat tight. It wasn't quite cold enough to steam her breath, but the dampness made it feel colder than it was. She stopped at the gate and flashed her credentials to the deputy.

"Agent Henning, FBI."

He checked it. A few raindrops gathered on the gold FBI shield. "Detective Kessler from Seattle is at the recovery site. He's expecting you."

"Where is it, exactly?"

"Straight down the path about a half mile. You'll see public rest rooms on your right. Turn left, then just head down the hill. You'll see the forensic team at work."

Andie thanked him and started down the path. She walked quickly, but not so quick that she couldn't take in the surroundings. The walk was slightly uphill, she noticed. It would have taken one hell of a strong man to carry a dead body this far.

At the top of the hill were the rest rooms the deputy had mentioned. Typical county park facilities made of cinder blocks. The largest wall had been hit by graffiti artists. DON'T CALIFORNICATE WASHINGTON, the spray-painted message read. Washingtonians certainly felt strongly about overdevelopment, but Andie was fairly sure it had nothing to do with the latest string of homicides.

The footpath ended at the rest rooms. Beyond was a steep embankment. A thick stand of tall evergreens darkened the slope, leaving the moss-covered ground in almost perpetual darkness. The embankment was so steep that Andie stood at eye level with the pointed tops of forty-foot fir trees rising from the ravine. Lakewood Park was a long way from Washington Park Arboretum, where the other body had been found. The setting, however, was remarkably similar.

Andie heard voices from below. She couldn't see through the woods, but the forensic team was evidently at work. She headed down the hill toward the recovery site.

At the foot of the hill, police tape marked off an area the size of a baseball diamond. Several deputies stood watch at various points, their hats covered in plastic, like shower caps, to protect the felt from the light rain. A forensic photographer circled the scene, covering every angle. Andie noticed the rope still hanging from a tree limb. A dark plastic bag lay atop the gurney on the ground. The fourth victim.

She approached Kessler, who was jotting down a few notes for himself. A dark blue jacket shielded him from the misty rain. His hair was wet and matted to his head, though he seemed oblivious to the elements.

"Thanks for the call, Dick."

"No problem. Like I said on the phone, outside the city of Seattle is more your jurisdiction than mine. I'm just looking for connections to Jane Doe."

"What do you think?"

"I think maybe you were right to cool my heels about Gus Wheatley. I think it's a good thing the King County sheriff's department is already part of our task force. And I think it just grew to include the city of Issaquah police."

He continued moving around the site, checking different angles, jotting down notes. Andie followed him, asking questions to fill in the blanks he'd left on the telephone.

"Must have been a strong guy to carry the body all this way from the entrance."

"You're assuming she was dead when they got here."

"Wasn't she?"

He shrugged. "Maybe. Tire tracks lead all the way up the footpath. He drove as far as the rest rooms, which suggests he was trying to shorten the carrying distance. Victim was dead or unconscious, I'd say."

"How'd he get his car past the gate? I only took a quick look, but the lock didn't seem busted to me."

"Gate wasn't locked."

"Why not?"

"Hardly ever is. The park director is on call twenty-four hours a day, but she's afraid to come out after dark and lock the gate. Reduced security is probably what lured our killer out of Seattle. Ever since we found Jane Doe, we had every park on alert, extra patrol cars going through at night. Decent chance somebody would have spotted him had he tried to string up another body in our neck of the woods. No pun intended."

"Who found the body?"

"Park director, on her rounds at sunrise."

He turned away and headed toward the tree. He was checking for hooks or nails, anything that would have helped the killer climb a massive trunk as straight up and down as a flagpole.

Andie asked, "How long has she been dead?"

"A day or so, I'd guess."

She surveyed the tree, top to bottom. "Scene sure looks a lot like the place we found Jane Doe."

"Yup."

"Does she?"

"Does she what?"

"Does the victim look like Jane Doe?"

"If you're asking whether it's Beth Wheatley, the answer is no."

"You're sure?"

"Positive. No abdominal scar."

Andie knew exactly what he meant. When she'd asked Gus about distinctive scars or moles that might help identify his wife, he'd mentioned their daughter's cesarean delivery.

Kessler said, "But to give a complete answer to your question, she does look a lot like Jane Doe."

"How so?"

"Brunette, brown eyes. Mid-thirties. Same height, build. Body left hanging in a tree, stark naked."

"Was she dead before he hung her?"

"Can't say till the autopsy comes in."

"You got a look at her neck, didn't you? You heard what the medical examiner said about the bruise marks on Jane Doe. What do you think happened here?"

"I think he strangled her someplace else, brought the body here, strung it up in the tree. This is a dumping site, not a murder scene. It's just like the other one."

Andie nodded. "None of that surprises me."

"I think it does," he said pointedly. "This shoots a huge hole in your bookend theory."

"What do you mean?"

"Jane Doe is victim number three. Now you got number four, and she isn't Beth Wheatley. But Beth Wheatley is still missing."

"And you think that kills my theory?"

"It does if we find Wheatley hanging from a tree. Who the hell ever heard of three bookends?"

He snapped his notepad shut, then turned and headed toward the body, leaving Andie alone by the tree.

Twenty-one

Gus was alone in the waiting room. He wanted to stay at Morgan's side while the dentist worked on her tooth, but his being there only seemed to make Morgan more upset that her mother *wasn't*. At the dentist's suggestion, he waited outside.

He sat on the couch and flipped through the usual stack of stale periodicals. No place like a dentist's office to catch up on *People* magazine's most intriguing personalities of 1991. Gus was too sidetracked to read anyway. He was still thinking about that scream from Morgan that had jolted him out of bed this morning. Beth had been missing for three days, and he didn't feel any closer to knowing what had happened than on the night she'd disappeared. The first reaction of everyone from his own sister Carla to homicide detective Kessler was that Beth had finally left him. The abuse allegations only fueled those suspicions. The lone dissident was Agent Henning. She was still clinging to the morbid possibility that Beth was the victim of a serial killer.

Now there was a dilemma. Hope for a serial killer so your friends will stop calling you a wife beater.

"Mr. Wheatley?"

Dr. Shippee was standing in the open doorway. Gus shook off his thoughts, rose from the couch. From the smile on her face, it looked as though everything had gone well. But you never knew with a dentist, even someone as gentle as Dr. Shippee. That gray hair and sweet grand-motherly demeanor were just a cover. Deep down was a sadist.

"Morgan's okay?"

"She's doing great. Little anxiety attack, so I had to use gas instead of novocaine. If you want to come inside and wait, she'll be clearheaded in about two minutes."

"Thanks." Gus followed her down the hall. She stopped before they entered Morgan's room. Her expression showed concern, as if something were on her mind.

"About that anxiety attack," she said. "She kept calling for Beth. Screaming, I should say. She wouldn't let me touch her. That's why I had to put her out."

"Since Beth disappeared it's been a bit of a crisis at home."

"I can understand. But are you sure the crisis didn't start before then?"

Gus blinked, not sure what to say. "Why do you ask?"

"Beth had two appointments last week, before she dis-appeared. Missed them both. Didn't even call to cancel."

"Must have forgot." He looked away, but her suspicious eye caught him. Lying to old Dr. Shippee was like lying to your mother. "What?"

"I don't mean to be presumptuous, but you know why she was coming here, right?"

"Something wrong with her teeth, I presume."

"She's been coming twice a week for the past month. Four more visits to go."

"For what?"

"I'm repairing the enamel. It was destroyed by digestive fluids. Stomach acids."

Gus checked her expression. She seemed to be telling him something. "I don't understand."

"It comes from excessive regurgitation."

"You're saying—what? She had a problem?"

"Beth suffered from bulimia."

He rocked back on his heels. "I had no idea."

"I didn't think you did. And as Beth's dentist, I technically shouldn't be telling you this. But now that she's missing, doctor-patient confidentiality be damned. This is something you should know. Any eating disorder is a sign of low self-esteem. It's not uncommon for someone with bulimia to engage in other forms of self-destructive behavior."

"Meaning what? You think she'd commit suicide or something?"

"The last thing I want to do is scare you. I'm not her psychiatrist, but from the condition of her teeth, I'd say her disorder was prolonged and severe. In that kind of mental state, a young woman shouldn't be out on the run. She should get help. I don't know what you're doing to find her. But if I were her husband, if she were someone I loved, I wouldn't just sit around and wait for her to come home."

Her words hit like an accusation, as if he'd already wasted too much time. "Neither would I," he said, looking her in the eye.

"Good." She turned and opened the door.

Morgan was awake but groggy, still in the reclining chair. A dental assistant stood at the rail to make sure she didn't fall out. From the hallway, looking through the doorway and into the room, it was like peering through a telescope. Morgan looked suddenly grown-up, perhaps because she was sitting higher than usual in the dentist's chair. He didn't focus on any single facial feature, the eyes or the nose. It was just an overall impression, a feeling that had never hit him so hard before.

She looked incredibly like Beth.

Dr. Shippee said, "There's your beautiful daughter."

He felt numb for a moment, so reminded of his wife. "*Our* daughter," he said softly as he entered the room.

* * *

Andie was on the phone again. When Isaac Underwood had told her she would be working with Victoria Santos, she didn't realize how much of the work would be by long-distance phone calls. Victoria was stretched thin. Seattle's bookend killer was just one of several hot cases. She'd spent most of the week in San Francisco trying to profile a serial rapist who was targeting high school girls. She was also trying to peg an arsonist in Sacramento and a kidnapper in Spokane. Of necessity, profilers were skilled jugglers who somehow managed to keep a ridiculous number of files in the air. At any given time it was estimated that upward of fifty true serial killers were actively plying their trade across the United States. Although the ISU staff had grown since the early years when it was called the Behavioral Science Unit, criminals still far outnumbered criminal profilers. Some things never changed.

It was late afternoon, and much had broken in the case since Andie had talked to Victoria yesterday. On the desk before her was a handwritten outline of specific points she needed to cover, just to make sure she didn't leave anything out. The complete files were handy, right beside her desk, in case Victoria fired any obscure questions. Since this morning the files had expanded by a good ten inches to include victim number four. The expedited autopsy was complete, the police reports were filed. Colleen Easterbrook had been positively identified by a friend who normally car-pooled to work with her. Police now knew more about the fourth victim than the third; Jane Doe was still a Jane Doe.

From her office in the Federal Building, Andie was finally able to track down Victoria at her hotel room in San Francisco. It was clear she was pressed for time. Andie tried to be as efficient as possible with her update. She was able to work smoothly through three of the eight items on her outline before Victoria took over with questions.

"Go to the autopsy," said Victoria. "Did Easterbrook have a ruptured eardrum?"

"Yes. Both of them this time. Jane Doe was just the right."

"What do you think caused it?"

Andie felt challenged. It sounded like a test, as if Victoria had already figured out the answer. "I doubt it's from listening to a loud stereo. Maybe some kind of blunt trauma to the head?"

"Don't talk like you're asking questions, Andie."

"Excuse me?"

"You raised your voice at the end of the sentence, as if you were asking a question. You have a habit of doing that. I noticed it in our task force meeting. Talk with more self-assurance. Your instincts are good. What kind of blunt trauma?"

Andie glanced nervously at her outline in front of her. This wasn't part of her prepared speech.

"Come on, Andie. You're right there with the killer. He sees Colleen. He's going to strangle her. What does he need?"

"Control. Control the victim."

"How does he get it?"

"A weapon?"

"No. His weapon is the rope. He needs control *before* he can use his weapon of choice."

"He surprises her. Sneak attack."

"And then she gouges his eyes out, leaves traces of his flesh under her fingernails for our DNA analysts. No good. Get back to the blunt trauma. The broken eardrums."

Andie blinked, searching her mind for whatever image she could conjure. "He stuns her."

"How?"

"Both hands. Has to be both hands. Both eardrums were broken. He slaps her on the ears, both hands simultaneously. Like those martial arts experts."

"Is he in front or behind?"

"I—I don't know."

"Go back to Jane Doe. The left eardrum busted. Only the left. Now what do you see?"

Andie squirmed, thinking. "He's standing right in front of her."

"How do you know?"

"I don't. Not for sure. If he's right-handed, he's stronger in his right hand, it lands with more force. Face to face, his right hand goes to Jane Doe's left ear, the one that ruptured. If he's standing behind her, his left hand goes to her left ear."

"Which means?"

"We have a right-handed killer who attacks from the front, or a left-handed killer who attacks from the rear."

Victoria was silent. Andie waited nervously for a response—like a pupil waiting on her grade.

"Well done, Andie. I had to talk to a martial-arts expert before *I* figured all that out."

"You led me exactly where I needed to go."

"Just take the compliment and shut up. There's very little stroking in this business."

"Okay," she said with a thin smile. "Thanks. Does that mean the quiz is over?"

"It's never over. What does this tell you about the men? No ruptured eardrums in either case."

Andie visualized it. "He must have overtaken them in some other manner. Possibly held them at gunpoint, then handcuffed them, then strangled them. Maybe that proved too easy. The next time around, he needs more thrills, more of a challenge. So he uses the martial-arts stuff on the women."

"I'll buy that. For now." Victoria checked her watch. "Listen, overnight the whole file to me here at the hotel. We can talk more once I've read it."

"One last thing," said Andie. "There's an interesting detail that may seem irrelevant at first blush, but I think it might be important in the big picture."

"What?"

"Colleen Easterbrook's employment. She was a hotel manager."

"So?"

"It may help further support our bookend theory."

"Are you saying you somehow divined that Jane Doe was also a hotel manager?"

"No. But consider this. I've had a few conversations with Gus Wheatley this week, the lawyer whose wife disappeared Sunday. Beth Wheatley is her name. A few years back Beth accused Gus of abuse. It got pretty ugly, but nothing came of it. And that's not my point, anyway."

"What *is* your point?"

"They separated for a few months. It's the only time Beth worked outside the house during their entire marriage. She took a job downtown. Get this. She worked in a hotel booking conventions. You might call it an assistant hotel manager."

"So that gives her something in common with Colleen Easterbrook."

"More than something. Same age, hair, eye color. Easterbrook was divorced, but she used to be married to a lawyer. Not as prominent as Gus Wheatley, but still a lawyer. And both victims took jobs as hotel managers."

"Except you don't know if Beth Wheatley is a victim."

"No. But she's still missing. Vanished."

"Andie, I hope you aren't groping for similarities just to bolster your bookend theory."

"To the contrary. It's like Detective Kessler told me. A third female victim blows my bookend theory. Especially if it turns out that Jane Doe worked in hotel management. That would give us one pair, followed by three of a kind."

An eerie silence came over the line, as if they both had the same sudden insight. Victoria asked, "Do you think we could have missed the first murder in this series? A solo shot?"

"Which would mean our killer is playing some kind of numbers game. The first strike is one victim. The second is two. The third is three."

"Each time he amplifies the experience, ratcheting things up. So that the fourth would be four, and on down the line, until we stop him."

"Which leaves one very intriguing question," said Andie.

"Yes, it does. And now you know the reason I do this godforsaken job. I have to know *why*."

Twenty-two

By seven A.M. Gus was dressed and ready to leave the house. He had to go into the office to check the mail and reroute a few assignments before the weekend. The rest of the day was set aside for the latest brainstorm on finding Beth.

He threw on his coat, grabbed his keys, and started down the hall. Carla was asleep in the guest room, the door shut. The door to Morgan's room, however, was half-open. He stopped and peeked inside. She was an ill-defined mound on the mattress, asleep somewhere beneath a heap of blankets. He stood in the doorway, watching in silence.

Yesterday, he had made several attempts to have that serious talk with her. The right moment never arrived— Morgan had made sure of it. She was surely in pain from the loose tooth she'd yanked out prematurely, but she was making more of it than she might have. She had spent the whole day in bed. Gus had visited her room a dozen times to talk. Light conversation was fine. Whenever he had tried to steer the conversation toward Beth, however, she suddenly needed sleep, another pillow, or a story read to her. It was frustrating, but he didn't want to force it. After the horror of that newscast on Tuesday night, talking on any level was a positive.

He checked his watch. He needed to get going, but his

feet wouldn't move. His gaze drifted across the room, a little girl's dreamland. Tiny ballerinas danced in synchronized patterns on the walls, the curtains, and matching quilt. Minnie Mouse guarded the toy chest beneath the window. Barbie was parked in her pink convertible beside the bed. Gus had paid for all of it. He had selected none of it. It was all Beth's doing. Morgan was *all* Beth's doing.

The room was so peaceful, deceptively so. He wondered what was going on inside her head, deep beneath the covers. He could only guess. One thing, however, rang clear in the silence. He had something to tell her. Something that couldn't wait.

Gently, he pushed the door the rest of the way open and stepped closer. A three-foot teddy bear was in the rocking chair beside the bed. Gus removed it and lowered himself quietly onto the quilted cushion. He whispered softly, almost mouthing her name. "Morgan."

She didn't stir.

He drew a deep breath. It didn't matter that she was asleep. He had to get it off his chest. His eyes closed, then opened. He spoke in a low, hoarse whisper.

"I came to see you last night," he said, a lump in his throat, "but you were already asleep."

The ball beneath the blankets was perfectly still, save for her breathing. He continued, "Your books were scattered on the floor, so I picked them up and put them on the shelf. That's when I noticed the little marks on the inside of the closet door. Little lines, all about a half inch apart. The first one was about two feet off the ground, the next one a little higher, up and up and up. Each one had a date beside it. Your mother's handwriting.

"I just stood there and stared. It shocked me. Seeing how you had grown, all the time that had passed. It was literally the writing on the wall. Your mother had been there for you every inch of the way. The first step, the first word, the first day of school. All the big days in your little life, and the not so big days. Day in and day out, your mommy was there."

He glanced toward the closet, his gaze unfocused. "And all I could think was . . . where the heck was I? I missed it. I've missed all of it."

His eyes welled, the voice cracked. "And when I woke up this morning, I felt even worse. I realized that Monday was the first time I'd ever picked you up from school. Yesterday with your bloody tooth was the first weekday morning we've ever spent together, just the two of us. I don't understand how that happened, how time gets away. I just wish it didn't take your mother's disappearance to make your father wake up."

He laid his hand on the covers gently, so as not to wake her. "I just wanted to say I'm sorry. I know it doesn't count when you're sleeping. But I truly am sorry. And I couldn't wait to tell you that."

He was motionless in the rocking chair. It was hard to say where the rush of emotion was coming from. But it was coming, unstoppable. It was as if the whole horrendous week were racing to a head. The fears about Beth. The rejection from Morgan. The sparring with Carla and snakes at the law firm. He was a smart guy. He could handle the law firm. Only with things that really mattered was he utterly powerless.

Slowly, he noticed movement beneath the covers. He didn't want to wake her, but he felt the urge to give her a hug. He waited for her to come around, but the movement stopped.

"Morgan?" he said softly.

He heard a click that sounded mechanical, followed by muffled music. He gently tugged the blanket, peeling away the top layer, exposing the back of Morgan's head. A black wire was tangled in her hair. It ran to her ear. She was wearing headphones, listening to music. She had turned it up so loud even Gus could hear it three feet away.

The sight crushed him. She had been awake throughout. She had heard everything. He waited a few moments, hoping her eyes would open. They didn't. The garbled music just kept coming from the headphones. Without uttering a word, her response was loud and clear.

She had nothing to say to him.

Slowly, sadly, he rose from the rocking chair and walked out the door.

Andie left the Federal Building around three-thirty, her first opportunity for a lunch break. Victoria hadn't asked for one, but Andie was preparing a summary of the common behavioral indicators exhibited in all four murders. She wasn't so presumptuous as to take a stab at the actual criminal profile, though she was quietly hoping that Victoria might suggest it.

Isaac Underwood caught her on her way out the door. Seems the lunch schedule for the assistant special agent in charge was also on a three-hour delay. He hustled down the granite steps till his gait was even with hers.

"Mind if I join you?"

"Actually, I was headed over to the market. Good deals toward the end of the day."

"Mind if I walk with you?"

"I was going to take the bus."

"Not a good place to talk business. Come on, the walk will do you good."

As they covered the long five blocks up First Avenue to Pike Place Market, Andie filled him in on the latest developments, including the rendezvous with Martha Goldstein. A light north breeze was in their face, but gloves, overcoats and a very brisk pace kept off the chill.

Traffic, both cars and pedestrians, got heavier as they neared the historic market. It was nothing like a sunny summer afternoon, however, when the chance of winning the state lottery was better than finding a parking spot. Pike

Place was the nation's oldest continuously operating farmers market, and with as many as forty thousand visitors daily it was to many the heart and soul of Seattle. The two-and-half-block stretch was prime for people watching, or it was just as fun to explore the many old buildings that had been strung together over the years by ramps, alleys and stairways. The city council had forbade singing by market vendors since 1947, but that didn't dampen the loud and continuous hawking of everything from Guatemalan cigars and Turkish pastries to African violets and Pacific Northwest salmon. No chain stores or franchises were allowed, which made it a true bazaar, not another mall.

Andie headed toward the main arcade, a semi-open area facing the street. About half of the fresh-produce stalls were there, side by side with the gleaming rows of fresh crab and halibut in angled, iced beds. The crowds weren't peak, but there was still a steady stream of shoppers. A magician performed tricks beneath the big market clock. A guitarist on the corner sang an old Jimmy Buffett tune. A fishmonger hurried by with a very recently deceased eel draped over each shoulder. Andie's eye was on the live Maine lobsters at the bottom of the big glass tank, but Isaac was still talking business.

"How are you and my old buddies at Seattle P.D. getting along?"

"Good, I think." She stopped at Arcade No. 8 to check out the homegrown Asian vegetables, one of the sure signs that spring was coming to Seattle. "You hear differently?"

"I had lunch with Detective Kessler yesterday. Tells me you learned a valuable lesson with that leak to the newspapers about the bookend theory."

"Yeah. Never again do I tell him anything that isn't fit to print."

"Actually, he thought you two had reached an understanding. If there's something you don't want in the papers, you'll tell him up-front in no uncertain terms. No more assumptions about what's confidential and what isn't. You remember what I used to tell you about assumptions, don't you? The minute you start making assumptions—"

"You make an ass out of U and umption." She smiled. "I remember."

"Good."

"I just wish Kessler hadn't put quite so much umption into making an ass out of me. Especially the very day Victoria Santos comes into town. I have an uneasy, bad feeling about that guy."

"That's funny. He thinks highly of you."

"Really?"

"He was impressed the way you came up with that bookend theory so quickly, even if it does turn out to be wrong."

"He never let me know he was impressed."

"He never would. Dick's kind of a pain. Even a bit of a whiner. But overall he's a damn fine detective. And if you're good he respects you. Even if he doesn't show it."

Andie bought some speckled Chinese eggplant and stalks of lemongrass, then wandered farther down the arcade, toward a stall filled with fresh and dried flowers. Isaac had stopped next door for a bag of pistachios. Her phone rang. She stepped behind a tall stack of wicker baskets and answered. It was Kessler. *Speaking of the devil.*

"You asked me to call as soon as we got anything on Jane Doe. Well, we got an ID."

Andie pressed a finger to her free ear to block out the market noise. "Who is she?"

"Name's Paula Jablinski. Just moved here from Wisconsin three weeks ago. She didn't even have a job yet. No friends or family in the area, which explains why nobody filed a missing-persons report on her. Her mother in Milwaukee notified us today. Said her daughter hadn't returned her phone calls in over a week. From the description and dental records she faxed, looks like a fairly positive ID."

"Smart choice of victim," said Andie. "No connections to the area, nobody misses her."

"Ideal victim. Especially if you're looking for a match for Colleen Easterbrook."

"Colleen didn't just move here."

"That's not what I meant. Get this. Paula Jablinski used to work for a Holiday Inn in Milwaukee. She was looking for work in Seattle in hotel management. Just like Colleen Easterbrook."

"Just like Beth Wheatley," said Andie.

"So, you think Jablinski and Easterbrook are a lone pair of bookends? Or are we just missing another cold one named Wheatley?"

"I don't know."

"I'm not a gambler," he said. "But my money's on the trifecta."

"Hate to say it," she said as she stared blankly at a bundle of crumbling dried flowers. "But I'm afraid mine is, too."

Twenty-three

He was dressed entirely in black, a sleek silhouette in the early evening darkness. The rear basement window was the obvious point of entry. There was no alarm, no dog. The light burning in the kitchen was the same light she routinely left on whenever she left the house, a beacon of welcome for any would-be intruder. He covered the window with duct tape, then tapped it quietly, shattering the pane. The glass peeled away with the tape. He unlocked the window and entered in seconds.

She was out for drinks after work, then probably dinner and a movie. He knew her routine, knew her circle of friends, knew she lived alone. Last night's stakeout had been only one of many. He had a pretty good idea when she would return home. It was just a matter of waiting, anticipating—preparing.

Without a sound he slid into the basement. Once his eyes adjusted to the darkness, he climbed the stairs. He had a pick with him, but the door was unlocked. It opened with a squeak. He peered inside. The oven light from the kitchen spilled into the hallway, dim but sufficient to guide him through the house. He moved quickly past the master bedroom, disturbing nothing. He went straight to the guest bedroom, again touching nothing. He slid the closet door open and stepped inside, closing it behind him. She wasn't likely to check there. She'd come home and go to bed in the master, completely unaware of what was waiting for her in the next room.

His heart was pounding. Anticipation always fueled excitement. The risk heightened the thrill, a winner-take-all scenario. If someone had seen him enter, if she could somehow sense his presence, he was trapped, literally backed into a corner. But if he had gone undetected—and he knew he had—the night was completely his.

Silently, he laid his leather bag at his feet. It contained everything he needed, his tools. He lowered himself to the closet floor and sat motionless. He noticed the clothes hanging overhead, could even smell them. This close to a kill, his senses were always heightened. Slivers of light seeped through the louvered closet door, painting stripes on his torso. From behind the closet door he peered through the slats and checked out the room. A streetlight outside the house gave the room a faint yellow cast. The bed was in the corner. The door was directly across. He'd left it open, as he had found it, so he could see into the hall.

He looked away. It could be hours before her return. He would have to stay alert. Usually, adrenaline kept him focused. Tonight, however, his mind wanted to wander. He closed his eyes tightly, then opened them, fighting off the distraction. No use. The setting was the problem. Hiding inside the closet. The clothes hanging overhead. The narrow slats of light beaming through the louvered closet doors. The darkness, the silence—it was beginning to play tricks. He closed his eyes to escape from the reminders, but there was no stopping the mental journey. He was going back in time, many years, to his childhood. He could see himself at home in his father's study—the one room in the house his father had declared off limits. He did his work there, reviewing confidential files and materials from the Torture Victims' Institute. It was only natural for a ten-year-old to be drawn to a room he was forbidden to enter.

And it was only natural to run and hide in the closet at the sound of his father's footsteps approaching in the hallway . . .

The door opened. He peered through the louvered slats and watched his father enter, praying he wouldn't check the closet. He didn't. He went straight for the window and pulled the blinds shut. The room darkened. The closet turned even darker. He could barely see out. His heart raced at the sound of footsteps again, his father crossing the room. He closed his eyes and braced himself for the closet door to open, but it didn't. He heard a dresser drawer slide open, then close. He opened his eyes. His father had something in his hand. A videocassette, which he inserted into the VCR. The television switched on. The room brightened with its flickering glow. His father sank into his chair, his back to the closet. He and his father were faced in the same direction, watching the same videotape.

The screen was pure snow at first, then a woman appeared. She was sitting on a chair, facing the camera. She wasn't too old, probably in her thirties. She had short dark hair and skin that looked tanned. She looked nervous. She licked her lips a lot; her hand was clenched into a fist. She wasn't beautiful but pretty. Prettier than his mother, anyway. Finally she spoke.

"My name is Alicia Santiago."

"And where are you from?"

The second voice startled him. It was his father. It was a taped interview, psychotherapist and patient.

"Bogotá, Colombia."

He watched for several minutes, never taking his eyes off the screen, almost forgetting that his father too was watching just a few feet away. The tape itself, with his father asking questions and the pretty woman answering, seemed more real. It intrigued him the way she would answer anything the therapist asked, even details about her marriage.

"Tell me more about your husband."

She drew a deep breath. "He was a judge in the criminal courts. Many drug cases."

It would have been boring for a ten-year-old to watch but for her expressions, her obvious pain. With each answer she seemed more distressed. The tone of his father's questions never changed. It was the same monotone, very methodical.

"Tell me about that night," his father said. "The night the men took you."

Her voice shook. "There were . . . three of them. I think. I don't remember exactly. I was asleep. They grabbed me in my bed. Put something over my mouth. I tried to scream but couldn't breathe. Then I blacked out."

"They drugged you?"

She nodded.

"What do you remember next?"

"Waking up."

"Where were you?"

"I don't know. I was blindfolded. It felt more like a cell than a room. A bare cement floor. Cold. Very cold."

"Were you dressed warmly?"

"No." She lowered her head, embarrassed. "I was naked."

"What happened to your clothes?"

"I don't know."

There was silence for a second. She sipped a cup of water. The camera never moved, locked on her distress. "Alicia, I know this is difficult. But I want you to tell me what happened next. After you woke up."

"I was afraid to move. I just lay on the floor."

"How long?"

"Hard to say. Maybe a few minutes. Longer possibly."

"Then what?"

"Then I heard something outside the door."

"Someone entering?"

She nodded, gnawing her lower lip nervously.

"Who was it?"

Her eyes welled. A hand appeared on screen, passing her a tissue. She took it and dabbed away a tear. "One of the men."

"You were still blindfolded?"

"Yes."

"What did you do?"

"I—nothing, really. Tried to cover myself, my breasts, with my arms. But nothing else."

"What did he do?"

"Came to me. I could hear his footsteps on the cement floor."

"Just one man, you're sure?"

"I—I think so. He walked very slowly, very close to me. Then he stopped."

"Did he say anything?"

She nodded, her face flushed with emotion. "He told me to kneel," she said, her voice cracking, "and to open my mouth."

"What did you do?"

"I did whatever he said."

"Then what?"

"I just knelt there, waiting. I could see nothing, but I sensed him standing right there. I was afraid. I heard his belt unbuckling. His pants unzip. And then he shouted at me. *Wider!* And I would open my mouth wider. It wasn't wide enough. He grabbed me."

"Where?"

"My jaw—prying it apart."

"Were you in pain?"

Tears flowed. "At this point I was numb. I just braced myself, expecting him to—you know, put it in my mouth."

"Did he?"

Her voice shook. "I couldn't see."

"What did you feel?"

"Nothing at first. I sensed something was in my mouth. But it was sort of—hovering."

"Then what happened?"

"He shouted at me again. *Close!* So I closed my mouth."

"And what did you feel?"

"Cold."

"Cold?"

She nodded. "It was long and flat."

"Flat?"

"Resting on my tongue, pushing on the roof of my mouth. After a few seconds I could feel the blood oozing from the corners of my mouth." Her eyes closed, then opened. She barely had control, her voice barely audible. "The edges were so sharp."

"A knife?"

She trembled, then nodded.

"He ordered me not to swallow. The blood gathered in my mouth. It had to go somewhere. My mouth was full. It was running down my chin."

"Then what happened?"

"The flashing."

"Lights?"

"I was still blindfolded. But it was like a strobe light seeping in around the edges."

"White light?"

"Yes."

"You were imagining it?"

"No, no. It was real. A bright flash of light, over and over."

"What was it for?"

"I don't know. I didn't know."

"Do you know now?"

She didn't answer.

He asked again, "Do you know what it was?"

She answered quietly. "Someone was taking pictures."

On screen, the sobbing continued. From the safety of the

closet, his ten-year-old eyes never looked away, barely even blinked. Here was a woman on the verge of hysteria. Yet he was strangely unfazed by the tears. For a second he felt guilty, mesmerized by this woman's suffering as his father reviewed it for study, so he could help her. But he couldn't tear his young eyes away from the screen.

The taped interview continued. "What happened next?" his father asked her.

"He pulled out the knife. Very fast. Cut like a razor."

"What then?"

"He asked me, 'Do you like the knife?'"

"Did you answer?"

"No. So he shouted again: '*Do you like the knife!*'"

"Did you answer this time?"

"I just shook my head. Then he shouted again. '*Say it loud! Say you don't like the knife!*' So I did. I shouted back. Over and over he made me shout it—'*I don't like the knife!*'"

"Then what?"

She swallowed hard. "He whispered into my ear."

"What did he say?"

"'Next time, be *glad* it's not the knife.'"

A deep groan emerged from the couch, clearly not from the videotape. The tape was switched off, controlled by the remote. Several seconds passed. His father didn't move. Then slowly he rose and turned around. The view from the closet was unobstructed. The look on his face was one of total exhaustion. But it wasn't his father's face that caught his attention. It was the unzipped fly, the spent erection. He was only ten, but he knew what was going on.

This was no professional study session.

. . . A thud on the window roused him from his memories. He was out of the past but still in the closet—a strange woman's closet. He peered through the slats in the louvered doors. Outside, the wind had kicked up again. A tree branch thrashed against the bedroom window. Nothing to be concerned about. Still, he chastised himself in silence. Too much at stake to let the mind drift away, especially into the past. He opened his eyes widely and stared toward the hallway, thinking only of the future. The immediate future.

When it would be better than videotape.

Twenty-four

Gus returned home after dinnertime. Morgan was in her room with one of her friends. Carla had invited her over. A good move, anything to take Morgan's focus off any child's worst fear. He knocked on her door and popped his head into the room. "Hi."

She looked up from her computer. She and her friend were trying out a new dinosaur CD-ROM. "Hi, Daddy."

"Who's your friend?"

"This is Hannah." Her eyes were telling. That he had to ask only reinforced the uncomfortable note he had left on this morning. "She's my best friend."

"Hi," she peeped.

"Hi, Hannah."

They stared back in silence. Gus felt decidedly unwelcome. He backed out awkwardly. "Well, you two have fun."

He closed the door. Even the simple exchanges were going badly. He slipped off his jacket and headed for the kitchen.

Carla was in the family room watching television on the big sixty-inch screen. One of those mindless magazine shows. *Hard Edition* or some such thing, where Armani-clad journalists ask megastars the really probing questions like, "Are you incredibly excited about your new movie?"

He got a beer from the refrigerator and leaned on the granite counter facing the family room. Carla remained glued to the television.

"I hired a private investigator today."

She switched off the TV with the remote control. "You did?"

"Spent most of the day with him."

"Are you unhappy with the job the police are doing?"

He opened the bottle, took a sip. "Honestly, they seem to have written her off for dead. I want to make sure they're not jumping to conclusions."

"You mean you're coming around to my first thought—that she left you?"

"I'm not ruling it out, though it does seem remote. Even if she was as unhappy as you say, that doesn't explain the way she left, leaving Morgan without a ride at the youth center, leaving without her purse or credit cards. It's all pretty confusing."

"And you think a private investigator can sort it out?"

"No one seems to have a clue where she might have gone. I'm beginning to think maybe someone is covering for her. If that's the case, I'm hoping the private investigator can help."

"I hope so, too."

He nodded, then set his half-empty beer bottle on the counter. "Carla, did you know Beth had an eating disorder?"

She recoiled, but only slightly. The question didn't seem to floor her. "Didn't you?"

"No. How long did she have it?"

"About as long as you've made her feel insecure, I guess."

"What did I ever do to make her feel so insecure?"

"You're the only one who can answer that."

"Did she ever say anything to you?"

"Lots of things."

"Anything specific? Anything she seemed preoccupied with?"

"Yeah. Two words. Martha Goldstein."

He went cold, recalling Martha's words in his office—the way Beth had shunned her at the firm Christmas party. "I was never unfaithful to Beth. Not with Martha, not with anyone."

"That's not the way Beth saw it."

"What did she tell you?"

"She didn't show me any photographs of you and Martha in compromising positions, if that's what you're wondering. And that's not what bugged her anyway. To be honest with you, I think she could have found a way to forgive you if you'd gotten drunk, lost your head and pulled a one-night stand with some woman you didn't care about. What she couldn't stand was the long, painful death. And it has to be painful, watching your husband slowly fall in love with another woman."

"I'm not in love with Martha Goldstein," he said with frustration.

"Maybe not. But somewhere along the line you fell out of love with Beth."

"I've always loved Beth. I still love her. If she doubted that, she should have talked to me about it."

"If you didn't hear her throwing up, I guess she figured you weren't listening."

Gus was looking at Carla but didn't really see her. He was really looking inside himself, seeing things he didn't like.

"I'm beat. I'm going to go lie down before dinner."

"All I made was soup and Jell-O. It's in the fridge. Morgan's tooth is still bothering her. She likes chicken soup and Jell-O when she's sick. Cherry."

All the little things he didn't know about Morgan. The thought of having to learn them from Carla had him feeling not so good himself. "Guess I'll just order a pizza or something. You eat yet?"

"No, but I need to get home. You think you can handle things on your own tonight?"

"I think so."

She grabbed her coat and started down the hall. Gus followed and opened the front door for her, then switched on the porch light. A chilly wind stirred the evergreens in the big front yard. Carla walked down the steps in silence.

"Thanks for watching Morgan," he said, standing in the doorway.

She stopped and looked back. "What's an aunt for?" She started down the steps again but stopped short, as if she had something to say. "Gus?"

"Yeah?"

She paused, measuring her words. "Let me just say this to you. You may never have stopped loving Beth. In your own loyal and convenient way, you may even still love her." Her eyes began to well, her voice even quavered. "But in the last six months you really stopped knowing her."

He watched in silence as she turned and walked to her car. The door closed slowly, leaving him alone with his thoughts in the dark and empty hallway.

Twenty-five

The profile arrived by fax. Six typed pages, double spaced. Andie read it several times. It was her job to disseminate it, not critique it. But she couldn't help herself. She at least had to compare it to what she had come up with.

On several key points she was on Victoria's same wave length. A man in his late twenties or early thirties. Caucasian, same as his victims. Higher than average intelligence. Doesn't know his victims. Likely to have experienced a recent stressful event in his life, such as job loss, divorce, or breakup with his girlfriend.

But the heart of it was somewhat different from what Andie had envisioned. Leads a normal and even respectable lifestyle by day. A roamer by night, possible insomniac. No felony convictions, but arrest record includes peeping tom or trespassing offenses. Fancies himself smarter than police. No formal police training, but probably self-educated through books and magazines on police procedures and perhaps even profiling techniques. Subscribes to detective magazines, frequents bars or restaurants where law enforcement personnel gather, may even befriend or strike up conversations with cops to fit in. A law enforcement reject, possibly a security guard who didn't make the police cut.

Andie's overall impression was disappointment. She

wasn't expecting a name and address. Profiles were by their nature generalizations. But this one struck Andie as a little too general. It didn't exhibit the genius Victoria Santos was.

But what do I know?

She scrambled to get the profile delivered to each of the local law enforcement agencies before six-thirty. Then it was off to her usual Friday routine: yoga classes. Andie rarely missed, especially when the stress level at work was high. Nothing like the downward-facing dog pose to get your mind off work, even if it wasn't nearly as kinky as it sounded.

Andie parked in the paved lot on the corner, across the street and a half block down from the studio. Beneath her coat she wore a clingy aerobic leotard. Her workout bag was over her shoulder. Inside were the usual yoga props: a thin rubber sticky-mat, a strap, and two wooden blocks. The yoga instructor banned cell phones and beepers from class. Fortunately, he had never said anything about the firearm an FBI agent was required to carry. That too was in her bag.

The yoga studio shared space with a ballet company in a low-rent area. The office building across the street was eighty years old and looked even older. The red brick warehouse next door was abandoned and slated for demolition. The handful of restaurants nearby were strictly for the lunch crowd, all closed by late afternoon. It wasn't an unsafe neighborhood, but it wasn't for the fainthearted, either. Most students came in groups. Andie, late as usual, came alone.

She locked her car and headed briskly down the sidewalk. Her sneakers squeaked on the damp cement. A lone car passed, spraying the curb with foul-smelling runoff. Andie danced out of the way and continued up the block. It was a straight shot to the studio, with the entrance to the dark alley beside the warehouse her only real safety concern. She made it a practice never to cross the street till she was past it. In less than a minute, she was there. Seeing no degenerates in the shadows, she jumped off the curb and cut across the street. A truck passed. The sound of tires on wet pavement faded behind her. It was replaced by footsteps.

Andie quickened her pace. The footsteps quickened. Leather heels, she could tell, probably a man. She slowed her pace, just to test. The footsteps were closing.

Paranoid already. All this serial killer stuff.

Just to be safe, she stepped off the curb, pretending to cross the street. The sound changed from the sharp click of heels on a cement sidewalk to the more muffled heels on asphalt. She hopped back on the sidewalk. Again, the footsteps followed.

This was *not* paranoia.

She unzipped her bag and grabbed her pistol, leaving it inside. She stopped and wheeled around. He stopped. She stopped. The gun was still inside her bag, but it was pointing at the chest of her ex-fiancé.

"Rick," she gasped, "what the hell are you doing?"

He wobbled slightly, as though he'd been drinking. "Just, uh. Nothin'."

His eyes were glazed. He'd definitely been drinking. "You're following me."

"I have something to say to you."

"Rick, leave me alone."

"I didn't sleep with your sister."

"I know you didn't. You fucked her."

He smiled, struggling not to laugh. But he couldn't hold it in. It was funny to a drunk. He finally got control of himself. "Oh, that was rich."

Inside the bag, her finger twitched on the trigger. Her darker side wondered if *this* could pass for justifiable homicide. "You think it's funny that you had sex with my sister the night before our wedding?"

The laughter faded. But the smirk was still there. "Come on, Andie. You hate your sister anyway. The only reason she was maid of honor is because your mother made you pick her."

"And that's supposed to make what *you* did okay?"

"She came on to me. I wasn't looking for it."

She checked her watch, ready to go. "What do you want from me?"

"What do you think?"

"Okay. You're forgiven. No hard feelings. Now drop dead and get out of my life."

She turned away. He stepped toward her and grabbed her arm. She stopped and shot a look. "Don't touch me."

He squeezed tighter. "You made a fucking fool out of me."

"You are a fool. Now take your hand off me."

His face reddened. His grip tightened. "What are you gonna do, Andie?"

She looked him straight in the eye. For a second he looked like he was going to kiss her. On impulse, her knee came up and caught him squarely in the groin. He doubled over and fell to the pavement. He was groaning, then dry-heaving. He got up on one knee but could climb no farther. His eyes filled with rage.

"You . . . are gonna . . . pay for this. Bitch."

She returned the glare. "Send me a bill," she said, then turned away.

"I mean it!" he shouted. "I'll make you pay!"

Andie just kept on walking.

"Listen to me!" His senseless shouting followed her down the sidewalk, ceasing only when Andie was inside the building.

After Carla left, Gus was tired enough to sleep, but his mind wouldn't allow it. The lights were off, the master bedroom was dark. He was flat on his back, eyes wide open, staring at the ceiling.

As his pupils adjusted to the darkness, the jewelry box on the bureau caught his attention. A thought crossed his mind that bordered on panic. He couldn't remember if he had told the FBI if Beth had been wearing any jewelry when she'd disappeared. Maybe he could tell from the box. A ring or some other distinctive item might conceivably help identify her—if the worst of Agent Henning's suspicions were true. He switched on the lamp and rose from the bed.

It was a beautiful antique box made of burled walnut. It used to play music, but that had died years ago. Metaphorical, in a way.

He opened it carefully and peered inside. It was well organized. Earrings and less expensive pieces were in the felt-lined squares on top; larger and more precious pieces filled the bottom. He noticed right away the engagement ring was there. The wedding ring was missing. He wasn't sure what to make of that, whether she'd worn it faithfully till the day she had disappeared or symbolically discarded it as she walked out the door.

It was difficult to account for everything, but as best he could tell, everything else he had ever given her was still there. A pear-shaped diamond necklace. A diamond and emerald bracelet. Some of the items were almost too precious to keep in the house. Strangely, the only stones that evoked any emotion were the smallest of all. He'd bought her a pair of diamond-chip earrings for her twentieth birthday, the first they had celebrated together. Years later, after he'd started making real money, it used to make him smile inside when Beth would still wear those tiny little earrings.

He held them in the palm of his hand. Two sparkling specks, not much bigger than flecks of glitter. Beth used to wear them on anniversaries of certain milestones in their early love life, silly little things like the date of their first kiss, the first time he'd said "I love you." It was a shame he'd never told her how good it made him feel to see them on her, how much he appreciated the sentimentality. She probably thought he hadn't noticed. He had.

He'd noticed most when she'd stopped.

She'd stopped when she'd gotten pregnant—when a lot of things seemed to change. It hadn't been an easy pregnancy, though it had started out happily enough. They had talked about furniture shopping together and painting the nursery. He'd even made it to the first three office visits and signed them up for Lamaze classes. He was adamant about being a partner in the experience. Then things blew up at work. He had to go to New York for six weeks to help save his biggest corporate client from a hostile-takeover attempt. When he returned home, Beth had changed. Not just physically, though the difference between her fifth month and the seventh was undeniably dramatic, especially to a husband who had been away. It was more a matter of her mind-set and personality. She seemed worn down by the constant nausea—and it did seem constant. Early in the morning and late at night, Gus heard the honking from behind the closed bathroom door. Beth had called it morning sickness, and he had accepted the explanation at face value, knowing better than to argue with a pregnant woman. Now, however, he wasn't so sure. He was thinking of what Dr. Shippee had said, how the enamel on her teeth suggested that her eating disorder had been going on for a long time. Those awful sounds from the bathroom might well have been the early signs of trouble. He remembered how Beth had almost seemed happy about the nausea in the first couple of months, because it had kept her weight down. In hindsight, she'd seemed unduly intrigued by the rare reported cases of women with nausea throughout their entire pregnancy. Maybe it wasn't nature that had extended her morning sickness beyond the normal thirteen weeks. It might well have been as vulgar as a finger down the throat.

Had he not been so busy, maybe he would have taken a different look at her obsession with gaining no more than eighteen pounds, her insistence on wearing her tight blue jeans just as soon as the cesarian scar healed, her crying jag when she couldn't button them. Something more than pregnancy and hormones was going on. But Gus had let it go.

He'd let too many things go in the last few years. And, as Carla had said, it came with a price: He'd stopped knowing his own wife. He wondered what exactly that meant. Was she criticizing him for not being sensitive to her needs? Or was she telling him that if Beth came back today, if he sat down and really talked to her, he'd literally find he didn't even know her?

Whatever she'd meant, the entire train of thought was leading him in one direction. He was becoming ever more intrigued by something he'd been afraid to check out, something he could never have believed was true. Until now.

Gus put the earrings back in the box and went to the walk-in closet. It was huge, with rows and rows of his business suits on the left. To the right was Beth's space. It was more like a room than a closet. A silk-covered settee faced the big triple mirror. The lighting was indirect candescent, not the fluorescent kind that made it more difficult to determine subtle shades of color in fabrics. The shelves and built-in drawers were solid maple. Nearly an entire wall was devoted just to shoes and sweaters. Hanging clothes lined the other three walls, organized from casual to formal, left to right.

He opened a few drawers randomly, seeing nothing unusual. He flipped through some skirts and dresses on hangers, then stopped. One dress still had the tags on it. He pulled it down. It had an empire waistline. Beth hated that style. He remembered how she'd nearly died when an old sorority sister had gotten married and all the bridesmaids had to wear burnt-orange gowns with empire waistlines. She'd felt like the long, glowing end of those flashlights cops used to direct traffic. It was funny at the time. Not so funny now.

Gus scanned the rack for a dress he was sure she had worn. He found the beaded evening gown she'd worn to the firm's Christmas party and checked the label. It was a size six. He glanced at the other dress. Size twelve.

He draped it over his arm and quickly searched the rack for more dresses with tags. He found a sundress, size ten. A wool skirt, size two. Quickly, he did the same with the shoes on the shelves against the other wall. He found a pair of heels she used to wear and a pair of hiking boots. Both size seven. On the bottom shelf was a leather boot with no mate, the tag still on the sole, never been worn. Size eleven. A beige pump, size four. Again, no mate.

He felt chills down his spine. He stared into the triple mirror, seeing himself from all angles, his arms full of odd-sized clothes his wife could never wear.

It was just as Morgan had said. She was stealing things just for the sake of stealing. Clothes that didn't fit. Odd shoes with their mate still in the back storage room at Nordstrom's. She was filling her closet with useless trophies of the hunt.

"Dear God," he said softly. "What happened to you, Beth?"

Twenty-six

She was alive. He could feel it. With two latex-covered fingers pressed against her neck, he detected a hint of a heartbeat. She was unconscious but slowly coming back for another round. The discovery thrilled him, as if her fading pulse were pumping the blood through his own veins. The icy-cold blood.

After weeks of anticipation, all the tedious preparation, this was the payoff. Everything had gone exactly according to plan.

For nearly three hours he had waited patiently inside the closet in the guest bedroom. Around eleven he'd heard her car pull up in the driveway. The front door opened and closed. The keys jingled in the lock; her heels clicked on the tile floor. Through the slats in the louvered closet door, he watched her pass in the lighted hallway. He heard the toilet flush, listened as she brushed her teeth. The lights went out. The bed squeaked gently beneath the weight of her body. The television played for twenty minutes, then was switched off. It was an instant rush—routine noises that telegraphed her complete unawareness. It made him want to spring early, but he contained himself, sticking to the schedule. He waited. With time, silence filled the house. He allowed another thirty minutes for her to fall asleep. And then he'd made his move.

Quietly out of the closet, then down the hall, dressed in a hooded black body suit that rendered him invisible in the darkness. The hunting knife was in its sheath, strapped to his forearm. A set of plastic handcuffs was in one hand. His strangulation stick was in the other. The bedroom door was open. He stood in the doorway, opposite the bay window on the far wall. Outside, a big full moon radiated just enough light to cast shadows across the room. A collage of framed photographs covered another wall. A queen-size bed faced the bureau. His analytic eye traced the gentle curve of her body beneath the blankets. She lay on her right side, facing away from him. She was surely asleep, but he would wait for the furnace to kick on before closing in. The hum from the blowers would muffle his footsteps. He stood motionless for several minutes, watching over her, never flinching a muscle. Finally, the furnace tripped. A stream of warm air poured from the vents. The lace curtains on the window began to stir. That was his cue. He hooked the plastic cuffs to his belt. He put his arm though the loop of his strangulation stick and brought it up around his right shoulder. Both hands were free. He took four steps closer, right to the edge of the bed. She was easily within his grasp.

Half her sleepy face was hidden beneath the covers, but he knew exactly what she looked like. He knew all about her. She met the essential requirements. Brown hair, brown eyes, mid-thirties. A very suitable selection, given the compressed time frame.

He took a deep, silent breath, then unleashed his fury in one fluid motion. He grabbed her hip and shoulder and jerked her backward, arching her spine against his knee with such force that it cracked the seventh vertebrae. He dragged her to the floor, flat on her stomach. Her limbs flailed as he mounted her, nearly two hundred muscular pounds planted firmly on her kidneys. He extended his arms, and with cupped hands he slapped her simultane-

ously on the ears. It stunned her long enough for him to
gain control and lock her wrists behind her back in the
plastic cuffs. He jerked her upward and sat her on the edge
of the bed. She screamed once. The strangulation stick
dropped over her head and tightened quickly, silencing her.
It was a simple but lethal device, a two-foot loop of nylon
rope attached at both ends to an eight-inch wooden handle.
It allowed him to twist with one hand and choke his victim,
leaving the other free to control her. He knelt behind her on
the bed as the rope twisted and tightened around her neck.
The blood flow to her brain stopped. She weakened with
each breathless moment. He propped her up with his free
arm around her waist, beneath the rib cage, like half a
Heimlich maneuver. As long as she was alive, he wouldn't
let her fall. She sat facing the mirror. He was directly behind her, facing the mirror, too, though his face was unrec-
ognizable behind the ski mask. There was just enough light
to show their reflection. In every attack, there had to be a
mirror.

It was the only way his victims could watch themselves
be strangled.

Her legs kicked, her body tightened with resistance. The
futility of her efforts only heightened his excitement, underlined his total control. This one had fought for nearly
half an hour. The fight, however, was on *his* terms. Every
few minutes he would give a twist of the right hand and
tighten the noose. She would groan and squirm, then
slowly lose consciousness. And then—at precisely the
right moment—he would release. The loop at the end of
the strangulation stick would loosen. Her swan-like neck
would lose the hourglass effect. The air passages would reopen. Blood flow to and from the brain would resume. The
purple ring of bruises around the neck would swell, then
throb. Slowly, her near-dead body would return to life. He
could enjoy it all over again. Three times so far.

And now she was coming back—*again*.

She coughed lightly. Once more she was gaining strength. He could feel the change in her neck and shoulders. She was no longer dead weight. This was unprecedented—four times, up and down, then up again. Either she was an amazing fighter, or he was getting better. More likely the former. He was already *the best*. He knew just how far to take it, how tight to squeeze, how long to hold it. It had taken years of training, much of it at the expense of his own neck muscles. All those afternoons in his garage as a teenager, standing on a ladder, hanging by the neck with his makeshift pulley. Practice had made perfect. He knew what it was like on the other side. The rope had taken him there. More important, he knew the way back. He could show others the way, too. He could bring anyone back.

Or not.

Her face was red and puffy. Blood oozed from her tongue and lips, where she'd bitten herself. Her eyes blinked open, locking with his in the mirror. Hers were glassy and bloodshot. His were dark, narrow slits. He gave the stick a swift turn, harder than the last time, farther than before. The noose tightened and crushed the larynx. Her body stiffened, then quickly went limp. She had little fight left. The struggle was over.

This one was *not* coming back.

He released the tension on the rope, staring closely at a face that no longer showed expression. The brief excitement faded, then turned to disappointment. The anger should have subsided, but it was only getting stronger. This close up, eye to eye with his victim, beyond the flurry of the kill, his mistake was evident.

This one just didn't look enough like Beth Wheatley.

Part Three

Twenty-seven

Andie finished her Monday morning run in record time. The clouds even parted as she crossed the imaginary finish line outside her town house. A quick three miles with a sprint-kick finish had left her sweaty and exhausted. The phone rang just as she reached her back door.

She had not yet caught her breath as she raced inside the kitchen and grabbed it in mid-ring. It was Gus.

"Good—morn—ing," she said, each syllable separated by heavy breathing.

"Did I catch you in the middle of . . . something?"

"No, not—it's not *that*," she said, realizing she had the distinct breathlessness of recent orgasm.

"I'd better call back later."

"It's okay, really." She drew a few more breaths. "I was jogging."

"Oh." He sounded relieved.

She pulled the scrunchie from her knotted hair, letting it fall. "What's up?"

"I hate to bother you at home so early, but I've been thinking about something all weekend that I really need to talk to you about. With your psychology background and all, I thought you might be able to help."

"Sure. Be happy to."

"It's about Beth. She seems to have been in some kind of

trouble. Even before she disappeared, I mean."

He had her attention. Andie sank into a chair at the kitchen table as he told her about the bulimia, the shoplifting. She got up once to grab the magnetic message pad from the refrigerator door, then jotted down a few notes with the phone tucked beneath her chin. It took him several minutes to recount everything. She listened carefully, interjecting only a few "uh-huhs" and "I sees" along the way. As he spoke, however, she was internally debating whether to tell him on the phone that the evidence was more than ever pointing to Beth as a likely victim. When he finished, there was silence.

Andie said, "Would you mind if I stopped by your house this morning?"

"That would be fine, I guess. What do you have in mind?"

She caught herself, careful not to use the term *victimology* with a man who might not be ready to label his wife a victim. "It would be helpful for me to see where Beth lived, how she lived. Maybe even look at some of those things you think she shoplifted. Then we can talk more."

"That sounds like a good idea."

"I can be there in about an hour."

"Great. See you then."

The Wheatley house was even more impressive than Andie had expected. The brick Tudor-style estate was set well back from the street, hidden behind an eight-foot hedge that lined the imposing stone fence and decorative iron gate. A long, curved driveway sloped up toward the house. It was set on the highest point on the heavily wooded lot, perched just above the neighbors' trees for unobstructed views of Puget Sound.

Andie parked beneath the portico and rang the doorbell. Gus answered. He looked tired, as though he'd barely slept all night.

"Come in," he said, letting her pass. The double doors

closed behind her. She stood beneath the crystal chandelier in the foyer, facing the living room. It was a dramatic room with vaulted ceilings that followed the steep lines of the Tudor design. The floor was oak with inlaid borders of teak and rosewood. A huge stone fireplace covered one wall. Museum-quality artwork covered another. The furnishings were expensive European designs she had admired only in storefront windows. In the center was a silk oriental rug big enough to carpet her entire town house.

"Nice place," she said as Gus took her coat.

"It's cozy."

Right. My Subaru is "cozy."

He asked, "Can I get you something? Coffee?"

"That would be perfect."

He directed her toward the kitchen, but they were practically ambushed halfway down the hall as Morgan emerged from her bedroom.

Gus said, "This is my daughter, Morgan."

Andie leaned forward to extend her hand. "I'm Andie."

"Andie? That's a *boy's* name."

"No more than Morgan," she said, smiling thinly.

That seemed to break the ice, as if they had a kinship. "I lost a tooth," she said as she pointed at the gap.

"Oh, my. Does it hurt?"

"A little. Enough to keep me out of school today."

"I see," said Andie, smiling with her eyes.

"Are you going to find my mommy?"

Andie and Gus exchanged glances. She sensed the FBI was as yet an unsettled matter between father and daughter. "I'm here to help your dad."

A phone rang. Morgan pulled a cordless receiver from her Barbie shoulder bag and answered, "Hi, Hannah."

"Sounds like somebody found a friend to play hooky with her," Andie said with a wink.

Morgan blushed, guilty as charged. She waved a quick good-bye and started down the hall, then stopped and glanced back. "You can come see my room sometime, Andie. If you want."

"I'd like that."

Morgan seemed to smile as she ducked into her room.

Gus watched, bewildered. "How the heck did you do that?"

"It's a girl thing."

"Works better than the lousy dad thing, I guess."

"Come on. Any dad who gets his little girl a pink phone can't be all bad."

She followed Gus into a kitchen that rivaled those dream spreads in magazines. Solid cherrywood cabinets. Lots of granite and stainless steel. An island the size of Hawaii. Andie pulled up a stool at the counter. Gus remained standing, too nervous to sit. A beam of welcome sunlight streamed down through the skylight, almost drawing a line between them.

"You haven't told Morgan the FBI's looking for her mother, have you?" It was a question, but her tone was judgmental.

"Not specifically. I was afraid the mere mention of something like the FBI would only make it more scary to her."

"You need to be honest. Kids are more intuitive than you think."

"Especially this one. If she's this self-aware at six, I'm dreading sixteen."

"A little extra maturity isn't at all unusual in an only child."

Gus poured two coffees, then came to the opposite side of the counter. "Morgan certainly has some adult-sized proclivities," he said, thinking of the little wooden horse that had disappeared from his office.

"How do you mean?"

"Nothing. Have you given any more thought to what I told you about Beth?"

"For the past hour that's all I've thought about."

"And?"

"The eating disorder, shoplifting. I'd say they're related manifestations of the same problem. Lack of self-esteem, purpose, identity. Sounds like a troubled woman crying out for help."

"I've heard of eating disorders. Even self-mutilation. But shoplifting?"

Andie sipped her coffee, then glanced at the surroundings. "She lived in a world where no material need went unfilled. Stealing a basic necessity like clothing was the ultimate way for her to break from what she was. Has she ever done anything like that before?"

"Stealing?"

"No. Has she ever shown any resentment for the kind of life you've given her?"

"Not that I know of."

"You have any idea why she would be so unhappy with what she was?"

"That's a more complicated question."

"Let me try to simplify it. Your wife did accuse you of spouse abuse some years ago."

"Yes, she did."

"Abuse has a way of making a woman do strange things. Especially if it occurs over many years. I've seen more than one abused wife snap and do some pretty strange things."

"Beth was not an abused wife."

She softened her tone, not looking for a confrontation. "Can we talk a little about that? You said the same thing the night we met at the medical examiner's office. I'd like to believe you. But why did she file that report?"

"Like I said. It's complicated."

She wondered if "complicated" meant Martha Goldstein. "I think it's important for me to know, don't you?"

He wasn't eager to reopen those wounds, but it was undeniably relevant. "After Morgan was born, Beth had terrible postpartum depression. Didn't come out of the bedroom for days at a time, didn't want anything to do with Morgan."

"That's more common than you would think."

He stirred a little sugar into his coffee. "That's what I'm told, but that didn't make it any easier. We needed double-shift nannies to take care of the baby, because Beth wasn't even taking care of herself. I tried to get her to see a psychiatrist, but she wouldn't go. It got to be a daily routine. I'd come home, she'd still be in bed where I left her. We started having arguments. Just the exchange of words, nothing else. She would cry and yell at me, saying I ignored her, I neglected her. It seemed like we were having the same argument, night after night. Except, after a while, she started using the word abuse. Things hadn't changed. If I was doing anything wrong, I was still busy at work—ignoring her, as she said. But suddenly she was calling it abuse."

"So you're saying that's the full extent of the abuse?"

"That's exactly what I'm saying."

"That's not what you'd infer from the police report she filed. She claimed you physically hit her."

"That was pure embellishment."

"Why would she make that up?"

"Why would she steal a size twelve dress from a department store?"

"Is that what you're hoping? That people will hear she was shoplifting and finally believe she made up the abuse allegations?"

Gus looked stunned, then angered. "I have no intention of making this public. I'm telling you this only because I hope it will help you find out what happened to Beth. I called you in confidence."

"Sorry. It's just that you're a very prominent attorney in this town. Kind of hard to believe you don't care what other people think."

"I did care. It bothered me a great deal the way people reacted back then. My friends, *her* friends. My own law firm. I almost lost my job over it. Somehow, a mere accusation was enough to convict me, even after Beth retracted it."

"It's hard for outsiders to know what to believe in those situations."

"Then why do they always want to believe the worst?"

"It's juicy, I guess. A high-powered lawyer who abused his wife. Or a desperate wife who makes the whole thing up to keep him from leaving her for another woman."

"Where did you hear that?"

"I can't say."

"You talked to Martha Goldstein, didn't you?"

"I really can't talk about that."

"*That's* her angle. She plants ideas in your head so she can honestly tell my partners and my clients that I'm under police investigation. It's all a ploy. She's using you."

"I don't know anything about that."

"I know it's Martha. She somehow fancied herself the other woman. Rumors like that only made it harder for Beth and me to patch things up and move forward. It is hard, even if you love each other. And I did love Beth."

"But not enough to change."

He stared into his coffee cup. "We just seemed to drift further apart."

"Over the Martha rumors?"

"No. The real difficulty was me. I never fully believed she made up the charges to get my attention or keep me from leaving her. When she filed that report, it was as if part of her were wishing I *had* crossed the line. I'm not saying she wanted to be abused. But I do think she wished the issues had been more black and white. It sounds crazy, but the real problem was that we had something really good a long time ago. I suppose she needed something really bad to make her finally give up on that. You know what I mean?"

His question hit close to her own personal disaster, her own recent pain at the altar. "I suppose decisions are easier when somebody does something horrendous. Like me and my ex-fiancé. Bam. I was out of there. No hesitation."

"What happened?"

"Not important. It was so unlike your situation with Beth."

"But you do understand?"

"I understand what you're saying. But if you really loved her, I can't say I understand how you let it get to that point."

He fell silent, absorbing the blow. "Neither can I."

"Daddy!" Morgan was sprinting up the hall. Gus turned and braced himself. She nearly ran him over.

"Daddy, you missed it, you missed it!" She spoke in short, panicky breaths, her voice shaking.

"Missed what?"

"I can't believe you missed it!"

Tears filled her eyes. Gus lifted her up and sat her on the counter. "Missed what?"

"Just—just now!"

"Morgan, calm down. What's wrong?"

"While you were talking, you just missed it!"

"Missed *what*?"

She shouted with all her breath, "Mommy called!"

He froze for an instant, then raced down the hall.

Twenty-eight

In seconds Gus was in his daughter's bedroom. Andie and Morgan were right behind. He snatched up the phone from the pink rug beside the bed, where Morgan had dropped it. The dial tone hummed in his ear.

"Does Morgan's line have caller-ID?" asked Andie. She was standing in the doorway.

"No."

"Hit star sixty-nine, then."

Gus had used the memory-call service before. It automatically dialed the number of the last incoming phone call. He punched the buttons and waited.

A young girl answered. "Hello."

"Who is this?"

"Hannah."

Confused, Gus covered the mouthpiece and asked his daughter, "Did your friend Hannah call you this morning?"

Morgan nodded slowly.

Gus returned to the phone. "I'm sorry, Hannah. This is Morgan Wheatley's father. We dialed a wrong number." He hung up and gave Morgan a stern look. "I thought you said your mother called."

"She did!"

He appealed to Andie, not sure what to do. Andie sat on the edge of the bed, at eye level with the six-year old. "Are you sure it was your mom who called?"

"*Yes*. It was her. It had to be her."

"This is very important. If she called, your daddy and I want to talk to her."

"She called. I know it was her!"

Gus took her hand gently. "What did she say, sweetie?"

"She didn't say anything."

The adults shared a moment of skepticism. "You never heard her voice?" asked Gus.

"No."

"Then how do you know it was Mommy who called?"

"The numbers."

"I don't understand. What numbers?"

"Nine–five–three–four–eight–eight–nine."

Andie asked, "Is that Beth's cell phone number?"

"No. Sweetheart, what are you talking about?"

Morgan picked up the phone and put it to her father's ear. "Listen." She punched out the numbers. It made a tune.

Gus looked at Andie. "Mary Had a Little Lamb."

Morgan said, "That's what I'm telling you. Mommy showed me how to do that, long time ago. She called me and hit the numbers. Just now. And then she hung up."

Gus felt a chill. "Did you ever tell Hannah about those numbers? Did she know how to play that tune, too?"

"No way. That was me and Mommy's secret."

He looked quizzically at Andie. "Why did I get Hannah when I dialed memory call?"

"People can buy devices to beat any of those phone-company services—memory call, caller-ID. We see it all the time with creeps who make obscene calls."

"So, it could have been made from a telephone that was outfitted with one of those electronic gizmos?"

"That would explain how you got Hannah when you dialed star sixty-nine. You would have pulled up the second-to-last call rather than the last call."

"Then it's possible it was Beth."

"It *was* Mommy. I know it was!" Morgan was so frustrated, she was about to hit him.

Gus was silent, but he sensed Andie had the same exact thought. She sprang from the bed. "I'll get one of our technical agents to see if he can track the call."

He tossed her the phone.

"Let's not use Morgan's anymore. I don't want to screw anything up."

"The kitchen," said Gus, leading the way. He spoke as they hurried down the hall. "If it was Beth who called, why didn't she talk?"

"I can't answer that."

They stopped at the kitchen counter. Fear was in his eyes. "You don't think this was some kind of prank?"

"That's what I hope my techies can tell me."

"But if it wasn't a prank—why the numbers?"

"I don't know. Maybe your daughter can help us with that."

"I don't think so. It's more a matter of thinking it through logically. A woman disappears for nearly a week. She's finally able to get to a phone. She's able to dial the numbers. But she doesn't speak. There are only a couple possibilities. Either she doesn't want to speak, or . . ."

"She can't."

The words chilled him. "Can't speak? Meaning what?"

Their eyes met and held. It was as if she were telling him there were any number of possibilities. None of them pretty. "Let's get the technical agents on the trail, all right? Then we can brainstorm."

Gus nodded, then swallowed the lump in his throat. "Okay," he said quietly as she dialed the number.

Andie was on the phone with technical agents when Carla rang the doorbell. In all the confusion Gus had almost forgotten he'd called his sister before Andie's arrival. He'd wanted her there to watch Morgan, just in case the FBI visit ended up taking all morning or required him to leave the house. Good thing he'd called—though he certainly hadn't anticipated *this*.

The house seemed chaotic, considering it was just the four of them. Andie was in the kitchen, actually speaking on two phones at once, her cellular and the Wheatleys'. Morgan was continually bopping between her room and Gus's home office, the two free lines. She was sure that staring at the phone would make it ring again, but she couldn't decide which one to watch. Gus trailed after her, letting her burn off the excitement. He gave Carla all the details as they traced the erratic steps of a six-year-old across the house.

Carla asked, "You sure Morgan isn't making this up?" They were standing outside Morgan's bedroom, the door open, keeping an eye on her inside.

"After those shoplifting allegations panned out, I don't have much room to doubt her word anymore."

Morgan hurried past them, then down the hall. Back to Gus's office. Gus and Carla followed at a safe distance behind so that Morgan couldn't overhear.

"Doesn't it scare you that she didn't speak?"

"Of course it does," said Gus.

"I mean, she would have said *something*. If she could have."

"That's sort of where Agent Henning and I came out."

"So . . . why couldn't she?"

They stopped near Gus's office, just off the kitchen. He glanced across the room at Andie on the phone, then looked down, unable to look Carla in the eye. "I have this image in my head."

"Image?"

"I keep seeing Beth on the floor, her hands and feet tied. Crawling to a phone. She knocks it off the hook. Her mouth is gagged, she can't talk. So she pecks out this tune on the key pad."

"That's brilliant," she said, impressed.

He shot a look. "It's horrifying."

A yelp of excitement drew their attention to the kitchen. Andie hung up the phone and hissed out a loud "*Yesssssss*," like a tennis pro who'd just served an ace. She shouted, "We pegged the call!"

Gus hurried into the kitchen. "Where?"

"It came from Oregon. A pay phone just across the state line."

"A pay phone?" So much for his image of Beth crawling on the floor.

"Yeah. They're on their way to check it out." She pulled on her overcoat and grabbed her car keys. "I'm headed there myself."

"I'm going with you," said Gus.

"You can't. What if another call comes?"

He agonized for a moment but realized she was right. "What if another one *does* come? What do I do?"

"We've set up a trap and trace on all three house lines now. If a remotely suspicious call comes on any one of them, keep it going as long as you can."

Gus led her to the foyer and opened the front door. "Call me the minute you hear anything."

"I will. But, Gus, please. Try not to drive yourself crazy with worry."

He watched from the top step as she turned and hurried to her car. Too late, he thought as her car sped away. I'm way beyond worried.

Twenty-nine

Andie drove alone to the northernmost nub of western Oregon. In these parts, the irregular path of the Columbia River defined the state line, which accounted for the little pocket of Oregon that protruded into southwestern Washington. Her exact destination was near the city of Rainier, forty miles north of Portland on the Oregon side of the river.

Most of the trip was interstate at high speed. She played no radio, no books on cassette. She was alone with her thoughts, mostly about Beth Wheatley. Her mind did wander somewhat. Exit signs for connections to Route 101 reminded her of the trip she and Rick had taken along the coast, Washington to San Francisco, the long and scenic route. She had hoped it would be romantic, but Rick kept brooding over the fact that she had vetoed his preference for nude beaches in Jamaica. In hindsight, she should have seen the early warning signs of a guy who wanted to put his girlfriend on display, as if to show the rest of the world what *he* was getting. So intent was he on going that it took a threat to settle the matter. She vowed to dissolve copious quantities of Viagra—the miracle cure for impotence—into his piña coladas. Rick backed off immediately. Nothing was more uncool than a cheesy-grinned tourist on a nude beach with a permanent erection.

The gray fog thickened as she crossed the bridge over the Columbia River, a far cry from sunny Jamaican beaches. Rain fell, then stopped, then started again as she drove through Rainier to a more remote area outside town. According to her technical agents, the call to Morgan's line had come from a pay phone along the highway. A public rest area, to be exact, just west of Rainier and situated at the foot of a forested preserve. She hadn't mentioned anything to Gus, but a pay phone was the last place she had expected the trace to have led them. With three dead women who looked so much like her, the thought of Beth Wheatley at a pay phone punching out "Mary Had a Little Lamb" just didn't add up.

Unless by some miracle she had escaped.

Rain gathered on the windshield, and the image in her mind was suddenly vivid. A desperate woman leaping from her captor's van as it rounded the corner. The rough pavement ripping at her flesh as she rolled into the parking lot. The mad dash to the pay phone, her attacker in pursuit. Her hands shaking as she frantically punched the buttons. The excitement of the call going through. The frustration of finding she couldn't respond to her own daughter's voice, couldn't speak at all. A gag, possibly. Or a rope around her neck. Her attacker grabbing her, pulling her back toward the van, but she hangs on long enough to bang out a tune her daughter would recognize.

Andie shook off the disturbing image and turned into the rest area.

It was a typical looking highway road stop, a flat roof perched on brown-painted cinder blocks. A bank of three pay phones was in the middle, flanked by men's and women's facilities to the left and right, respectively. The entire building, parking lot, and neighboring curtilage had been marked off as a crime scene with yellow police tape. A forensic team was already at work. Two men were casting a mold for a tire track near a puddle. Another was scouring the pay phone for fingerprints. Four teams had fanned out in all directions, searching the surrounding area for articles of clothing, footprints, blood, weapons— anything of interest.

Andie parked near a squad car on the opposite side of the highway. She stepped out, shocked for a moment by the cold wind. The tall stand of pines behind the building blocked any view of the river, though it was near enough to feel its damp chill.

Andie cinched up her trench coat, crossed the highway and started toward the shelter. A deputy sheriff stopped her before she could duck under the tape. She identified herself and flashed her credentials. He was expecting her.

"This way," he said, then led her around back the long way, outside the yellow-taped perimeter. The wind was blowing harder. Her nose started to run. She stayed a half step behind him so he wouldn't notice.

"Anybody see anything?" she asked, still walking.

"We got the word out to local news asking people to come forward if they were near the rest area this morning. But I wouldn't get your hopes up."

They stopped at a ridge about fifty meters behind the rest area. The stand of pines was behind them. A steep cliff was at their feet. Thick, gray clouds moved slowly through the valley like the ghost of a glacier.

The deputy offered his binoculars and pointed to an area deep in the valley. "Down there. Through that clearing."

With the naked eye she noticed a team converging near the bank of a winding stream. She trained the binoculars toward a wooded area that had shed its leaves for winter. She peered intently, though by now it was a scene she could have described without looking.

Through the tangle of branches, the ravaged body of yet another nude brunette hung limply from a tree.

* * *

For Gus, the minutes passed like hours. Andie had been gone for more than two hours, and he had yet to hear anything. It was a long drive to Rainier, he knew, but he had hoped for more frequent updates. Finally, the phone rang.

Gus started in his chair but didn't answer. It rang again.

Carla snapped, "Answer it."

He was frozen for a moment by the possibility of bad news. He grabbed it on the third ring.

"We found a body," said Andie.

"Oh, my God."

"It's okay. It's not Beth."

Gus was relieved at first, then felt guilty about it. True, it wasn't Beth. But it was *someone*.

Carla was nearly draped over him, concerned. "Did they find her?" she asked.

He covered the mouthpiece, quickly told her what he knew, then continued with Andie. "Who is it?"

"We don't know yet. Identification might take time. Another one exposed to the elements."

"Let me guess. She looks like Beth."

"Not quite as much as the others, but yes. In a general way, there's a resemblance."

"Do you know anything about her?"

"Really nothing as yet."

His head was pounding. "I guess there are a couple of things we'll never know."

"What's that?"

"Whether she has Morgan's number. And whether she knows how to play 'Mary Had a Little Lamb' on the phone."

There was silence on the line, as if Andie didn't know what to say. "I gotta go, Gus. I'll keep you informed."

"Thanks." He hung up and looked straight at Carla.

She asked anxiously, "What's going on? Is Beth okay?"

"They sure as hell don't know." He looked away, focused on nothing, really. But his gaze intensified. "And I'll be damned if I'm going to wait around for them to find out."

Thirty

Late Monday afternoon Andie drove to the airport Hilton to meet with Victoria Santos and Isaac Underwood. It wasn't a scheduled meeting, but Victoria diverted from her case in Sacramento for a much needed brainstorming session. Isaac brought Alex Gould with him, a retired special agent who had served as profile coordinator for the Seattle field office. Gould was trained at the FBI Academy and had done some impressive work in his day. But for his personality, he might well have been selected to join the profilers in Quantico. The unit was too small and too elite to reward another insufferable know-it-all, however talented.

It was an unusual move, dusting off a retired agent. That made Andie a little nervous. She wondered if Isaac still deemed her up to the task. To his credit, he made a point of pulling her aside before the meeting to reassure her.

"Just wanted another perspective on this, Andie. Don't get paranoid on me."

She wanted to accept that, but it wasn't just Gould who had her nervous. It seemed strange that Isaac would personally attend a meeting like this—a little too hands-on for the office ASAC. Perhaps he was trying to show Victoria how important this case was to the office. Perhaps he wanted to evaluate the performance of his former protégé firsthand. Either way, Andie felt under the microscope.

For Victoria's convenience, they met in a hotel suite right at the airport. An occasional commercial jet streaked across the sky outside their seventh-floor window, but not even the space shuttle would have broken their concentration. Victoria sat in an armchair near the television. Isaac sat across from her, preferring the desktop itself to the chair behind it. Andie was seated on the couch with Gould. They were at opposite ends, but Gould was such a large man they were still closer than Andie would have liked. For a man who had joined the FBI in the height of the image-conscious Hoover era, he had certainly let himself go in retirement.

Andie updated them on the latest victim outside Rainier. The group listened and fished little goldfish crackers from a bowl on the coffee table, the bulk going to Gould. When she had finished, Isaac took over.

"The basic question is, why would the killer lead us to the recovery site with this strange phone call to a six-year-old?"

"Let's take a broader look," said Victoria. "We have two contacts. The latest one is to Morgan Wheatley. But the first was to the Torture Victims' Institute." She glanced at Andie. "How is your follow-up in Minneapolis coming?"

"It's pretty much done."

"Excuse me," said Gould. He brushed the gold layer of cracker crumbs from his bulging lap onto Andie, as if she were a dustpan. "I went over the whole file just this morning and didn't see anything to suggest it's pretty much done."

"Maybe you missed it." She brushed the crumbs back at him.

"Maybe it isn't pretty much done."

She glanced at Isaac, as if to say, *You invited this jerk?* "Mr. Gould, I assure you I've worked very hard on this case."

"I'm sure you've done your best."

"What is that supposed to mean?"

Isaac interjected. "Andie, what's happening in Minnesota?"

She let it go. "The Minneapolis office put two agents on it. They reviewed records, interviewed current staff. To the extent possible they interviewed former staff and even some former patients. They focused especially on people who were fired or disciplined, anyone who showed any bitterness toward the institute, any individuals or organizations that opposed the type of work that was going on there. They've also done follow-ups with certain victims to determine whether any of their torturers might currently be in the United States."

"Any leads?"

"Nothing promising."

Isaac said, "We have to look at everyone who was ever an employee of the institute. Not just the ones who were fired. Check *everyone*."

"We did," said Andie. "But I'll double-check."

Victoria asked, "What about the International Center for Victims of Torture in Denmark? Have they received any messages that might be from our killer?"

"None they've identified."

"You've actually checked, then?" said Gould.

"Yes," said Andie. "I checked. There's nothing."

Gould rose and started to pace, his look pensive. He moistened his finger and gathered the last few specks from the cracker bowl. "That may tell us something in and of itself."

"Like what?" asked Isaac.

"From what I saw in the file, Miss Henning's initial theory was that his e-mail to the national institute in Minnesota was simply his way of telling us that his signature is torture."

"That was actually my theory," said Victoria.

Gould said, "That's quite all right, we all make mistakes, Vicky."

"It's Victoria. And where's the mistake?"

Gould was still pacing, stroking his double chin. "Think about it. If our killer was simply trying to convey the message that torture is what gets him off, why would he limit his e-mail message to the torture institute in Minnesota? Why not the international center in Denmark? It's every bit as accessible on the Internet. It seems more likely that he has a connection of some sort to the national institute. All the more reason to turn up the scrutiny there."

Isaac said, "Maybe he just doesn't know about the international center."

"That's possible, too," said Gould. "In fact, that fits neatly with my own preliminary take on this guy. He's got no time to do any homework. He's too rushed. That's what I see here. A guy in a hurry. He's showing signs of a spree killer, like that young fella who killed Gianni Versace."

"Cunanan."

"Right. Andrew Cunanan. Someone who's killing people in rapid succession, no cooling-off period. Usually these types are at the end of their run when they kill this rapidly. They know they're going to be caught. They want as big a splash as possible when they check out."

"It's a fine line," said Victoria, "spree versus serial. Serial killers often have shorter cooling-off periods toward the end of their run too."

"Let's not get hung up on labels," said Isaac.

"It's not just semantics," said Victoria. "It's a whole different psychological profile. If we have a serial killer— even one at the end of his run—we're still talking about a psychopathic sexual sadist. That's what serial killers are, and that's what I see here. As much as Hollywood likes to cast them as clever geniuses who enjoy a deadly game of cat and mouse with law enforcement, the truth is, they kill because they're driven by uncontrollable sexual fantasies and a warped sense of values that makes their own ten-second orgasm more important than the life of the average thirty-five-year-old woman. A spree killer is different. Who the hell knows what drove Andrew Cunanan to kill Gianni Versace?"

"Spree, serial, whatever," said Isaac. "Let's get back to my original question. What's the point of phoning Morgan Wheatley and dialing 'Mary Had a Little Lamb'?"

Gould said, "With all due respect for Agent Santos, I believe this phone call is indeed the game of a spree killer who's looking for a showdown. He's dropping little bread crumbs as clues along the way, luring us closer, bringing this thing to a head."

"I disagree," said Andie.

Gould smirked. "Oh, that takes courage. Jumping on the Santos bandwagon."

"I'm just thinking logically. If the killer wanted to taunt us with clues on how to find him, he could have simply picked up the phone and called us himself."

"I didn't say he was trying to make it *easy* for us," said Gould. "He knows that Mr. Wheatley has been dealing with the FBI, and he assumed the phone lines in his house were being monitored. Maybe he feared voice identification."

Isaac said, "He could have let Beth speak."

"Too risky," said Gould. "She could have talked too long, ensured a trace."

"We got a trace anyway," said Isaac.

"Which is exactly what the killer wanted," said Andie.

Gould scoffed. "What, now you're on Isaac's bandwagon? You're all over the map, Henning."

"I'm not on anybody's bandwagon, you blowhard."

He backed off, indignant. "Hey, I'm here as a favor. I don't need your grief."

The room was silent. Andie said, "I'm sorry. I admit I don't have the experience of the rest of you, but I've thought about this case more than anyone on the planet, with the possible exception of Gus Wheatley. I feel like I have something important to say about it."

"Then say it, Andie."

"As I see it, this breaks down to two questions. First, why did he call from that pay phone? The answer: he wanted us to find the body."

"Why would he want that?"

"If you look at the pattern on the map, these recovery sites keep moving south. Seattle. Issaquah. Now Oregon. Maybe he's just trying to point us in the wrong direction."

Victoria nodded, which energized her. Andie continued, "Which leads to the second question. Why didn't he just dump the body on the highway where somebody would quickly find it? Or if he felt the need to use the phone, why didn't he just call 911 or the newspaper and tell them where the body was? Why did he call Morgan Wheatley and play a tune on her phone? There's only one explanation I can come up with. He wants us to know he has Beth Wheatley. Really has her."

Isaac asked, "You mean sexually?"

"I'm talking beyond the realm of the physical. He wants us to know he's been inside her head, knows everything about her. Right down to the secret code she uses to communicate with her daughter. He wants us to know he controls her."

They exchanged glances in silence. No one challenged her. It made sense.

Andie continued, "This isn't a spree killer looking for some suicidal showdown on the evening news. He's a serial killer asserting his control. He doesn't want us to catch him. To the contrary. He doesn't think we can."

The silence turned uneasy. It was the familiar fear that lurked in the mind whenever a killer fancied himself uncatchable: He might be right.

"The question is," said Victoria, "does he still control her?"

"Meaning?" asked Gould.

"Meaning, is it purely the memory of Beth Wheatley that fuels this psychopath's fantasy?"

"Or," said Andie, "is he keeping her alive?"

A sudden chill swept over them, as if no one were quite certain which would be worse.

Thirty-one

Gus met his private investigator at Café René. Despite the French name, it was about as continental as French toast and French fries. It was a dive of a joint, with dank walls of exposed red brick and hanging light fixtures that looked like they might drop from the ceiling at any moment. The sagging wood floor was in such disrepair that years of foot traffic had worn paths in the polish. Private booths and bottomless cups of coffee, however, made it Dexter Bryant's favorite meeting place. That, and the fact that they never enforced the rules against cigar smoking.

Dex was a former Seattle police officer who had specialized in child abductions and teenage runaways while on the force. As a P.I. he was a reputed crackerjack at finding missing persons. To look at him, you'd think *he* was a missing person. He hadn't shaved since retiring, and he'd grown back the ponytail he'd worn as a teenage hippie, before he'd sold out and joined the police force. In his own mind, however, he had never completely sold out. His heart went out to the lost souls he searched for.

They took an isolated booth in the back, where Gus gave him the latest. Dex lit up a cigar and listened. He didn't just smoke his cigar, he admired it, checking out the burn as his client talked on. He took a long, slow drag when Gus had finished. Thick gray smoke poured from his lips as he spoke.

"We need to go on the offensive, try to develop some leads. You got media contacts?"

"Sure."

"My advice is to use them."

Gus sipped his coffee, waved away the cloud of smoke. "I did already. Ended up with a very interesting piece on wife beating on the tube."

"Oh, yeah. I saw that. Screw those sneaky reporters, then. Go the advertising route. You can afford it."

"Advertising?"

"Yeah. Just buy a big ad, put your wife's picture on page three of the *P-I*. You know, the space those fancy department stores buy every other week for their once a year sale. Offer a reward for information that leads to her return. I'll bet dollars to doughnuts that'll prompt some calls for me to follow up on."

"Can't hurt."

"Here, I brought some samples for format." He opened his briefcase and spread them across the table. A clump of ash fell from his cigar, which Dex brushed away.

Gus thumbed through the samples. Nothing particularly creative, much like the side of the milk cartons he'd never really paid attention to.

Dex said, "I got the template on my computer. We can plug in your wife's picture and information and have it over to the paper in time for tomorrow afternoon's *Times*, Wednesday morning's *P-I*."

"Shouldn't I run this by the FBI first?"

"What for? So they can run it up their bureaucratic flagpole and come to the same decision we did, only three weeks later. That's why you hired me, Gus. To do the right thing and to do it right now."

Gus hesitated, then figured what the hell. "Okay, let's go with it."

"Great. I'll need a little advance, of course."

Gus pulled out his checkbook. "How much?"

"Just make it out to the *Seattle Times* and leave the amount blank. I'll fill in whatever the ad costs. And by the way, while you've got the checkbook out . . ."

Gus looked up suspiciously.

"Now, don't go looking at me like that," said Dex. "I told you I was a full-service private investigator. I'm just throwing out ideas. This one's a little off the wall, but I know this psychic."

"A psychic?"

"Yeah. Someone who can hold a piece of jewelry or an article of clothing, pick up on some vibes or whatever, maybe help you find your wife. I think it's a little hokey, but some police forces use them, so why shouldn't you? If you're serious about pulling out all the stops, that's just an option I want to make available to you."

"I'll think about that. Let's see where the ads take us first."

"Sure. It's your call."

Gus handed over the check, then took a closer look at the sample ads scattered on the table before him. A seventeen-year-old girl. A boy in kindergarten. A half dozen others. Wives, sons, and daughters. Just a bunch of names and faces on paper, the black-and-white legacy of families torn apart.

"Were any of these people ever found?"

Dex chomped nervously on his cigar. "Yeah, most of them."

"How many alive?"

He answered in a quiet, serious tone. "A few."

Gus leaned back, his expression vague. Dex said, "There's no guarantees in this business, Mr. Wheatley."

"You're telling me," Gus said with concern.

Andie's meeting lasted till almost five. They walked out together and separated in the hotel lobby. Victoria took a cab back to the airport, promising Isaac she'd probably have some revisions to her profile. Gould headed for the bar, mumbling something about the prospect of finding more of those tasty little goldfish crackers. Isaac walked Andie to her car.

Andie enjoyed spending time with Isaac again. Since his promotion to ASAC, she hadn't seen him nearly as often as when he was her direct supervisor. The more they were together, however, the more she realized it wasn't his supervision she missed. It was his company.

The rain had cleared, but the pavement was still wet. It was just beyond dusk, and the sun had disappeared without ever really appearing. Andie walked the brightest path to her car, beneath the center line of street lamps.

"So, what's up with Gould?" she asked.

Isaac buried his hands in his coat pockets, walking at her side. "Like I said, I just wanted another perspective on this."

"That sounds like bull."

"I know. But it's true. Gould has more profiling experience than anyone I know outside of Quantico. He's a pain, but I think he helped us focus."

"I thought maybe you brought him in because you're unhappy with me."

"Not at all." They stopped at Andie's car. "It's Victoria I'm worried about."

"Victoria?"

"She's spread too thin. All the ISU profilers are."

"I have to admit I wasn't all that impressed with the profile she prepared. Not as insightful as I had expected."

"You're being kind, Andie. It was pure boilerplate, the usual stuff about serial killers that someone like Victoria can rattle off in her sleep."

"So you brought Gould in to help her?"

"Heck, no. I brought Gould in to kick her in the ass."

"She's not going to take orders from Gould."

"You're missing the point. Gould is the last guy on earth

she wants upstaging her. You think she wants it getting back to Quantico that it was a retired old fart like Gould, not her, who cracked this case? You can bet she'll give our case top priority from here on out."

"So, is Gould on or off the case?"

"He's off," Isaac said with a chuckle. "He served his purpose. You can rest easy."

"I can't say I exactly took a liking to the old guy, but I almost feel a little sorry for him. You used him."

"The guy had a ball. You think he would have been brushing cracker crumbs all over you if he'd thought this was a long-term relationship?"

"What does that say about me? I brushed them right back."

They laughed as they recalled the moment, both of them leaning against her car. The laughter was over, but their eyes met and held. They were sharing a smile, but it didn't feel like their usual kidding around. This seemed more serious.

"What?" said Andie.

"Nothing."

"Come on, Isaac. What's that look for? What are you thinking?"

"I . . . I don't know."

"It's okay. You can tell me."

He chuckled nervously. "Tell you what?"

"Where do we go from here?"

It was a wide-open question at an ambiguous moment. It could have roped in anything from "What's my next assignment?" to "What are you doing Saturday night?" Maybe it was the age difference. Maybe it was just Isaac's sensitivity to his new position of authority. He whiffed.

"That phone call from Oregon changed the entire complexion of the case."

Andie had to refocus. Back to work. "How so?"

"This is no longer just a matter of providing support and

expertise to the local police in their homicide investigations. We got a possible kidnapping across state lines. It's a category seven. This is our jurisdiction. The FBI is taking the lead."

"Does that mean you're reassigning it?"

"You've done three kidnapping cases, counting that First Federal bank robbery that turned into a hostage situation. You did a bang-up job on all of them. Why would I reassign?"

"This is pretty high-profile."

"Extremely high-profile. This could be a career maker."

"Wow. I don't know what to say."

"You want it or don't you?"

" 'Course I want it."

"Then you can have it. Just one condition."

"What?"

"Don't fuck it up."

His words seemed harsh, but she understood the message. No matter what their friendship might someday become, she had to make the grade. "You got nothing to worry about."

Gus drove straight home from his meeting. The Magnolia district could be quite dark on a moonless evening, especially near the waterfront estates on the western edge, what little light from the heavens being blocked by the trees. Trees were in abundance, none of them magnolias. Surveyors back in the nineteenth century had mistaken the madroñas for magnolias. One expansive estate after another, dressed with madronas, oaks, elms, huge Douglas firs. Cherry hedges galore. Even a stand of bamboo. But no magnolias. It was fitting, thought Gus. A magnificent bluff with everything a homeowner could conceivably want, named for the one thing it didn't actually have.

The Mercedes slowed as Gus turned into his driveway. He stopped at the iron gate. Two huge lanterns glowed atop the imposing stone pillars on either side of the drive. The gate was an antique, a true work of art. Only on very close inspection of the elaborately curved design was the letter C discernible, the family initial of the original owners. This particular estate had been in the same family forever. Gus had admired it since he was a kid, thinking it was the most amazing house ever built.

He remembered the night he had first shown it to Beth. It looked much the same then as now, at least from this vantage point, right outside the gate. The night was very similar, too, cloudy and cool with a fine mist in the air. But things between them were beginning to change. Morgan was still in diapers. Gus was an eager young partner at Preston & Coolidge. They were on their way home from dinner, celebrating the fact that Gus had just been elected to the firm's executive committee. Gus was on the right track—the fast track. He took a detour through Magnolia driving from the restaurant and stopped right before the gate.

"Why are you stopping?" asked Beth.

Gus glanced toward the estate, then back at Beth. "We're here."

"Where?"

"Home."

"Whose home?"

"Ours."

She laughed. "What bank did you rob?"

"You like it?"

She gazed across the manicured lawn in the moonlight, toward the huge Tudor-style house on the hill. It looked like something out of a fairy tale. An expensive fairy tale. "What's not to like?"

"Someday soon I'm going to buy it for you."

She smiled, but it wasn't as wide as he'd expected.

"I mean it," said Gus. "I'm going to buy this house."

"I don't doubt that for a minute."

"You don't sound all that sure."

"I'm completely sure." She looked away, toward the house again. "It just scares me a little."

"What scares you?"

"You. And this job. This new position."

"It's a great opportunity. I'm the youngest lawyer ever elected to the executive committee. I swear, I'm going to run this damn law firm. Next step, managing partner. And then I'm going to buy this house."

She looked out the passenger-side window. "Let's go, okay?"

"What's wrong?"

"Nothing."

"No. Something's wrong. Tell me."

She looked at him coolly. "Have you noticed lately how often you talk about what *you* are going to do?"

"I'm sharing with you. These are my plans. My dreams."

"It just seems they used to be more about *us*."

"They are about us."

"What? Because you plan to buy me things, that makes it about us?"

He nearly groaned. "I just took a huge step up at the firm. Can't you be happy about it? Share it with me?"

She blinked, lowered her eyes. "I'm sorry. You're right. I should be happy for you."

"But you're not."

Her eyes were moist, glistening in the flickering light from the lanterns. "Do you ever look back on our days in that one-bedroom apartment and think those were our happiest times together?"

"It wasn't the apartment that made us happy."

"Exactly. So why should I be happy about moving into a house so big my husband has to work seventy hours a week to pay for it? A house so damn big that when you close the front door you actually hear an echo. It's like a constant reminder of how alone you really are. I don't want that. I don't want to hear the echoes."

The iron gate started to open, rousing Gus from his memories. Carla must have seen him on the security camera and opened it from inside the house. The gate was fully extended, inviting him home. But he didn't pull forward. He was still thinking of Beth's words, so clear in his memory. His response was just as clear, chiseled in his mind. He had leaned across the console, brushed her cheek, and kissed her. Then he looked her straight in the eye and spoke softly, "I promise you, Beth. I will never let that happen."

Only now, years later, did it finally occur to him. Yet again he had been telling her what *he* was going to do.

Thirty-two

Half of Andie's brain was still fried from the meeting at the hotel; the other half was swirling from the confusing exchange with Isaac. He had been right to nip things in the bud. Isaac was rising fast in the bureau and didn't need a reputation for hitting on female agents. She considered taking the onus off him and asking *him* out on a real date, but that wouldn't be fair either. If he was going to be put in the position of dating a subordinate, it should be on his own initiative. Why tempt a friend to go somewhere he really didn't want to go?

She picked up a pizza on her way home, flopped on the couch, and caught the tail end of a Sonics basketball game on television. They were winning by eight, but she would have bet her last two slices that they'd blow another fourth-quarter lead.

The phone rang with less than a minute to play. The score was tied. The bad guys were closing. With the game in the balance she was tempted to ignore the phone, but she had watched this unhappy ending unfold too many times this season anyway. She rolled from the couch and answered. Good thing. It was the crime lab.

"Got a read on those fingerprints," he said.

She sat up immediately. "Which set?"

"The thumb and index finger from the phone. It took a

while to isolate something readable. That's just the nature of a public phone."

"What did you pull up?"

"The buttons were too smudged, but we got a read and a match from the mouthpiece."

"Who is it?"

"You're gonna be surprised. Beth Wheatley."

Andie was stunned into silence. She thanked him for the quick work and hung up, confused. Little over an hour ago, she had convinced Isaac and everyone else at the meeting that the killer was a mind-control expert who had crawled inside Beth's head, gotten the secret code she and Morgan used to communicate, and dialed the number himself. Now this. She wracked her brain, but her theory and the facts were irreconcilable. Fingerprints generally don't lie. Beth had held the phone in her hand. One way or another, she had been there.

And then disappeared. Again.

Andie phoned Gus with the news that same night. He had scores of questions, none of which she was prepared to answer. She left him frustrated but grateful for the call.

She spent most of Tuesday in the office just getting organized. Isaac had told her to make the Wheatley kidnapping—they were calling it a kidnapping—her top priority. Fortunately, most of her thirty-three other cases were relatively dormant, but she knew that could change at any moment. She got commitments from other agents to cover the ones most likely to blow, which her supervisor approved.

Her supervisor was Kent Lundquist, who had taken over as the violent crimes squad supervisor upon Isaac's promotion to the number two position in the office, assistant special agent in charge. Lundquist reported to Isaac, and he rather frequently reminded Andie that she didn't. It wasn't unusual for an agent to appeal a supervisor's decision to the ASAC, but Andie and Isaac's unusually close relationship made Lundquist quite defensive whenever she went over his head. He seemed fearful that Isaac had more confidence in her than him. On technical or procedural matters that required an experienced eye, that wasn't the case. For decisions that drew on interpersonal skills and raw intelligence, his fears were justified.

There was no kidnapping squad as such in the office. Like Andie, plenty of other agents in the violent crimes squad had relevant experience. Andie met with three other agents assigned to the Wheatley case, briefing them on each of the known homicides, the Wheatley family, the peculiarities behind Beth and her disappearance. By the end of the day they had carved out specific areas of responsibility. Everyone had plenty to do. Andie's first task, however, was a direct order from Lundquist himself. He had been in his office reading the afternoon edition of the *Seattle Times*. He had seen the huge ad with Beth's picture and the offer of a reward.

"What the hell is this?" he asked.

Andie sat across the desk from him, staring at the page. "This is the first I've seen of it."

"Damn it, Henning. You can't let the family haul off and do things like this without coordinating through you. Now get control of your case. Or you're going to lose it before you get started."

"I'll meet with Gus Wheatley tonight."

"And another thing," he said, grousing. "Make damn sure Gus Wheatley plans to make good on two hundred fifty thousand dollars. It's his private reward, but I know how these things play out in the press. If he reneges after we make the arrest, it'll reflect badly on the FBI."

"I understand your concerns."

"You better. Because I'll hold you responsible."

"I wouldn't have it any other way." She answered in a tone that made it impossible to tell if she was gung-ho or a smart-ass.

He glared for a moment, then returned to his newspaper, dismissing her. Andie went straight to her car, speaking to no one on the way out.

Andie stopped by the Wheatley residence on her way home from work at the height of dinner hour. Gus greeted her at the door and took her to the dining room, where Morgan was slouched in her chair and poking her peas.

"Hi, Morgan," said Andie.

"Hi," she said weakly.

"Sorry to interrupt your dinner."

Morgan pushed her plate away. "It's okay. We're done."

"Done?" said Gus. "You've hardly eaten."

"I'm not hungry."

"You have to eat, sweetheart."

"Why?"

"Because if you don't eat, you'll get sick."

"Is Mommy sick?"

Even she had noticed the eating disorder. Just one more indicator of just how oblivious Gus had been.

"We're not sure how Mommy feels. But Agent Henning is going to help us find out."

"That's what you said yesterday."

Andie said, "We're working very hard. It just takes time."

"How long?" Her voice had lost its defiant edge. It had even cracked.

Gus scooted onto her chair beside her, put his arm around her, and stroked her head. "We're going to keep looking as long as it takes."

They both looked at Andie, as if seeking a commitment. "That's right," she told them. "As long as it takes."

Some of the anxiety faded from Morgan's expression. The little grown-up was more like a kid again, though her heart was clearly aching. "Dad, can I feed my goldfish now?"

"Sure."

She gave Andie a little smile as she rose from the table, then scampered down the hall.

"Don't feed them too much," he called out, but she didn't answer. He glanced at Andie and said, "If those fish get any bigger, I'll have the friends of Willy outside my door demanding I set them free."

Andie smiled. Gus checked his empty wineglass and said, "Like some cabernet?"

"Can't. I'm on duty. I'm actually not much of a week-night drinker anyway."

"Neither am I. Normally."

"I understand."

Gus excused himself and retreated to the kitchen for a refill. Alone at the table, she canvassed the opulent surroundings while contemplating how, without insulting him, she could confirm that Gus was good for the reward. The crystal chandelier was undoubtedly Steuben or Baccarat. On the wall opposite Andie was an antique mahogany-and-glass cabinet that displayed the Wheatley china. The pattern was distracting at first, as no two plates looked alike. Then Andie realized that each plate was a small piece of a larger picture, Adam and Eve in the Garden of Eden. It was as though someone had cut twelve perfect circles from a huge painting, keeping the plates and discarding the rest. It was a spectacular effect, like something out of a museum. *That alone could cover a good chunk of the reward.*

"Did you see my ad in this afternoon's paper?" Gus asked as he returned to his chair.

"Yes," she said, startled. "I'm glad you brought that up."

"I thought you'd be pleased."

"A quarter-million-dollar reward seems a little hefty, don't you think?"

"If it brings Beth back, I can afford it."

"I'm sure you can. But maybe a hundred thousand would have been enough."

"I'm not looking for the blue light special here. I'm trying to get my wife back."

"I know that. But an overly generous reward can make the bad guys see dollar signs."

"I don't understand."

"That's because you're thinking like a victim. You need to think like a criminal—like a kidnapper. There's been no ransom demand yet, but you could get one any day. Imagine him sitting out there somewhere trying to figure out how much to demand. There's no science to this. Maybe to him a quarter million sounds like a good number. He thinks that's a ton of money. Then he picks up today's newspaper and sees you offering two-fifty as a reward to any Joe Blow off the street. Suddenly, his sights are much higher."

"I hadn't thought of that."

"That's why it's so important that you never do anything like this again without calling me first."

It was a little harsher than she'd intended. Gus said, "You sound ticked off."

"I just want us to communicate better. I know it's your personality to be proactive, but I'd like you to check with me before you do anything. Agreed?"

Gus nodded, but she'd clearly put him on the defensive. "All right. I can agree to that. So long as the communication flows both ways."

"I've been keeping you informed."

He raised an eyebrow. "Have you?"

"Yes, as best I can."

"Then tell me what's going on with Beth's fingerprints."

"I told you. We found a match on the phone."

"Thank you, Joe Friday. Now can you get beyond the facts and tell me what you're thinking?"

"We think they're hers."

"Come on," he said, eyes narrowing. "Don't be cute. Surely you must have developed some theories as to how they got there."

"Gus, some aspects of an investigation have to remain confidential."

"I promise, I don't work for *Newsweek*."

"I'm serious. Some things I can't share with anyone. Not even the victim's family."

"Ah, yes, I forgot. That's the eleventh commandment, isn't it? Or perhaps it's an addendum to the Magna Carta. Or no—I remember now. It's just administrative bullshit some law enforcement bureaucrat made up."

Andie nodded, unoffended by his wit. *"Touché."*

He sipped his wine, then turned more serious. "You must be able to understand my need to know."

"Of course I do."

His gaze tightened. It wasn't a stare, or even a glare. It was just a long, hard look. "I didn't sleep a wink last night. Up all night after you called. I kept thinking about those prints, wondering how the hell they got there. My first thought was that the worst had happened. Kept thinking he brought her there, forced her to dial, then killed her, too."

Andie couldn't tell him much, but she couldn't let him twist in the wind either. "We searched for any signs of a second victim at the site. Nothing, beyond Beth's prints."

"Which triggers a number of other not so pleasant possibilities."

"Such as?"

"He brought her there to terrorize her. He let her call home, dial up her daughter's line and punch out their secret message. Just when she thinks maybe he'll set her free, he shows her the other victim hanging in the tree, his way of telling her how she'll end up if her husband doesn't meet his demands."

"What demands?" she asked, alarmed. "You didn't say anything about any demands."

"Relax. There are none yet. But like you said, a ransom note could arrive any day."

"That's true."

He finished his wine, a long sip. "So, for a guy whose stomach is tied in knots, I've come up with some pretty good theories. Don't you think?"

"Pretty good."

"You got any better ones?"

Andie didn't have to answer, but she suddenly felt as though he had a right to know. Suffering was its own right of passage. "None better," she replied. "Just different."

"How so?"

"You're not going to like it."

"Try me."

"It's a remote possibility, but we can't rule it out."

"I'm listening."

"It's something we feel we have to consider, in light of your wife's history."

"History?"

"The bulimia, the shoplifting, the postpartum depression, the false accusations of spousal abuse against you. Her general psychological instability."

"I don't see how any of that explains how her fingerprints ended up on a pay phone in Oregon."

She hesitated. It was Lundquist's theory, one she didn't fully embrace. It pained her to repeat it. "It raises the possibility that she was there willingly."

"What the hell are you saying? She's an accomplice?"

"Remote possibility. But yes."

"That's preposterous."

"It might explain why she's alive. Assuming she's alive."

"My wife is no killer."

"It could explain why there's no ransom demand."

"Are you seriously considering this?"

"It is a theory."

"It's a terrible theory," he said sharply.

"I sincerely hope you're right."

"I know I'm right." His face was flushed, both from the

wine and adrenaline. He said nothing for a minute or two, staring blankly at his empty glass. Finally, he spoke again, though he sounded a hint less sure of himself. "That just can't be."

Thirty-three

On Wednesday Andie decided to start at the very beginning: victim number one.

Fears that Gus's wife was a victim had shifted their focus toward the Beth Wheatley look-alikes, victims three, four and five. But if she was an accomplice, maybe the answer lay with the men—the first two victims.

Early that morning she arrived at 151 Chatham Lane, home of the late Patrick Sullivan. He had been the first of two brown-eyed fifty-òne-year-old, Ford pickup truck–driving, divorced men to have been handcuffed in his living room, strangled on the couch, and stabbed exactly eleven times. A far cry from the three women found hanging in trees. If it wasn't for the same triple braided three-quarter-inch yellow nylon rope, police would never have made the connection.

Andie spent more than an hour at Sullivan's house, taking notes, some on paper and some mental. Detective Kessler acted as tour guide. He had been over the house thoroughly and repeatedly as part of his homicide investigation.

Around nine o'clock they finished and headed to the vacant home of Victor Millner, victim number two. The house was near the Sammamish River in north-central King County, an area popular with hot air balloonists who could be seen peacefully drifting overhead on most any summer day or clear autumn evening. Winters were another story. The day had started gray and stayed that way, showing occasional signs of movement from dull to threatening. No breeze to speak of. A light mist was floating more than falling, not near enough to warrant an umbrella. The slow and steady saturation had turned everything darker. The asphalt blacker. The canvas awning greener. Her mood gloomier.

Andie stood at the end of the sidewalk for the broad view. It was a relatively new single-family home, one more box in a building craze that had tripled the Redmond-area population in the last two decades. Structurally, it looked like many of the new frame houses in the same development. The most striking thing, however, was how strongly it resembled the first victim's house, miles away in a different part of town, a totally different neighborhood. The similarities weren't in the architecture or general design. They were in the details. The green awning that extended from the garage. The wooden flower boxes on the windowsills. The hanging plants and latticework around the front porch. Andie had read the police reports that had noted the curious similarities, but words could leave the reader with the impression that it was mere coincidence. She had seen the photographs, too, but they hadn't captured the feeling. A personal visit left no room for doubt. The killer had very specific criteria.

He profiled his victims.

"You just gonna stand in the rain?" said Kessler.

She started, her concentration broken. "I'm sorry, what?"

"You want to go in?"

"Yeah, of course."

She followed him up the sidewalk and climbed the three stairs on the front porch—the same number as the last house. Kessler pulled aside the crime tape and reached for his key. At that moment Andie focused on one of the major differences between the two crime scenes.

"No forced entry," she said, thinking aloud.

"It's noted in the first officer's report," he said. "That shouldn't be news to you."

"It's not. My perspective is just changing a little."

"How so?"

"One of the things Victoria Santos tried to reconcile was the fact that at Sullivan's house the lock had been picked and the door broken open. Here, there was no sign of forcible entry. Yet the crime scene looks exactly the same."

"It's probably like Santos said. He forced his way inside the first time, talked his way in the second. Both guys ended up handcuffed. It's the same ritual once you get the victim under control."

"That explanation makes sense if you're trying to understand why a work-alone killer would change his entry m.o."

"You got something else in mind?"

"Just testing my supervisor's accomplice theory."

Kessler shook his head, smirking. "Look, I'm the last guy to cross a potential suspect off the list willy-nilly. But Beth Wheatley is no serial killer's sidekick."

"That's the same reaction I had. At first. But we have to look at the evidence. One scenario suggests that whatever con or ruse the killer used to gain access the second time didn't work with the first victim. He had to force his way in."

"Maybe the first victim was more careful than the second, more savvy."

"Possibly," said Andie.

"Or maybe practice makes perfect. He had a little more polish on his ruse the second time. He was more persuasive with victim number two."

"Or maybe he had help the second time."

He nodded slowly, seeming to pick up her drift. "Like an

attractive thirty-five-year-old woman. Someone who could knock on the front door, say her car broke down, and ask to use the phone. A fifty-one-year-old man would be more willing to open the door for an attractive woman in distress."

"For that matter, so would another woman."

Again, he read her mind. "As in the next three victims, all female."

They exchanged a long look, as if each were waiting for the other to say it was ridiculous. Neither one did.

Kessler raised an eyebrow, intrigued. "So, where does that leave us?"

Andie watched as he turned the key and opened the door. It was like unsealing a tomb. Dark and silent. The residual odor of death wafted from the living room.

"Confused," she said as she stepped inside.

Gus didn't leave the house all day. The prospect of a phone call kept him there. Beth. Her kidnapper. Someone responding to his ad.

The ad had run again in this morning's *Post-Intelligencer*, identical to yesterday afternoon's ad in the *Times*. A smaller version would run again tomorrow in Seattle and in the *Portland Oregoner*. After all, Beth's fingerprints had been found on an Oregon pay phone. Agent Henning had told him to run everything by her, but she had also told him the FBI considered his wife a possible accomplice. That had changed the whole ball game in Gus's eyes, heightening the need for self-help. To that end, he borrowed one of the computer experts from his law firm to help load pictures and information about Beth in all the right places on the World Wide Web, along with the offer of the reward. He even purchased an ad from America Online and other major Internet services. For the next twenty-four hours his would be one of a half dozen advertisement icons that popped on the screen when subscribers logged on. People wouldn't have to read the actual ad unless they clicked on the icon and opened it, so he had to be creative. "Win $250,000!" was what he came up with. It was a little slick perhaps, but the idea was to get people to click and read. "Have you seen this person?" wasn't exactly catchy.

Less than an hour of his day had actually felt wasted. That was how long it took to return phone messages from the office. It was something he had to do, so in that sense it was productive. But when he had finished, it hardly felt like an accomplishment. He had voluntarily reassigned his case load to other partners so that he could focus on finding Beth. That left little in the way of legal responsibilities. And last week's bloodless coup had shifted all his managerial responsibilities to Martha Goldstein. For the first time in his life he wasn't the point man at the office.

It was liberating in a sense, knowing how easily he could divest himself of responsibility and chuck it all, if he wanted. No one would be hurt, not the firm or his clients. On the other hand, such freedom didn't exactly stroke his sense of self-worth. It reminded him of the so-called Preston & Coolidge revolt some years ago. Gus had ruffled a few feathers by deciding to run for managing partner at the relatively young age of thirty-eight. He challenged his own mentor, a senior partner with twenty years more experience. Eleven other senior partners threatened to resign if Gus were elected. Gus ran. And he won. The old guard made good on their threat. They left in a huff to open a competing firm right across the street. They did everything they could to hurt what was left of Preston & Coolidge. They reviled Gus in the newspapers. They made job offers to the firm's top young associates. They tried to lure away clients. Their actions created chaos and panic throughout the firm. For about two days. Then the reporters moved on to stories more newsworthy. The lawyers went back to practicing law. The clients stayed put. It took about a week for the buzz around the watercooler to switch from "Do you think we're going to make it?" to "Do you think those crazy old fools are going to land on their feet?" In a month it was as though the infamous "Geriatric Dozen" had never worked at the firm, their influence as remote as the very dead Mssrs. Preston and Coolidge who had founded the firm a hundred years earlier. That was the beauty of the institution. No one was indispensable.

Not even Gus.

"We're back," Carla announced as she entered the house. She was carrying a bag of groceries in each arm. Morgan was behind her, toting a smaller bag. Gus met them in the kitchen.

"Hi, Morgan."

"Hi," she said softly.

"Can Daddy have a hello kiss?"

"I'm pretty dirty right now. I have to wash up before dinner." She hurried from the room before Gus could think of something to say. He looked helplessly at Carla.

"Is it my imagination, or am I actually losing ground with her?"

Carla set the bags of groceries on the counter and removed her jacket. "She's a little upset today."

"Is it the ad in the paper?"

"That could be part of it."

"What's the other part?"

"I haven't been able to get anything out of her, but I think maybe somebody said something to her at school."

"Like what?"

"I don't know. Kids can say mean stuff."

"Maybe I'll have a talk with her."

"I'd leave her be for a while. I worked her over pretty good in the car. She's not ready to talk about it."

He nodded once, reluctantly. "All right. Later."

Together they unloaded the groceries. Carla was like a machine, pulling things out in short and jerky motions, setting them down on the counter with a little too much force.

"You mad about something?" asked Gus.

"I was thinking about what you said this morning."

"Which was . . . what?"

"How the police are even considering the possibility that Beth has something to do with her own disappearance. That really frosts me."

"Hopefully, they won't waste too much time on that."

"You know they will. It's always been that way."

"It's always been what way?"

"Everyone always wants to blame Beth."

"No one wants to."

The bag was empty. She looked directly at Gus. "But that's what they're doing. It's the same thing they did five years ago, when you two had your . . . your blowup. Beth's a wacko. Beth needs a shrink. Beth needs a life. It's always *her* fault."

"This is not the same thing as five years ago."

"How is it different?"

"I'm not a serial killer, for one."

"That's only a difference of degree. Beth was a victim both times."

"*I* was the one she falsely accused."

"You were the one who drove her nuts."

Gus angrily folded the paper sack, then shoved it in the cupboard and slammed the door. "I thought we were past this, Carla."

She drew a deep breath. "I'm sorry. I'm not blaming you." She paused, then added, "No more than you do, anyway."

"What does that mean?"

"Come on. A reward of two hundred fifty thousand dollars? Even the FBI told you that was excessive. What prompted that, love?"

"Frankly, yes."

"And you want others to see how much you love her."

"I'm not trying to prove anything, if that's what you're suggesting."

"People who feel guilty always have something to prove."

Had someone else said it, Gus would have erupted. But there was no fooling Carla. Not his own sister. Not Beth's best friend.

"I don't see what good it does to say things like that."

"Maybe it will help you understand why your daughter won't kiss you hello."

Gus stopped to think. "You think she blames me, too?"

"Of course she does. And she always will. So long as you mope around blaming yourself."

"I'm not moping around. I haven't stopped looking for Beth since she disappeared."

"And that's all terrific. But I'm talking about the very private moments, the way you act around Morgan. The way you look at her. The things you say to her. The things you *don't* say to her. Guilt is dripping off of you."

"I just want her to know I'm sorry."

"No. You want *Beth* to know you're sorry. But it doesn't work that way. Morgan can't grant you Beth's forgiveness. So stop looking to her as if she can. Or you're just going to drive her further away."

He thought of his mea culpa at Morgan's bedside and her headphone response. Maybe Carla had a point, harsh though she was.

The phone rang, giving him a start. He answered in a detached voice. A woman was on the line.

"I'm calling about that ad in the paper."

Gus was suddenly alert. "Yes?"

"I know Beth Wheatley. I think I can help."

"Who are you?"

"Shirley Borge."

Gus searched his mind but couldn't recall the name anywhere in Beth's past. "How do you know Beth?"

"Seen her around."

"Where?"

She didn't answer. From across the kitchen he felt

Carla's stare. She stood motionless, listening, sensing the urgency in his voice. He asked again, "Where have you seen her?"

Still no answer. His voice hardened. "Is this a crank?"

"Your wife had bulimia."

For a second he couldn't speak.

She added, "And she's the dumbest shoplifter in King County."

His throat tightened. "What else do you know?"

"Plenty."

"Where is she?"

"I got a pretty good idea."

"Tell me."

"Uh-uh. We gotta work out a deal first."

"If you're worried about the reward, don't. I'll even sign a contract with you. I'll promise to pay you a quarter of a million dollars if the information you give me leads to Beth's return."

"That would help."

"Where would you like to meet?"

She laughed lightly. "I'd like to meet in Mexico. But I think it's best we meet right here where I live."

"Sure. Where is that?"

"Gig Harbor."

He hesitated. "Isn't that where—"

"Yeah. I'm at the Washington Corrections Center for Women. Is that some kinda problem for you?"

"Under the circumstances, I'd say that only enhances your credibility. I can be there tonight."

"Good. But don't come if there's only money on the table."

"What do you mean?"

"There's only so much chewing gum a woman can buy. I want outta here."

He froze, not sure what to say. "I don't think I'm in a po-sition—"

"I'm gonna hang up."

"Don't, please!"

"You sound desperate, Mr. Wheatley."

"My wife is missing. How do expect me to sound?"

"Then help me. And I'll help you."

"All I was trying to say is that it really isn't my place to negotiate your release. Something like this needs to be worked out between your lawyer and the state attorney's office and the department of corrections and whoever else is involved."

"Fine."

"Do you have a lawyer?"

"Yeah."

"Who is it?"

"You."

"*What?*"

"You are a lawyer, aren't you?"

"Yeah, but—"

"But you've never done anything like this. So what? This is about influence, not experience. Guy like you has plenty of influential friends. A lot more than that incompetent little twit of a public defender who landed me here in the first place. You expect me to go back to *him*?"

"All I know is you're asking for an awful lot. If you want money, you got it. But on something like this, I just can't guarantee anything."

"Your guarantee is that you'll work harder than anyone to put this deal together. Because there's not another lawyer on the planet who has more incentive to get me out of here."

She had a point. He at least had to try. "What are you in for?"

"Conspiracy."

"Conspiracy to do what?"

"Murder."

"It's not going to be easy to spring a murderer from jail."

"I'm not in for murder. It was conspiracy to commit murder."

"So what are you saying? Someone else was the trigger person?"

"I'm saying no one got murdered. It was a conspiracy. Just a plan. The police got wind of it before anyone got killed."

"It's still not going to be easy."

"You want your wife back or don't you?"

"Of course I do."

"Then get me outta here."

"Okay," he said, his heart racing. "I'll see what I can do."

Thirty-four

It was a J-shaped drive from Seattle to the Washington Correctional Center for Women, down the interstate to Tacoma, then back up to Gig Harbor on the western side of Puget Sound. In good weather and light traffic the trip normally took about two hours.

Gus made it in record time.

Gig Harbor was a quaint harbor town with bite. It had plenty of lovely old-fashioned shops, restaurants, and bed-and-breakfasts. Getting there, however, meant a trip across the mile-wide Tacoma Narrows, where winds whipped so furiously across the water that the original bridge had twisted and turned and toppled into the sea just months after opening in 1940. It had been replaced by the world's fifth largest suspension bridge, but Gus couldn't cross without one or two panicky visions of "Galloping Gertie," the ill-fated predecessor that had galloped too much.

The prison was located just outside of town, a recently renovated compound that spread across several acres of cleared evergreen forest. Of Washington's twelve major correctional facilities, WCCW was the only one exclusively for women. Medium- and minimum-security facilities housed nearly seven hundred female inmates, their crimes ranging from property theft to murder.

It was well after normal visitation hours when Gus ar-

rived. Gus had spoken to Andie en route by car phone and
told her all about Shirley Borge. Andie had called the Department of Corrections. If this inmate might help catch a
serial killer, the warden was all too happy to allow an after-
hours meeting.

Gus entered the compound at the close-custody reception unit, a long building that resembled old army barracks.
A corrections officer led him down the hall to the attorney-
client visitation area and checked him in. Gus entered
booth number one, a small room with one chair. The door
was behind him. White walls on either side. A glass partition separated him from an identical room on the lockup
side. It was empty for the moment. He scooted his chair
closer to the glass, closer to the phone box on the counter.
He waited.

He heard a noise on the other side of the glass. The handle turned and the metal door opened. Gus started to rise,
forgetting for a second that there would be no handshake.
He settled back in his chair. Shirley Borge entered. She
looked right at him. The door closed behind her. She sat in
the chair and faced him, saying nothing. For a moment
they just studied each other from opposite sides of the
glass.

She looked younger than she had sounded on the telephone. And she was much prettier than Gus had expected.
She had sandy blond hair and mysterious brown eyes. The
face was thin with attractive lines, the lips full. Still, she
was a hardened twenty-five. Andie had pulled her police
record and shared it with Gus. Shirley had been convicted
on conspiracy charges but had a history of prostitution. A
long scar ran from her left temple and down across her
cheek. Someone had cut her badly, perhaps with a razor.
Deep in her eyes, the anger was still there. Gus looked
away, not wanting to be caught staring at her misfortune.
His eyes drifted down her neck. Inmates didn't wear uniforms at WCCW unless they were in segregation. Shirley

was dressed in baggy cotton sweats that were unzipped at the collar to the base of her cleavage, where a small purple tattoo clung to her left breast. The breasts were round and firm, but the tattoo was horrendous, presumably an in-house jail job. Again, Gus tried not to stare, but there was magnetism in this abomination.

She tapped on the window, giving him a start. Gus looked up, embarrassed. The phone was pressed to her ear. Gus picked up.

"You like the tattoo?" she asked.

He blinked, even more embarrassed. "I'm sorry. I was just trying to figure out what it was."

"What does it look like?"

"Kind of like a flower."

"Not a bad guess. It's my genitalia."

"Excuse me?"

She leaned forward, pointing and offering a closer look, as if she were an anatomical chart. "I know it looks a little strange, but it's dead-on accurate. My labia minora is much larger than my majora. A lot larger. They call it a full-blown rose."

He wasn't sure what to say. "I guess I'd never heard of that."

"Me neither. Till I got locked with seven hundred other women."

He squirmed, which she seemed to enjoy.

"You think I'm kidding?"

"I don't really care. I'm here to find my wife."

Her smile turned sly. "You surprise me. Being married to a shoplifter, I thought maybe you'd have a soft spot for the plight of us convicted felons."

"How do you know so much about Beth?"

"How are you going to get me out of here?" She was glaring, but it wasn't contempt. It was just negotiations.

"Bottom line is that I can't make this happen overnight. I spoke to the FBI at length on the way over here. They don't just spring you from jail because you claim to have information that will help solve a crime."

"Then you've got your work cut out for you, don't you?"

"Yeah, but you have to work with me. It's like any transaction. The FBI has to know what it's buying. Which means you have to show them what you've got."

"Where I come from, you get the cash on the dresser before you show the bootie."

"This isn't the happy mattress hotel. You can't just walk down the street to the next john and work out a better deal. You have one customer. That customer makes the rules."

She thought for a second, but she seemed a little less tough, as if starting to understand. "So I tell them what I know. Then what?"

"The FBI uses your tip. If it turns out to be true and helps them find my wife, they write a letter to the parole board telling them to please take your cooperation into consideration at the next parole hearing."

"But there's no guarantee."

"No. The board can still deny parole."

She thought for a second, then the eyes narrowed. "Fuck 'em, then."

"What?"

"They don't do the deal my way, I don't do it."

"That's not smart."

"Who are you to say?"

"I'm your lawyer."

"You're whatever I say you are."

"I'm here to help you."

"You're here to help yourself."

"We can both win."

"I don't care. Just fuck the FBI. Fuck you, too."

"This isn't about me and the FBI."

"Damn right it isn't. It's about *me*."

"Go to hell, lady. It's about a six-year-old kid who misses her mom."

Their eyes locked. He noticed the slightest twitch in her eye.

"You got a kid?" she asked.

"Yeah. Morgan's her name."

Shirley fell quiet.

He added, "She's full of questions, you know. Half the time she wants to know why someone would take her mommy away. The other half she wants to know why her mommy would leave her. Hard to make a six-year-old understand."

The silence lingered. They were staring at each other, the phones pressed to their ears. Then she blinked.

"I got a little girl, too. She's four."

"Girls are great."

She nodded. "Don't get to see her much."

"I'm sorry."

"Yeah, me too," she said with a mirthless laugh. "Pretty hard to make her understand why her mommy has to live *here*."

Gus started to say something, then let it go. Shirley was thinking, weighing things in her mind, perhaps even agonizing. He could see it in her eyes. In a minute, she had shaken it off. "Tell you what, Mr. Wheatley. I won't just spill my guts to you like some fool. But I'm gonna give you a chance."

"That's all I'm asking for."

"Here's the deal. The FBI has to prove itself to me, convince me that they're willing to deal. So I want you to tell them to get me some privileges here. If they can do that, I'll talk. That will show me they're dealing in good faith."

"What do you want?"

"I want to get back on the prison pet program."

"What's that?"

"It's a special program here. Some of the inmates get to keep dogs in their cells and train them. Then we give them away to handicapped people as pets. It's a nice thing.

Makes you feel like you're doing something worthwhile. I
did it for about a year or so. They kicked me off."

"How come?"

"I let one of the dogs lick me."

Gus looked confused.

She added, "You don't want to know where."

"I see."

"It was stupid. Just a spur of the moment thing that
grossed me out immediately. My luck I got caught."

"We all do stupid things."

"Anyway, I want back on the program. So this is a good
way for the FBI to show me some good faith. If they can do
a little something for me now, then I'll know they're taking
me serious. Then you and me can talk."

"You can't just put the FBI to the test. You have to give
up something in return."

"I told you, I'm not going to spill my guts for nothing."

"Just give them something little. This is a negotiation,
Shirley. You can't expect people to do something because
you want to test them. You have to horse-trade."

She studied him, thinking. "Okay. I'll give you a little
something."

His eyes lit. "Tell me."

"In Yakima there's a used-clothing store called Second
Chance. Lots of migrant workers shop there. Mexican apple pickers, some Indians, too."

"What about it?"

"Check it out."

"Check it out for what?"

"Just check it out. Check it out yourself. That's all."

"What do you mean, that's all?"

"That's all I'm going to tell you for now. You get me
back on the prison pet program, I'll tell you more. You get
a promise to reduce my sentence, I'll tell you everything."
She leaned forward, arching an eyebrow. "You get me out
of here tonight, I'll show you my full-blown rose."

Gus just stared.

"I'll wait to hear from you." She pushed away from the table, then hit the call button. A guard outside opened the door. She shot one more look, then disappeared behind the steel door.

Gus gathered up his things and hurried out in search of a phone.

Thirty-five

Early Thursday morning Andie and her supervisor were in Isaac Underwood's office. She had told Lundquist all about the WCCW inmate and her unusual demands. Right off the bat they were in disagreement over how to follow up on the clothing-store lead. Andie felt strongly enough about it to appeal to the ASAC. Lundquist felt strongly enough to follow right along.

Isaac was seated behind his desk, directly in front of what was known throughout the office as "the wall of teeth and honor." Isaac had earned more award plaques and letters of commendation than any agent in the office, many of which were displayed in sprawling collage format behind his desk. In the center of it all were the teeth—the huge, gaping jaws of a tiger shark he had fished from the Indian Ocean. For such a nice guy, Isaac had become quite facile in the art of office intimidation.

Isaac was especially busy this morning. Though as ASAC he was technically second in command, he had been running the office since the special agent in charge had retired. Headquarters had yet to name a replacement. Isaac gave Andie ten minutes, not a second more. Run over the time allotted and the deadly jaws would come clamping down on your head. Andie spoke fast, summarizing for Isaac's benefit, then framing the issues.

"Granted," she said, "the fact that the inmate is incarcerated at a state penitentiary only complicates things. To do this by the book, we'd have to go through the U.S. attorney's office, which would contact the state attorney general's office, which would probably sit on it till Beth Wheatley dies of old age. Gus Wheatley's instincts are right, I believe. The situation doesn't give us the luxury of months, weeks, or even days to hammer out a deal with the bureaucracy."

Isaac asked, "Has anybody considered the possibility that we're dealing with some bored inmate who's yanking everybody's chain for the pure entertainment value of it?"

"Then how would she know about the bulimia? The shoplifting?"

"Valid point," said Isaac. "What are you proposing, Andie?"

"First, I need to get you on board. If this inmate's story starts to check out, it will take someone at least at the level of an ASAC to make some phone calls and get the bureaucracy moving."

"We can deal with that after things check out. So get out of here and go follow your leads."

Lundquist said, "That's really why we're here. There's some disagreement as to how we should check out that used-clothing store."

"You got three special agents on the Wheatley kidnapping team. Rock, paper, scissors. The loser drives to Yakima and pokes around. Any more executive decisions you'd like me to make for you?"

"That's where we disagree," said Andie.

"Fine. The *winner* drives to Yakima."

Isaac was being a real hard ass. It must have stemmed from last night, the brief lapse in the parking lot when he'd let his guard down. *Definite overcompensation*, thought Andie.

"The issue isn't who goes," she said. "It's how. I don't

think it's smart for the FBI to march into this store and start flashing badges and asking questions. From all indications we're dealing with a fairly intelligent serial killer. We don't know the nature of his connection to this clothing store."

"If any," snapped Lundquist.

"True, if any. But we could blow everything if we walk in as straight agents. We need to be more subtle, more creative."

"This is a pretty flimsy tip to start spending the taxpayer money on surveillance."

Lundquist piled on smugly. "That's exactly what I said."

"Doesn't have to be surveillance. I can do a cameo appearance. The store caters to lower-income Hispanics and Indians. I'm half Indian. I can play the part."

"What's wrong with that, Kent?"

Lundquist made a face. "Because I can see how this is going to turn out. She'll do a cameo for an afternoon, then she'll ask for another day, then for a week, on and on. Before you know it, we'll be into a group-two undercover assignment to the tune of seventy thousand bucks, and in six months the auditors will come crashing down on my head."

Isaac raised his eyes to the ceiling. "Did I hear someone say the sky is falling?"

"Come on, Isaac. You know that's the danger of these cameos."

"To some extent, you're right." He glanced the other way. "How about it, Andie? Can you look me in the eye and tell me this is a one-afternoon cameo, nothing more?"

She would have liked to say yes, but she never suckered Isaac. "Can I make a suggestion?"

"Sure."

"Just so we're not arguing about extensions day after day, let's just agree up-front on a time limit."

"How long?"

"Give me three days. If nothing turns up, I back off the assignment."

Isaac nodded. "Seems reasonable. You okay with that, Kent?"

He thought for a second, then said, "Fine. Three days."

"Good." Andie rose and started for the door before any-one could change their mind. "Thanks, Isaac. I'll pick you up a nice secondhand shirt or something."

"Don't forget about Kent."

"Oh, yeah," she said with a thin smile. "I'll put his on six-month layaway."

"Three days!" he shouted, but she was already out the door.

Gus had hoped to hear back from Andie quickly, but as the day dragged on and last night's phone conversation played over and over again in his mind, he was no longer sure she even owed him a call. He had her assurance that she would do everything possible to work a deal with Shirley if her tips panned out. He could only assume that nothing had firmed up.

That afternoon he picked up Morgan from school. During the ride home he tried to follow up on the hunch Carla had raised yesterday—that someone was bothering Mor-gan at school. He asked general questions. How's school? Everything okay with your friends? The car was both the best and worst place for this kind of conversation. He had her captive, but with her riding safely away from the air bags in the backseat he couldn't read her face or check her body language. He wasn't getting anywhere, so he let it go for now. He wasn't going to pop the hard questions and try to gauge her reaction in the rearview mirror.

They were home by three o'clock. Morgan went to her room. Gus checked the answering machines in the kitchen and his study. Nothing.

He gave Morgan a few minutes to settle into her room, then checked on her. The door was half open, enough for him to see completely inside. Morgan sat cross-legged on the floor, her back to him. The television was playing. He watched the back of her head, her thin neck, the slight shoulders that made it ever so clear what a little girl she still was. Then he watched the screen. It was the sound that had caught his attention more than the picture. She was playing one of her old videocassettes. Very old. It was called *More Baby Songs*. Gus remembered it because Morgan used to play it all the time. She was little more than two and had just learned to use the VCR. It was kind of a family joke, but at twenty-six months she knew how to operate it better than her parents did. *More Baby Songs* had been her favorite video, and her favorite song was the one Beth had taught her. It was right about the time Beth had decided to go back to work for the hotel. The song was about a working mother who leaves her daughter at day care for the day. The daughter cries when she leaves, but the song taught her not to. *Because my mommy comes back. She always comes back. She always come back to get me.*

Morgan's voice was cracking as she sang along. Gus watched from the doorway, his heart breaking.

Because my mommy comes back. She always comes back. She never would forget me.

Gus wanted to go to her, scoop her up in his arms, and hold her, tell her yes, Mommy would be back. But then she would see the doubt in his eyes, his own uncertainties about Beth. That would only make things worse. For the moment, Morgan was better off without him. She was better served by her videos and her songs and her memories of her mother's unconditional promise.

He suddenly felt the chill, then the warmth of an ironic sense of solace, as if the very thought of Beth's promise erased any doubt of her return. It occurred to him that in this family *he* was the promise breaker. Not Beth.

He watched a moment longer, then turned and walked away, a little more sad and yet a little more hopeful.

Thirty-six

His general direction was south, but it had been a zigzag route through Oregon. He had no specific destination in mind, so long as it was well south of the last dump site. Over the past three days he'd moved from town to town, hotel to hotel, shopping mall to shopping mall. He was a compulsive planner but above all a realist. Selection of the next victim always involved a certain amount of luck.

Lucky you, he thought as he sifted through the purse of his latest target. He'd stolen it yesterday, having followed her to a crowded happy hour after work. One minute it was on the bar stool beside her, the next it was gone. Afterward, he'd stayed around to check her reaction from afar. The moment of panic, the frantic search, the realization that it was gone. He could tell a lot about a woman by the way she responded to a minor crisis like a stolen purse. Whether she took charge or crumbled. Whether she got angry or just sobbed. Whether she was a fighter or an easy mark.

This one would be so easy.

And she was a pretty good match, too. She was the right age and build, and the eye and hair color were the same. She was the exact height, according to her driver's license. She didn't work at a hotel like the others, but it was getting too damn hard to match them up that closely. He was cutting corners, admittedly, but time was of the essence.

He waited on the east side of her house, dressed in black and nestled between trash cans. Low-hanging pine limbs blocked out the moonlight and shrouded him in darkness. A thick row of evergreen shrubs stretched from the fence to the house, presumably to keep the garbage cans out of view. It was the perfect hiding spot. Through the branches he could see the driveway, which was empty. He had expected her home by now, but she was late—or at least later than the previous three nights he'd stalked her.

It was getting colder by the half hour. He could see his breath. The rubber gloves were stiffening as the night neared the freezing mark. Finally, just after nine o'clock, her car pulled up. The head lamps switched off. She stepped out and slammed the car door shut, then headed up the sidewalk with her house key in hand. The very sight sent his heart pounding. He could have jumped her right there, but that would have been an unnecessary risk. Women were always on guard during that trip from the car to the front door. Better to wait till she was inside, snug and oblivious, completely unaware of the killer outside her door.

She appeared nervous as she climbed the front stairs. The locks had been changed, he knew; he had tried the key from her stolen purse. The new house key shook as she aimed for the lock. All that shivering might have been the cold night air, except that she was bundled up in a heavy winter coat and a warm knit hat. More likely, the theft of her purse yesterday had left her paranoid. She probably thought some guy with a knife was hiding in the bushes beneath her bedroom window.

What an imagination.

She finally opened the door and disappeared inside. A string of windows brightened one after the other as he monitored her movement from the foyer to the living room, down the main hall, and finally to the back bedroom.

He knelt outside her window and peered inside. The blinds were raised a half inch above the sill, just enough for him to see inside. She was seated on the edge of the bed, but the way the blinds were adjusted he could see her only from the waist down. For the moment, that view was just fine. She kicked her shoes off. The skirt dropped to the floor. She worked the sheer pantyhose down her long legs. It seemed to gather for a second at the calves. Very nice calf muscles. A jogger for sure, maybe some dance training. She pitched the hose aside and crossed the room to the full-length mirror.

He could see her whole body now, her face, her hair. *The hair!*

Outside, the change had been hidden beneath her winter hat. The brunette was gone. She'd colored it. *Son of a bitch!*

Three days of preparations and planning for nothing. He was furious at first, until he realized it was of his own do-ing, a manifestation of the immense power he wielded. The publicity had gotten to her. Yet another woman unnerved by reports of a serial killer who targeted thirty-something brunettes and who was apparently working his way south from Seattle. He wondered how many other women had been affected the same way and were now driven by fear, though he realized the purse snatching had probably driven this one over the edge.

He watched as she slipped into her robe and admired her new color in the mirror. He was tempted to go through with it, just out of anger. After all, the last one hadn't been such a perfect match either. Then inspiration struck. He could kill her and dye it back to the rich shade of brown it used to be. That would send a message that no one was safe. If you didn't look the part, the killer would remake you. Blondes and redheads were no longer immune. No more hiding be-hind your bottle of Lady Clairol.

It was a stupid idea, giving a corpse a dye job. He had no

interest in playing beautician. In fact, he had nearly lost interest in this one altogether. Those self-proclaimed expert profilers would probably say he was in some supposed cooling-off period. They'd say he was still too sated from the last one to get excited about the next. The FBI thought it had everything figured out, as if every serial killer on the planet went into hibernation after a kill and needed time to rejuvenate before the next strike. Some of them did. Some slept for days. But he wasn't like them.

They didn't share his energy.

Quietly, as secretly as he had come, he sneaked away from the house. This wasn't a failure, his walking away. His lack of enthusiasm had nothing to do with timing. It wasn't even the dye job that had ruined the excitement for him. At bottom, he was simply losing patience with the whole scheme. After three dead look-alikes he had to know.

Was Beth Wheatley with him? Or was she against him?

Part Four

Early Friday morning found Andie at Goodwill shopping for secondhand clothes. She bought two pairs of old jeans, one black, one blue; hiking boots; a stained sweatshirt; two sweaters; and a brown winter coat with a torn pocket. She returned to the office at mid-morning and met with a backup technician to construct her cameo persona. They didn't bother with the phony driver's license, Social Security number, apartment, telephone number, employment history, credit record, bank account, and other trappings of identity that came with a full-blown undercover operation. For such a short assignment she needed only a name and a story. For the next three days she would be Kira Whitehook, a high school dropout who had drifted in and out of trouble and part-time work for the past ten years. It was not the kind of past to be proud of, which was perfect. She couldn't be expected to answer many personal questions.

It took some effort to look the part of a transient. She did most of the work herself in one of the office changing rooms. She stripped the polish from her nails and cut them down jagged, till they looked bitten to the quick. She had a few calluses from the weights at the gym. She roughed them up with a pumice stone and gave her knuckles a few nicks with the car keys. The hair was next. Too stylish. She trimmed it at the ends, making sure the ends were slightly uneven. She wet it and blew it dry for nearly a half hour, till it looked baked and over-processed. Finally, the face. The eyebrows were far too perfect, but she couldn't *un*-pluck them. She shaved off the very outside tip of the left one. Nothing too distracting, just enough to create a little asymmetry, as if she'd been in some kind of brawl at some point in her life. She washed off every bit of makeup, but the *Cover Girl* complexion wasn't exactly in role. She did a caky, over-brushed job on her cheeks. A waxy brown lipstick helped harden the soft mouth.

She checked the mirror and nearly screamed. Then it seemed funny. She imagined herself sneaking up on Isaac and telling him this was what she looked like on the morning after. Suddenly, it wasn't so funny. Two weeks ago she would have joked at her own expense, but now for some reason she wouldn't think of letting him see her like this.

Life is too damn complicated.

She wore the beige cable-knit sweater and baggy blue jeans, no jewelry. The rest of her belongings went in the duffel bag, along with two hundred dollars in cash, the entire budget she had managed to squeeze out of Lundquist. She left her FBI shield and credentials behind in her desk. The gun, a Walther PPK .380, she strapped to her ankle inside her pant leg. It was smaller than her usual Sig-Sauer P–228, more suitable for undercover work.

She left the office during the lunch hour, sneaking out the back so no one would ask her where she was headed or what the new look was about. No one outside the Wheatley kidnapping team, her supervisor, and Isaac would know she was working undercover. It was simply too dangerous to divulge a secret like that, be it to the victim's family, outside law enforcement agencies, or other FBI agents who didn't need to know. As much as she would have liked to assure Gus that she was following up his lead, phoning him was out of the question.

The Greyhound bus left Seattle at 3:10 P.M. She probably could have driven, but the safest course was to stay in her role from the minute she left the field office.

She was one of eleven passengers scattered about the bus. Andie had a window seat in the middle. She rode in silence, save for the occasional outburst from the two young boys with their grandmother up front. The creepy guy across the aisle made eye contact once, smiled, and pulled a big wad of chewing gum from his mouth.

"Want some?"

Andie looked away and ignored him.

It was a four-hour bus ride over the mountains. Seattle was separated from central and eastern Washington by the North Cascades, a beautiful range reminiscent of the Alps, which extended seven hundred miles from northern California to the Fraser River in southwest Canada. The western slope was the windward side, green and lush and given to wet weather. Abundant water only heightened the beauty, creating huge reflecting lakes, rushing rivers, and impressive falls like the one at Snoqualmie, an avalanche of water more than a hundred feet higher than Niagara. Skiing at White Pass had been excellent this winter, and the views were astounding all year round. Mount Rainier near Seattle was the most impressive peak, permanently snow-capped and visible in all directions from two hundred miles. There were six others of note, including Mount St. Helens, famous for having blown its top in 1980. The volcanic ash had drifted for hundreds of miles, falling like gritty urban snow in places as far away as the Yakima Valley in central Washington.

The Yakima Valley was technically a desert on the leeward side of the mountain, where thick forests and green mosses of the windward side gave way to sagebrush and cactus on a brown, dusty plain. It was harsh country, given to extremes, cold in winter and hot in summer. Creeks could run dry or at a trickle most of the year, then gush with muddy torrents of sudden melted snow or unexpected summer rain. That a great flood had once converted the entire valley into a vast lake was both Indian legend and geological fact. The rest of the legend was just legend, there being no proof of the giant canoe that had landed atop Snipes Mountain and the young Indian couple it had brought to repopulate the valley.

Whatever the lore, the Yakamas—not Yakimas, as they were later mislabeled—had indeed roamed the wind-billowed grasslands from time beyond memory, surviving on fish, berries, and camas-root cakes. They had been nomads, the premier horse breeders and trainers of the Pacific Northwest. The white man had arrived in the mid-nineteenth century, bringing cattle and farming and development and conflict. A land once without fences was now neatly sectioned off into huge quadrants of irrigated farmland. Row after row of fruit trees covered the hillsides. Apples in particular put Yakima on the modern-day map.

That, and crime.

Andie had seen the FBI crime stats on Yakima, a city famous for its orchards but notorious for its violence. With roughly fifty thousand residents, it was, per capita, one of the nation's most dangerous cities. At the risk of political incorrectness, some saw the violence as an inevitable offshoot of the daily clash of cultures. Native Americans wrestled with the problems that attended the stresses of reservation life, including a rate of alcoholism much higher than the general population. Hispanic migrant workers arrived in droves for the harvest seasons. They were poor, as in any transient population, and a few were outright dangerous. Most were law-abiding but through no fault of their own brought out the worst in people who didn't speak their language. The white population was divided within itself, with plenty of hardy and longtime residents living in double-wide trailers right across the road from the beautiful new vineyards of the wealthy and visionary landowners who had pioneered Washington's trendy wine industry.

"Yakima," announced the bus driver.

Andie was one of only three remaining passengers. The others had gotten off earlier in Ellensburg.

Andie put her coat on, slung her duffel bag over her shoulder, and stepped down to the sidewalk. It was colder than Seattle, just a half hour of daylight remaining. Her breath crystallized in the crisp, dry air. A chilly gust of wind stung her cheeks. She wished she had invested in a pair of gloves, but that could be remedied at the used-clothing store. She had studied a map during the ride and knew which local bus she needed. The number five bus was stopped at the traffic light just a half block away. With a ten-second burst she reached the bus stop at the corner just in time to board. In five minutes she reached I Street and North First Street.

The bus rumbled as it pulled away, leaving her on the corner by the AM/PM mini-mart. From her research Andie knew of the shootings there, at least one fatality. Farther north toward the town of Selah was an old hotel that had been converted to a mission. Good intentions, but a definite up-tick in derelict foot traffic. Andie saw two of the homeless huddling in cardboard boxes in the empty parking lot across the street. She checked her watch. Quarter till five. They were bedding down for the cold night, no doubt. Andie would have to do the same soon. Just up the street were clusters of rundown motels and low-rent apartments, popular with hookers and boozers. To keep in role, she'd take a room there. But she was in no hurry to check in. The Second Chance clothing store was a couple of doors down. She was eager to pay a visit.

It was a typical storefront with a plate-glass window. The dresses on display were on hangers, not mannequins. Andie peered inside from the sidewalk. The store was long on inventory, short on decor. The overhead lighting was stark fluorescent. The old tile floors were cracked and stained. You could see where the previous tenants had kept counters and other fixtures that had long since been removed. On the shelves along the far wall were folded pants, T-shirts, and sweaters. Most of the clothes were hanging on the five metal racks that ran the length of the store. Dresses and skirts on one, button shirts on another. Kids' clothing, winter coats, and miscellaneous items filled the rest. A few wedding dresses were on display in the very back.

As Andie entered, the bell on the door announced her arrival. An old woman came out from behind a curtain in back. She was quite the sight. Wrinkled white skin, like an albino rhinoceros. Jet black hair, as if she'd dyed it with shoe polish. She said nothing, just watched. Andie simply acted like a customer.

It was a strange feeling. There she was, browsing through used clothes, needing nothing, pretending to be someone she wasn't, not really sure how any of this might help her find a woman she had never met, a woman named Beth Wheatley.

The logical thing was to strike up a conversation and see where it went. She found a pair of gloves, which she needed.

"How much are these?"

The woman wasn't far away. She'd been hovering like a security guard, not about to be shoplifted. "Whatever the tag says. You buy a few more things, I'll knock a little off."

Andie tried them on. "These are nice."

"I guess," she said.

"I'll take them." She handed them over, smiling.

The old woman started toward the cash register. Andie followed and stopped before the counter. It was a glass display filled with costume jewelry, none of it very valuable. Andie shot a longing look at a string of faux pearls. "I've always wanted a necklace like that."

"All it takes is money."

"How much is it?"

She punched the register, ringing up the gloves. "More than you can afford."

"How much?"

"I can let you have it for forty dollars."

"Oh." It wasn't worth half that, but Andie played dumb. "I'm sure that's a fair price. But I'm afraid I don't have that kind of money."

"Tough break."

"Yeah. I'm kind of out of work right now."

She gave Andie the once-over, judging her appearance. "What a surprise." The register clanged as the cash drawer opened. "That'll be three bucks for the gloves."

Andie dug in her pockets for two singles and some loose change, acting as though it were her last three dollars. She counted out the dimes on the countertop, then handed it over. "Maybe I could work here."

The woman raised an eyebrow. "Don't think so."

"Looks like you could use some help around here un-loading boxes, cleaning up, whatever."

The old lady just glared. "I don't hire strangers."

"I work cheap."

"You all do," she said wryly. "When you work, that is."

It was a racist jab, something Andie wasn't accustomed to. But she let it go. "I'd even work free for three days. You can stay right here and watch me, get to know me. If you like me, you keep me and give me the necklace for three days' salary. If you don't like me, you let me go. You pay me nothing."

She studied Andie carefully, quizzically. It was a great offer. Three days of work for a nine-dollar necklace. With the option to screw her in the end. *Dumb Injun.*

"All right," she said finally. "I got some boxes that need unpacking, price marking, folding. You can start tomorrow."

"Thanks."

"Hold it," she said, halting Andie in her tracks. She grabbed a baseball bat from behind the counter and pointed it at Andie, snarling. Andie took a half step back.

"Got only one rule here, young lady. You rip me off, I crack your skull. Understand?"

Andie nodded.

"Good. What's your name?"

She started to say Andie, then caught herself. "Kira Whitehook."

"I'm Marion. Call me Mrs. Rankin. I'll see you tomorrow."

"Okay. Tomorrow." She turned and headed out the door, struggling not to show how very pleased she was that Kira Whitehook had found herself a job.

Gus was getting edgy. He had called Andie several times that afternoon and left messages on her voice mail. He had spoken twice to the receptionist, who either didn't know or couldn't tell him where she was. The last time he'd demanded to speak to her supervisor, but he too was unavailable. Something weird was going on.

Carla came by to fix dinner, but his stomach was too knotted to eat. He felt out of the loop, out of control. He wanted to call back Shirley Borge and tell her the prison pet program was hers and she could have any damn dog she wanted, as many as she wanted. Just give up the information. But he couldn't tell her anything without the okay from Andie.

Why the hell doesn't Henning call back?

Time was wasting. Either the FBI was dragging its feet and letting an opportunity slip away, or they were up to something and keeping him in the dark. Either way, he didn't like it.

"You want me to keep that warm for you?" Carla asked. She was standing at the oven with another one of those spaghetti casseroles that Morgan loved.

He looked up, elbows on the kitchen table. He hadn't touched his food.

"Mix it with the Jell-O," said Morgan. "It's good that way."

Gus forced himself to smile. Any communication from Morgan needed affirmation and encouragement. "Maybe later," he said.

The phone rang. He glanced at the wall phone, but that one wasn't ringing. He jumped from his chair and ran down the hall into his office. He grabbed it on the third ring, nearly diving for the phone before the machine picked up.

"Hello," he said eagerly. There was silence. "Hello," he repeated.

Still no answer.

He paused, confused. "Hello? Is someone there?"

It was a strange silence. Not the dead kind of silence that precedes the dial tone. He could tell the line was open.

"Who is this?" he asked.

There was no response. But Gus didn't hang up. He waited. Seconds passed, then nearly half a minute. His confusion turned to anger. "Damn it, *who* are you?"

He thought he heard a crackle on the line. Could have been the sound of his own breathing. Then he had a thought. "Beth . . ." His voice shook. "Is that you?"

No answer. But the caller didn't hang up.

His mind raced. He thought of the last call, the nursery tune she had played. He thought of all the horrible things that could have kept her from speaking. His voice turned frantic. "Beth, if it's you, hit any key three times."

After a few seconds he heard it. Three long tones.

"Beth!"

The line clicked. The caller was gone. Gus slammed down the phone and, one last time, dialed Agent Henning.

Thirty-eight

Andie ate dinner at a fast-food joint, then walked around the block to check out the neighborhood. The night was clear but cold. Yakima's version of rush-hour traffic had subsided, and the streets seemed lonely. Two cars waited at the Wendy's drive-thru, big clouds of exhaust spewing from the tailpipes in the chilly air. Three other cars were parked on I Street, one that looked as if it hadn't moved since the Bush administration. The gutters were packed with three or four inches of crusty brown ice, the melted and refrozen remnants of last week's snowfall. At the light Andie crossed the street. The two homeless guys were still in the parking lot, huddled in an empty cardboard box for a refrigerator. It looked as though three or four buddies had joined them. In numbers there was warmth, if not strength.

Around seven o'clock she found a hotel just up the street from Second Chance clothing store. It was a rundown one-story unit with a permanent sign that proclaimed VACANCY. Room rates were posted outside the door. By the month. By the week. By the night. By the hour. It was exactly the kind of place Kira Whitehook would patronize. Andie headed up the sidewalk and stepped inside.

The lobby was warm but smelled of old dust. A middle-aged Hispanic man sat behind the front desk reading a newspaper. He didn't look up. Across the room, the usual business of the night was well underway. A young Indian woman, not more than nineteen, was leaning against the wall. Her shirt was unbuttoned far below her breasts. Three men were pawing her. Andie could hear them haggling.

"Uh-uh," said the girl, "not three at once."

"Aww, come on, bitch."

"Gets too crazy. One at a time."

"I'll throw in an extra rock," he said, meaning crack.

His buddy grabbed his crotch. "I give you two rocks." They all laughed, even the girl. It was like wheeling and dealing with the old lady in the clothes store. Everything was for sale in this part of town. Everything was negotiable.

The desk clerk looked up. "What's it gonna be?"

"Huh?" Andie answered.

The clerk looked past her and raised his voice. "I'm talking to those jerks. You boys want a room or don't you?"

The bald one answered. "We're working on it, okay? I'm this close to talking Gives-Great-Head into changing her name to Fucks-Three-At-Once."

They all laughed again. The clerk said, "Take it out of the lobby, pal."

The man was still laughing as he stepped to the counter and opened his wallet.

Andie stepped back and waited, watching the Indian girl. The eyes were glazed. Her mouth was partly open, as if it required too much effort to keep it closed. One of the men held a rag to her nose, from which she sniffed. It almost sent her spinning. The tall one had his hand inside her shirt, caressing her soft, young belly. They were dirty, rough hands, soiled from work in the fields. But the girl didn't flinch. She was beyond not caring. She was numb to it. Whatever she'd inhaled had made her night livable, her life bearable.

"Hey," said the one at the counter, "one of you losers got five bucks?"

Andie could hear them haggling as they pooled their money to cover the room and the girl. Her eyes, however, never left the girl.

It was a painful sight. Andie felt for her, but she also felt for herself. She thought back to the remark that old woman at the clothing store had made, something to the effect that you—meaning Indians—all work cheap, at least when you're working. Prejudice was something she had never come to terms with, the ridiculous views that crime and un-employment and a host of other social ills were simply a part of the Indian culture. But she knew next to nothing about the traditions and values that were her real heritage. Nine years of foster care had taught her only about sur-vival, and the nice white family that finally adopted her had raised her as their own, with the best of intentions but without regard for where she had come from. She knew only that her father was white and her mother was Native American, but she didn't even know which tribe.

Strangely, she had never pursued her past. That was something her ex-fiancé had found puzzling. They had talked about it once, when she and Rick had talked about having kids of their own. Rick had asked point-blank if she'd ever wondered who her real mother was. . . .

"At times," Andie told him.

"Ever try to find her?" Rick asked.

"No."

"Why not?"

Andie thought for a second. "Just out of respect."

"Respect for who?"

"My adoptive parents. I think it would hurt their feelings if I started looking for my biological parents."

Rick scoffed. "That's stupid. You would put their feel-ings above everything else?"

"It's just not important to me."

"Come on."

"Honest. I don't really need to know."

"Maybe you just don't want to know. I think you're afraid."

"Afraid of what?"

"Afraid of what kind of woman your mother was. Afraid she was a hooker or druggie or something."

"Go to hell."

"I'm sorry. You're right. It doesn't matter. You are what you are. Not what your mother was." He leaned close and took her hand, as if his sudden about-face was supposed to be the sweetest thing she'd ever heard. As if she was supposed to melt in his arms and marvel at his sensitivity. As if he really believed the future was all that mattered. Andie just looked away and wondered. . . .

"Hey, doll face." It was the clerk behind the counter pulling her back to reality. He had finished with the three-some and their nineteen-year-old prize. "You're next."

Andie didn't move. She watched as the men gathered around the girl in the hallway. The debate had shifted to which of them would be first.

"You want a room or not?" the clerk asked.

Andie didn't answer. Watching that girl had triggered the irrational fears her adoptive mother had drummed into her head. Fears about who—or what—her biological mother had been. Fears that Andie would have been the same if she hadn't been adopted.

Confusion boiled inside her. She felt compelled to do something. The pistol was strapped to her ankle, but that would be stupid. She had to think like Kira Whitehook, not Agent Henning. Kira would just let them go. Can't save the world. Save yourself. *Screw Kira.*

"Hey, asshole," said Andie.

The men froze. The biggest one shot her a look. "Who you think you're talking to?"

"An asshole, apparently. You answered."

The attitude amused him. "Whadda we got here? An-other whore muscling in on her sister's territory? Maybe a little head-to-head competition?" He laughed at his own pun.

"Get your hands off her."

His eyes narrowed. He pulled his hand from the girl's shirt. "Now, exactly who's gonna make me do that?"

Andie felt the urge to pop him. Before she could speak, the girl stepped forward and glared with contempt. Her speech was slurred from whatever she'd inhaled two minutes ago. "Get outcha here, bish. Dis is my trick."

Andie froze, not sure what to say. There was a rumble behind the desk. The clerk had a shotgun on the counter.

"Get out," he said, aiming at Andie. "Or you're a stain on the wall."

Andie glanced again at the girl. She was barely able to stand but mad enough to shout. "Beat it, slut!"

The hammer cocked on the shotgun. The clerk meant business. Andie hoisted her duffel bag, turned away, and left. The door slammed behind her.

"Get lost, bish!"

The night air chilled her face. For twenty paces down the dark sidewalk the shouting followed her. It wasn't the men. Only the girl continued to deride her, showering her with slurred profanity.

She kept walking. The shrill voice faded, but the knot in her stomach tightened.

Kira had lost a turf war. Andie had found her demons.

Thirty-nine

The FBI had set up a trap and trace on all of the Wheatley phone lines, so Gus knew they were immediately on the call, even if it was just three tones and a hang-up. An agent he had never met, some guy named Mel Haveres, had called to tell him they were pursuing it. Haveres couldn't say where Agent Henning was, and Gus still couldn't get her to call him back.

For whatever reason, the FBI was being awfully cagey as to Andie's whereabouts. Gus talked it over with Dex, who suggested they try someone outside the FBI, like Detective Kessler. Gus didn't exactly feel like he had a rapport with Kessler, not after their rocky start. It only made sense to let Dex do the digging.

At eight-thirty Dexter Bryant came by the house to report back. A face-to-face meeting was the only reliable way to make sure the FBI wasn't listening. They sat at the kitchen table. Carla served coffee, a polite way of trying to invite herself into the conversation. Ever since Gus had confided in her about Shirley Borge, she seemed to think she was automatically in the loop. But Gus had a feeling she was a pipeline to Morgan, telling her things she didn't need to know. So out she went.

"What did you find out?" asked Gus.

Dex poured a generous amount of milk into his steaming

cup. "He doesn't know what's up with Henning. Didn't care to speculate either."

"Does he know about Shirley Borge?"

"I don't think so. But I had to tap dance around that subject pretty lightly. If the FBI hasn't brought him into the loop, I didn't want to be the one to come out and spill the beans."

"I just wish somebody would tell me they're following up on her tip."

Dex sipped his coffee, then added even more milk. "Kessler can't help you there."

"I can't believe they would just drop the ball."

"I don't think they have," said Dex.

"What makes you say that?"

"Just the way this is playing out. Kessler's in the dark. You're in the dark. I think Henning is probably snooping around Yakima as we speak."

"You mean like an undercover thing?"

"That's the way the FBI operates. Don't tell anybody squat. Which sucks from your perspective. But that's why they so rarely lose an agent."

"But that's just your guess, right? There's no way to verify that they're taking Shirley's tip seriously."

"I can't call FBI headquarters and get a list of everybody working undercover this week, if that's what you mean."

Gus rubbed his face, groaning. "So what do we do? Sit here and wait?"

"That's one option," said Dex. "Or I could go to Yakima."

Gus perked up. "Or maybe I should."

"Gus, you're a lawyer. A *corporate* lawyer."

He was suddenly pensive, not listening. "It makes sense. That's what Shirley was telling me. She said, check it out. Check it out *yourself*. She was saying *I* need to go."

"You're reading too much into that."

"Think about it. Let's say Andie Henning is over in

Yakima now. What in the world is she looking for? If there's some clue over there about Beth, I'm the one who's going to recognize it. Not some FBI agent who's never met her."

Dex didn't argue.

"It's settled, then," said Gus. "Carla can watch Morgan. I'm going to Yakima."

Andie took a room at the Thunderbird Motel, which catered more to business people than the drunk-and-falling-down crowd. It was over budget and definitely out of role for the cameo she was playing, but she didn't care. She needed to get away from that girl and that neighborhood, at least for the night.

From her room she called her contact agent, Mel Haveres. Mel was one of the agents assigned to the Wheatley kidnapping team. As long as Andie was undercover, she was required to check in with him. It wasn't a supervisor-subordinate relationship. She just brought him up to date and let him know she was safe. Likewise, he kept her abreast of real world developments.

"The Wheatleys got another weird call tonight."

"How weird?"

He explained Gus's one-sided exchange and the three long tones, then added, "We traced it back to southern Oregon. Another rest area pay phone. This one just north of the California border."

"Dear God, not another body."

"None yet. They'll keep looking."

"You think it was really Beth Wheatley on the line?"

"No way to know for sure," he said. "There's no fingerprints this time, and there's no magic to punching a button three times. Anybody could have done that in response to Gus's question."

"I can't believe I missed this. I need to get back."

"Lundquist wants you to stay put. Isaac agrees."

"With the killer on his way to California? Why stay here?"

"We think you're in the right place."

"I don't get it."

"The call was a little too cute, too convenient. Nobody talks, but the line stays open just long enough for us to trace. Then it disconnects."

"Meaning what?"

"According to Isaac, you said it yourself in that last meeting with Victoria Santos. There's a steady geographical pattern moving south from Seattle. Could be the killer is just diverting our attention from where we should be looking. Maybe he has an inkling we've targeted Yakima, and now he's trying even harder to shift our attention all the way to California."

"How would he know we've zeroed in on Yakima?"

"That inmate at WCCW could be shooting her mouth off, bragging about pulling down the reward money. Wouldn't surprise me if our killer is plugged into the prison grapevine."

Andie thought for a second. "That's possible."

"We think it's more probable than possible. Your orders are to stay put. Play out the cameo for the full three days and see what turns up."

"All right," said Andie. "I'm on the inside track at the store, so if there's anything to Shirley Borge's tip, I should flush it out."

"Good. Check in again tomorrow morning."

"I will."

"Oh, one more thing. Don't take it the wrong way. It's just that Isaac really does think you're in the right place, so he wanted me to be sure to pass this along."

"What is it?"

"He says, be very careful."

She smiled weakly with appreciation. "Tell Isaac he worries too much."

*   *   *

Gus left Seattle at five A.M. and reached Yakima before nine. He found a parking space a half block down from the Second Chance clothing store. His investigator had warned him it wasn't in the best part of town, but this was rougher than he'd envisioned. He stepped down from his car and paused, wondering if he'd still have tires on his Mercedes when he returned. He set the alarm and walked up the sidewalk.

The store was closed. No hours were posted, but he assumed it would open at nine. He could wait five minutes.

The day was gray and overcast, cold enough to make him consider waiting in the car. The wind kicked up, stirring some stray newspapers in the gutter. Gus cinched his coat to stay warm. He turned at the sound of footsteps behind him.

"Gus? What the hell are you doing here?"

He did a double-take. Her appearance had thrown him, but the voice he recognized. It was Andie. He answered, "I'm here to check things out."

"That's my job. Get out of here."

"Why didn't you return my calls?"

"Gus, you're blowing my cover. Now get out of here before the owner shows up."

"That's exactly who I want to talk to. I brought some pictures of Beth. Just thought I'd show them and see if the owner knows anything."

"That's a terrible idea. For all we know, this store owner is the killer's mother. If word gets back to the killer that you or the police are closing in, that's bad news for Beth. He could panic, cut bait, and send your wife's body floating down the river. Now get out of here. I mean it."

He didn't move, but he didn't argue.

"Go," she said sternly.

He turned slowly, then stopped. The display in the storefront window had caught his attention.

"What now?" asked Andie.

He stepped closer to the window, his eyes locked like radar. "That black dress."

"What about it?"

His face was ashen. "It belongs to Beth."

Forty

Andie was alone outside the shop when Mrs. Rankin arrived to open up. She played in role as Kira, having decided to stay undercover. It would be easier to find out about the dress as a dumb employee than an FBI agent.

"You actually showed?" the old woman said with surprise.

"Not like I have anyplace else to be."

"Just remember, you're working for the necklace. Don't try hitting me up for money at the end of your three days. Because I won't pay."

"Fine by me."

She gave Andie a curious look, then unlocked the door and headed inside. Andie followed. It was dark and drafty inside, nearly as cold as the outdoors. Mrs. Rankin switched on the heater and then the lights. The old fluorescent tubes hummed and flickered overhead until they finally brightened the store.

Mrs. Rankin sat on her stool behind the counter. She seemed amused to be able to bark out orders from atop her throne. "Let's see," she said ponderously. "What can I get you started on?"

Andie looked for something toward the front, near the dress in the window. The long shelf of sweaters looked in disarray. "How about those sweaters? I could fold them up neat for you."

"Yeah, that's good. Had a couple of women in here yesterday who tore through every last one of them. Didn't buy a darn thing, but left the place a mess, they did."

"I'll take care of it."

"Twenty minutes. That's all it should take you. Nobody putters around in this store. I hate putterers. You're not a putterer, are you, Kira?"

"No, ma'am." Andie turned and rolled her eyes. Yesterday the old lady was on her own. *Today she's a union buster.*

The noisy heater had not yet warmed the store, so Andie left her coat on. She folded the sweaters into neat stacks, working diligently from left to right, ever the eager new employee. She didn't stop until she had worked halfway across the store, even with the dress in the window. She stopped and touched it, as if admiring it. Discreetly, she checked the tag. It was a Donna Karan, easily worth several hundred dollars new. She flipped the tag over. The dry-cleaner's marking was written with indelible ink. Her heart skipped a beat. It read, "B. Wheatley."

No denying it. The dress was Beth's.

"Don't get any ideas, girl."

Andie started. "What—what do you mean?"

"That dress. You'd have to work here a month to pay that one off."

That was a relief. The old woman had thought she was dreaming, not snooping. Andie stroked the fabric. "Where did you get something like this?"

"Girl named Shirley. Good kid. Used to be one of my best suppliers. Not just quantity but real quality. Storefront Shirley is what I used to call her. Everything she brought went right in the front window. My best merchandise."

"Think Shirley can get me something in red?"

The old lady snorted. "Even if you could afford it, I wouldn't expect anything from Shirley anytime soon."

"Why not?"

"She's locked up. For a long time."

Andie looked away, feigning disappointment. She checked the label again. "Who's this B. Wheatley?"

"I don't know. Somebody sells me a dress, I don't ask those kind of questions. You shouldn't either."

That was for sure. Andie was starting to sound too much like the heat. She went back to folding sweaters, but her mind was still on the dress. Things were starting to fit together. She couldn't waste the morning.

"I'm hungry," she said. "I'm going over to Wendy's. You want something?"

"You just got here."

"I was so excited about starting this morning I couldn't eat. And now I'm hungry."

"Oh, all right. Ten minutes, no more. And I'm taking it out of your lunch hour. Bring me back a biscuit or something."

"Okay." Andie hurried out the door and across the street. The pay phone was around back near the drive-thru. She didn't call her contact agent. She didn't even call her supervisor. She dialed the ASAC directly.

"Isaac," she said in a serious tone, "I think it's time to cut a deal with Shirley Borge."

Gus was halfway back to Seattle when his car phone rang. It was Andie.

"You were right," she said. "The dress was Beth's."

Gus eased up on the accelerator without even realizing it, slowing well under the limit. Traffic started to fly past him on the interstate. "What does this mean?"

"The owner told me she bought the dress from a woman named Shirley, who is now in jail. That's obviously why Shirley told you to check out the store."

"But Shirley has been in jail for six months. How could she have known that Beth's dress would still be there?"

"It's high-end designer merchandise, not the cheap stuff

that moves fast in a store like this. That's why it was on display in the window. And Shirley might not even have had this particular dress in mind. The owner told me that Shirley brought her lots of nice clothes. If we look around, we might find dozens of things in that store that belonged to Beth."

Big, wet snowflakes began to splatter on the windshield. Gus switched on the wipers. "The better question, I guess, is how did Shirley get her hands on Beth's dress in the first place?"

"That's why I called. At the moment you're the only one Shirley is talking to."

"She's not going to say another word until you cut her a deal."

"I think we can probably get her back on the prison pet program."

"She doesn't care about the dogs. That's just a test. If we're going to get any real answers, you're going to have to come up with a lot more than that."

Andie was careful not to speak out of turn. She still had to clear things through the bureau. "I'm working on it."

"That's what you want me to tell Shirley? You're working on it?"

"Gus, let me be honest with you. The FBI will promise to write a nice letter to the parole board on Shirley's behalf only on two conditions. One, if her information helps us find Beth. And two, if she was totally uninvolved with Beth's disappearance."

"That's fine."

"Don't you see? The fact that Shirley sold Beth's dress to this used-clothing store could make it hard for me to convince my supervisors that she had nothing to do with Beth's disappearance."

"She was in prison. How could she be involved?"

"People have run the Mafia from inside prison walls."

"Shirley's practically a kid. She's not a mobster."

"You don't know anything about her."

"Well then, maybe it's time I found out."

"What are you suggesting?"

"Just tell your supervisors to keep an open mind. I've closed tougher deals than this one." He hung up and hit the accelerator, surging well above the speed limit.

Forty-one

Gus didn't have to persuade her. Maybe she thought it would be fun or that it was a prerequisite to earning her reward. Maybe she simply thought she could beat it. Whatever the reason, Shirley expressed no reservations about sitting for a polygraph examination.

Andie's challenge had immediately triggered the idea of a lie-detector test. Shirley wouldn't talk unless she had a deal. The FBI wouldn't cut a deal unless she had nothing to do with Beth's disappearance. The polygraph was the answer.

Irving Pappas—Pappy, they called him—was the best in the business. He was a few years older than the last time Gus had seen him, but he looked the same. Warm, aged eyes. White hair and big, bushy white eyebrows. With his grandfatherly looks and a name like Pappy, he had a way of putting his subjects at ease, which only heightened the reliability of his test results. That was crucial. When dealing with the government, the reputation of the examiner was just as important as the results of the test.

Only once before in his legal career had Gus ever asked anyone to take a lie-detector test. Years ago the Justice Department had targeted one of his clients for a criminal antitrust indictment. Gus hired Pappy. His client passed, and Gus shared the results with the government. Although the results would not be admissible at trial, prosecutors and the FBI often gave the tests considerable weight outside the courtroom. The plan worked. There was no indictment. Gus had earned himself a very powerful and loyal client— until Martha Goldstein poisoned the ear of Marcus Mueller and swept him away. Hard to believe that was just two weeks ago. It was even harder to believe that Gus almost didn't care. All he cared about right now was getting Shirley through the test, getting the results to Andie, and getting one step closer to Beth.

They met in a special room reserved for attorneys who needed face-to-face contact with their clients, no Plexiglas between them. Usually that meant preparation for trial. Rarely did it mean a polygraph exam.

Shirley sat in an old oak chair made more uncomfortable by an inflatable rubber bladder beneath her seat and another tucked behind her back. A blood-pressure cuff squeezed her right arm. Two fingers on her left hand were wired with electrodes. Pneumograph tubes wrapped her chest and abdomen.

Pappy sat across from her, watching his cardioamplifier and galvanic skin monitor atop the table. The scroll of paper was rolling. The needle wobbled as it inked out a warbling line. "All set," said Pappy.

"Should I leave?" asked Gus.

"Only if you're making Shirley nervous." Pappy looked right at her. "Does Gus make you nervous?"

"Hell, no." The needle barely swerved, but it was too soon for that to mean anything.

Pappy said, "It probably would be best if you waited outside."

Gus stepped out and closed the door. But he didn't go far. With an ear to the door he listened. In such a stark room voices carried clearly. Gus could hear everything.

Pappy had the voice of a consummate hypnotist. He

never came right out and told Shirley to relax. He just
talked to her about innocuous things that would put her at
ease. Did she ever watch television? Did she like dogs?
The questions were so far from the point of the inquiry that
Shirley probably didn't even realize the test had begun. As
she spoke, however, he was monitoring her physiological
response to establish the lower parameters of her blood
pressure, respiration, and perspiration. It was a fishing ex-
pedition of sorts. The examiner needed to quiet her down,
then catch her in a small lie that would serve as a baseline
reading for a falsehood. The standard technique was to ask
something even a truthful person might lie about. Have
you ever smoked pot? Cheated on your taxes? Thought
about sex in church? Most people lied, and the examiner
got his baseline. No problem for the average Joe. Big problem for a drug-using ex-prostitute who had tattooed her left
breast with the peculiar likeness of her own genitalia while
doing time for conspiracy to commit murder. Finding that
one sensitive subject that tapped into her sense of shame
and would make her squirm was going to take some inge-
nuity on Pappy's part. Gus listened through the door as
Pappy made his move.

"Is your name Shirley?"

"Yes."

"Do you like ice cream?"

"Yes."

"Are your eyes brown?"

"Yes."

"Have you ever stolen anything?"

"Yes."

"Have you ever taken money for sex?"

"Yes."

"Have you broken any of the rules here in prison?"

"Yes."

"Are you a good mother?"

She hesitated, then answered weakly, "Yes."

There was a break in the rhythm, silence in the room. Outside, Gus felt a little sorry for Shirley. That hadn't taken long. Pappy had his control question. She had lied. Pappy knew what it looked like when she did. Now he could fish for the really big lie.

"Have you ever killed anyone?"

"No."

"Is today Saturday?"

"Yes."

"Are you twenty-one years old?"

"No."

"Have you ever met Beth Wheatley?"

"No."

"Are you sitting down now?"

"Yes."

"Are you a woman?"

"Yes."

"Do you know where Beth Wheatley is?"

"I might."

Pappy grumbled. "You have to answer yes or no."

"Sorry."

"Are you blind?"

"No."

"Are you in prison?"

"Yes."

"Do you know where Beth Wheatley is?"

"No."

There was another pause, but Gus could only guess at what it meant.

Pappy continued, "Do you smoke cigarettes?"

"Yes."

"Is your mother alive?"

"I—I don't know."

She'd thrown him a curve in response to what was intended as a neutral question. Pappy moved on. "Can you speak Japanese?"

"No."

"Do you know how to swim?"

"Yes."

"Do you own a car?"

"No."

"Did you have anything to do with Beth Wheatley's disappearance?"

"No."

Outside, Gus felt his weight nearly falling against the door. He was weak at the knees. It was over. He had his answers.

But was it the truth?

Forty-two

Andie had hoped to hear that a deal with Shirley Borge was a slam dunk. Instead, Isaac had turned the heat right back on her. If Andie could continue to cultivate her own leads, they wouldn't have to cut a deal with an inmate. The thrift shop seemed like the logical place to keep mining. Another day or so undercover wouldn't kill her, though she wasn't a hundred percent sure she could say the same about Beth Wheatley.

Mrs. Rankin, of course, had found enough projects to keep Andie working undercover till they carried her out on a gurney. She'd actually made a handwritten list with little boxes on the side for Andie to check off each project before moving to the next. By mid-afternoon Andie had swept out the storeroom, laundered a box of baby clothes, and ironed a full rack of dresses.

She had saved the most undesirable job for last, stitching lost sequins back onto a used wedding dress. She couldn't help but wonder what had happened to the woman who had worn it, what made her get rid of it. Money problems possibly. Divorce probably. Or perhaps she had never really liked it in the first place. Andie had shopped weeks for her own dress, mainly to please her mother. The one Andie had wanted was too sexy for Mom's taste. Her mother's first pick was way too traditional. They settled on a thousand dollars worth of satin and lace that was now rolled in a ball and stuffed in the closet where Andie had thrown it after she'd raced home from the church and ripped herself out of it.

The bell on the door tinkled. A customer entered, bringing a rush of cold air through the door with her. Andie looked up. It had been a fairly slow day, but she had made a point of discreetly checking out everyone who visited the store.

It was a woman, Andie noted, at first blush much like the others who had come and gone today. Her clothes were clean but old. She was dressed in layers, like someone who spent a good deal of her time outdoors or in a poorly insulated home. Her face showed no smile, no discernible expression at all.

She went straight for the sweaters Andie had folded that morning. She walked with polish—or like someone who used to have polish. Her appearance was anything but. The hair was short and lacked style. She wore no makeup, no polish on her fingernails. Her face was tanned and windburned, like a migrant worker. The ears were pierced, but she wore no earrings, no jewelry of any kind. Everything about her was functional with no excess. Yet she seemed different from the others, oddly out of place.

Andie rose from her chair and started toward her. She'd offer some help, maybe strike up a conversation. Of all the customers who had come by today, this one was the most intriguing.

"Get out!" shouted Mrs. Rankin.

Andie froze. The bossy old woman was standing a few steps behind her. The customer looked up, nervous. Mrs. Rankin hurried past Andie. "I said, get out of here."

The woman seemed flustered. "I was just—"

"I told you not to come around here no more. Now, get out."

Her hands shook as she placed the sweater neatly back

on the stack. She glanced at Mrs. Rankin, then at Andie. She was embarrassed, not at all confrontational. Quietly, she walked to the door, opened it, and left without a word.

Andie watched through the window as she crossed the street, then turned and faced Mrs. Rankin. The old woman just glared, as if to say, *Don't ask.*

Andie didn't.

Mrs. Rankin returned to her stool behind the counter. Andie went back to sewing sequins on the wedding dress, wondering what that was all about.

The corrections officer took Shirley back to her cell. Gus and Pappy met alone in the attorney-inmate conference room to discuss the test results.

"Well?" asked Gus.

Pappy looked up from the long scroll of paper on the desk. "The good news is, I'm confident the results are reliable."

"And the bad news?"

"No real bad news. The results are just interesting."

"Good interesting or bad interesting?"

"Mixed."

"Cut to it, will you, Pappy?"

"Any polygraph is good for about three, no more than four test questions. We had four. Two questions came clean. Whether she'd ever met Beth. And whether she had anything to do with Beth's disappearance. She said no to both."

"True or false?"

"No sign of deception there."

"Good. That should satisfy the FBI's concerns that they're dealing with an inmate who was behind Beth's kidnapping. What else?"

"I also asked her if she knew where Beth was. First she said, I might. Then she said no."

"What's your take?"

"I can't tell whether she might know. But I can tell you

this. I saw no sign of deception when she said she didn't."

Gus felt a wave of disappointment. "So you're saying she's bullshitting me? She can't lead me to Beth?"

"I wouldn't read it that way. She probably was able to say no because she isn't a hundred percent certain where Beth is."

Gus nodded slowly, wanting to agree. "That's why she initially said she might know. She has a theory about what happened to Beth. Probably a pretty good theory. But she can't say for certain."

"I think that's a fair interpretation."

"Which only reinforces the notion that she had nothing to do with Beth's disappearance. This is perfect. I want you to type up your report right away, Pappy. I can't wait to show this to the FBI."

Pappy made a face. "You might want to give that some thought."

"What are you talking about?"

"There was a fourth question. I didn't expect it to elicit any reaction, but it did."

"Which one was that?"

"I asked if she had ever killed anyone. She said no."

"That's the truth. She was convicted of conspiracy to commit murder, but the murder never happened. They nailed her for planning to kill someone, not for murder."

"Then she must have had another body in mind when she answered this question."

"I don't understand."

"She was lying, Gus. She has killed someone."

Gus couldn't ask Pappy to leave that out of the report. The guy had too much integrity. He knew, however, that the FBI wouldn't be eager to cut a deal with a woman who had apparently gotten away with murder.

"You want me to type up the report?"

Gus thought for a second, then said, "Hold on, Pappy. Let me look into this first."

Forty-three

There was no panic at midnight, no missing glass slipper. Even so, if Mrs. Rankin made her mop the floors once more, Andie was going to change her alias from Kira to Cinderella.

The store had been closed on Sunday, but Andie had worked a full day just cleaning the place up. Monday had started the way the weekend had left off, one menial task after another. In the make-believe world, Kira was about halfway to earning that necklace the old lady had promised her. In the real world, Andie was trying to find a discreet way to get the story behind that innocent-looking woman Mrs. Rankin had run out of the store Saturday afternoon.

Andie squeezed the soapy brown water from the mop into the bucket. Mrs. Rankin stood over her and inspected the damp and shiny floors.

"Not bad," she said, arms folded across her sagging bosom. "Corners need some work."

Andie rose and leaned defiantly on her mop handle. She'd about had it. "The corners are just fine."

"They're fine when I say they're fine."

"This is a thrift store. Not an operating room."

"Don't sass me. Or I'll fire you on the spot."

"You'd like that, wouldn't you? A nice power rush."

"Watch yourself," she said sternly.

"What is it with you? You sit on your butt all day long just waiting for the chance to jump down somebody's throat."

"I'm warning you, Kira."

"No, I'm tired of it. You abuse me, you abuse your customers. Like that woman in here yesterday, just minding her own business."

"Don't get into that."

"She wasn't hurting anybody. Just looking at sweaters."

"Shut your trap. You don't know what you're talking about."

"I was standing right there. I saw what happened."

"I had every right to throw her out of here."

"Well, people also have the right to be treated with a little respect. A little kindness. Maybe you should try it sometime."

"Maybe you should zip it up before I fire you."

"Maybe I'll quit if you don't start treating people nicely."

"What's your problem? You don't even know that woman."

"Makes no difference. She seemed nice enough to me."

The old lady was steaming. She grabbed Andie by the arm.

"Let go of me!" said Andie.

She squeezed harder and led Andie to the door.

"What are you, crazy?"

She flung open the door and led Andie outside. "Come on!" she said harshly. "You think she looks nice, huh? You want to be friends with that woman, do you? You be my guest." They stopped at the lamp post a half block away. A flyer was tacked to it at eye level. Mrs. Rankin snatched it down and shoved it at Andie.

"Here you go, you stupid brat. You want to be chummy with her, you go right ahead. Just don't ever step foot in my store again."

She turned and stormed back to her shop. Andie stood at the curb, confused. The printed flyer was a crumpled ball in her hand. She unfurled it and read it. Instantly Andie knew her work was done at the thrift shop.

Tomorrow night there was someplace else she had to be.

Gus couldn't stop thinking about the polygraph results.

His first instinct had been to summon Shirley and confront her. As a lawyer, however, he knew that cross-examination without preparation was a recipe for disaster. He needed to gather his thoughts, review the information he had. Unfortunately, nothing in his possession offered any insight into whether Shirley had ever really killed anyone. He had a copy of her criminal record. He had all the newspapers relating to her arrest and trial. He could turn his private investigator loose to scrounge for more, but that would take time. Too much time.

He returned to the Washington Corrections Center for Women on Monday morning, a little calmer but otherwise no better disposed to interrogate Shirley than he had been on Saturday. As he sat behind the Plexiglas partition, even the calmness disappeared. She had kept him waiting nearly twenty minutes. Finally, the door opened behind him.

The guard said, "Shirley doesn't want to meet with you."

"What?"

"She says she doesn't want any visitors this morning."

"I drove all the way over here to see her."

"Sorry."

"What else is on her schedule, lawn tennis at Wimbledon?"

"Hey, if she doesn't want to see you, I can't make her."

Gus rose, struggling to contain his anger. He took two steps closer and invaded the guard's space. The guard was little more than a kid, less than half Gus's age, much smaller in stature. "Get her."

The guard took a half step back.

"Get her right now," said Gus. "Or I have no choice but to call the warden and tell him you are interfering with confidential communications between an attorney and his client."

"Don't do that. I just got this job."

"Then don't let an inmate jerk you around. Bring me Shirley Borge."

He blinked nervously as he backed out through the door. Gus went back to his chair in front of the glass. His anger was rising. Shirley was toying with him, playing games about whether she did or didn't know where Beth was. Concealing the fact that she had indeed murdered someone. Maybe she was even lying when she denied any involvement in Beth's disappearance and had simply fooled the machine. Now she was pulling this "I don't want to see him" crap. It was time for Gus to get in her face.

The door opened and Shirley entered the room on the other side of the glass. She stepped forward and stopped, glaring at him from five feet away. Gus's anger turned to confusion. Her face was purple and puffy. The left eye was nearly swollen shut. A nasty split on her lower lip had been stitched closed.

They picked up their phones. "What happened to you?" he asked, both curious and concerned.

"I fell out of bed." She was deadpan, then added, "I got the shit beat out of me, what does it look like?"

"Who did this to you?"

"Nobody in particular. Nobody likes a rat in prison."

"What are you talking about?"

"Word got out I took a polygraph."

"I'm sorry. I don't know how that happened."

She looked at him with contempt. "I know what you're doing, Mr. Wheatley. Very clever plan. You have me sit for a polygraph, then have a guard or someone leak it to the other inmates. That's a sure-fire way of putting pressure on me to cooperate. Now I have two options. Take a beating every day for being a rat. Or I can talk to you and hope the FBI will at least transfer me to another prison."

"That's not at all what happened."

She shook her head, clearly unconvinced. "You cost me big-time. I had some respect in this place. When I got busted, I could have shaved five years off my sentence if I just ratted out my partners. I wouldn't do it. I took the rap myself. That's a badge of honor inside here. Now I've lost it."

"I swear to you. We took every precaution to keep this quiet. We didn't leak a thing."

"Right," she scoffed, glaring through the glass. "Good luck finding your wife now, asshole." She slammed down the phone and turned away.

Gus wanted to call out but couldn't. He felt numb, helpless, as she crossed the room and disappeared behind the door.

Forty-four

Andie arrived at the Eagle Trace Motel in Yakima just before eight o'clock on Tuesday evening. She went straight to a room called the governor's hall, which had nothing to do with the governor. It was just an impressive-sounding name for an unimpressive meeting room.

There was a slight backup at the door. A young woman was passing out pamphlets to each person as they entered. Andie was fifth in line. It moved quickly.

"Welcome," said the woman. "Please sit anywhere you'd like."

Andie took the pamphlet and went inside. It was an unadorned room. No artwork on the walls. Basic beige carpeting. She counted twenty rows of folding chairs, ten on each side with an aisle down the center. About half the seats were filled with adults of all ages, about an equal number of men and women. Some were dressed as Andie was, as though they didn't have much in life. Others wore the kind of clothes Andie might wear in real life. Some had come as couples, but it seemed most had come alone. Very few were talking to each other. Most had left an empty seat between them and the nearest person.

Andie sat on the far right side on the very end about halfway toward the front. An old man was seated to her left. He looked straight ahead at the podium, though no one was there. Andie removed her coat, folded it in her lap, and read the pamphlet the girl had given her at the door. It was simply a reprint of the flyer that had been tacked to the pole outside Mrs. Rankin's store.

In bold letters it read, "Tap the untapped energy within and around you." That sounded innocuous enough. It went on: "If you have ever entertained the idea that humans can indeed acquire the kind of energy that is necessary to transition to a level beyond human, you will want to attend this gathering."

Any doubt as to the true purpose of the meeting was eliminated by the fine print: "This is not a religious or philosophical organization recruiting membership."

Right. And the Congress was not controlled by special interests.

Straight up at eight o'clock, the doors closed. The lights dimmed. The crowd fell silent. From the back of the room, a beam of light blazed over the audience and illuminated the podium. It cast a faint circle of light at first, but it grew stronger as the ambient lighting continued to dim. It was like watching the moon rise, a white ball of light rising over the podium, shining brilliantly against the reflective backdrop. In a matter of moments the audience was shrouded in total darkness. The white globe around the podium was the only light.

Without warning, the spotlight went out. The room was black. Just as suddenly the light returned. It cut like a laser through the darkness and shined on the man who had almost magically appeared behind the podium. He stood with arms outstretched and his head tilted back, his eyes to the ceiling. He brought the microphone to his mouth and shouted in a deep, resounding voice, "I am the god of hell fire, and I bring you . . . fire!"

Music erupted from the large speakers in the back. It was the 1968 rock 'n' roll smash by the Crazy World of Arthur Brown, with its shrill organ music and swift beat.

He sang of fire and burning in a voice that sounded almost demonic. The man at the podium moved not an inch, frozen in the light. The music pounded for another ten seconds and was building to a crescendo. Then it ended abruptly with the sound of a phonograph needle scratching on vinyl.

The lights came on. The music was gone. The room was back to normal. The bemused man at the podium stood with his hands at his sides. A handsome man, not much older than Andie.

"I am the god of hell fire?" he asked incredulously. A smile crept to his lips. "I don't think so."

A few members of the audience chuckled uneasily.

"Had you all going there for a moment, though, didn't I?" He approached an elderly couple in the front row and said playfully, "Come on, admit it. I saw you kind of lean into your wife and mutter between your teeth: 'Get your purse, Ethyl, the man's a lunatic.'"

The old man laughed. Others laughed with him.

"What's your name, sir?"

"Bob."

He shook his hand. "Good to meet you, Bob. My name's Steven Blechman." He smiled and returned to the podium. "And I am not a god. And this meeting is not about hell fire. In fact, it has absolutely nothing to do with what *I* am. It's about you and the direction of your life." He let the words hang for effect, then added, "And there is nothing more important than that."

Andie watched carefully, listened to his every word. He was a curious blend of television evangelist and stand-up comedian. Riveting. Captivating.

"I'm curious. Does anyone here believe there is energy in the universe?"

A few people answered, "Yes."

"Come on. All of you believe *that*. The stars shine. The planets rotate. Comets soar. There *is* energy."

Many people nodded.

"Congratulations," he said, smiling. "You've all passed physics for idiots one-oh-one. But now answer this question for me. Privately. Honestly. As honest as you can be with yourself." He paused and leaned forward, as if putting the question to each member of the audience individually. "Do you feel *connected* to that energy?"

The audience was silent. He had them thinking. He waited nearly half a minute, then said, "Perhaps some of you think you are. But do you feel *so connected* that if you left this earth today, it would carry you to the next level? The level beyond human?"

He waited again. The silence was palpable.

"I see some doubtful faces." He smiled again at the old couple up front. "Look at Bob, everyone. He's got that look on his face again. 'Ethyl, get your coat. The guy's off his rocker.'"

Blechman smiled. Others smiled with him. Then he turned serious. "But am I? In this universe, how does something get from one place to another? How does one thing *become* another?"

The question lingered. "Energy, right? All living things have energy. In casual conversation, you've heard people say they can feel your vibes. Or they might say, he or she is giving me bad vibes. The Beach Boys even wrote a song about it. Well, there's something to that, folks. Each one of us is constantly vibrating with energy. We vibrate at different levels, depending on how connected we are to the source of that energy. A proper connection to the source, ladies and gentlemen, is vital to our ability to transcend our humanness, to move up to the next level."

He returned to the podium and sipped water from a glass. To Andie, even his drinking seemed calculated, designed to make the audience thirst for his next word.

"Many things can break our connection with the source. Temptation. Greed. All of the worldly possessions that delude us into thinking that being human is the ultimate form of existence. That self-absorbed outlook is what keeps us vibrating at a human level, a lower level of energy."

A few people lowered their eyes, seemingly embarrassed, as if he had touched a nerve. He softened his tone. He was no longer judgmental.

"But perhaps the most important point for you to understand is that you don't have to be a bad person to be disconnected from the source. Strangely enough, the most kind and giving people are often the most disconnected. Why? Because the most dangerous break between humans and the source is caused by people we allow to rule our lives, dictate our emotions, and literally suck the energy right out of us. People who profess to love us but are only parasites."

All eyes followed as he walked from one end of the room to the other, then back to the podium. "So, I return to my original question. Are you so connected to the source of energy in this vast universe that if you left this earth today you would transcend to the next level, the level beyond human?" He looked again toward the audience, locking eyes with each member. "I can tell you this. If you cling to the things that define you as a human. If you pander to others who enslave you as human. If there is anything or anyone on this planet you could not bear to leave behind. Then you are not so connected."

He was looking right at Andie, or so it seemed. She forced herself not to flinch and was glad he moved on to someone more enthralled.

"What does all this mean?" he asked in a voice that was hushed for effect. "It means you must prepare yourself for the long and difficult road ahead. The good news, folks, is that each and every one of you has the power to succeed. Just go back to the source. You can do it. I know you can."

He smiled warmly, not overdoing it. "Now I'd like you to meet some friends of mine. Two people who, not long

ago, were sitting in the audience like you are tonight. Two
people whose lives have been transformed. They can help
you understand what this journey is all about. Ladies and
gentlemen, please give a warm welcome to Tom and Felicia."

The audience applauded. Andie applauded, then froze.
Felicia was the woman who had been kicked out of the
thrift store.

They looked like two very normal people. He wore jeans
and a flannel shirt; she wore slacks and a sweater. They
weren't great public speakers, but they talked intelligently,
honestly. The man spoke first, then Felicia. She was particularly interesting. Earlier, Andie had been right on the
money when she'd guessed the woman was out of place in
a thrift store. It was no surprise she walked with polish. Felicia was a college graduate. She had run her own travel
agency for nine years. She had been married to an architect
who lived in Seattle. She hadn't been unhappy. Just disconnected. She gave it all up for one simple reason.

"Steve Blechman changed my life."

"No, no," said Blechman. "*You* changed your life."

"Right," she said, as if he were *always* right. "I did it."

Blechman thanked his friends and opened the floor to
questions from the audience, which took another twenty
minutes. Most people asked legitimate questions. A few
were cynics who just wanted to rattle him. Friend or foe,
Blechman treated each of them with respect. His message
never wavered. He never lost his cool. It was impressive.
The man could talk.

Felicia explained his gift. "He's better connected to the
source than you or I."

Blechman smiled modestly and laughed it off. He
checked his watch. Their hour was up. He returned to the
podium.

"Ladies and gentlemen, I hope this has been more than
just a form of entertainment for you. For me, Tom, Felicia,

and many, many others, it is a lifelong cause. As we've stated all along, we do not recruit members. We leave it up to each of you to decide for yourself whether you want to take that big first step. If anyone is interested, we are having a retreat this weekend. We leave Friday night and return Sunday. It's not a pleasure trip. There are some cabins in the mountains. It's cold, but there are wood-burning stoves and plenty of blankets. There's no fast food, only what nature provides. It's about getting back to the source. The purpose isn't for you to learn more about us. It's a chance to learn more about yourself. We'd love to see you there. Thank you all for coming."

Blechman left the room to a warm but not overwhelming ovation. A few people didn't applaud at all. They headed straight for the exits, shaking their heads. Others were more intrigued. They milled about the exit, taking more pamphlets and asking questions of the girl at the door. She had a sign-up list for people who wanted to receive additional information in the mail. Several people signed. She also had videotapes for sale, for those who wanted to relive the studio version of tonight's experience or share it with their friends. Andie bought one, then followed the dozen or so others who drifted toward the front of the room. Tom and Felicia were answering questions. Tom had a clipboard with a sign-up list for the retreat.

Andie made her way toward Felicia, who was talking to a college-age man, telling him what to pack for the weekend and what to expect. Andie waited behind him. When they finished, Andie moved up. Felicia immediately recognized her.

"Hello. You work at Second Chance, don't you?"

Andie smiled shyly. "Yeah. Sorry about what happened."

"That's okay. Mrs. Rankin doesn't think much of our group."

"I'm afraid Mrs. Rankin doesn't think much of anyone."

They shared a laugh. Felicia asked, "What's your name?"

"Kira."

"Well, Kira, are you going to join us this weekend?"

She wanted to appear indecisive, unsure of herself. The kind of person they'd prey upon. "I don't know," she said with a shrug.

"Come on. I think you'd be perfect."

"You really think so?"

"I know so."

Andie blinked demurely. "Will Steve be there?"

Felicia smirked. Another smitten young woman. "Of course."

"Well, what the heck? What do I got to lose?"

"Atta girl. Just check in with Tom. He's got the sign-up list and all the info."

"Thanks."

"You're welcome. I'll see you Friday."

Andie drifted toward Tom. He was talking to the old couple Blechman had teased during his presentation. The wife was lukewarm, but the husband was excited and ready to sign up. Andie, too, was excited, though she tried not to show it. She had a sixth sense about Blechman and his teachings. Beth Wheatley's disappearance was taking on a whole new face. She couldn't wait for Friday.

Just remember your name is Kira.

Forty-five

Gus met his investigator for an early Wednesday breakfast. Dex picked Café René again, his favorite. It was starting to grow on Gus, too. There was something endearing about a place so unpretentious that it printed its dubious review from *Seattle Weekly* right on the menu: "The food and service are equally bad, but at least the atmosphere's lousy."

Dex gorged himself on a thick slice of Canadian bacon and a mountain of scrambled eggs smothered in ketchup. Gus nibbled on a side order of toast as they hashed out Shirley Borge.

"First thing," said Dex with his mouth full. "You gotta decide just how important Shirley really is."

"There's only one way to read that polygraph. She may not know for certain where Beth is. But she either knows some people or knows something about Beth that gives her a pretty good idea what happened to her."

"Maybe she'll cool off in a day or so and talk to you."

"I don't think so."

Dex added even more ketchup. "You could play hardball. Get the FBI to put some pressure on her till she comes back and talks to you. Solitary confinement. Move her to a cell with a backed-up toilet. One thing about life in prison. It can always get worse."

"Those kind of games might just push her further away."

"Or maybe she'll just cough up what she knows."

"Or she'll be even more ticked off and Beth will get killed."

Dex gulped down half his glass of orange juice. His eyes bulged as the stomach erupted in scrambled-egg revolt, but he managed to keep it silent. "You got two choices. You either gotta go through Shirley Borge or around her."

It sounded like mindless jock talk. "What is that supposed to mean?"

"Shirley has information you want. You're telling me you can't beg it, force it, or buy it out of her. So go around her. Find someone else. Someone who knows her secrets."

"Like who?"

Dex shrugged. "The usual suspects. Friends. Lovers."

"That's a list I don't have."

"Don't need the whole list. Just one person she might have confided in somewhere along the line."

Gus sipped his coffee, thinking. Then his eyes brightened.

Dex smiled thinly. "You got one already?"

Gus lowered his cup, then answered, "I think maybe I do."

Sympathy got Gus an immediate meeting with Kirby Toombs. Rarely did he make himself available on a moment's notice, but he made an exception for a fellow member of the bar whose wife was missing.

Kirby had read about Gus's plight in the newspapers. Though he had seen the reward advertised, he was completely unaware that Shirley Borge had responded to it. After Gus explained his predicament on the phone, Kirby couldn't blame him for wanting to talk to the lawyer who had represented her.

Kirby had been a rookie public defender at the time of Shirley's trial. Many talented lawyers had come out of the

P.D.'s office, but Kirby wasn't one of them. He'd been fired four months ago, couldn't find a job, and was now in the process of setting up a solo criminal defense practice. From the looks of things, he had a long way to go. His office was near the state courthouse in a decaying brick building that looked ready for the wrecking ball. Gus knew it well, since one of his clients owned it and was waiting on a historic designation that would make renovation worthwhile. About half the building was vacant. The rest was filled with questionable tenants, many of whom weren't even paying rent. The sign outside Kirby's door read VENTURA ENTERPRISES, the name of a former tenant, probably not even the most recent former tenant. Gus rang the buzzer outside the door. It didn't buzz. He tapped on the glass. Kirby answered from behind the closed door.

"Who is it?" He sounded as though he were talking into a trash can.

"It's Gus Wheatley. I just got off the phone with you."

The chain rattled. Three dead bolts clicked. The door opened. Kirby was standing in the doorway. He was perhaps two years out of law school, still sporting the chubby look of a kid who drank too much beer in college. He wore a bad brown suit, the exact shade Gus told the young lawyers in his firm never to wear unless they wanted to look like a walking turd.

"Come on in."

Gus thanked him and entered. The dowdy suite bore no resemblance to a law office. It was two rooms, counting the tiny reception area. There was no receptionist, just an ugly metal desk and an answering machine.

"Want some coffee?"

The pot on the credenza looked as if it had been there since Mr. Coffee was in diapers. "No, thanks."

Kirby poured himself a cup and led Gus to the main office. Dusty venetian blinds cut the morning sun into slats on the rug. Overloaded banker's boxes were stacked on the desk and couch. Kirby made room for Gus on the couch and took a seat in the squeaky desk chair.

"Just moving in?"

"No," he said, a little offended.

"I'm sorry. I just thought—"

"I know, I know. It doesn't look like the cherry-paneled offices of Preston and Coolidge."

"That's not what I was going to say."

"You didn't have to. It was written all over your face."

"Really, it's not like that at all. I have a lot of respect for a young guy who tries to strike out on his own."

"Yeah, sure you do. I think you mentioned that somewhere in the rejection letter I got from you in law school. Dear Mr. Toombs. Thank you very much for your interest in our firm. It gives us all great wracking belly laughs to dump on the drones who aren't top ten percent and law review."

Gus turned cautious. The guy was a little off. "It's a competitive market, Kirby. You can't take rejection personally."

"How else am I supposed to take it?"

"It's . . . business."

"Easy for you to say, hot shot. Do you have any idea what it feels like to be fired?"

Gus felt a twinge inside. He thought of the way the executive committee had so abruptly removed him as managing partner and replaced him with Martha Goldstein. "I can imagine."

"No, you can't. It hurts, man. And I'm not just talking about your ego. The word gets out on the street. You're damaged goods. I wasn't a bad lawyer. I just didn't get along with the more important people over at the P.D.'s office. So they fired me. Now look at me. There's not a law firm in the city who wants a reject from the public defender's office."

"That doesn't mean you can't land on your feet."

He leaned forward, anger in his eyes. "Look around, asshole. I'm practicing law out of the trunk of my car."

"Who knows? I may be joining you someday."

"Go right ahead. Make jokes."

He wasn't joking, but there was no point in explaining. He changed his tone. "Is this why you wanted to meet in person? You want to chew my ass out because you can't find a job? Well, let me tell you something. Two weeks ago I would have been the last guy to say this, but there are worse things in life than losing a stupid job. So if we don't start talking about Shirley Borge in the next thirty seconds, I'm walking right out that door. I don't have time for this."

Toombs leaned back smugly, as if it pleased him to irk a man of Gus's stature. "You want to talk about Shirley Borge? No problem. I'll tell you anything you want to know."

"Thank you."

"All I need is a check."

"A check?"

"Yeah. My time is money."

"You want me to pay you for information about Shirley Borge?"

He shook his head, grimacing. "That has such an un-seemly connotation, the way you put it. Let's just say I want to be compensated for my time and inconvenience."

Gus didn't have time to lecture the kid on ethics. He laid his checkbook on the desk and started writing. "Fine. I'll pay you for an hour of your time."

"Sounds reasonable. Make it five thousand dollars."

His hand froze. He stopped writing. "You're joking."

"Do I sound like I'm joking?"

"This is robbery."

"That's probably what your clients say when they see your bills. Payback sucks, doesn't it, Mr. Wheatley?"

Gus hated to give it to him, but he thought of Beth on the other end of the phone, unable to speak, maybe even tied up and gagged. He thought of Shirley slamming the door on him, taking her secrets about Beth back to her cell. This was no time to stand on a five-thousand-dollar principle. He wrote the check and signed it.

Kirby reached for it. Gus snatched it back.

"First, you answer my questions."

Kirby clearly wanted the check first, but the harsh tone made him back away. "All right. What has Shirley told you so far?"

"Not much. Most of what I know is from my own research, newspaper accounts of the trial and such. I know she was convicted of conspiracy to commit a murder that was planned but never carried out."

"That's the bare bones of it."

"Then fill me in."

"Supposedly, Shirley and some friends saw some movie on television where homeless people started getting whacked, so they decided that might be a fun way to liven up their weekend."

"They were just going to kill a homeless person at random?"

"That's the story."

"How did they get caught?"

"Well, they didn't just rush out and do it. They started planning it. They got hold of a gun. And then Shirley started bragging at bars and places that they had this plan."

"So that's who turned them in? Someone from the bar?"

"No, actually it was Shirley's mother."

Gus suddenly recalled the polygraph exam, where Shirley had said she didn't know if her mother was dead or alive. "Why?"

"Shirley had always been a problem kid. So when her mom heard she was getting mixed up in some plan to kill a homeless person, that was the last straw. She decided to put a little scare in her daughter. She went to the police. Turns out the police had more in mind that just scaring her.

They put a wiretap on the home phones and recorded Shirley talking about her scheme. The conversations were pretty explicit. Not an easy case to defend. They talked about the time of the hit. The weapon they would use. How they'd dispose of the gun. What they would do with the body."

"So they arrested Shirley before the murder."

"Yeah."

"Why didn't they arrest her friends?"

"It was only one friend, actually. At least that's all they had on the tape. No one knew who he was. Both he and Shirley were very careful never to mention his name on the phone. Whenever he called Shirley, he always called from a pay phone, so there was no way to trace it."

"That's the guy the police wanted Shirley to identify?" asked Gus.

"Right. We could have gotten Shirley off pretty easy if she had given up the guy's name. But she wouldn't. So she's living at WCCW."

"She did mention how she refused to rat out her friend. She seemed proud of that."

"I don't know if it was pride so much as fear that kept her quiet."

"Why do you say that?"

"Good reasons."

"Let's hear them."

"Let's have the check."

Gus reluctantly laid it on the table. Kirby grabbed it, stuffed it in his coat pocket, and said, "You didn't hear this from me, okay?"

"Whatever."

"Everything I just told you is the story that came out in trial. But that's not the real story."

"That's what I'm here for. What's real?"

"Shirley was mixed up with something weird. This

wasn't just some friends who watched television and decided it might be fun to kill a homeless person."

"What was it?"

"I don't know exactly. Some kind of gang, maybe."

"Shirley told you this?"

"Not in so many words. This is mostly my take on it."

"Why did they want to kill a homeless person?"

His expression turned very serious. "There was never a homeless person."

"But what about the recorded phone calls? Surely they must have mentioned the target was a homeless person."

"They did. But it was like a code, you know. The homeless lady. Like Monica Lewinsky referring to Bill Clinton as the big creep."

"Then who was the real target?"

"I don't know for sure."

"Who do you think it was?"

"The woman who turned her in."

"Her mother?"

Kirby nodded. "Her mother."

The wheels were turning. Gangs. Serial killings. Targeted mothers. Missing wives. It wasn't quite as good as Shirley telling him precisely how she knew where Beth was, but it was another promising lead. "This could be very helpful."

Kirby rose. "I aim to please. But if you'll excuse me, I actually have a client to meet at the courthouse in less than five minutes."

"I won't keep you."

Kirby flashed a cheesy smile. "If there's anything else you need," he said as he tapped the pocket that held the check, "I'm sure we can work something out."

He extended his hand. Gus didn't shake it.

"I'll see you around, Kirby." He let himself out and headed down the stairs. As he hurried from the building, the words scum bag came to mind, but he settled on two others.

Stop payment.

He jumped in his car and sped away.

Forty-six

Andie caught an overnight bus back to Seattle and was back in the office on Wednesday in time for an impromptu but important team meeting. So important, in fact, that Isaac Underwood cleared his calendar to attend, along with Lundquist, her supervisor; Haveres, her contact agent; and two other members of the Wheatley kidnapping team. At Isaac's request, Victoria Santos participated by speaker phone from Quantico. Based on the advance briefing Andie had given him by phone, he expected to call on the expertise of a profiler experienced in the ways of New Age cults.

They met in a small, windowless conference room adjacent to the ASAC's office. Isaac made short work of the preliminaries and turned the meeting over to Andie. She quickly summarized the experiences at Second Chance clothing store that had led her to the gathering at Eagle Trace Motel, then spent several more minutes describing the impressive performance of Steven Blechman. She offered to play the videotape she had purchased, but it was too long for this meeting. The real groaning started when she mentioned the weekend retreat she wanted to attend. It was from Lundquist.

"I knew it," he said, shaking his head.

"Knew what?" asked Isaac.

"This is the problem with using inexperienced agents for

317

cameos. We send her out on a three-day assignment, and before her three days are even up she's back asking for an extension. Before we know it, we're into a full-blown undercover operation with no way to pay for it."

Isaac said, "The most this could ever amount to is a Group Two operation with a seventy-thousand-dollar maximum. We don't even need headquarters approval for that."

"We don't even need anywhere near seventy thousand dollars," said Andie.

Isaac hedged, as if he knew how quickly costs mounted. "Let's put the budget aside for now. I want to know what you plan to accomplish and how you plan to do it. You got the floor, Andie. Sell us."

She silently thanked him, then moved the speaker phone closer so Victoria Santos could hear. "None of this makes any sense unless you back up and take a look at a few key facts about Beth Wheatley.

"First, she has some signs of emotional instability. She falsely accused her husband of spouse abuse, she suffered from bulimia, and she was apparently the most wealthy shoplifter in the history of Nordstrom department stores.

"Second, she physically resembles and shares some other personal characteristics with all three women who have fallen victim to our serial killer. But unlike the others, she may be alive. We've never recovered her body, her daughter got the 'Mary Had a Little Lamb' phone call, and Beth's fingerprints were found on the pay phone in Oregon from which that call was made.

"Third, Beth had some connection to the Second Chance clothing store in Yakima. One of her dresses was found there.

"Put that all together, you're left with an emotionally unstable woman who mysteriously disappeared, who may be alive and held captive by a serial killer, and whose dress is sitting in a thrift shop frequented by members of a New Age cult."

"Andie?" The voice came from the speaker box. It was Victoria.

"Yes?"

"Has anyone checked to see if any of the serial killer's victims had friends or family members who disappeared? By disappear I mean they just ran off and never came back, the way people sometimes do when they join a cult."

Lundquist answered, "That's one of the projects our team is undertaking."

"Actually," said Andie, "I already checked. None of the decedents had friends or family members who are unaccounted for."

"Good," said Victoria. "Ruling out the obvious is always a good place to start. Now, tell me more about this supposed cult itself. I understand the philosophy, but what about its size, its makeup, its physical location?"

"We have some information on that from the Yakima County Sheriff's office. They own an old farm just outside Yakima. About thirty people live there. We have photos of some of the members because they were arrested in a peaceable civil disobedience where they chained themselves to the pipes when Water and Sewer tried to put an irrigation drainage ditch across the land adjacent to their property. According to the arresting officer's report, they seemed like a rather peaceable but paranoid bunch, thinking the whole drainage-ditch project was just a government ruse to spy on them."

"Any other trouble with the law?"

"No."

"How about the individual members? Any arrest records in the bunch?"

"Not one of those arrested on the civil disobedience charge had a prior arrest record. They were just ordinary people, much like the people I saw at the meeting last night."

Isaac interjected. "So I take it this Shirley Borge over at

WCCW has no official connection to the cult?"

"None that we know of. She wasn't part of the civil disobedience group, anyway."

"Not to ask a stupid question," Victoria followed up.
"But I don't suppose Beth Wheatley's picture was among
the photos of cult members who were arrested."

"No," said Andie. "And that's not a stupid question. To
address Isaac's question at the outset, one of the things I
want to accomplish with this assignment is to determine
whether Beth Wheatley is a victim. Or an accomplice."

"Accomplice to *what*?" asked Lundquist. "Let's not lose
sight of the fact that this whole theory is based on a tip
from a convicted felon who wants to get out of jail, collect
a quarter of a million dollars in reward money, and move to
Tahiti. We don't have any evidence that Steve Blechman or
anyone else from this so-called cult has ever met Beth
Wheatley or any other of the victims of this serial killer."

"Which is exactly why I need to go on this retreat," said
Andie.

Lundquist said, "Working in a used-clothing store in
Yakima undercover was one thing. Infiltrating a cult is
quite another."

"What are you saying?" asked Isaac. "That the assignment is foolhardy?"

"I say that if it's evidence we're after, we get a search
warrant and go look for it."

"You know as well as anyone that a search warrant has
to be specific. We have to list exactly what we're looking
for in our affidavit."

"How about Beth Wheatley? That's pretty specific. If we
really think Beth Wheatley could be at the farm owned by
Mr. Blechman's cult, I say we get a search warrant and turn
the place upside down till we find her."

Andie was about to speak, but Victoria beat her to it.
"Bad idea," she said loudly over the box. "Any overt action
by the FBI could prompt the cult members to turn the place

into a poison drinking fest, like Heaven's Gate or Jonestown, or a deadly inferno, like David Koresh in Waco. Cult members are by definition suicidal, since they have already killed off their past life. From what Andie told us of Blechman's teachings, this cult is no different. He preaches the need to sever ties with family and friends—everything that keeps you vibrating at a human level. Based on what I've heard, Blechman isn't afraid to die. And he isn't afraid to take his followers with him— whether they're willing or unwilling."

Lundquist grimaced, seemingly unconvinced. "I'm just trying to strike a reasonable balance here. We have a serial killer who could strike again at any moment. I don't want to get sidetracked on some expensive and protracted undercover operation that turns out to be totally beside the point."

"That's a valid concern," said Andie. "But storming the compound isn't the answer."

"I didn't say *storm* it," snapped Lundquist. "I said get a search warrant. Don't twist my words."

"Sorry. But I think the point Victoria was making is that the distinction might be lost on a paranoid group of cult members who went so far as to chain themselves to an irrigation pipe in order to stop the government from spying on them."

Lundquist was searching for a reply but was coming up empty. "Smartass," he muttered beneath his breath.

"Come on," said Isaac. "Let's not get personal."

"On the contrary," said Lundquist. "Now is precisely the time to get personal. I sense that you're leaning toward some kind of undercover approach. So the next logical question is, who is the right man for the job?"

"At the risk of sounding like a bumper sticker, I'd have to say the right man is a woman."

"Is that so?" said Lundquist. "Andie, why don't you relate to us your previous undercover training and experience?"

She had none, but she felt compelled to say something. "I did some acting in college."

"Wonderful. You can be Eliza Doolittle in the cult revival of *My Fair Lady*. Isaac, how'd you like to play 'enry 'iggins?"

"Enough," said Isaac.

"I'm not just taking potshots," said Lundquist. "I like Andie. I think she's got real potential. I just don't want to see her killed on an assignment she's not qualified to handle."

"I'm up for it," said Andie.

"Think before you talk, kid. You're going inside a cult. Once you're there, you're on your own. Our surveillance agents can't see through walls. And we can't wire you. If they pat you down and find a wire, you're dead. I'm not saying this to be a sexist pig. But with two dead men, three dead women, and another woman missing, maybe you'd better think twice before you walk into a cult that may have spawned a serial killer."

She looked at Lundquist and then at Isaac. "I have thought about it. This is what I want to do." Her gaze fixed on Isaac. He'd been with her so far, and she expected his approval. She waited. Several seconds passed. She suffered through the silence, begging with her eyes.

He said finally, "Let me think about it."

"But—"

With a quick wave of the hand Isaac cut her off. Concern was evident in his eyes. Lundquist's speech had gotten to him. "I said I'd think about it."

Andie watched with disappointment as he rose from the table and left the room.

Forty-seven

Gus had been awake since three A.M. That was when Morgan had finally fallen asleep. The nights were getting increasingly difficult. For a six-year-old, a week and a half was an eternity. Beth had been gone so long that Morgan was seriously beginning to doubt her return.

For the most part, Gus had managed to keep his own doubts to himself. The advice he'd gotten was to remain positive in front of Morgan. That didn't mean walking around the house with an ear-to-ear smile. Nor did it mean lying to her. She could see the worry in his face, so there was little point in telling her he wasn't concerned.

Last night, however, he might have been a little too honest. It was on their third late-night go-round, after the story-reading session at eleven o'clock and another glass of water at one A.M. Morgan was still wide awake. Clearly, something was weighing on her mind. Gus carried her from the bed and held her on his lap as they rocked in the glider. Her head lay on his shoulder. He could feel the warm breath against his neck, the baby-fine hair brushing against his skin. They rocked in the glow of her Little Mermaid night light. It took a few minutes, but finally she opened up. She spoke without looking at him, her cheek against his chest.

"Daddy?"

"Yes."

"What's a reward?"

He knew where this was headed, so he answered carefully. "It's like a prize that you give to a person who does a good deed."

"A kid at school said there was a reward for Mommy."

"That's true. If anyone can bring Mommy back to us, that would be a good deed. So I'll give them a reward."

"What are you going to give them?"

"Money."

"How much?"

"A lot."

"All the money we have?"

"No. Not all of it."

"Why not?"

"Because we don't have to give that much."

"How do you know that?"

"I just know."

"But Mommy isn't back. What if your reward isn't big enough?"

"It's big enough. But if they ask for more, we'll give it to them."

They rocked in silence, then she asked, "How much more?"

"Whatever it takes."

"Would you give them your car?"

"Absolutely."

"How about the house?"

"If we had to, I would."

"Would you give them Aunt Carla?"

That elicited a half smile. "No, honey. We can't do that."

"Would you give them me?"

"Never," he said firmly. "Not in a million years."

She nuzzled the nape of his neck and asked softly, "What about you?"

"What about me?"

"If they wanted you as their reward, would you go?"

He didn't answer right away. Not because he didn't know the answer, but because he had never thought of it in those terms. "Yes. I would."

He felt her cling tighter. Her voice filled with urgency. "You would go, too?"

"No. I would go instead of Mommy. Mommy would come back."

Her body shivered. "But what if it was a trick? What if *both* of you went away?"

"That's not going to happen. Don't worry about that. I promise you that will never happen."

She nearly crawled inside him. She pressed as much of her body against his as was physically possible. This close, he could practically see her thoughts. He could definitely feel her fears, and it made him regret having said he might go away under any circumstances. All he could do was hang on tight and reassure her. They remained that way for almost two hours, till Morgan finally fell asleep.

After putting her down, Gus didn't even try falling back to sleep. He needed something to occupy his mind. Predawn television didn't cut it. The newspaper had yet to be delivered. His eyes drifted toward the framed photographs on the dresser. There were at least a dozen of them. The frames were old, some of them from the days when he and Beth were just living together. Over time, however, the pictures had changed. It was an interesting progression, he thought. It used to be him and Beth. The two of them snow skiing. The two of them at Haystack Rock. Then came the engagement and wedding pictures. The baby pictures followed. Morgan in her bassinet. Morgan and Mommy. He scanned the entire dresser.

There wasn't a single picture of him and Morgan.

Curious, he went to the closet and dragged down the old shoe boxes that held all their photographs. Over the next several hours, he went through them slowly, box by box, oldest to newest. The old ones were familiar and brought back memories. The new ones, however, were truly new to him. He hadn't been the photographer for any of them. He wasn't *in* any of them. He hadn't even seen most of them before.

He returned to the older ones, back to a time when he was still part of the family. His favorite was one he had taken of Morgan in her crib when she was just eight months old, before things really started to tank between him and Beth. A ray of sunlight streamed through slats on the Bermuda shutters. It angled perfectly toward her crib, shooting like a laser beam. Morgan stared at it intently, reaching for it, trying to grasp it in her tiny fingers. Gus snapped a perfect shot that captured the moment exactly. Friends and family who saw it had the same reaction. "Just like her dad. Mad because she can't have everything."

Looking at it now, Gus saw it differently. There was no anger or frustration in baby Morgan's eyes. It was simple fascination. The look of determination was so strong that if you stared at the photo long enough, you couldn't help but put aside your own grown-up notion of the laws of physics. You'd swear she could reach out and grab it, even bend it and twist it as she wished. She had the innate gift of making the impossible seem possible, but that didn't make her a hopeless overachiever like her dad. As the years had made clear, she also had the wisdom to leave certain things be and enjoy them for what they were.

That made her more like her mother—the Beth he remembered.

"Daddy?" He looked up, startled. Morgan was standing in the doorway, still in her pajamas. "Are you going to take me to school?"

He checked the clock and groaned. It was already after nine. "Oh, boy. We're late." He quickly started stuffing photographs back into the boxes. In his haste he spilled a bulging stack all over the rug. Morgan came to help gather them up. She handed him one after the other. It was slower that way, but Gus liked the teamwork.

"Thank you," he said as she handed him the last one.

"Should I get ready for school?"

He was about to say yes, then reconsidered. She probably hadn't noticed that her father wasn't in a single one of the dozen photographs she'd just handed over, but he certainly had. He had planned to take another run at Shirley Borge, but she probably could use another day to cool off anyway. "Morgan, why don't you and I take the day off?"

"And do what?"

"Anything you want. Go ice skating. Go to the zoo. Anything at all."

Her eyes brightened. "You mean we're going to play hooky together?"

"Yeah," he said with a thin smile. "I think it's about time."

It took just minutes to fill his duffel bag with the basic necessities, though everything was folded and arranged with precision. One change of pants, two clean shirts. Extra thermal socks and underwear. Three long-sleeve cotton turtlenecks and a heavy wool sweater. A toothbrush and toothpaste. A straight-edge razor with just a bar of soap, no shaving cream. A Swiss Army knife, flammable steel wool, and some waterproof matches.

His weekend in the mountains would require little more. The retreat was just one day away. Already, he could feel the increased flow of energy, feel the change in his level of vibration. Energy was power. Power was his sustenance—his power over others.

The window shade was drawn and the room was dark, though not completely black. A four-watt bulb in the bathroom cast a faint glow that reached all the way to the bed. He could see only because his pupils had adjusted, and he could see quite well. The pattern on the bedspread. The curves beneath the covers. Her head resting on the pillow.

He took a silent step forward, then another, till he was at

the edge of the bed and standing directly over her. She was sound asleep. No surprise. After what she'd been through this past week, she couldn't possibly know night from day.

That was power.

He laid his packed duffel bag on the chair, then rested a black leather bag atop the dresser and zipped it open. Inside was a pair of rubber gloves. A three-foot stick. A length of rope. A longer stretch of the same yellow nylon rope. And a knife.

This too was power. But it was the easy way.

This time there could be no props or tools, no worldly instruments of any kind. He would have to summon deeper powers. He was certain he could do it. He had that gift, he knew. All he had to do was *will* it. And it would be so.

He drew a deep cleansing breath, closed his eyes, and focused. Slowly, he exhaled. His lungs emptied, but he continued to exhale. His body called for air, but the mind said no. The lungs began to burn, but he refused to draw a breath. He struggled with the pain until it became a numbness. Dizziness set in. He felt rocky on his feet. Just at the point it seemed unbearable, the blackness became a vision. He could suddenly see the tightness in the rope, the pressure around the neck. He could feel the woman's body twitching, hear the pounding of her heart. He drew on all his powers of concentration, his powers of vibration— every ounce of mental strength and energy. Beads of sweat gathered on his brow. His face showed signs of strain. His grip tightened on the dresser's edge. He grimaced one last time and fell to his knees, barely conscious.

He groaned, gasping for air. He gobbled it up in quick, erratic breaths. After a few moments, he regained control. He took another deep cleansing breath and smiled to himself, his eyes still closed. It was the thin smile of the victor. His success was palpable, as real as ever before. The deed was as good as done. Such was his power over others.

The power of the source.

Forty-eight

Andie was reasonably patient, but by mid-Thursday afternoon she could wait no longer. More than twenty-four hours had passed since Isaac's announcement that he wanted to think about the undercover assignment. She wasn't about to let him think it to death. The FBI was like every place else in that respect: too many decisions were made by not making a decision.

"Got a minute?" she said, standing in the open doorway.

He didn't look surprised to see her, but he didn't look thrilled either. He waved her in and signaled to close the door. She did, then sat in the armchair facing his desk. He leaned back in his leather chair and said, "You want my decision, I take it."

"Not to be pushy, but Blechman's retreat is tomorrow."

"I can think of plenty of reasons to let you go. You're the logical choice, since you've already got your foot in the door. For my money you're the most talented young agent in the office. And to be perfectly frank, I don't have a slew of agents willing to put their lives on hold and infiltrate a cult. Which makes me wonder. Why do you want to do this?"

"Because I honestly believe it will lead us to Beth Wheatley."

He leaned forward, elbows on the desk. "No, I mean why do you *really* want to do this?"

"You mean, do I think it will be a professional challenge? Good for my career? Better than another weekend of rented movies and microwave popcorn?"

"I'm being serious. This is a dangerous assignment. I don't want someone going into it for the wrong reason."

"What would be the wrong reason?"

"Oh, I don't know. But hypothetically, let's say someone was still feeling a little hurt or embarrassed about a wedding that literally turned into a brawl at the altar. Maybe she'd jump at an undercover assignment as a convenient escape."

She was momentarily speechless. "That has nothing to do with this."

"Don't be mad. I just want to be sure you're going into this with a clear head. That's my professional responsibility."

"I know it wasn't that long ago. But emotionally Rick is so far behind me it isn't funny."

"Are you sure?"

"Are you sure your interest is purely professional?" She wasn't being accusatory. Just giving him another opening.

Isaac softened his expression but remained all business. "This weekend retreat is probably the kind of place where new recruits are expected to talk about themselves. If I approve the assignment, you understand you'll need a lot more than phony IDs. You'll have to create a whole family history."

"That's easy. I'm adopted, remember? No one has given more thought to another life than an adopted child. Don't think I'm crazy, but I have plenty of imaginary parents to choose from."

"Cults tend to prey on the emotionally wounded. You'd have to invent something on the dysfunctional side."

"No problem. Going to Yakima has already triggered some thoughts along those lines."

"How do you mean?"

She was thinking of the drunken prostitute at the hotel, but she saw no point in sharing her fears about the mother she'd never known. "It's nothing, really. Just believe me, I can construct a phony family so dysfunctional they'll name me cult recruit of the month."

"You wouldn't want to overdo it. One of the biggest problems for an undercover agent is remembering the story she tells. It's a good idea to stick to the truth as much as possible, at least on things that don't matter. Like, do you have any brothers or sisters? Did you take dance lessons as a girl? What does your father do for a living?"

"Am I a half-breed who was adopted and raised by middle-class white parents?"

"Now that you mention it, that is a rather plausible background for someone who might have issues later in life. Someone who might eventually be drawn to a cult." He saw the expression on her face, then backpedaled. "I didn't mean you—"

"It's okay."

"I don't want you to think you have to embrace any particular back story just to earn my approval. If I were doing this assignment, I'd obviously have to go as a black man. But you look white, you were raised white, you can *be* white. Or you can be Indian. Or you can be mixed. You have that unique luxury."

"It's no luxury," said Andie.

"Bad choice of words, sorry."

Very bad. She could have told him how in college she'd gone to a powwow on the U.W. campus and was shunned as just another horny white chick on the prowl for a brown Indian warrior. How the scholarship committee had rejected her claim of Native American status because she had no idea what tribe her mother belonged to. How as a girl she'd kept an Ai-Ya-To-Mat, a hemp string diary that marked the most important days of her life with knots and colored beads, only to have her mother take it away and

burn it out of fear that it was linked to some kind of devil
worship.

"Isaac, are you giving me this assignment or not?"

"Yes. I am."

"Thank you." She was startled but pleased.

"You're welcome. But you should probably thank Victoria more than me."

"Victoria?"

"I had a talk with her about an hour ago, just to see what she thought about you taking the assignment. She's been down in the dumps lately, which accounts for her lackluster performance on this case. I think she sees some of her old self in you. You play your cards right, you might just find yourself a mentor."

"She'd want to mentor *me*?"

"She's already looking out for you. Doesn't want to see you passed over as a young and inexperienced female for risky assignments like this one, never getting the chance to build the kind of record you need to make it all the way to the top."

Andie knew about Victoria's failed bid for chief of the Child Abduction and Serial Killer Unit, knew that no woman had ever been chief of a profiling unit at Quantico. "Funny, my toughest critics have always been women. It's nice to have one on my side. Thanks for passing that along."

"You're welcome. And again, I apologize for my stupid comments about cults and your mixed heritage. I was out of line."

"Forget it. It's just complicated when you're adopted. You wonder about different things, like brothers or sisters who might have been raised elsewhere. Maybe their lives were more difficult than mine, but maybe they also understand who they are better than I do. Does that make any sense?"

"Sure."

They sat in silence, as if there had been enough said about that. Andie checked her watch. "If it's a go, then I'd better pay the tech guys a visit."

"Definitely."

She rose and started for the door.

"Oh, Andie?" he called.

She stopped and turned. Isaac shook his head, half smiling and half scowling. "Damn it, Kira. You flunked your first test."

"That will never happen again, sir." She smiled and gave a mock salute as she left the office. *At least I hope not*, she told herself, her smile fading to concern.

It was a foggy Friday morning on Puget Sound. The sun wouldn't rise for more than an hour, so the thick gray shroud hovering over the Washington Corrections Center for Women hadn't even begun to burn off. In the pre-dawn silence, the bare cement floors and cinder-block walls were at their coldest.

Most inmates were asleep in their cells. Several dozen, however, spent the night in the large common sleeping area, a temporary arrangement to alleviate overcrowding in the minimum-security unit. Row after row of metal beds stood draped in white sheets and blue blankets. The unlucky women near the security lights lay with pillows over their eyes to block out the perpetual glow. Those bunked beside the snorers had their ears stuffed with wadded toilet paper.

At five A.M. a corrections officer passed through for a head count. He walked at such a slow and steady pace that the rhythmic clicking of his heels was like the ticking of a giant clock. He passed each row, disturbing no one. Most slept right through the inspection. The few who were awakened quickly rolled over and went back to sleep. His pace slowed even more as he reached the back row. It was darker there, farther from the security lights and harder to see. The head count continued without pause till he reached the ninth bunk. It looked lumpy but strange. He switched on his flashlight. The bed was empty. By itself that wasn't cause for panic. It wouldn't have been the first time an inmate had stolen away to the bathroom or crawled in bed with her lover. But then he noticed something else. He pulled back the blanket. The bed sheet was gone.

That did alarm him.

He grabbed his walkie-talkie and alerted the command center in a voice filled with urgency. "Security breach in unit one! Lights on!"

The pulsating alarm sounded as the emergency lights switched on to full intensity. Dozens of drowsy inmates grumbled and rolled out of bed. A team of correctional officers raced down a secured corridor to the sleeping area. As the electronic doors slid open, they broke into pairs and dispersed throughout the unit in systematic fashion.

"Line up!" they shouted. The inmates stood at some semblance of attention as the guards checked off each one and searched under the bunks. They found only one per bunk; no one was caught sharing. That meant one inmate was still missing.

Three guards rushed into the bathroom. Their footsteps echoed off the bright white walls. "Anyone in here?" shouted the senior guard.

A quick visual inspection revealed no one at the long row of sinks or toilets. They entered the large community shower room and froze.

The missing bed sheet was taut and twisted like a rope, tied to a water pipe overhead. A woman was hanging by the neck, her toes dangling just six inches above the shower drain. She was completely naked, her clothes balled up and stashed in the corner.

"Get her down!"

The biggest guard supported the limp body as the others unfastened the makeshift noose around her neck. They laid her on the floor and checked the pulse. There was none. In desperation one of the guards started CPR, but the other stopped him. The body was too cold. She was clearly beyond resuscitation.

The senior guard stepped away and shook his head, angry and distraught. "Damn it, Shirley. What in the hell made you go and do that?"

Part Five

The bus left Yakima at ten A.M. It was an old yellow school bus that had been painted a dull blue. The windshield had a long, elaborate crack in it that resembled the Big Dipper. The rubber flooring had worn away to bare metal in the most heavily trafficked spots. Years of juvenile graffiti covered the seat backs. JOEY + DONNA. DONNA STUFFS. JOEY IS A HOMO.

Andie recognized two men and three women from Tuesday night's gathering. She counted six other women and five men, including the driver. Based on the familiarity they demonstrated toward one another, she presumed these eleven were already members. Felicia and Tom, the two who had spoken to the group on Wednesday, were in charge. They had made sure everyone was accounted for, that their baggage was stored properly, and that each recruit had taken the appropriate seat on the bus. Seats were assigned. There did seem to be a plan and structure.

As they headed out of town, Felicia stood at the front of the bus and addressed the group over the rumble of the noisy old motor. "Now that we're finally underway, I want to officially welcome each one of you and thank you for coming. Retreats are a time for newcomers to find out what we're all about and for existing members to revitalize their energy. For some of you, this could be the most important weekend of your life. Don't be frustrated if you don't immediately feel changes in your flow of energy or your level of vibration. Look at this weekend as a first step, not the complete journey.

"The bus ride should take about three hours. We've tried to mix the bus evenly with experienced members and newcomers. So please take the time to meet your neighbors. Talk if you like. Or just look out the window and relax. Any questions?"

The group was silent. Finally, an old man raised his hand, the guy Blechman had teased at Tuesday's meeting. His wife wasn't with him. "Exactly where are we going?"

That was something Andie, too, had been wondering. Their precise destination had never been disclosed.

"The source." Felicia paused, as if to emphasize that nothing more needed to be said, then smiled smugly and returned to her seat.

For the first ninety minutes of the bus ride, Andie made small talk with the man behind her and two women across the aisle. None of them struck her as particularly loony. The women were young, practically girls. They had worked a variety of odd jobs, not sure of what to do with their lives. The man was a musician who played nightclubs in second-rate hotels. Andie talked only of her recent experience at the Second Chance clothing store, which was as far back in Kira's employment history as she needed to go. It wasn't long before Andie realized that undercover work was a lot like dating. To be successful, all you had to do was act interested and get the other guy talking about his favorite subject—himself.

Throughout the ride Felicia had been making her way from the front to the back, stopping to visit individually with each newcomer for ten or fifteen minutes. Andie was about two-thirds of the way back. Felicia reached her at the two-hour mark, right on schedule.

"Can I join you for a minute, Kira?"

"Sure."

Felicia took the seat on the aisle but said nothing. Andie surmised it was her job to ask the questions.

"So, how often do you have these retreats?"

"About once a month. Sometimes twice a month in the summer."

More often than Andie would have guessed. The fact that they were having a retreat the same week she had gone to work at the used-clothing store wasn't quite the lucky coincidence she had thought it was.

"Is this a good turnout?"

"Pretty decent, yeah."

A million questions swirled in Andie's head, but she didn't want to come across as overly inquisitive, too much like a cop. After a minute of silence, Felicia asked, "Anything special you'd like to know, Kira?

Where the hell is Beth Wheatley? she thought. "Nothing specific that comes to mind. I'm just taking your advice. You know, taking things one step at a time."

"That's really the only way. One step at a time."

"Just out of curiosity, how many steps are there?"

Felicia smiled, as though the question were naive. "That depends on the individual."

"I hope you don't mind me asking, but how many steps have you taken?"

"One of your goals is to figure that out for yourself. By the end of this weekend you should be able to interpret the energy given off by others and determine their level of vibration."

"Does that mean you know my level of vibration?"

"Yours is the most basic level, Kira. Very human. But don't be discouraged. We all started at the beginning. Even Steve Blechman."

"He'll be here this weekend, right? When I asked at the orientation meeting, you said Steve was coming."

"He's coming."

"Why isn't he here on the bus?"

"He just has to be very careful on retreats."

"What do you mean?

"He has to limit the time he spends with us."

"We'll all get to meet him, right?"

Felicia hedged. "I'm afraid you won't. None of the new-comers will."

"Why not?"

"He'll be spending his time with the more experienced members."

"He can't even take the time to say hello to us?"

"It's not that simple. Before you go one-on-one with Steve, you have to be prepared. Without the proper prepa-ration, newcomers tend to feed too strongly off his energy. They become leeches. That sort of overindulgence is not what this is all about. You must know exactly how much to take. And you must take no more."

"How do I begin my preparation?"

Felicia seemed pleased that she had asked, as if her ea-gerness were a good thing. "You will begin tonight."

"I can't wait," she replied, and she truly meant it.

News of Shirley's death had left Gus numb. Friday was the day he had planned another visit to follow up on her lawyer's insights about the conspiracy to commit murder. Whether she was in a gang or not wasn't all that crucial. He simply wanted the names of her co-conspirators. He wanted to find out if they, like Shirley, had known Beth. Perhaps they even knew what had happened to her. Shirley and her unnamed co-conspirators had seemed like his best lead. Until this morning.

Throughout the morning Gus repeatedly phoned Andie and left messages, but she didn't return any of them. He did finally get a call back from Agent Haveres, who said he had taken over Agent Henning's responsibilities on the Wheatley case. That didn't sit well with Gus. Something

was amiss, and he wasn't getting any answers by telephone. At lunchtime, he headed to the FBI building downtown and demanded to speak to Andie's supervisor.

Lundquist kept him waiting in the lobby for almost an
hour. Finally, when it was clear Gus wasn't going to give
up and go home, a receptionist brought him back to the supervisor's corner office. The introductions were brief, the
small talk nonexistent. Gus got directly to the point.

"Where is Agent Henning, and why won't she return my
calls?"

The bluntness startled Lundquist. "She's been reassigned."

"To where, Siberia?"

"To a case and location that is confidential. Just as Agent
Haveres told you this morning."

"He didn't tell me squat. All he said was that he's taken
over Andie's cases."

"That's really all you need to know, isn't it?"

"What I need to know is why the sudden change in the
way the FBI treats me? At the beginning I felt totally informed. Ever since my wife called from that pay phone in
Oregon, it's as if somebody has cut the phone lines."

"There's a balance we have to strike, Mr. Wheatley. On
the one hand, the FBI wants to keep the victim's family up
to date. On the other, we can't jeopardize the investigation
with leaks."

"I'm part of the investigation. If I'm in the dark, we
can't help each other."

"That's why I encourage you to pass along any information you have, no matter how trivial you think it might be."

"And all I expect in return is for the FBI to answer a few
questions for me."

"I'll do my best."

"Does Agent Henning's sudden disappearance have anything to do with the fact that Shirley Borge was found dead
this morning?"

"I can't answer that."

"That's what this is all about, isn't it? You all think Shirley was part of some group that has something to do with Beth's disappearance."

His insight surprised Lundquist. "I'm afraid that's not on the table for discussion."

"Andie is working undercover, isn't she?"

"I can't talk about that."

"Would you rather have me speculating about it? In public?"

Lundquist shot a nasty look. "It's not in the best interest of your wife or Agent Henning for you to go shooting your mouth off about a cult."

"A cult? I thought it was a gang."

"Why would you think there's a gang involved?"

He was about to mention Kirby Toombs but dropped it. "I don't anymore. So stop playing word games and tell me what makes the FBI think this is cult activity."

"Many things, most of which I'm not at liberty to delineate. Suffice it to say that certain evidence suggests to our experts that we could be dealing with some kind of group agenda that is effectuated through homicide."

"What do you mean, like the Manson family?"

Lundquist did not respond, but he didn't have to. Gus said, "My God. Let's hope you're wrong."

"Mr. Wheatley, I don't want you to spend a lot of time worrying whether there's a cult involved in these killings. For you, the question boils down to something far more personal. Something that should perhaps help you understand why the flow of information between you and the FBI hasn't been quite what it used to be."

"I don't understand."

"You need to ask yourself the same question we're asking. Is your wife a victim? Or is she an accomplice?"

"Excuse me?"

"You heard me."

With that, the proverbial line in the sand had been drawn at his feet. Gus was suddenly glad he hadn't mentioned his talk with Kirby Toombs. If his wife was some kind of suspect, he had to be very careful about the things he told the FBI. He needed to leave before saying something he'd regret.

"Thank you for your candor," said Gus, rising.

"You're welcome."

Gus started for the door but stopped. "Let me say just one thing to you and the whole damn FBI. If you think for one second that my wife had anything to do with these murders, you're out of your mind."

"We'll see," he said coolly.

Gus glared across the office till the agent blinked. He closed the door on his way out, nearly slamming it in his wake.

Fifty

They were somewhere in north-central Washington, exactly where Andie didn't know. They had traveled the last half hour without so much as a road sign. Although the trip had taken three hours, she sensed they were nowhere near a full three hours from Yakima. The journey had been circuitous. Had she wanted to turn back and go home, it would have been impossible. If she had wanted to retrace her journey three weeks hence, that, too, would have been impossible. To that extent, the meandering had a certain paranoid logic to it.

It was more in the hills than the mountains. Nine rustic cabins with stone chimneys overlooked an ice-cold river that snaked between bumps on the terrain. With the first day of spring less than two weeks away, clusters of blue and yellow wildflowers were starting to push through the earth's brown winter crust. The ground had that spongy, thawing quality that sucked boots right off your feet. By nightfall the hilltops would freeze over. Plenty of snow still covered the mountains in the not too distant background. The bus would never have made it through the back roads above the snow line. Surely, Blechman had been aware of that when he'd promised a retreat "in the mountains." A little white lie to make sure those who stayed behind were left with misinformation as to the actual destination.

Andie was assigned to a cabin with three other women, all newcomers. Two of them were the young women Andie had spoken to on the bus. The other was a fifty-something widow named Ingrid. Andie checked for a bathroom, but there was none. The only source of water was a hand pump in the kitchen. A single outhouse for nine cabins was in the woods near the river, mercifully downwind. The cabin had no phone or electricity either. Three small windows and a candle on the mantel provided the only light. The fireplace evidently worked, still holding the charred remains of someone else's fire. The beds were merely canvas cots, no mattress. They were preassigned, avoiding any arguments over sleeping arrangements.

Everything they would need for the weekend had been laid atop their bunks and was waiting for them upon arrival. A blanket. A bar of soap, toothbrush, and toothpaste. A pair of boots and set of clothes, neatly folded. They weren't new clothes, but they were clean and in good condition. They looked like the stuff Andie had been selling at the Second Chance. Some of it undoubtedly had come from there.

"Everything okay?" asked Felicia as she entered the cabin.

"Fine," they answered in unison.

"Thanks for the extra clothes," added Andie.

Felicia said, "They're not extras. They're replacements."

Ingrid, the older woman, inspected her replacement sweater, probing a hole the size of a golf ball with her finger. "I kind of prefer what I brought."

Felicia ignored her and handed each of them a paper shopping bag. "Change into your new clothes and stuff everything you brought with you into the bag. The welcome dinner is outside in thirty minutes. Bring the bag with you." She left without another word, closing the door behind her.

The two younger women immediately started changing

clothes, no questions asked. Andie and the older woman exchanged glances.

"Well, I'm not putting on this ratty old stuff," said Ingrid.

She was clearly looking to Andie for some show of solidarity. Andie looked away, then started peeling off her clothes and stuffing them into the bag.

Gus's anger only swelled as the day went on. He suppressed it long enough to pick Morgan up from school, but by the time Carla came by to fix dinner he needed to vent.

"I'm beyond mad," he said from his seat at the kitchen table. "I'd like to kick his ass."

Carla stirred the sautéed vegetables. "Geez, why didn't you think of that earlier? That will solve everything."

"Fine. Be sarcastic. But when Beth disappeared, the police thought I was a wife beater who killed my wife and dumped the body. Now that they've moved beyond that theory, they think Beth is a cult member and accomplice to serial murders. I don't know why they keep treating us like criminals."

"They're just being thorough, I guess. Exploring every possibility."

"Do you honestly think Beth could have been mixed up with a cult?"

"No more than I think you're a wife beater."

"Meaning what?"

"Nothing."

"I'm tired of the little digs, Carla. I'm sorry your old boyfriend used to hit you, and I feel sorry for you for having lived through it. But I'm not him, and I was never like him."

"This is not about him."

"Why do you protect the man who beat you?"

"I don't protect him!"

"Yes, you do. I don't know how to explain it, but I get

this feeling that all the things you wish you had said to him, you say to me. You're misdirecting your anger. Damn, sometimes I would swear you still love the guy."

She glared and said, "Don't presume to psychoanalyze me."

"I was just—"

"Just doing what you do best. Blaming people for their own misfortune so you don't have to help them."

"What are you talking about?"

"There are a lot of brothers who look out for their sisters. Who aren't so wrapped up in themselves. Who wouldn't have been so quick to believe that all those black eyes and bruises came from falling off a horse."

He wasn't sure that was fair. But if laying the guilt on him was a way of putting her own past behind her, so be it. "I'm sorry."

"Just forget it."

"No, you have a point. Based on no evidence at all, I haul off and suggest my sister still loves the guy who beat her. Yet in the same breath I'm outraged at the cops for twisting the evidence about my wife."

"I wouldn't worry about Beth being accused. That's just one of many theories, I'm sure."

"But once the cops get it in their heads that maybe she's a willing participant in some cult murders, the danger is they'll start looking for evidence to support their theory. If they don't see what they want to see, they'll cross their eyes, squint, stand on their heads—they'll look at it every way imaginable until they see it in a light that supports their theory."

Carla lowered the burner to simmer and covered the sauce pan. "Well, for Beth's sake, I hope you're wrong about that."

"I'm not wrong. And the real shame is that I'd love to tell them all the things Shirley's lawyer told me."

"What kind of things?"

"That the real target of the conspiracy to commit murder wasn't a homeless person but her own mother. That her unnamed accomplices were possibly gang members. The gang theory sounds even more interesting now that the FBI is talking about a cult. But if I mention it now, you know what will happen?"

"What?"

"Think about it. If I give them inside information about Shirley's conspiracy to commit murder, they'll probably think Beth was one of Shirley's unnamed accomplices."

Carla shot a look across the kitchen, then returned to cooking. It was a brief exchange, but Gus seemed to know what she was thinking.

"I have to do this, don't I, Carla?"

"Do what?"

"If I'm going to debunk the FBI's suspicions about Beth, the first thing I have to do is prove she wasn't part of Shirley's little group."

"I didn't say you had to do anything."

"You didn't have to."

It was the darkness of a new moon. Miles away from the glow of city lights, just an hour past sunset seemed like the dead of night. With each passing moment, another cluster of stars seemed to emerge in the ocean of blackness overhead.

Andie, Ingrid, and their two younger roommates walked together from their cabin to the camp area near the river. As instructed, they had their paper shopping bags with them, filled with their belongings. It was a large campfire with flames that reached eye level. The group was seated around it, just close enough to bask in its glow and feel its warmth. They eagerly expanded the circle to make room for the newcomers.

Andie didn't see Blechman among the group. The meal had begun without him. No one was talking. The group was taking its cue from Felicia and the other "lieutenants," as Andie had labeled them. As long as the honchos ate in silence, so would everyone else.

Several baskets of food were passed around. Andie watched and imitated Felicia. The drill was to take something from each basket as it passed, place it on a big cloth napkin on the ground before you, and eat at your own pace. Andie took one of everything, leaving her with an assortment of delicacies. She first ate the smoked salmon, which was more like a jerky than the delicacy served in restaurants. The dried berries were tasty, left over from last summer. The meat—some kind of stringy and pungent game—she left for last. She tried something that resembled a cookie, somewhat sweet but very dry.

"It's a camas-root cake," said Felicia, breaking the silence. She had been watching Andie pick over her food.

"It's good," said Andie.

"Camas root is the bulb of lilies indigenous to this area. It has been a natural source of nourishment for peoples of the land for thousands of years."

"How do you make them?"

"The roots are dug from the ground and baked in an oven over well-heated stones. Then you pound them till the mass is as fine as cornmeal, knead them into cakes, and dry them in the sun."

"Sounds like a lot of work."

"You'll have help."

Andie realized she'd just been volunteered. Felicia asked, "Who wants to help Kira make the camas cakes for tomorrow's meal?"

Andie's eager young roommates thrust their hands into the air.

"Very good," said Felicia. "Ingrid, how about you? Care to make it a project for your whole cabin?"

The older woman hedged. "Oh, I'm not much of a cook, I'm afraid."

"Then you can gather the roots," she said reprovingly.

Ingrid nodded nervously. "Whatever you say."

Andie leaned toward her and said quietly, "It's okay if you don't want to."

The older woman smiled awkwardly and whispered, "She seemed a lot nicer at the sign-up."

They ate in silence for several minutes more. When the last among them had finished, the baskets were passed around again to gather the leftovers. A young woman collected the baskets and took them away. At Felicia's direction, a man stoked the fire and added a few more logs. Finally, Felicia rose to address the group.

"We have six newcomers with us tonight, and the principal purpose of tonight's banquet is to welcome all of you. We don't have a secret handshake or password or anything like that. None of us is big on ceremonies and rituals. But there is one tradition that has developed over time. This is something we have done on the first night of every retreat for as long as I can remember. It does have a certain symbolic significance. But more important, it will put each of you in the proper frame of mind to get the most out of this retreat.

"At this time, I would ask each of the newcomers to please stand."

Andie and the others rose. Ingrid was at her side. Her other two roommates were down to her right. Two men were standing on the opposite side of the fire.

Felicia continued, "Each of you heard Steve Blechman's speech earlier this week. Obviously, it touched you in some way, or you wouldn't be here tonight. But none of us is here simply to be moved or inspired. We're here to be transformed. If you listened to Steve carefully, you understand that to be transformed, you must rid yourself of the worldly things that bind you.

"When you arrived this afternoon, each of you was given everything you will need for the weekend. You placed everything you had brought with you in a paper bag. Did you bring those bags with you?"

One of the men answered, "Yes." The others just nodded.

"Ingrid?" said Felicia.

The older woman started.

"Place your bag in the fire."

Ingrid clutched it like the payroll. "You want me to burn my things?"

"Yes."

Her eyes darted nervously. She was suddenly digging into her bag. "Well, okay I guess, but let me get my wallet—"

"Burn it," she said firmly. "Burn *everything* you brought with you."

"But I have credit cards and photographs—"

"Burn them."

She froze. All eyes were upon her. "I don't want to be difficult, but—"

"Ingrid. Throw the bag in fire."

"At least let me keep the pictures of my husband."

"You mustn't cling to the things of this world."

"They're my memories. They're all I have."

"They're all you'll *ever* have. Be seated."

Ingrid was shaking, seeming to shrink as she returned to her seat. Andie wanted to go to her and tell her not to be intimidated, that she'd done the right thing. But now wasn't the time.

"Kira?" said Felicia.

Andie looked alert.

"Will you take the first step?"

Andie could feel the gaze of the group turn toward her. She hated to make Ingrid feel even more like an outcast, but she knew what she had to do. She took her bag, stepped forward, and pitched it into the fire. The flames shot higher as they consumed all of Kira's belongings. The group seemed transfixed by the ceremonial burning. Andie stepped back, her task complete.

"Wait," said Felicia.

Andie halted and looked up inquisitively.

Felicia said, "The ring."

"What?"

"The ring on your finger. You brought that with you, didn't you?"

"Yes, but—"

"It has to go."

Andie hesitated. The struggle wasn't staged.

"Kira, it must go. Feed the fire."

With some obvious reluctance she pulled the ring from her finger, held it for a moment, and then tossed it into the flames.

Felicia smiled. She clapped her hands, and the entire group promptly applauded her. One by one, each of them rose from their place in the circle and stepped forward to embrace her. Warm, full embraces, each one taking a full ten seconds or more. They said nothing, but their actions said it all. Nothing she had ever done in her life had earned her such immediate acceptance and approval.

When the last had embraced her, she faced Felicia. She smiled with her eyes, but she did not rise to embrace her. The clear implication was that a newcomer had to travel much further to gain the praise of the inner circle.

"Welcome, Kira," she said simply.

Andie gave a quick nod and returned to her seat. She listened as Felicia called out the name of the next newcomer, but she was so fixated on the fire that their voices faded behind the hissing and crackling of logs. She stared at the dancing yellow flames, searching helplessly for the ring. It wasn't just any piece of jewelry. It was a very special ring. Hidden inside it was the tiny electronic tracking transmitter that Isaac Underwood had insisted she carry for her own safety. And now it was incinerated.

Kira had won acceptance. But Andie was truly on her own.

Fifty-one

Gus called his investigator at home early Saturday morning. Dex was on his way out the kitchen door, fishing pole in hand. It was his first weekend off in months, and he had planned to make the most of it. Gus had other ideas.

"I need you to find Shirley Borge's mother for me."

Naturally, he wanted to know why, and Gus explained in less than a minute.

Dex said, "As I recall from Shirley's polygraph results, she didn't even know if her mother was still alive."

"That's true. But if she is, I want to talk to her."

"Is the FBI looking for her?"

"They don't even know she was the real target of Shirley's conspiracy to commit murder. That was something Shirley's lawyer told me. If I shared any of that with the FBI, they'd have Beth tagged as one of her unnamed co-conspirators."

"You think your wife could have been?"

"No," he said harshly.

Dex was silent, as if giving his client time to think about it.

"No way," said Gus, this time a little less firmly.

"It's all right. This isn't the first time someone has hired me to find out if a spouse is really involved in a crime rather than sharing their information with the police."

"That's not what I'm doing."

"You may not realize it. But that *is* what you're doing."

"You're starting to make me mad."

"Don't be mad at me. Don't be mad at the FBI either. With that phone call from Beth, her shoplifting and her clothes found in a thrift shop where Agent Henning is working undercover, it seems plausible that a cult or a gang could have played a role in these murders. And that Beth might be . . . involved."

"Beth couldn't hurt anyone."

"She could have played a more passive role. She is an attractive woman."

"What does that have to do with anything?"

"I'm just talking hypothetically here. Remember, the serial killer's first two victims were men killed in their homes. No sign of forced entry at the second one. Sending an attractive woman to the door is a good way to catch a man off guard, get inside. I've used that ruse myself. Hired myself an attractive cocktail waitress who pretends her car broke down, knocks on some guy's door, and asks to borrow the phone. Once inside, she plants a bug for me."

"You're saying Beth is the one who opened the door for a serial killer?"

"All I'm saying is that she doesn't have to strangle someone with her own hands to be involved in these killings."

"Yet another possibility," said Gus. "Someone wants the police to *think* she is an accomplice. He is planting evidence of Beth's involvement, like that phone call to Morgan."

"But why?"

"I don't know. Maybe to throw the cops off the track. Maybe to make the FBI think they should be looking for a cult in Yakima when they should be chasing down Shirley's little gang in Seattle. That's just one more thing I have to find out."

"You want me to tackle that one?"

"I just want you to find Shirley's mother. Can you do that fast?"

"Piece of cake."

"Call me when you do," said Gus.

It was an unusually warm Saturday afternoon for early March. The valley had been in winter's icy grip since Thanksgiving, but over the last week or so temperatures had been steadily rising in anticipation of spring. The humming of lawn mowers could be heard in the nearby town of Selah, the first cut of the year. It was time to store away the snowmobiles till next season, a good day to leave the jacket inside and feel the warmth on your skin.

It was Flora's first day out of the house in more than a week.

There was always plenty of work to do around the farm, and today was no exception. Two hundred newly hatched chicks had been delivered to the coop last week. In six weeks the pullets would be grown and tender and ready for slaughter. This afternoon her job was menial but necessary. In a way, it was even philosophical. They called it culling. Every delivery of chicks included some infirm ones. It wasn't wise to wait for the weak to infect the strong. Every day someone had to walk down to the coop, select the weaklings, and snap their necks. As clichéd as it sounded, it really was all in the wrist. The fuzzy little body fit easily in one hand. A little squirming, a few innocent chirps. With one quick jerk it was all over.

She had hated it at first but had grown accustomed to it. It wasn't so much the killing that bothered her anymore. It was the odor. Nothing smelled worse than a chicken coop.

To her credit, she could at least come and go without holding her nose, a vast improvement over her first visit to the compound more than a year ago. Of course, it wasn't the thought of raising chickens or picking apples that had drawn her there. It was the typical laundry list of personal problems. Trouble at home. An unhappy marriage. A husband who had become a stranger. She'd attended dozens of enlightenment workshops and lectures, none of which had lasted more than a day. Over time she had found herself drawn to a different kind of family, to the group's teachings. Working in the orchards or tending to the farm was therapeutic, though she had never honestly planned on staying.

Now leaving was out of the question.

"Flora?" the man's voice echoed from the farmhouse. He was standing on the back porch nearly a quarter mile away.

She didn't answer. He called again, this time more sternly. "Flora!"

The second time it hit her. He was calling *her*. Despite the drilling, she wasn't used to her new name yet.

Quickly and without a word, she tossed the last of the dead culls into her basket and obediently started toward the house. This was the part she dreaded. She knew the pattern by now. Every time he gave her something, like free time, he laid another burden on her. The burden of guilt.

Her steps grew heavier as she crossed the yard, knowing what to expect when she returned to her room. The photographs. The innocent victims. More mind games to play on her conscience. Those women had been strangers to her at one time. By now, however, she knew their names, their faces, and every detail of their horrible deaths. Most disturbing of all, she knew there would be more. That much was clear from what he'd told her all along. *"Only you have the power to stop it, Flora. It's in your hands."*

With her head down she climbed the back steps and entered the house, feeling anything but power. Feeling like anyone but "Flora."

Andie was exhausted. They had spent the morning digging for camas roots to make cakes. At this higher elevation, the ground was frozen in spots, half-frozen in others, which made it a chore. Still, they had managed to pull out more than the eight bushels with their long, hooked knives. They were quite an efficient tool. Andie couldn't help but wonder how efficient they might be as a weapon.

By late afternoon her knuckles ached from pounding the roots into meal with large stones. She and her roommates had shaped the meal into cakes until it became almost mechanical. By mid-afternoon the cakes were drying in the sun. Felicia came by and gave her approval. Ingrid and Andie's two younger roommates went back to the cabin to clean up. She held Andie back to talk.

"You're a good worker," said Felicia.

"All four of us worked hard."

"Not really. The girls think this is just fun. Ingrid—I'm surprised she lasted all day. But you have the seriousness of purpose that we like."

"Thank you."

She invited Andie to sit on the ground atop a blanket of dried leaves. Facing one another, Felicia asked, "Why are you here?"

"You mean, on this earth, or at this retreat?"

Felicia smiled. "I like the way you think. At this retreat."

Andie sensed she was being quizzed. She wanted to give the right answers. "I'm here to learn more about your group."

"What have you found out so far?"

She checked her battered hands. "That getting back to the source can cause blisters."

"What else?"

Andie turned more serious. "That whatever it takes, it's worth it."

"How do you know that?"

"I have good instincts."

"Congratulations, Kira. You've taken the first step: learning to trust your instincts."

"What's the next step?"

"That is something that will come to you in the normal course. After you have focused your energy."

"How do I focus?"

"Through meditation and reflection."

"What do I reflect on?"

She was staring into Andie's eyes, but it was more of a warm gaze than a cold glare. "Let me tell you something about us. We are not about comets or the passing of the millennium or other such things that have driven the hundreds of ufology groups that have come and gone in recent times. We don't believe that a spaceship is going to come down to earth and take us all to the next level beyond human. By changing our own level of vibration, we strive for a connection with a higher source, which requires an emotional disconnection from the negative energy that keeps us on the wrong life paths."

"Where does that negative energy come from?"

"Frankly, the usual source is the traditional family. A controlling parent, a manipulative spouse. But for each individual it's different. You must analyze and reflect on the sources of negative energy in your own life."

It sounded as though Felicia were fishing for something about Andie's past. She had her phony background memorized, but the more she talked, the higher the risk of eventually being caught in inconsistencies. Andie answered vaguely, "That sounds like a very insightful way of thinking."

"Yes. But I assure you, it is utterly impossible to identify the true source of negative energy in your life if you return to your same old environment."

"That's logical. One has to step back in order to be objective."

"That's exactly the opportunity I'm offering you."

"I don't understand."

"The retreat ends tomorrow morning. Most of the newcomers will return home. They will never evolve beyond their present selves. But you are different, Kira."

"How so?"

"We'd like you stay with us. Come back to the farm and continue your journey."

"What about the others?"

"Don't worry about the others. You have been chosen, not them."

"I don't know what to say."

She squeezed her hand. "Say yes."

Andie hesitated, not wanting to appear overeager. "Okay. I accept."

"Of course you do." Her tone was matter-of-fact, as if yes were the only acceptable answer.

"Thank you, Felicia."

"Don't thank me. Thank Steve."

"I'm not sure I know how."

"You will learn," she said in the same flat tone. "*That* I can promise you."

Fifty-two

The bus returned to Yakima early Sunday morning. Of the six newcomers, Andie and one of the men, the aspiring lounge musician, were the only ones invited back to the farm. The others were dropped at the parking lot where they had left their cars on Friday.

The bus would leave for the farm in fifteen minutes, just a short break to give everyone time to use the bathroom after the three-hour ride back to the city. Andie knew she had to make a phone call before they reached the farm. Her supervisors hadn't authorized an undercover assignment beyond the weekend. She considered just going to the pay phone and calling, but she didn't want the others to get suspicious. She pulled Felicia aside to be up-front with her in an undercover way.

"I have to call my mother," said Andie. "I told her I was going away just for the weekend. If she doesn't hear from me, she'll worry."

"Why call her?"

"Like I said, she'll be worried. Heck, who knows? She might even call the police and report me missing."

"I understand. Whenever we invite a newcomer back to the farm, we encourage them to notify their family of their decision for precisely that reason. But phone calls can be problematic. We prefer that you simply write a letter."

"You don't know my mother," said Andie. "She will never believe this was my decision if she just gets a letter in the mail. She'll want to hear it straight from my own mouth."

Felicia shot a judgmental look, as if to say that Andie's mother was one of those controlling family members with negative energy who needed to be eliminated. "All right. Call her if you must. But be strong. Do not let her talk you out of something that you know is right."

"Thank you." Andie started for the pay phone across the street.

"Kira?" she called, stopping her. "Tell her you won't be calling home again. Tell her that if she hears from you again, it will be by letter."

"I will," she said, then continued toward the phone.

The phone rang at the Underwood residence. Isaac was in the kitchen with his daughter cooking breakfast and watching *Sesame Street*. It was one of his two weekends a month, one of just two dozen annual opportunities to prove that divorced men can do Sunday morning pancakes. He lowered the volume on the TV and took the call while tending to the griddle.

It was Andie, which relieved him. The word from his technical agents—that the transmitter in Andie's ring had been stationary all weekend—had worried him. Andie explained the ceremonial burning and more, glancing every now and then toward the bus to make sure no one could overhear.

Isaac said, "What you're saying blends with the updated profile from Quantico."

"What does Santos think now?"

"She's getting back to the fact that all of the victims display wounds consistent with personal-cause homicides. The killer is acting out of personal anger against the victim. The killings may not be random, as Santos had originally thought. The killer—or killers—may have a very specific agenda. That's especially interesting when you're talking about a cult."

"Which is why I need to stay on this assignment."

"What?"

"I'm sorry not to run this through the usual channels, but the fact is, I have just one phone call, my contact agent doesn't have the authority to extend my assignment, and Lundquist's balls are barely big enough to get him into the men's room. So what do you say?"

"How long?"

"As long as it takes."

The pancakes were burning. Isaac snatched up the griddle and dumped the smoldering mess into the sink. "Andie, as long as there's the threat of a serial killer making another hit, you're going to have to move fast. Normally, I'd say take some time to build contacts. In this case you're going to have to be aggressive, which means you could blow your own cover."

"I understand."

"I don't think you do. Not fully. You know that videotape you bought at Blechman's orientation meeting? I sent it out for analysis by an audio expert. Specifically, a psychological stress evaluator."

"I was under the impression the bureau didn't use PSEs."

"I had a few of them done when I was with Seattle P.D., and I thought it might be right in this circumstance. You're familiar with the test, then?"

"Yeah. It measures variations and tremors in voice patterns that are inaudible to the human ear."

"Right. In fact, the machine actually charts the variations and creates a kind of voice print. Which is what I did with your tape. We had a voice print created for Blechman, and also for Felicia and Tom, the two lieutenants who spoke at the meeting."

"What did you find?"

"Blechman is off by himself, which is normal. He's the leader. It's Tom and Felicia who are interesting. They have almost an identical voice print. The expert could barely tell them apart."

"What does the expert make of that?"

"Two possibilities," said Isaac. "One, these characters are skilled actors who are delivering a very well-rehearsed pitch in a very controlled and identical manner."

"Or . . . ?"

"Or they are programmed exactly alike. I mean *exactly*. Someone has done a real mind-control number on them."

"Someone named Blechman."

"I'm not trying to scare you, Andie. I say this only because . . . well, you know why."

"Do I?"

"I think you do."

She smiled, but it was strained. *Boy, is this not the time.* "I'll watch my back. Don't worry."

"Well, since you don't have eyes in the back of your head, I'm going to set up spot surveillance around the farm. It won't be twenty-four hours, but it's still too expensive to run this forever. I want you to check with me no later than Wednesday. Just somehow get yourself to a phone. If I don't hear from you, I'm pulling the plug."

Isaac sensed her hesitation, as if she were suddenly distracted, perhaps being watched.

"It won't be easy," she said finally. "But I promise I'll stay in touch."

It was one of those mornings that Gus felt like going straight back to bed and staying there. Not the typical lazy Sunday morning with a cup of coffee and the *Post-Intelligencer*. More like Sunday, the two-week anniversary of Beth's disappearance.

Martha Goldstein's timing was a piece of work. A letter hand-delivered to his house on the very day she knew he would be at an emotional low. "Dear Gus," it read. "I know you're busy with other things, but could you please make

time to come into the office this week to assist in the orderly transfer of your files?"

What a manipulator. The message was handwritten on
her personal stationery rather than typed on the firm's let-
terhead, as if that would disguise the fact that it was purely
a "cover your ass" letter designed to put Gus on legal notice that if anything slipped through the cracks while he
was out searching for his wife, his professional neck was
on the line, not hers. *Nice touch, Martha. You forgot to
draw in the smiley face under your signature.*

In the big picture, he knew that the "orderly transfer of
files" was one more step toward his permanent removal as
managing partner and eventual break with Preston &
Coolidge. The same thing had happened five years ago
when he had taken the helm and sent his successor packing. It would be best if he just resigned, less embarrassment for the old manager and fewer hassles for the new.
The thought of dragging things out sickened him, knowing
he'd have to endure the slow parade of partners who would
stop by his office, tell him he'd gotten screwed, tell him
they admired his fight, and then ask for dibs on his office.
The distastefulness of it all had Gus yearning for a clean
break. This was his chance to realize one of his oldest
dreams, something he would never have found the nerve to
try unless forced to do it. Starting his own law firm. Now,
that was a professional dream worth his sweat.

Just as soon as he found Beth.

The phone rang. It was his investigator, Dex. "I found
Shirley's mother."

Gus was suddenly over the law firm. "Dead or alive?"

"Most definitely alive, about an hour's drive from here.
More the sticks than the suburbs. If you want, I can pay her
a visit today, see if she'll talk."

"No," said Gus. "I'll do it myself."

"You sure?"

"Yeah," he said as he hopped out of bed. "I'm sure."

Fifty-three

The farm was on twelve acres that looked like a hundred. It was surrounded by open prairie, and had it not been for the barbed-wire fencing, its boundaries would have been indiscernible. A long and dusty driveway led to a barn large enough to hold the old school bus, a tractor, two cars, and nine horses. Adjacent to it was a white two-story frame house. It was old but freshly painted and well maintained, its original Victorian-style details still intact. On the other side of the barn were a dozen small, boxy-looking units with aluminum siding. They reminded Andie of a minimum-security prison.

The bus pulled straight into the barn. The group filed off and walked toward the smaller living quarters. None went to the main farmhouse.

"Come on," said Felicia. "Let me show you around."

Andie followed her on a brief walking tour. To the east was a five-acre orchard, apples and apricots. The trees had been pruned in hat-rack fashion, but spring buds were emerging. A vegetable garden covered another two acres. Felicia mentioned a variety of spring vegetables, but it was too early to tell what had been planted where. The animals were around back. A chicken coop was all the way against the back fence, its odor well away from the main house. A half dozen horses and cows were munching grass along the

fence line. They kept a healthy distance from the wire.
Andie noted the electrodes. It was electrified.

They continued down past the chickens to a pond and a
stand of trees. Behind the trees Andie noticed a small rectangular building.

"What's that?" she asked.

"We can't go there," said Felicia.

"Why not?"

"We're not ready. It's a special place for meetings and
ceremonies. Only the members who have reached the
highest level can go there."

"Even you can't go there?" asked Andie.

"You think *I'm* the highest level?" she asked, amused.
"Far from it, girl. I have a long way to go."

"How many levels are there?"

"You pass through as many levels as are necessary to
purge yourself of the human irritations, frustrations, and
anxieties that must be overcome to reach beyond the human realm."

"So it's different for each person?"

"Yes, because we all come here with different baggage.
Remember, the ultimate goal is to physically change your
level of vibration so that you can receive the flow of energy
directly from the source. Everyone has different circumstances that keep them vibrating at a human level. Some
people are married. Some have children. Some just live in
the past, thinking about what they used to be like when
they were eighteen or twenty or thirty-five. Your attach-
ment to other people or even to your own past will keep
you from evolving."

"You mean, I have to forget who I was?"

"Absolutely."

Andie took a breath. "That's quite a commitment."

"Yes. And each level you attain brings additional commitments."

"What kind of commitments?"

"You'll see."

"How long does it take?"

"No set time frame. When you're ready to move up, he will know. And he will tell you."

"He?"

"Steven Blechman, of course."

"Oh, of course."

"Come on, Kira. Let me show you to your room."

Felicia led her back to the plain barracks on the far side of the barn. Each of the twelve units looked exactly alike. Felicia took her to the last unit, farthest from the barn. The door had no lock, but it was stuffy inside, as if it hadn't been lived in for some time. Four bunks lined the wall. Clothes and other essentials were laid out on the bed, just as they had been at the cabin on the retreat. There was a bathroom, though it wasn't much bigger than the closet beside it. The thought of sharing this space with three other women didn't thrill Andie.

"It will be just the two of us for a week or so," said Felicia.

"We're living together?"

"Everyone gets a partner when they first arrive. It's my job to help you through."

"Thank you."

"You're welcome." She gestured toward the bathroom. "Maybe you'd like to clean up a little?"

"I'd love a shower."

"There's a towel in the bathroom. Feel free."

The shower stall was small, but Andie didn't care. A hot shower was the closest thing to normal she'd experienced in three days. She ran it until the hot water was gone, which wasn't long. Less than two minutes. It was on a timer to keep her from overindulging.

Andie stepped out and toweled off. She stood and faced what should have been the mirror, that space right above the sink. But there was none.

She stepped out, wrapped in a towel. Felicia was seated on the bed. Laid out atop the towel resting on the bed were a brush, a comb, and scissors.

"Did you know there's no mirror in here?" said Andie.

"We don't have any."

"No mirrors?"

"Come, sit here."

Andie seated herself on the bed. Felicia said, "How you see yourself is not important." She started combing Andie's hair in a way Andie had never combed it, parting it on the wrong side. "What matters is how *he* sees you. We groom each other in the way that pleases him."

Andie froze as her new partner reached for the scissors. She wanted to protest, but she quelled her instincts. She had to submit. Kira would submit.

"Are you saying every woman who comes here has changed her appearance?"

"Every woman and every man."

The thought chilled her. She had looked carefully, but perhaps not carefully enough. It was entirely possible that she had already seen Beth Wheatley and not recognized her. Then again, maybe she was one of those less accessible members at the higher level.

With a snip of the scissors, long strands of wet hair began falling to the floor.

The pea-gravel driveway was empty at the home of Meredith Borge, and no one answered when Gus knocked on the door. He had decided against an advance call for fear that she might not want to see him. He thought it best to catch her cold.

Meredith lived in a rural area at the end of a gravel road, just one of two houses on the entire route. The driveway was rather ill-defined, just two dirt ruts in the ground that cut across the lawn and ended at the front porch. Gus parked near the culvert at the turn-around at the end of the road and waited. Through a thin stand of pine trees he could see the house clearly. An hour passed, and not a single car came or went. The rain started and stopped a dozen times before a twenty-year-old pickup truck finally pulled into the driveway. A woman stepped down and walked up the pathway. She appeared to be in her forties, slim and brunette, right in line with Dex's description. Gus jumped out of his car.

"Mrs. Borge?"

She stopped and turned but did not respond. Her suspicious gaze stopped Gus in his tracks. "Excuse me for bothering you," he said. "But I'd like to talk to you about your daughter."

"I don't have a daughter."

"I know. I'm sorry about her death."

"You are? Why?"

"My name's Gus Wheatley. My wife disappeared two weeks ago today. Your daughter and I were involved in some discussions about her possible whereabouts before she died."

Her stare was ice-cold. "I have nothing to say to you."

"Mrs. Borge, please."

Gus followed her halfway up the front steps, but her glare only intensified. "Get off my property before I call the police."

"It's important that we talk. Please, just a minute of your time."

She unlocked the door. For an instant it seemed she was about to say something, more nervous than hostile.

"Please," said Gus.

"Do us both a favor. Go away." She stepped inside and slammed the door, leaving Gus alone on the front porch.

Andie hadn't eaten since early Saturday afternoon, but there was no breakfast or lunch on the Sunday menu. On the retreat they had kept her up late and woken her early, allowing her little more than seven hours of total sleep since Thursday. Rest, however, was not on Sunday's schedule either.

Felicia was her constant companion. Neither one of them left the unit. They spent hours together sitting on the floor, eyes closed and legs crossed. Felicia taught her several breathing exercises to help her relax and meditate. Every half hour or so she would ask Andie to join her in repeating three times aloud, "I am going to rise above and overcome my human desires and activities and transform my being into something more than physical." They had no other conversation. The goal was to channel Andie's thoughts and energy. Her thoughts were definitely focused, though all Andie could think was, *What in the hell have I gotten myself into?*

By late afternoon, sitting in the same posture had left her legs cramped and her knees on the verge of explosion. She had already passed the hunger stage when Felicia announced it was time to eat. They didn't have to leave the room. Felicia opened the door, and a tray with two camas cakes was waiting on the door step, seemingly on cue. Felicia took one and offered the other to Andie. She ate neither quickly nor slowly, matching Felicia bite for bite.

When they finished, Felicia again led her in the same chant, *I am going to rise above and overcome . . .*

Andie joined her. She could hear herself speaking but no longer felt her mouth moving. The light in the room suddenly gave way to a black buzzing. She felt dizzy and disoriented. In the background she heard Felicia's voice, but it was the very distant background. Andie focused, as if the words from Felicia's mouth were her life line back to reality, as if she could see herself climbing hand over hand from the dark, swirling hole.

Finally, the dizziness passed. She was shaking but coherent. Her eyes opened. Felicia was staring at her, checking her out. Andie could still feel the tingling in her fingertips. That was no ordinary camas cake.

Or had she simply experienced a breakthrough?

"It's time," said Felicia.

"For what?"

"Your meeting with Steven Blechman."

"One on one?"

"Yes."

"Oh, my gosh. Am I ready?"

"Yes."

"I'm so nervous."

"Don't be," said Felicia. "The first meeting is the same for everyone."

"What happens?"

"He just gives you a lie-detector test."

Andie rose, feigning eagerness, hiding her true feelings. *Now what do I do?*

Fifty-four

Gus had waited outside Mrs. Borge's house for only ninety seconds before realizing he didn't need a stalking charge piled upon his alleged spouse abuse. She had told him to get lost and seemed to have meant it. A failure, he drove away reluctantly to think through his options.

Once home, it was immediately obvious that he wasn't the only one haunted by the fact that this Sunday afternoon marked two weeks since Beth had dropped off Morgan for tumbling class and disappeared. Gus needed to get his daughter out of the house. The Sonics were in town, and Gus had season tickets that he routinely gave away to clients and rarely used for himself. Morgan was more into soccer than basketball, but it turned out to be a pretty effective way of keeping her focused on something other than Beth. The same could not be said for Gus. His mind was barely on the game.

It ended with a Sonics victory, which left the fans in an upbeat mood on the way out of the stadium. Gus carried Morgan through the heavy foot traffic, but she wanted to walk once they got outside. He led her by the hand as they flowed with a thousand others to the parking garage across the street.

"That was fun, Daddy."

"Yeah. We'll do it again soon."

Their car was just ahead. No sooner had these words left his lips than he noticed the ticket on his windshield. He swallowed several bad words in Morgan's presence, wondering what horrible offense the traffic gestapo had nailed him for. Parking too close to the line? Forgetting to straighten his wheels? Failing to run over the visiting team's fans?

He put Morgan in the backseat and checked his prize beneath the wiper. It wasn't a ticket at all. It was a note, much like the pizza flyers and other junk he'd often discarded without even reading. This one, however, caught his attention. His name was written on the outside. He opened it and froze.

Stay away from Meredith Borge. Or I end up like her daughter.

Icicles ran up his spine. He scanned the garage instinctively, as if whoever had placed it there might actually be stupid enough to hang around and watch him read it. He saw only happy Sonics fans on their way to their cars. Carefully, he placed the note in his jacket and got in the car.

"What was that, Daddy?"

"What was what?"

"That thing on our windshield."

He had to gather his wits to answer, still shaken. "It was . . . just nothing, really."

"Why did you keep it?"

"Because there's no garbage can. I'll throw it out when we get home."

"Can we stop for ice cream on the way?"

"Not tonight, sweetie. We have ice cream at home. Daddy has to get back."

Gus wasn't sure if he should call the police or his investigator. He had to do something, but not in front of Morgan. He merged aggressively into traffic. With a little attitude behind the wheel, he could have them home in fifteen minutes. As they cruised up I-5, Gus dissected the note in his mind, particularly the last part. *Or I end up like her daughter.* Shirley Borge had committed suicide. Why would his discussions with Meredith Borge prompt another suicide?

Or maybe that was the point. Shirley's death had not been a suicide.

"Daddy, can I get a cat?"

He checked her in the rearview mirror. A couple of years back Morgan had asked for one. The answer had been no. "We can't get a cat, remember? Your mother's allergic."

"Are you 'lergic?"

"No."

"Is Aunt Carla 'lergic?"

"No."

"Then why can't we have one now?"

She was testing him to see if he thought her mother was really coming back. If he hadn't been so distracted, if the whole damn situation hadn't been so sad and pathetic, he would have thought she was a pretty clever kid.

"Morgan, if we get a cat, we would just have to get rid of it when your mother comes home."

She wasn't satisfied. She knew her trick had been foiled.

The iron gate at the end of their driveway opened, and the car pulled up to their house. Once inside, Morgan went to her room. Gus went straight for the telephone.

The red light on his answering machine was blinking. One message. He hit the PLAY button. "This is Meredith Borge calling for Gus Wheatley."

There was a long pause. Gus moved closer to the machine, as if willing her to continue. Finally she said, "Meet me in the coffee shop at the Red Lion Hotel by the airport at eight o'clock tonight. Just you. I got no interest in talking to the police."

More silence, then the digital voice announced, "End of messages."

It was a cryptic message, all the more eerie on the heels of the note on his windshield. Gus wasn't sure what to make of the pair. Bizarre coincidence? Some kind of setup? He checked his watch. Not quite six. Plenty of time to drive out to the airport and meet her.

Car keys in hand, he picked up the phone and called his investigator.

"Dex, we need to meet. Someone left a note on my windshield this afternoon. It's signed by someone named Flora. But I'd swear it's Beth's handwriting."

Fifty-five

The chill of night had covered the valley, yet Andie felt numb to the cold as Felicia led her to the main farmhouse. It was either the fortified camas cake or the apprehension over the lie-detector test. Or both.

Andie knew polygraphs could be beaten. The problem was, she wasn't sure *she* could beat one.

They walked around to the back of the house and stopped at the cellar doors. They weren't actually going inside the house. It was off limits to the likes of Felicia and certainly Andie. Those were the rules, she knew, but that didn't take the edge off the thought of being trapped in the basement with a possible serial killer.

Felicia opened the cellar doors. "He's waiting for you."

It was one of those defining moments for an undercover agent. Andie hadn't been at it nearly long enough to know when to step out of role and run for it.

"Are you coming with me?"

Felicia shook her head. "Just you and Steven."

Andie glanced down the dark cement staircase, then back at Felicia. "Wish me luck."

"There's no such thing as luck, Kira."

Then why do I feel so shit out of it? thought Andie. She started the climb down into the cellar. The instant she reached the bottom stair, the doors closed behind her. Total darkness. She waited for the eyes to adjust, but there was no adjustment to the complete absence of light. Her heart raced. She was about to make a dash for the doors, somewhere up the stairs behind her. Then a light switched on.

Steven Blechman was standing just three feet in front of her. She started, nearly panicked.

"Welcome," he said as he extended a hand.

She struggled to bring her adrenaline under control. "You scared me."

"There's nothing to be scared of."

"Easy for you to say."

"Yes, it is. Fear is a human bondage I shed long ago."

"I guess I'm not quite on your level yet."

"That's okay. You're learning." He took a half step closer, again offering his hand. "Come."

Andie met his gaze. Funny, but he didn't have yellow eyes, blazing eyes, eyes that glowed in the dark. He looked like just a normal guy.

"Where are we going?"

"Nowhere. We're staying right where we are."

"Do we have to do this down here? It's kind of cold."

"You're nervous," he said with a half smile.

"Wouldn't you be?"

"Sure. Everyone is."

"So, Felicia was right? You give everyone a lie-detector test."

"Absolutely."

Andie looked around. The lighting from the lone bulb hanging from the ceiling was dim, at best. Still, Andie could see everything in the cellar. A sump pump. A couple of old bicycles. Two chairs. But nothing that resembled a polygraph.

"Where is your equipment?"

"My what?"

"Your polygraph equipment."

He chuckled. "You thought I was going to hook you up to all that mechanical stuff?"

"Yeah. I don't know of any other way to give someone a lie-detector test."

"I do." Something in his response had chilled her. He turned and went to one of the two chairs behind him. "Sit down, Kira, and face me."

Slowly, Andie came forward. Only when she sat did she notice that her chair was a few inches higher than his, leaving them exactly at the same eye level. Blechman stared into her eyes. Andie blinked.

"Don't look away from me," he said.

Andie met his stare. It was a penetrating gaze, as though he were looking inside her.

He extended his arms toward her. "Grab my wrists."

She reached forward, and their hands interlocked. Each of them had the other by the pulse, right hand to left wrist, left hand to right wrist. Still, Andie was more aware of her own racing heartbeat than his.

"Now just relax," he said.

She took a deep breath. It was okay that she was shaking. *Kira would be shaking.*

"Do I frighten you, Kira?"

"Yes."

"Why?"

"I don't know."

"Are you afraid of what I might ask you?"

"No."

His grip tightened around her pulse. "You're lying."

"I'm just . . . nervous."

"How old are you, Kira?"

"Twenty-seven."

"Where were you born?"

"Seattle."

"Tell me about your parents."

"What do you want to know?"

"Everything."

Andie concentrated. It was crucial to recite her phony

background accurately. Should Blechman check, she wanted to make sure she checked out.

"My mother taught high school for over thirty years. She's retired now. My dad worked at Boeing most of his life, till he died six years ago."

"What kind of relationship do you have with your mother?"

"Normal."

"Do you have your own apartment?"

"No."

"You think it's normal for a twenty-seven-year-old woman to live with her mother?"

"So long as you're a little embarrassed by it, I guess it is."

He didn't crack a smile. "Where does your mother live?"

"Tacoma."

He asked a series of questions about her mother's background and lifestyle. It would all check out. The FBI had enlisted a retired agent to pose as Kira's mother.

"Do you love her?"

"Yes. Of course."

"Did you love your father?"

"Yes."

"Have you ever loved anyone outside your immediate family?"

They were outside the phony FBI background now. Andie thought of her ex-fiancé. "I would say no."

He smirked. "I would say yes."

Andie flinched. Blechman bore down. "You've recently ended a relationship, haven't you?"

"I've never been married, if that's what you mean."

"A broken engagement?"

She squirmed, amazed he had figured that out.

Blechman said, "You don't want to talk about it, do you?"

"There's not much to talk about."

"Let's go back where you feel safe, then. Do you have any brothers or sisters?"

She hesitated for an instant. Again, the real world was closing in around her. Truthfully, she didn't know. She gave the FBI's answer. "No."

"Are you sure?"

"Of course I'm sure. I would know if I had brothers or sisters."

"Were you adopted, Kira?"

The insight floored her. He continued, "Do you sometimes wonder about your real parents?"

"I don't know what you mean."

His stare tightened. "The green eyes are a nice cover."

"They're not a cover. They're mine."

"How does an Indian girl get green eyes?"

"What?"

"You are part Indian, aren't you? I can see it."

Not everyone could, not even some Native Americans. But if he was on to it, there was no sense denying it. "Part, yes."

"Which part? Body or spirit?"

"I don't know how to answer that."

"What tribe are your ancestors from?"

"I don't know."

"You *were* adopted, weren't you?"

She suddenly regretted the *I don't know*. She should have just picked Cherokee or some other tribe that didn't have good recordkeeping, one that Blechman could never have verified. Not knowing your tribe was a red flag for adoption. "Yes, I was adopted."

He seemed to smile faintly, confident he was getting somewhere. "If I were to guess, I would say you're Yakama."

"Why?"

"The word Yakama means runaway. Are you a runaway?"

"No."

"You're running from something, Kira. Tell me what it is."

"I really don't know what you mean."

"Are you running from something you've hidden in your past? Or are you running from the fact that you *don't know* your past?"

"The past is just the past."

"No, Kira. Until you've transcended the human level, you are defined by the past. It's who you are."

He looked deeply into her eyes. "Who *are* you, Kira?"

"What—what do you mean?"

"You're not who you say you are. Tell me who you are. Who you *really* are."

Her fear soared to another level. Either he knew she was a phony, or he was on verge of figuring it out. She broke from his grip and sprang from her chair, ready to run for her life.

"Stop!" he shouted.

Andie wheeled, ready to defend herself.

"It's okay," said Blechman.

Part of her said run, but she fought the impulse. Her cover wasn't completely blown yet. At least she didn't think so.

His voice and demeanor were unthreatening. "Kira, many of my most devoted followers lied to me at first about their pasts. Some were simply unable to talk freely about past abusive relationships. Others were afraid I would reject them if they revealed their previous life of crime, drug abuse, sexual promiscuity, or whatever."

She felt a wave of relief. He didn't even suspect she was FBI. Just another loner with a checkered past. "I'm sorry I lied to you."

"I'm sorry I made you uncomfortable. But to come on this journey, you have to break with the past. To break with the past, you have to confront your demons."

"That's what I want to do."

"Good. And don't be afraid. You won't go through this alone. Felicia will help you. I will help you. And as you progress from one level to the next, you will find others to help you overcome the human traits that torment you."

"I'm not really tormented by anything."

"Yes, you are. That's why you're here. Only when you rid yourself of those past vibrations can you vibrate at the next level. Do you want to reach the next level?"

"Yes. Of course."

"Then make that your sole objective for all your remaining days on this planet. Not to become a better human, as your parents and teachers instructed you. But to become more than human. As long as you are human, it makes no difference whether you are a prostitute or a scientist, a minister or a murderer."

She cringed inside at the mention of a murderer. "I understand."

He rose and stepped toward her. Andie took a half step back, but she was suddenly in his grasp. She stiffened with fear, but it was just a warm embrace. He held her for nearly a full minute, then whispered softly, "Your name is now Willow, and you belong to us."

Fifty-six

Gus had his investigator tail him to the meeting with Meredith Borge, fully armed, just in case. Though it would be illegal to record their conversation without Meredith's consent, Dex wired him up anyway. No telling what direction this might take. He wanted it all on tape.

The coffee shop was nearly empty, just two men at opposite ends of the counter and a family of five sucking down the spaghetti special at a corner table. Meredith was alone in a booth by the revolving pie display. Gus arrived precisely at eight o'clock, as instructed.

"Got your call," he said.

She looked up from her coffee and gave a sideways glance toward the door, as if checking to make sure he hadn't been followed. "Have a seat."

The waitress poured him a cup and freshened Meredith's. After she'd gone, Gus asked, "Why the change of heart?"

"Why were you so stupid as to come to my front door in broad daylight?"

Gus wasn't sure how to respond, but after the message on his windshield this afternoon, it was a fairly astute question. "Guess I wasn't thinking."

"That's a dangerous way to live."

"I'm no stranger to danger. At least not lately."

"I know all about your situation."

He wondered if that included the alleged spouse abuse. "Don't believe everything you read in the papers or see on television."

"I don't. But my daughter was a very reliable source."

Gus stopped in mid-sip. "Shirley told me she didn't even know if you were alive."

"We didn't talk for quite some time, that's true."

"You mean after she conspired to kill you?"

His knowing surprised her. "That put a crimp in the relationship, yeah."

"So when did you get over it?" ·

"When she called and told me you were going to pay her a quarter million dollars."

"If she could help me find my wife."

"Which is precisely the reason she called me."

"I don't follow you."

She smiled wryly. "No way Shirley was going to find her without my help."

"Do you know where my wife is?"

"No."

"Stop playing games with me."

"It's not a game. It's a theory. Shirley's theory, to be exact. But she couldn't prove it without me. I know what you need to know."

Gus was tiring of her coyness. "Are you talking about the cult?"

"My, you have done your homework."

"What do you know about it?"

"You mean the one in the Yakima Valley, right? The one on ten acres of land with the old white farmhouse, big barn, apple and apricot orchards? Chicken coop out back?"

"Either you're totally making this up or you've been there."

"I *lived* there."

"When?"

"Long before your wife started shoplifting and donating clothes to the Second Chance."

"Are you still . . . involved?"

"No. It's been years. Used to be a very positive environment. I got out when Blechman took over."

"Blechman?"

"Younger guy. Very ambitious. Likes to think he pioneered the cult's thinking, but he's just another egomaniac with a pulpit."

"How do you mean?"

"He wrote this manuscript he thought was going to sell fifty million copies and spend two years on the *New York Times* bestseller list. Over a thousand pages. I'm sure it's been rejected by every publisher on the planet. Not that there isn't a market for this secular evangelism stuff. You've seen all these books lately that tap into the wave of spiritualism and enlightenment without conventional religion. Anyway, Blechman thought he could parlay the book into a weekly magazine, CD-ROMs, audiotapes, his own worldwide television talk show. So far the only place the philosophy seems to have caught on is on his farm."

"What's the philosophy?

"Can't say. Never read the book."

"I would think you would have gained some insights just from being around the farm."

"You would think," she said vaguely.

"What's the book's title?"

"His *manuscript*. There's no book. He calls it 'The Echoes.'"

"The echoes? What does that mean?"

"Maybe you should read it and find out."

"Can you get me a copy?"

"Sure. On sale. A mere fraction of what you offered Shirley. Twenty-five thousand."

"For a stinking unpublished manuscript?"

"You want to find your wife or don't you?"

"You're saying the book will tell me where Beth is?"

Her sly smile was back. "I think it just might explain everything."

"Why should I believe that?"

"Why do you think my daughter was murdered?"

"Your daughter's death was suicide, not homicide."

"Then why didn't they find any step stool or chair or anything like that around her? How did she suspend herself from the ceiling all by herself?"

"I don't know anything about that."

"You met Shirley. You really believe she hanged herself?"

Gus didn't answer, but the woman had a point.

She leaned closer, elbows on the table, her voice low. "This cult is like a fucking octopus. It's got arms that reach everywhere. Prisons. Thrift shops. Even perfect little neighborhoods like yours."

Gus met her stare. "How soon can I get my hands on that manuscript?"

"Just as soon as you can get me the cash."

"Tomorrow."

"I'll call you," she said. "Don't call me. Don't come by my house. And don't you dare tell anyone we talked. I don't want to end up like my daughter. Understand?"

"Yeah," said Gus. "I'm beginning to."

They left separately, first Meredith, then Gus a few minutes later. Gus called his investigator from his car phone. "You heard?"

"Yeah," said Dex. His car was just a block away. "The wire worked perfectly."

"What do you think?"

"I think someone was watching you."

"What?"

"I had my eye on the green Mercury across the street from the hotel. It sat there the whole time you and Meredith talked and then pulled away when you did. Could be FBI. Could be someone else."

Gus checked his rearview mirror. Pairs of headlights scattered across three lanes behind him, but in the dark it was impossible to tell if any belonged to a green Mercury. "You think they followed me here or Meredith?"

"Depends on who *they* are. And whether Meredith is still part of them."

"Meaning she could still be part of the cult?"

"Think back to the last thing she said to you: 'I don't want to end up like my daughter.' Interesting coincidence that she used almost the same language that was in the letter you got on your windshield."

Gus stopped at the traffic light. "I don't think she's with the cult anymore, Dex. You heard her words over the wire, but only I could see the anger in her face. She hates this Blechman, the way she ridiculed his writings, emphasizing it wasn't a book, just a crappy manuscript. If you ask me, she's even forgiven her daughter for conspiring to kill her. I think she blames the cult for that."

"That's a lot of assumptions," said Dex.

"I don't think it's an outrageous assumption. Especially the part about Shirley's death being murder rather than suicide."

"I'm with you there," said Dex.

"Good. Because if Shirley was killed, that might even explain that note on my windshield this afternoon."

"How so?"

"It's in Beth's handwriting, so let's assume she wrote it. She warned that if I talk to Meredith Borge, she'll end up like Shirley. That makes no sense if Shirley committed suicide. But it makes total sense if Shirley was murdered."

"I would agree with you if she had signed it in her own name. But she signed it as Flora. That sounds like a cult name to me."

"That's my whole point. Someone in the cult forced

Beth to write the letter. It's a warning to me in Beth's own handwriting that my wife will be killed if I talk to Meredith. It means they're holding Beth against her will."

"Or it means Beth is happy being Flora in her new life with the cult and wants you to back off. Because if her husband keeps snooping around, she's afraid they might decide she's more trouble than she's worth."

"I like my theory better."

"Don't be so sure," said Dex. "If you're right, they'll kill her if they find out you're talking to Meredith."

The traffic light changed. Gus pulled onto the expressway ramp. "If I'm right, she's as good as dead if I *don't* talk to Meredith."

Fifty-seven

The old farmhouse was quiet by day, still as death at night. Occasionally a floorboard would creak in the hall outside the bedroom door. Water could sometimes be heard rushing through old pipes in the wall. The furnace would kick on and rattle against the cold. For Beth Wheatley, those were the familiar sounds of the night.

That, and the VCR at midnight.

She lay motionless beneath the blankets. The double bed was in the corner. Her back was to the door, her face to the wall in a windowless room. The television screen provided the only light. It would last just twenty minutes. As it had every night. At the same time. For the past two weeks. This had become a silent nightly ritual—and tonight was no exception.

The lock clicked and the door opened. The room brightened just a bit with light from the hallway. Beth didn't stir. The door closed and the room returned to darkness. Heavy boots pounded the wood floor, then halted. She felt watched, as though someone were standing over her. Her heart raced, but she didn't dare move. After a long minute, she could sense her visitor back slowly away from the bed and rest in the chair facing the television.

As if on cue, it started.

For nearly twenty minutes Beth listened in the darkness,

lying on her side, her back to the television and her nightly visitor. After fourteen nights she knew the tape by heart. Not the video. Just the audio. She had forced herself never to steal a glance at the screen. She had tried not to listen either, but that was impossible. It was some kind of taped interview. A man and a very frightened woman. The man talked like a psychiatrist, maintaining an even and professional tone as the woman's story unfolded like a nightmare, a tale of torture and a phallic knife that ended each night with the same horrible crescendo.

"What happened next?"

"He yanked the knife from my mouth. Very fast. Cut like a razor."

"What then?"

"He asked me, 'Do you like the knife?'"

"Did you answer?"

"No. So he shouted again: 'Do you like the knife!'"

"Did you answer this time?"

"I just shook my head. Then he shouted again. Say it loud! Say you don't like the knife! So I did. I shouted back. Over and over, he made me shout it—I don't like the knife!"

"Then what?"

"He whispered into my ear."

"What did he say?"

"'Next time, be glad it's not the knife.'"

Beth cringed beneath the blanket. Experience had taught her that the end of the tape only triggered the worst part. The self-indulgent groaning. The climax and release. Tonight, as on past nights, those sounds filled the room, deep and guttural. She didn't have to peer out from beneath the sheets to know what was going on. The unmistakable noises sent her imagination racing as to the perverse mind in the chair beside her. One thing, however, her ears were sure of. The intruder was a man.

The television blackened. The chair squeaked. His boots

shuffled across the floor. The door opened and closed behind him. The lock clicked from the outside.

Again, she was alone in total darkness.

Andie hardly slept that night. She lay awake troubled by the ease with which Blechman had detected things as personal as her adoption and broken engagement. Was it possible he did have some kind of gift? She had heard of people like that, though it seemed just as likely that he had been toying with her, somehow knowing all along she was an undercover agent. Then again, virtually all of his followers were recovering from failed relationships and family trouble of some kind. An experienced palm reader might have done as well as he had.

At five A.M. there was a knock on the door. Felicia answered it without a word, as though she had been expecting it. A man entered. Andie's eyes slowly focused. It wasn't Blechman. It was Tom, the other lieutenant who had spoken with Felicia at Tuesday night's recruitment meeting—the man whose voice imprint had been identical to hers.

"Let's go, Willow." It took Andie a moment to realize he was talking to her. Andie a.k.a. Kira was now Willow.

"Where are we going?"

"Put your clothes on, and let's go."

She was wearing only a nightshirt and skimpy running shorts. Tom caught an eyeful on her way to the bathroom. It was a lecherous glare, something to be expected from one of those fifty-year-old loners who got kissed once a decade and cruised in a van with a bumper sticker that read, IF IT'S A' ROCKIN' DON'T COME KNOCKIN'.

You could use a little work on losing earthly desires, bucko.

They were out the door in five minutes. Felicia stayed behind.

Sunrise was more than an hour away. The ground was damp from patchy fog. Their boots made a swooshing sound as they walked through the coarse, ankle-high grass. Tom stopped and lit up a cigarette as they reached a safe distance from the house.

"They allow smoking here?" asked Andie.

"You got a problem with it?"

"It just seems like it would be one of those forbidden self-indulgences."

"Rule number one, Willow. Thou shalt not judge thy superiors."

Interesting, thought Andie. A smoker. A peeping Tom—literally. Yet his voice imprint had been virtually identical to Felicia's. He was either a believer with some weaknesses, or a nonbeliever with incredible acting skills. Either way, Andie wanted to explore.

They continued over a hill toward the chicken coop, where they were greeted by the ammonia-laden odor of fowl excrement and the incessant chirping of hundreds of week-old chicks. Like ants they climbed over each other at various feeders and waterers spaced evenly throughout the coop. Little yellow fuzzy balls, wall-to-wall cuteness. It made Andie think of Easter, till she looked more closely. A few lay dead on the ground. The weak stumbled about, too timid to make a serious charge toward the source of nourishment.

"Pick up the dead ones," said Tom. "Put them in the bucket."

Andie took the bucket and entered the coop, careful not to crush the live ones. With each step she sent clusters of chicks scattering. Every few feet she found a dead one. She felt a mixture of pity and disgust, especially for the eviscerated ones that had been cannibalized by their sisters. Each carcass weighed practically nothing, but soon her bucket was heavy. She finished in a few minutes and returned to Tom.

He took the bucket and handed her another. "Now get the weak ones."

"In a bucket?"

"Yeah. Like this." He grabbed a chick that was stumbling around the fringe. It chirped pathetically in his hand. With one quick jerk he silenced it, then tossed it in the bucket.

Andie had seen much worse in her career, but Tom seemed to expect some revulsion from Willow. He somehow seemed to think he was impressing her. She played along. "I can't kill an innocent little chick."

"Yeah, you can."

"But I don't want to."

"It's your job, Willow."

"But you do it so well."

"And with a little practice, you'll be every bit as good." He winked.

It wasn't easy to flirt with an obvious loser like Tom, but it seemed like a way to open the door. "I would think picking up chicks comes pretty naturally to a guy like you."

"That was my other life," he said with a smile.

"Quite the heartbreaker, were you?"

"Hmmmm, I had my fair share."

"And now you're . . . celibate?"

He quickly deflated. "Felicia will talk to you about that."

"I just assumed that was part of the deal. All this talk about weaning oneself of earthly desires. Sex has to be right up there with cable TV and ice cream."

He was obviously uncomfortable. Andie asked, "Am I making you nervous?"

"Just, men and women aren't supposed to have this discussion. Felicia will talk to you."

"I'm sorry. Somehow I just felt at ease talking to you."

That seemed to please him. "Really?"

"Yeah. You know how you just get a good feeling about a person?"

"Uh, yeah."

"But hey, if you're uncomfortable, let's just go back to killing baby chickens."

"No, I wasn't rejecting you."

"I hope not," said Andie. "It would be nice to have a friend."

"I don't think there's anything in the rules against that."

She glanced at his cigarette. "Not that the rules are written in stone."

"Smoking is a minor infraction," he said defensively. "More serious stuff can get you kicked out."

"Like what?"

"Like . . . sex."

"Why is that so bad?"

"Because it not only depletes your energy, but it takes you further away from the source. That's the whole problem with satisfying your worldly urges."

"So this entire belief system is based on abstinence?"

"No. It's based on fulfillment. But it comes in ways you've never experienced before."

"If it's so fulfilling, why do you still enjoy things like smoking?"

"Because I'm still human. To be honest with you, I don't really enjoy smoking all that much. I just do it. That's the way it is with everything that binds us to this world. That's the cornerstone of Mr. Blechman's philosophy. He teaches us that our emotions, our impulses, our desires—they're like an echo."

"An echo?"

"Yeah. Any experience is most intense and gratifying the first time. Each subsequent experience is mere repetition, growing weaker and weaker, like an echo, until we are totally disconnected from the source of energy that inspired us to try something new in the first place."

"I don't want you to think I have a one-track mind, but I wouldn't say the best sex I ever had was the first time I had it."

"Get beyond sex, will you, please? Think of the first time you saw the ocean. The first time you rode a bicycle. The first time you flew on an airplane."

"The first time you killed?"

He was taken aback.

"Like a baby chick, I mean," said Andie.

"That works too. Anything that makes you feel a rush of energy and changes your level of vibration. After a while we simply become numb to it. But we keep doing it, hoping we can get some glimpse of the thrill we experienced the first time."

"You get a thrill from killing?"

"I didn't say thrill."

"I'm sorry. I thought you did."

He was nervous again, drawing on his cigarette though it had burned to the filter. "All I'm saying is that we shouldn't be wasting our energy through repetition. We should be redirecting our energy."

"Toward the source?" said Andie.

"Yes." He crushed out his cigarette. "But you and I shouldn't be having this discussion. I'm getting way ahead on your program. You know a lot more than someone is supposed to know at your level."

Much more, she thought.

A band of clouds broke on the horizon. Golden rays of morning light pierced the coop's slatted walls. As Tom glanced toward the rising sun, Andie studied his profile. She couldn't quite place it, but he looked strangely familiar. He caught her staring, and she quickly looked away.

Andie picked up her bucket and returned to her task, watching out of the corner of her eye as Tom methodically moved about the flock and culled out the weak.

Fifty-eight

It wasn't yet sunrise, and Gus was in Beth's side of their master bedroom closet. Ever since he'd uncovered the fruits of her shoplifting, he'd wondered what other clues to Beth's whereabouts might be hiding in there. Over the past two weeks he'd examined jewelry, photographs, memorabilia, and thousands of other little things that had found their way into the drawers and boxes that lined the walls of their oversized closet. Having sifted through some items for the third or fourth time, he realized this was becoming less a hunt for clues than a way to reconnect with Beth. It was his sanity in another sleepless night.

Tonight he had more focus. Something about that letter from Martha Goldstein yesterday had gnawed at his memory. It was more the paper itself than the message she had written on it. The unusually high linen content of her personal stationery lent the distinctive fuchsia blend a marble-like appearance. Somewhere he had seen it before. It had taken several hours of lying awake in bed to realize where.

Beth had kept a junk drawer of things related to his law firm. He had blown past it quickly in nights past, figuring it couldn't possibly contain anything important. As he thumbed through the drawer this time, however, his opinion quickly changed. Tucked behind some old programs from past firm banquets was a fuchsia envelope. The post-

mark told him it was more than a year old. Neither the envelope nor the stationery inside bore a return address. It
had been written anonymously on one of those blank extra
sheets that come with each box of personal engraved stationery. It was an unsigned letter to Beth—penned in the
same handwriting and on the same fuchsia stationery Gus
had seen yesterday in the letter from Martha Goldstein.

He read eagerly, his anger rising in the second para-
graph. *"It doesn't matter who I am,"* she had written.
*"What's important is that your husband has given himself
to me, and it's time you faced the truth."*

He stopped, stunned. She had chosen her words carefully, "given himself." It was consistent with Martha's
view of them as soul mates. Yet the implication—the intended message to Beth—was that Gus was having sex
with another woman. The whole deceptive package was
classic Martha. The letter was unsigned, which meant Beth
would have had to confront Gus if she wanted to know
who had written it. It was written in her own script so that
Gus would know it was Martha. Forcing him to tell his
wife that the "anonymous" author was Martha would only
make the letter more believable to Beth.

Somehow, Beth had figured out it was Martha on her
own, since she'd filed the letter away in the drawer of law
firm–related junk. Beth had never said a word to Gus.
She'd internalized it, which went a long way to explain her
paranoia about him and Martha.

A noise stirred him. In the pre-dawn darkness, the wind
whistled through branches outside the bedroom window.
The clock ticked in the hallway. All else was still.

He thought immediately of Dex's warning that someone
had followed him to the Red Lion Hotel last night.

He stepped quietly from the closet and checked the
alarm panel on the wall. It was armed, no sign of intrusion.
He left the bedroom and peered down the hall. Again, only
silence. He walked slowly to the front door and peeked

through the beveled glass. The car was still in the driveway. No one scurried across the lawn. He headed for the kitchen. The wind was kicking up outside, but the branches against the house didn't sound at all like the noise that had roused him from sleep. He switched on the kitchen light and started.

The rubber trash can had been pulled out from under the sink and left near the dishwasher—not its usual place. It was upright but bulging, nearly overflowing. Something that resembled a tail was curling out from under the lid. Gus stepped closer and checked inside.

It was Garfield. One of Morgan's big stuffed animals was in the garbage.

He pulled it out. Tigger was in there, too, along with a fuzzy cub from the Lion King collection, two more stuffed felines, and a ceramic Sylvester. They weren't ripped, stained, or particularly worn out. They'd just been summarily discarded.

He hurried to Morgan's room. The door was open and her light was on. "Morgan?" he said with urgency.

Her head popped from beneath the covers. "I can't sleep."

"What's wrong?"

"Nothing."

"Does this have anything to do with what I found in the garbage can?"

"You didn't take them out, did you?"

"Yes."

"Daddy, no! Put them back."

"Why are you throwing them away?"

"Because."

He recalled their earlier conversation in the car about getting a cat. "Morgan, your mommy's allergic to real cats. Not stuffed animals."

"I know. But if I keep all these fake cats around, I might forget."

With soulful eyes he came to her and sat on the edge of the bed. "Sweetheart, you will never forget your mommy."

"I don't want to forget *anything* about her. Even little things. Like, I don't ever want to forget she's lergic to cats."

"Don't worry about that, okay? I'm going to do everything possible to bring Mommy home. And then you won't ever, ever have to worry about forgetting anything."

She was silent for a moment, then quizzical. "Have you forgotten things about Mommy?"

He wasn't sure how to answer. He settled for the truth. "It's funny, but since your mother disappeared, I actually remember more about her. That's a good thing, I guess. You can get back the things you forget."

"If you really strain your brain?"

"Not so much the brain, sweetheart."

"Which part?"

He held her close. "The part I haven't used in a very long time."

After breakfast Felicia drove Andie into town in the old station wagon. In the backseat was a woman at Felicia's supervisory level and a nineteen-year-old girl who was in her second month of training. Tom and his young male recruit drove separately in an SUV. Monday morning was when the cult purchased groceries and essentials that couldn't be produced on the farm. It was viewed as grunt work reserved for the newest members, under the strict supervision of their mentors, of course.

They stopped at a big price-cutting warehouse that sold everything from radial tires to cinnamon rolls, mostly in army-like quantities. Andie had been to a similar place in Seattle with the bare cement floors and huge pallets of Twinkies and paper towels stacked sixty-feet to the ceiling. She felt like a Lilliputian.

They broke into teams of two, each recruit with a mentor.

Each team had a list of things to retrieve from different parts of the warehouse. They were to buy only what was on the list. Salt, flour, and raw sugar. Soap. Toilet paper. Matches and batteries. Basic medications, such as aspirin and rubbing alcohol. All of the things Blechman regarded as necessities.

Andie pushed the shopping cart as Felicia retrieved items from the shelves. They talked very little. Andie couldn't stop thinking about "the echoes" concept. Her bookend theory had been out the window for some time, but "echoes" seemed apt. Two men and three women had been murdered in echo-like fashion.

Her discovery made her restless and eager to brainstorm. Isaac had given her until Wednesday to check in, but she wasn't sure when she might get away from the farm again. She had to seize the opportunity.

"Felicia? I'm going to use the bathroom, all right?"

"Okay. I'll be right here."

The rest rooms were in the rear of the store, near the butcher department, behind a pair of swinging doors and at the end of a long corridor. Andie hoped there would be a pay phone nearby. There was. She quickly dialed Isaac's private number.

"Isaac, it's Andie."

"Are you okay?"

"I'm fine. I can't talk long." She feared Felicia would burst through the doors any second. In two minutes she summarized her weekend, focusing mainly on "the echoes."

Isaac said, "Of course, even if his philosophy spawned the murders, it doesn't mean Blechman is our serial killer."

"I wondered what your take would be."

"It could be one of his demented followers. It might even be some psycho who read or heard about his teachings and is simply mocking the echo idea. After all, his seminars are open to the public. Who knows what kind of demented ideas people get?"

"That's what I want to find out." With a nervous glance she checked the hall, thinking she'd heard footsteps.

"Andie, you've done a good job. But for your own safety, I think it's time we pull you out and just move in."

"But I haven't seen a single sign of Beth Wheatley yet. I couldn't even tell you if she's here."

"Then maybe she isn't."

"But if she is, she could be dead the minute the FBI starts knocking on the door."

"We might consider a more aggressive takeover. Take them by surprise."

"That's a terrible idea, and you know it. Remember Waco?"

"You've been inside. You think there's a potential for mass suicide?"

"I don't know. But think of what you said earlier. What if the killer is just someone who might have passed through the cult and is no longer here? The FBI will want the cult's cooperation in identifying people who came to their meetings. Invading their compound is not going to endear them to the FBI and make them want to cooperate."

Isaac was silent. Andie checked the doors again at the end of the corridor. Through the little diamond-shaped window she could see Felicia coming down the aisle. This was taking too long. "Just give me forty-eight more hours. And give it to me *now*, before they catch me on the phone."

He was thinking. Andie's heart pounded as Felicia neared the doors. "Isaac, *please*."

"All right, you got it."

"Thank you. Gotta go." She slammed down the phone and started walking toward the doors just as they swung open.

"There you are," said Felicia.

Fifty-nine

Beth lay alone in the darkness. It was a helpless feeling, but she had learned not to pound on the walls or scream for help. That kind of behavior would only get her handcuffed and gagged. One night she had carried on so long he had revoked her lights-on privileges. Two days of total darkness, including meals and bathroom breaks. She guessed it was two days, based on the number of meals she had eaten. With no clock or windows there was no way to be sure.

Good behavior did seem to have its rewards. The lights used to come on only during each meal and bathroom break. Now she seemed to get a grace period before and after. Once, she had even been allowed outdoors to work at the chicken coop, albeit not without the electronic belt locked around her torso. It worked like those invisible fences for dogs, only this one would hit her like a stun gun if she got too close to the electrified boundaries. It had been good to get outdoors, though the farm had been strangely deserted that day. Almost everyone was away, perhaps on a retreat. Beth knew about retreats. It was how she'd gotten caught up in the first place.

In hindsight, it was easy to understand the initial appeal of Blechman's philosophy. She had been tired of wasting her energy trying to put the magic back in her marriage. It *was* like an echo, intense at first, then fading over time. It was as if each anniversary were just another hollow ring in the distance, each one a little weaker and farther from the source, until it was completely inaudible, nothing left. The idea of redirecting her energy and changing her level of vibration had been a revelation. She was revitalized for a time that included many a day-long visit to the farm when Gus was out of town. On the positive side, they had helped her identify and talk out her anxieties. Ultimately, however, she and her mentors came to a bitter disagreement over the root cause. They saw it as a huge problem, but she didn't see it as a problem at all.

She still loved Gus.

The way they wanted Beth to handle *that* problem was something she could never bring herself to do. The result was solitary confinement. She wasn't getting much direction from the leaders, but she assumed the idea was to isolate her from worldly influences until she channeled her energy properly. All of this time alone, however, had only separated her further from their way of thinking. With no one to talk to, she conjured up pleasant images from her past. Morgan was a frequent subject. There was quite a lot of Gus and the way they used to be. Had they read her mind, her mentors would have been furious.

Today her thoughts were not so pleasant. Almost against her own will, certain sounds were replaying in her mind. They revolved around the nightly ritual she had come to dread so much. She blocked out the ones that frightened her—the woman on tape, the sounds of his enjoyment. Instead, she focused on things that confused her. In particular, the sounds of his leaving.

In her mind, she could hear him rise from the chair and switch off the television. Hear him cross the room and open the door. The door shutting and locking from the outside. Those were the sounds she had heard every night. Last night, however, something had been missing. There had been a break in the routine. She didn't hear that familiar hydraulic sound of the VCR ejecting the videotape. She focused harder, this time on his arrival. Come to think of it, she hadn't heard him *insert* the videotape either. And it wasn't just last night. It had happened on the last several nights, at least. That explained the mechanical whining upon his arrival, the sounds of the tape rewinding.

For some reason, he had been leaving the tape in the VCR.

It could have been an oversight on his part, but that was unlikely. Very little happened on the farm without a purpose. If he was leaving the tape in the VCR, it was for a reason. There was only one she could imagine.

He wanted her to watch it.

The prospect didn't seem as frightening without him in the room. She had heard it so many times, seeing it couldn't be that disturbing. Slowly, she slid from the bed and stepped onto the floor. The room was black, but she knew the way from memory. She took small steps, almost sliding her feet across the room. She groped with her hands in front of her until she felt something. It was the television screen. She poked and probed until she found the on-off switch and hit it. The screen lit up with snow. She quickly muted the volume so that no one in the hall could hear. The set wasn't hooked up to a cable or antennae, of course. It was a good source of light, but up until now she had been afraid to use it for fear of breaking the rules. Curiosity, however, had emboldened her. It wasn't so much that she wanted to see the tape. She wanted to know why *he* wanted her to see it.

She hit the Rewind button and waited as the tape whined to the beginning. It took only a minute. Then she hit PLAY and stepped back. She stared at the screen as the image appeared. A woman was seated on a chair, facing the camera. She seemed nervous, but it wasn't her demeanor that struck Beth.

"My name is Alicia Santiago," she said.

Beth shut it off, her hand shaking. Ten seconds into the video and she had seen enough. The woman was gone, but the television screen was glowing with a dark blue background. It enabled Beth to see her reflection in the glass. She hadn't seen her likeness since her arrival. She brought a hand to her face and felt the contours of her cheeks, the curve of her mouth. She touched her hair. The short, dark hair. It was obvious now why they had cut it. The resemblance was chilling.

Beth looked almost exactly like the woman in the video. She switched off the television and returned to darkness.

Sixty

Monday was slipping away, and Gus had yet to hear from Meredith. He had the money for Blechman's manuscript, twenty-five thousand dollars. He found it hard to believe she would just walk away from that much cash. She had warned him not to call, but he was beginning to worry. From his home office he dialed her number.

No answer. That could have meant any number of things—none of them good.

Again he picked up the phone and hit speed dial. "Carla, it's Gus. Can you come over and watch Morgan? I need to go out for a while."

Andie was alone in her unit when she heard a knock on the door. Felicia had gone to some kind of meeting. It was Tom, and he looked angry.

"We need to talk, Willow."

She felt threatened by his tone. "Okay," she said, but she didn't invite him in.

"Inside."

"Is there a problem?"

"You know what the problem is." He quickly had her by the arm, led her inside, and nearly pushed her on the bed.

"What are you doing?" she asked.

He was pacing, getting more worked up. "You got Felicia in one hell of a lot of trouble, you know that? Steve is giving her what-for right now."

"What are you talking about?"

"Don't deny it," he snapped.

"I—deny what?"

"That phone call you made from the grocery warehouse. You were being watched."

Watched was okay. It was listening that Andie worried about. "So . . . they heard?"

"We don't have to hear. We know you weren't calling for the time and weather. Who was it? Your mother again?"

She struggled to contain her relief. She lowered her head. "Yes," she peeped, as if ashamed. "I promised Mom I would call home first chance I got."

"I knew it."

"I just didn't want her to worry." She flashed her repentant, sultry look. It worked.

He stopped pacing. His voice lost its edge. "Darn it, Willow. You have to stop worrying about people and things you've left behind."

"I've only been here a few days. You can't expect miracles."

"A clean break is the only way. If you try to wean yourself a little at a time, you'll never make it."

"Is that how you did it?"

"That's how we all did it."

"Didn't you miss some things?"

"Yeah. My pickup truck."

"You had to give up your truck?"

"That was my contribution when I joined the group. We all make contributions to keep the cause financed. One woman gave over her house."

"I wish I had something to contribute."

"That's not important. Right now all that matters is that you follow the rules. Phoning your mother . . . well, that's a lot worse than sneaking a cigarette now and then."

He cracked a faint smile to make her feel better.

She returned the smile, then turned serious. "Can I ask you something?"

"Sure."

"I've been wondering about something for a while. That talk we had this morning only made me more curious."

"What is it?"

"It just seems I hear a lot of talk about sacrifice and giving up earthly desires. The purpose is to get to the next level, right?"

"Right."

"So let's say I do everything right. I stop calling my mother, I let go of all the selfish inclinations that make me so human, I do all the things I'm supposed to do. What happens next? How do I get from this level to the next?"

He looked away, hedging. "That's really getting way ahead of your program."

"But maybe it would help me be more disciplined if I knew. Those things you told me this morning about the echoes were ahead of schedule, and they really helped me."

"I really can't discuss the transformation with you."

"There must be something you can tell me. Is it like traditional Judeo-Christian beliefs, where they say you have to die before you can go to heaven?"

"No. It's not like that at all."

"So the transformation comes when you're alive?"

"Yes." He hesitated but then seemed compelled to explain. "But we're not like many of the ufologists who believe that you must be fully conscious."

"I don't understand."

"You've heard of these groups who believe that a UFO will come down and take those who are ready to the next level. They believe you must be fully conscious to make that journey."

"Blechman has said all along he's not a ufologist. So what is he?"

"I can't explain everything to you, but trust me. It makes so much sense."

"It makes no sense. If he doesn't believe you have to die, but he doesn't believe you have to be conscious, what is he saying? You need to be in a coma?"

He became deadly serious, as if offended by her remark. "He's saying there is a window of opportunity between life and death. You've heard of people who were near death and who claim their whole life passed before their eyes?"

"Sure."

"These flashbacks are the echoes that Steven talks about. Your entire life echoes before you, and in this one lucid moment you understand where you have come from and where you are going. Now, you've also heard people say they have passed over to the other side and seen a white light or were embraced by the light?"

"Yes."

"Those people are going nowhere, Willow. If they don't see the echoes, they have no understanding. They don't reach the next level."

Things were starting to make sense to her—specifically, the hangings. "Is it the same window of opportunity no matter how you die? Or is it beneficial to linger for a time between life and death?"

"That's something I can't talk about."

She nodded, backing off. "I understand. This was helpful. Thank you."

"You're welcome. I need to get back to the house, check on Felicia."

As he started for the door, she gave him one more of those disarming smiles. "Hey, Tom?"

"Yeah?"

"Just out of curiosity, what kind of pickup truck did you used to have?"

"Ford. Hated to lose it, but—hell, it's not important."

"Good night."

"Good night," he said, closing the door behind him.

She remained seated on the bed, thinking. Maybe the truck wasn't important to him, but it was to her. The physical resemblance was part of it, his brown eyes and graying hair. But it was the personal data that had triggered the recognition, the little things she had put together from conversations with him and others. He was divorced. Early fifties. He had even driven the same vehicle, a Ford pickup.

Tom was a match for the serial killer's two male victims.

Sixty-one

Gus reached the Borge residence in under an hour. Dex followed separately and parked a short distance up the road, out of sight in the darkness. If Meredith was home, it was important that Gus appear to be alone. If something was amiss, alone was the last thing he actually wanted to be.

Her car was parked in the driveway, but the porch light was not burning. No lights were on inside either, as far as Gus could tell. The house was completely dark.

He walked up the front steps, rang the doorbell, and waited. No one answered. In fact, he didn't even hear the bell ring. He knocked, but still no one came. He cupped his hands to the oval window in the front door and peered inside. It was too dark to see past the foyer. He backed away from the door, thinking he had heard an approaching car. The gravel road was deserted. A door slammed, and he realized it had come from a neighbor's house on the next road over. Sounds traveled well in this rural area, just one or two houses on each long and curving unpaved street.

He signaled up the road to Dex, who was watching from a distance through night-vision binoculars. Gus climbed down the front steps and continued around to the back of the house. It was even darker in back than in front, farther from the streetlight. A rattling from the trash cans sent his heart leaping to his throat. A hungry raccoon scurried away. In the return to silence he gathered his wits. Once again all was quiet. Certainly quiet enough for his knocking to have been heard. If she was home. If she could still hear.

He sidestepped the spilled trash and checked the back door. He was about to knock, then stopped. One of the small rectangles of glass was shattered—the one right above the door lock. It looked as though someone had forced their way inside.

His instincts said run, but his feet wouldn't move. "Meredith?" he called out. His voice sounded hollow even to him. There was no reply. He tried again, louder. "Meredith Borge?"

Dex came quickly from the other side of the garage, his voice filled with urgency. "Electricity's been cut! Call nine-one-one!"

The door flew open as Gus reached for his cell phone. It was an explosion without explosives, like horses out of the gate. The door and whoever was behind it sent him tumbling backward down the stairs. He was suddenly wrestling on the lawn with a man in a sleek black body suit.

"Freeze!" shouted Dex, his gun drawn.

A gunshot pierced the night. Dex went down. Falling, he fired off several return rounds. The attacker fired back as he raced across the yard and leaped over the fence.

Gus hurried to Dex, who had been hit in the shoulder and was writhing in pain.

"Did I hit him?" asked Dex.

"I don't think so."

"Damn! Who the hell was that?"

"Sure wasn't Meredith. Are you going to be okay?"

"I will be," he answered, groaning. "But my shoulder's DOA. Call nine-one-one already."

The phone had landed just a few feet away in the scuffle.

Gus grabbed it and dialed. "Yes, operator, there's been a shooting at the Borge residence on Rural Route sixty-seven."

"Is there a better address?"

"That's the best I can do."

"Someone was shot with a gun, you say?"

"Yes, a man."

"Is he alive?"

"Yes. It's a shoulder wound."

"Was anyone else hurt?"

He glanced at the house, thinking of Meredith. "Quite possibly."

"Exactly how many people have been injured, sir?"

"I don't know. One for sure. For God's sakes, are you coming or not?"

"I'll dispatch police and paramedics right away."

"Thank you. Hurry." He hung up and dialed home. His sister answered.

"Carla, is everything okay there?"

"Yeah, everything's fine."

"Something terrible has happened."

"What?"

"Just—that's not important. I want you to grab Morgan right now. Both of you get in the car and drive to the police station as fast as you can."

"Gus, what's going on?"

"Just do it!"

"All right, all right."

"I'll meet you there as soon as the paramedics arrive."

"Paramedics! Gus—"

"Get going, Carla!"

"Okay. I'm leaving right this second."

I hope that's soon enough, he thought, but he didn't dare say it.

Across the lawn, Dex lay languidly across the sidewalk, his shoulder bathed in blood. Gus went to him and draped his coat over his body to keep the chill off and prevent shock.

"One more call," Dex said weakly.

"What are you talking about?"

"It's time you told the FBI about that note on your windshield."

The warning in Beth's handwriting suddenly blazed in his mind: *Stay away from Meredith Borge. Or I end up like her daughter.* That it had been signed "Flora," however, still complicated matters.

Dex grabbed him with newfound strength. "You have to call them. Even if it does make it look like Beth might really be part of that cult."

Gus grabbed Dex's gun. "First I have to check on Meredith."

"You're not going in that house."

"I have to check on her. It could take ten minutes for the cops to get out here in the sticks. If she's hanging by her neck, another minute could make all the difference."

"And if there's another guy with a gun in there, you're both dead. Don't risk your life to save that woman."

"That woman might know where my wife is!"

"Face it, man. Your wife joined a cult."

"Shut the hell up! Or I'll shoot you in the other shoulder."

"Fine, be a hero. I just hope to hell she's alone."

"And alive," said Gus as he started toward the house.

Sixty-two

Andie hadn't moved from the bed. In her mind she was sorting through the talk with Tom, trying to reconcile the cult's philosophy with the physical evidence in the serial killings. Two dead men. Both resembled Tom. Three dead women. All resembled Beth. A cult premised on the notion that all worldly experience was like an echo and that transformation to the next level came about only during that window of opportunity between life and death—a window that was wide open while hanging by the neck.

If it was all that simple, then why wasn't Beth Wheatley on the farm? Or if she was there, why was she nowhere to be seen?

Andie tried to sleep but couldn't close her eyes, too many questions pounding inside her head.

Beth's room was black when the music started. She had no control over it, no more than she controlled the room temperature or anything else in her environment. Over the past two weeks various classical pieces had played over two large speakers in the ceiling, coming and going at different times of the day for no apparent reason. At first she had thought it was a reward of some kind. Lately, it seemed more like a way to keep her from hearing what was going on outside her room.

It seemed so long ago that she had dropped Morgan off at the youth center, driven to meet Carla for a Sunday lunch, and parked her car in the garage. It had all happened so suddenly. A few quick footsteps behind her, a strong arm around her neck, a rag to her face that smelled of chemicals. Some time later—she couldn't say how long— she'd awakened in this very room.

The lock clicked, and the door suddenly opened. Beth backed against the far wall. The man in the doorway was just a silhouette in the shadows.

"Who's there?" she asked in the darkness.

"It's Tom."

She knew a Tom from the early meetings, the ones she had attended voluntarily, before she realized it was a cult. Back then he had seemed like a nice man. She was less frightened but still cautious. "What do you want?"

He raised the lights from the outside, then closed the door. "Steve wants the tape."

So it was him. She had never been face to face with her nightly visitor, but she had suspected it was Blechman.

"You watched it," he said with surprise. He was holding the tape, which she had neglected to rewind.

"I—" she said nervously. "I thought he wanted me to."

"He did. He's always wanted you to know."

"Know what? That I looked just like that poor woman?"

"That you were destined to join his inner circle."

"I don't want to join anything. That's why I stopped coming to the monthly meetings."

"You stopped coming because your husband made you stop."

"My husband didn't know anything about this."

"He is exactly the kind of domineering spouse that Steve warned us about. He controls you even when you don't re- alize you're being controlled."

"And I suppose this is a better way to live? Boxed up like an animal?"

"You have the power to free yourself, Flora."

"My name is *not* Flora. And I'm tired of hearing how Flora has the power to free herself. The power to stop innocent women from being killed. What *power*? All I want is to go home. Is anyone ever going to let me go home?"

He glared at her and said, "I've never liked you, *Beth*."

She blinked hard, shocked at the way he had spat out her real name. "What?"

"I knew you would never do what it takes to join the inner circle."

The madder he got, the more inclined he seemed to talk. It was risky, but she dug deep for courage and tweaked him good. "As if a dope like you would know what it takes to join the inner circle."

"I *am* the inner circle."

"Oh? And what did you do to get there? Promise to wash Steve's car for life?"

His face reddened. For a second she thought he would come after her, but he just clenched his teeth and said, "I killed for him. *That's* what it takes to make the inner circle."

She withdrew timidly. She'd seen the pictures of those murdered women.

He said, "Steve and I did, together. We cut the cord between my old and new family. I killed my old self."

"So, you didn't really kill anyone," she said, hoping that the photos had been phonies. "It's all symbolic?"

"The process is symbolic. But the murders are real."

"You . . . you actually killed someone?"

"And the real beauty is that the cops will never figure it out. I have no apparent motive. Never even met the victim. Chance resemblance is the only connection. He was fifty-one, so was I. He was divorced and lived alone, same with me. He represents my old self. The part that must die before you can reach a higher level of vibration."

"You just picked out some poor guy and killed him?"

"Steve picks. He picked both victims."

"Both?"

"Of course. Steve would never ask his most devoted followers to do something he hadn't already done himself. He kills the first one and shows you the way. And you duplicate it."

"Like an echo," said Beth, recalling the allusions to Blechman's manuscript in the speeches she'd attended.

"Now you're catching on."

She was almost too frightened to speak. "Is that why he killed those women, the ones in the photographs he showed me? He was showing me the way?"

"Yeah. Only he's tired of trying to lead you by example. He gave you three chances. Each time he told you the power to stop the killing was in your hands. All you had to do was follow his example. Kill your old self. And the echoes would stop."

"Why in the world would he think I was capable of murder?"

"You did steal for him."

She was suddenly queasy. The shoplifting from Nordstrom's. "Steve made it sound as innocent as those antisocial things you do for research in a college psychology class, like singing on a bus just to see the reaction of strangers."

"It was your first step toward breaking with your old self."

"And it obviously failed."

"Yes. Your failure is now obvious to everyone. Including Steve." He took the videotape and started for the door.

"Wait. What are you going to do with me?"

His eyes narrowed as he clutched the videotape of that tortured woman who looked eerily like Beth. "That's entirely up to Steve," he said, then shut the door and locked it.

The light switched off from the outside, and she was again alone in the darkness.

Sixty-three

Andie started at a noise outside her window. She looked out toward the main house. Past evenings on the farm had been tranquil to the point of dull. Tonight, however, the old farmhouse was filled with commotion. Lights were on. Doors were slamming, people coming and going. Men on ladders were bolting shutters to the second-story windows. The shutters appeared to be made of solid metal, not the old wood-slatted kind. From the way the men were straining to hoist them up, Andie would have guessed heavy-gauge steel.

Bulletproof? she wondered.

She stepped outside. A man was rushing by her unit, one of the young recruits. "What's going on?" she asked.

He stopped just long enough to catch his breath, winded but elated. "Preparations!"

"Preparations for what?"

He sprinted away without an answer. Andie called after him, again asking, "Preparations for what?"

He shouted back, "The transformation!"

As he ran toward the house, Andie stood and watched with a sinking sense of dread.

"Meredith?" Gus stood in the doorway, half inside and half out. The flashlight from his car was in one hand. The gun was in his right. The door was hanging by one hinge. Broken glass was scattered across the landing.

There was no reply. Not that he'd expected one.

Cautiously, he reached around the door frame and tried the kitchen light switch. Nothing. Dex was right. The electrical lines had been cut.

He switched on his flashlight and took just two steps inside. The narrow beam of light cut across the refrigerator and cabinets, then came to rest on the kitchen table. There were four chairs, but only one place setting. A good amount of food was on the plate. The water glass was nearly full. The napkin was neatly folded, seemingly unused. The intruder had apparently caught her at dinnertime. Or perhaps Gus had caught *him* at dinnertime.

Was that bastard cold enough to whack her and hang around to eat?

With each step forward, broken glass crunched beneath his feet. The thought of Meredith clinging to life, barely hanging on, drew him in. The thought of another intruder lurking around the corner made him freeze in his tracks.

"I have a gun," he said loudly, as if that would scare a murderer into surrender.

He aimed the flashlight and leaned forward to see down the hall into the living room. The sofa was straight. No lamps were tipped over. No sign of any disturbance at all. No sign of Meredith either.

He walked the other way, across the kitchen and toward the dining room. Crystal and silver glimmered as the flashlight cut across the breakfront to the display cabinet. A collection of framed photographs stood like dominoes on the credenza, one after the other. A wedding picture. Some baby photographs. None recent. The flashlight zipped past the last one, then zipped right back. It was a five-by-seven of a woman and a teenage girl. The girl was Shirley, five or so years ago. But it was the woman who intrigued him.

He picked it up and studied it. The woman had to be

Meredith, though she barely resembled the skinny woman with short hair he'd come to know. Seeing what she looked like with long hair and an extra seventy-five pounds was a watershed for him.

He'd just made the connection.

Sirens and swirling lights in the front lawn interrupted his thoughts. The police had arrived and were pounding on the front door.

"Police, open up!"

Gus stole one more look at the old photograph, then stuffed it in his jacket and hurried out the back.

The Op Center at the FBI office in Seattle was up and running by the time Isaac Underwood arrived. The phone call from Gus was but one of the triggers.

"What do we got?" asked Isaac. He entered like the wind with two assistants in his wake.

Lundquist answered, "Meredith Borge is confirmed dead. Strangled."

Isaac moved to the big table in the center of the room. A bright light from the ceiling illuminated a detailed drawing of Blechman's farm and a series of aerial photographs. "What's the latest from Yakima?"

"Our surveillance agents report a high level of activity at the compound, especially for night. They're placing shutters on the windows of the main farmhouse," he said as he pointed at the corresponding box on the drawing. "They appear to be bulletproof."

"Any sign of Andie?"

"No."

"Any chance she snuck away?"

Lundquist shrugged. "If she did, she hasn't made contact with us."

"Any concrete insights as to what the hell set these people off?"

"If we're to believe Gus Wheatley, Meredith Borge was

the one person who could link Blechman's group to his wife's disappearance. No doubt that got her killed. But maybe they're afraid they didn't shut her up soon enough and anticipate some kind of offensive from law enforcement. That scenario would be especially consistent with the theory that they're holding Beth Wheatley against her will."

"Yes. That's one possibility."

Both men were silent. Lundquist said, "I think we both know the other."

Isaac looked to the middle distance, speaking to no one in particular. "Or they finally figured out Andie is FBI."

"I'm afraid that's the way I see it too, sir. What do you want to do?"

"Start a dialogue."

"Specifics?"

"I want a negotiation team activated. Set up a mobile unit as our forward command post."

"Problem is, there's no phone service to the farm."

"Then get a chopper to drop a cell phone on their fucking heads. If that doesn't work, use a loudspeaker. Just stay out of sniper range."

"What about our own snipers?"

"Advance two of them. Just to observe at this point."

Lundquist didn't jump.

"Let's move!" said Isaac.

"Isaac, I'm all for opening up the lines of communication. But let's not forget that somebody on that farm is in all likelihood responsible for the strangulation of at least five people. Six if you count Meredith Borge, seven if you count Shirley. If they know Andie is an FBI agent, talk isn't going to get her out."

They locked eyes, then Isaac said, "Put SWAT on alert. Two teams. If we have to go in, I want them in position."

"Will do. Anything else?"

"Yeah," said Isaac, his voice low and serious. "No show

of force till I give the word. We negotiate as long as possible. In the meantime, be damn sure that SWAT stays out of sight."

Andie watched from the doorstep outside her barracks, feeling like the only person on the farm who wasn't in high gear. One after another, a stream of men and women hurried past her. They carried nondescript boxes of food and supplies from the barn to the main house. Some of them looked frightened. Others were angry. All of them seemed to know what to do.

"Come on, Willow! Give us a hand!"

A group of women raced by her, but Andie couldn't match the voice to a face. Standing around wasn't the kind of thing Willow would do. But Andie had a growing sense that she wasn't long for the role.

Obviously, something had made the cult leaders feel as though an attack from outside were imminent, but she couldn't say what specifically had triggered the decision to fortify the compound. In her last phone contact, Isaac had promised to set up spot surveillance of the farm. Maybe they had discovered one of the agents. Or perhaps Isaac had decided to increase the pressure without telling her. Some new break in the serial killings could easily have triggered a roadblock or even the deployment of SWAT around the perimeter. Andie needed to get up high where she could see what was going on.

She ran from her unit to the back of the barn. A ladder led to the hayloft. She climbed quickly and moved to the opening in front, where she hoped she might be able to see out to the main road. Tonight it was too dark to see to the end of the driveway. If law enforcement was out there, it was a furtive effort with no show of force. There were no swirling lights, not even the glowing orange dot of a cigarette in the darkness. From this vantage point, however, she did have a better look at the men on the ladders who were

putting the shutters on the main house. They were thirty
yards away, but Andie could see the automatic pistols hol-
stered at their sides.

A gunshot cracked through the barn wall. Another pop,
another shattered board. Suddenly the walls were explod-
ing from a barrage of gunfire across the face of the barn,
the old wood splintering like kindling. Andie dived low as
shots whistled over her head. Screams erupted from the
main house, where the metal shutters rattled with fully automatic gunfire. Andie looked up just as one of the men on
the ladders was hit several times. He tumbled down the
rungs and hit the ground with a thud. He didn't move.
Dead. Two others lay dead on the roof.

An attack! Why?

The semi-organized human supply line from the barn to
the house had now completely scattered, people running
scared. "Get inside!" someone shouted from below.

Andie smelled smoke. Flames erupted behind her. A fire
was ripping through the barn, devouring the loose and
baled hay in the loft. She couldn't go back to the ladder.
The flames were out of control behind her, but the front of
the barn was still being pelted by gunfire. With no other
choice, she jumped from the loft and ran from the flames,
keeping low to the ground. Frightened horses raced from
their smoke-filled stalls and nearly stampeded her. Another
barrage of gunfire cut down a woman just twenty feet
ahead of her. Andie ducked behind one of the sleeping barracks. Others screamed and ran for the house or the barracks, any place they could find cover.

A spray of gunfire shattered the windows above Andie's
head. She pressed her whole body to the ground, as low as
she could get. She was frightened but even more shocked.
The FBI had fired first. No warning.

What in the hell are you idiots doing?

Sixty-four

The Op Center had erupted in confusion. A half dozen agents were on the phone, each in a different shouting match, each trying to find out what all the shooting was about. Isaac was the center of the storm, directing his wrath at Agent Lundquist.

"Who the hell did you put in charge out there? Lieutenant Calley?"

Lundquist was at a loss. "It's not us who did the shooting."

"Who is it then? Yakima Sheriff's office? Everybody and their brother has a SWAT team these days."

"No one from the sheriff's office has been deployed. I'm telling you straight, Isaac. No paramilitary law enforcement unit is even in place yet. Not even our own SWAT."

Realization slowly washed over him. Isaac walked to the map and uttered softly, "They're firing upon themselves."

"What?" said Lundquist. "Why the hell would they do that?"

"Why did they start the fires at Waco? To trigger an apocalypse."

Lundquist stood silent, stunned.

"Deploy the SWAT," said Isaac. "It's time to save these people from themselves." He looked down, concerned. "Or at least save Andie."

* * *

A pulsating alarm pierced the night, echoing like an air-raid siren across the compound. Andie was lying in a depression in the earth that barely provided cover. It would soon be a shallow grave if she didn't move to a safer place. Bullets were missing her by inches, kicking up dirt all around her. Then there was a break, as if they were reloading or regrouping. On impulse, she made her move. She rolled to the front of the barracks and shoved the door open. Gunfire shattered the door above her, but she rolled inside and pushed it closed. She huddled on the floor, then looked up and gasped.

Three bodies were suspended above her, hanging by the neck at the end of a rope. One man, two women. They twitched every few seconds as bullets whistled through the shattered windows and riddled the corpses. They turned slowly on the rope, and finally Andie saw a face. One of them was Felicia.

The apocalypse had begun.

Andie was frozen, unable to look and at the same time unable to tear her eyes away. Suddenly, she smelled smoke again. It wasn't coming from the barn. It was from the back of the barracks. The unit was on fire.

The door burst open. She jumped to defend herself, but a man grabbed her. He was armed and wearing a flak jacket. He was dressed in fatigues and had his face covered with greasepaint. Instinctively, she hit him twice, landing a solid blow to his jaw.

"Willow, stop!"

She recognized him. It was Tom. And he still thought she was on his side.

"Let's go. Everybody inside."

She wasn't sure what was going on, then it clicked. She recognized the fully automatic AK–47 rifle and the full metal jacket ammunition he was carrying. *You son of a bitch. You were firing on your own people.*

"Come on, damn it! Inside the house!" He grabbed her and nearly dragged her out the door.

Sixty-five

The driveway was empty when Gus arrived home. Carla's car was gone. On the phone from Meredith's, he had tried to convey the requisite urgency without scaring her to death with news of a killer on the loose. It wasn't as if the killer were outside the Wheatleys' front door. Carla had plenty of time to get Morgan to safety before the attacker could get to his car and drive all the way from Meredith's house.

Unless he had a partner.

Gus's heart was suddenly racing. In all the confusion—fighting off the attacker, Dex getting shot—the possibility of two killers striking in tandem had eluded him. He hurried inside and called out from the foyer.

"Morgan, Carla?"

No reply. The house had a deserted feel to him. He closed the door and switched on the lights. Morgan's room was the first stop. Empty. He grabbed the cordless phone and dialed the police station, just to make sure. He continued to the master bedroom as the call went through.

"Hello, my name's Gus Wheatley. I'm checking to see if my six-year-old daughter and my sister are there. This may sound strange, but I told them to go there because something happened and they were afraid to stay here at the house alone."

"I'll check, sir. What are the names?"

"Wheatley is the last name. Morgan and Carla."

Gus heard a click, then elevator music. He was on hold. The line crackled as he entered the master closet, but the cordless reception soon cleared. With the phone tucked under his chin he pulled Beth's big box of old photographs down from the shelf, sat cross-legged on the floor, and dug in.

It was the same box he had gone through the other night while reminiscing about Beth and the way things used to be. Some he had lingered over. Others he had breezed through. At first he had focused only on pictures of Beth and him or Beth and Morgan. By the end of the night, however, he had gone through nearly every photograph. Some had been taken before he and Beth had even started dating. That night had been his rediscovery of Beth, a chance to meet friends of hers he had never met before.

One of those friends was now the focus of his suspicion.

If his memory was correct, she was in just one photograph among thousands. The other night it hadn't meant anything to him. Just another old snapshot of Beth with friends. He probably hadn't looked at it for more than five seconds. But earlier tonight, when he had seen that five-year-old photograph of Meredith Borge in her dining room, it hit him. He would have sworn that somewhere in Beth's stack of old photographs was a picture of her and Meredith. If it was really there, Gus had to find it. He had to know how Beth had gotten mixed up with a cult.

He wasn't sure which packet contained the right photograph. Like a Vegas card dealer he flipped through one stack after another with lightning speed. Finally, he stopped. He had found it. He laid it on the carpet beside the five-by-seven he had taken from Meredith's house and compared the two. No doubt about it. The woman in the photo was a younger and much fatter Meredith Borge with long brown hair. The woman on her right was Beth. Curious, he checked the remaining shots from the same roll of film, photos that had seemed so meaningless he hadn't even bothered to look at them the other night. He found another one of Beth and Meredith. But this one was different. There was a third woman, one with her arm around the woman he now knew was Meredith and who seemed particularly chummy with her.

It was Gus's sister.

The operator came back on the line. "Sir? There is no Morgan or Carla Wheatley here."

Before he could speak, Carla interrupted. "Hang up the phone, Gus."

He whirled. She was standing in the closet doorway with a gun pointed at him. The phone was in the other hand. She had been listening to the call.

"Sir?" asked the operator.

Carla said, "Tell her everything's fine, and hang up. *Now.*"

"Sir, are you still there?"

"Uh—you know what, operator? They're pulling up in the driveway right now. Thank you for checking, though."

He hung up and snapped, "What did you do with Morgan?"

"She's fine. And she'll continue to be fine if you just do as I say."

"Are you crazy? What are you doing?"

"I tried to warn you. That note on your windshield. You just ignored it."

"That was in Beth's handwriting."

"You don't think I know what her handwriting looks like?"

"You were behind the 'Mary Had a Little Lamb' message from that pay phone, weren't you? You're the only one who could have known Beth and Morgan's little secret."

"Just shut up, Gus. *I'm* in control now."

Sixty-six

Ash and burning cinders floated like glowing snowflakes from the barn. A cool wind carried them toward the farmhouse, where a dozen frantic people scurried to the backyard. Two men wearing camouflage fatigues like Tom stood at the open cellar doors and herded them below. Andie knew from her lie-detector meeting with Blechman that the cellar wasn't nearly big enough to hold all the cult members. Between the hangings and gunfire, the ranks had seriously thinned.

Culled, she thought, recalling the term Tom had used at the chicken coop.

The gunfire continued but was erratic, as if they were missing intentionally. Andie crouched low as she and Tom crossed the yard toward the house. Hot cinders landed in her hair and burned her face. It was only a matter of time before the house would be ablaze. Just ahead, people hurried into the cellar, eager for protection. It was certain to be a death trap. She had to break loose.

An argument broke out at the cellar doors. A woman refused to go below. From somewhere in the field a burst of gunfire erupted, killing her instantly. The crowd scattered. In the confusion Andie broke free from Tom's grasp and ran. She dived toward the shrubs alongside the house, where one of the slain workers had fallen off his ladder. He was stone dead, but his pistol was still in its holster. Andie grabbed the gun and stuffed it in her jacket.

Tom barked out some orders to his subordinates, then turned and saw Andie. "Willow!" He hadn't seen her take the gun. She ignored him.

"Get in here!" he shouted.

Andie ran the opposite way, up the back porch and into the house, baiting him to follow. He did. She continued at full speed through the kitchen and down the main hall. The house had been evacuated and no lights were on. Steel shutters covered most of the windows, but not the one over the kitchen sink. That was the only source of light, a faint and flickering glow from the burning barn some thirty yards away.

Or had the house caught fire?

Andie posted herself in the hallway beneath the staircase. She checked her pistol. It was fully loaded. Out of sight in the darkness and with her back to the wall, she waited.

A bullet ricocheted off the shutters on the front picture window, but she didn't flinch. Some of Blechman's lieutenants were apparently still in the field stirring up trouble.

The kitchen door flew open. "Willow!" Tom shouted. "Get your ass down in the cellar."

She didn't answer.

"I'm giving you five seconds to come out."

She counted off in her mind but didn't make a sound. Exactly on the count of five, Tom popped the spent ammunition clip from his rifle and attached a new one. "Have it your way, baby," he said loudly, then started across the kitchen.

They were in the large dressing area of the closet. Beth's clothing was on shelves and hangers all around them. Gus lay flat on his stomach on the floor, as Carla had directed. She stood over him with the gun aimed at his back. She was tugging at a robe, trying to remove the belt so she could tie his hands.

Gus looked up at her. "You're the one who got Beth into the cult, aren't you?"

"Brilliant, Gus. How many years did it take you to figure that one out?"

"You and your buddy Meredith. She's dead. Do you know that?"

She smiled thinly, as if her brother were stupid. "Of course I know. Meredith hasn't been my buddy since she turned against us and pulled her daughter off the farm."

"Is that why Shirley tried to kill her?"

"It wasn't Shirley by her lonesome. She just took the fall, and like a good kid she didn't name names. She was loyal to the group. Until you waved a quarter million dollars under her nose."

"You're the one who got Shirley killed. You told Blechman she was talking to me."

"Careful. Don't go figuring it all out. You were much safer as the workaholic attorney married to his job."

"That was my ticket to safety, huh? Just stay busy and happily oblivious while you indoctrinate my wife into some cult."

"If it makes you feel better, she never really joined. Our teacher has been working on her since the day I brought her by the farm. He's still working on her. He likes her look."

"If this *teacher*," he said angrily, "so much as lays a hand on her—"

A scream broke the tension. It had come from somewhere in the house. In that same instant Gus vaulted toward Carla and knocked her backward into the hanging clothes, legs and arms flailing. She tried to gouge his eyes with her nails as they wrestled for the gun. When the tumbling stopped, Gus was on top with the gun in her face.

"What was that scream?" He spoke sharply but quietly.

"I don't know."

"Where's Morgan?"

"She's okay, I swear. I locked her in the basement until . . ."

"Until you got rid of me?" he said with disbelief.

There was another scream. It seemed to have come from the basement. With the gun to her head he lifted her up and pushed her toward the door. "Come on. You're going with me."

Andie barely breathed as she waited beneath the stairs. The darkness was her only real shield. It wasn't totally black but dark enough to conceal her. Tom crossed cautiously. One step. Stop. Another step. Stop. Each step a little closer, a little louder than the next. Finally, she could see him in the shadows, his image slowly gaining definition. The entire house seemed to be brightening, and it wasn't just her eyes adjusting to the darkness. The fire outside was intensifying, blazing more light through the kitchen window. She heard a rumble outside, like the barn collapsing. The sudden burst of flames was like a flare in the hallway.

Their eyes met, and she knew she was toast.

She made a dash for the living room. Tom fired and missed. Andie fired back. A hit to his right hand sent his gun flying. Andie vaulted toward him and knocked him to his back. She tried to pin him. He squirmed beneath her.

"Freeze!" she shouted.

He swung wildly in defense, but his shattered hand was useless. She brought a knee to his groin and shoved her pistol in his face. "I said, freeze!"

Tom groaned and went limp.

"Take me to Beth Wheatley."

"Who?" he said, breathless.

She cocked the hammer and pressed the barrel into his eye socket. "Take me to Beth Wheatley or I'll blow your eyeball out the back of your head."

Andie wasn't sure Beth was there. She wasn't even sure if Beth had been taken against her will. She hoped the bluff would work.

"She's in the attic."

It *had* worked. She rose slowly and kept the gun on him. "You make just one move I don't like, you're dead. Now let's go," she said as she directed him toward the stairs.

They climbed the main staircase to the second floor, then a smaller staircase to the third floor. At the top of the stairs was a semiprivate sitting area that led to an outdoor widow's walk. The rear half of the sitting area had been enclosed in an ugly fashion. It was clearly built for security, not aesthetics. The door had a deadbolt that locked with a key from the outside.

"She's in there," said Tom.

If she really was in there, it was clear she was a prisoner. "Unlock it."

"I don't have a key."

"Lie down on the floor, facedown."

He got down. Andie called out, "Beth Wheatley, are you in there?" No one answered. "If you're in there, stand away from the door."

With one quick shot Andie blew the lock off. A woman screamed inside. "Beth, you're safe. It's the FBI!"

Tom shouted, "It's a trap, Flora!"

Andie turned the gun on him. "Shut up!"

"She's the enemy, Flora! They're killing all of us!"

Andie said, "Beth, come out now!"

"Stay down, Flora!"

Andie yanked him up by one arm. "Come on, we're going in."

She kicked the door open. Beth screamed even louder. She was huddled in the far corner beneath a boarded-up window. "Leave me alone!"

Gunshots suddenly pelted the metal shutters outside. Just as Beth screamed, Tom whirled and flung Andie over his shoulder. She hit the floor hard. Her pistol slid across the room. Beth sprang from the corner and grabbed it.

"Stop!" she shouted.

Andie and Tom froze, both on their knees. Beth was shaking and confused, moving the gun back and forth from Andie to Tom erratically. She wasn't treating Tom like a friend, but Andie still had to convince her she wasn't the enemy.

"I'm Agent Andie Henning with the FBI. Please, I'm here to help you."

"She's no FBI agent, Flora. She's leading the revolt. They've come to kill us all."

Beth aimed unsteadily at Andie. "If you're with the FBI, then show me your badge."

"I don't have one. I'm working undercover."

"She's one of the rebels," said Tom. "Kill her before she kills us both."

"Keep away from me!"

"Shoot her, Flora! You've already killed for us. Kill one more."

"I never killed anyone!" She looked at Andie, pleading, but still not convinced she was an FBI agent. "He's lying. He's trying to box me in."

"I believe you," said Andie. "Now just let me stand up, and give me the gun."

"No!" Beth shouted. "Both of you, just stay where you are!"

Tom rose and started toward her slowly. "Come on, Flora. You're one of us."

"No, I'm not!"

"Give me the gun."

"Stop! Don't come any closer."

He kept coming slowly. "It's time to break with the past. Join the inner circle."

"Not another step! I'll shoot!"

"That wouldn't make Steve very happy, now would it?"

Her face flushed with anger at the mere mention of his name. It was clear he'd played the wrong card. He leaped toward her and reached for the gun. A shot erupted, then another. Andie ducked. Tom fell. Beth tried to speak, but her voice merely quaked. A pool of blood oozed from beneath Tom's twisted body. He didn't move.

Beth dropped the gun, almost threw it down. Andie slid across the floor and grabbed it. Beth cowered against the bed, sobbing. Andie checked Tom's pulse and got nothing. Cautiously, she approached Beth and gently touched her arm.

"It's all right. It's over."

Beth was crying as she struggled to regain control. "Are you sure?"

"Yes. I'm sure."

"Where's Blechman?"

Andie felt a chill. She didn't know. "Everything is under control," she said, doing her best to mask her own concerns.

Sixty-seven

The basement door squeaked on its hinge as it slowly swung open. Gus wanted to rush down and get Morgan, but he feared a trap. He stood at the top of the stairs with Carla in front of him like a human shield, the gun pressed to the back of her skull.

"Morgan, are you down here?"

The silence confirmed his fears. She wasn't alone.

He switched on the light. The single low-watt bulb barely illuminated the top half of the steep and narrow wooden staircase. Beyond the tenth step was total darkness, the bowels of an unfinished basement that smelled of mildew and gave up not a sound. There was only one way in or out—through this door.

"If there's somebody down there, I called the police," said Gus. "They're on their way."

Gus waited, the seconds ticking in his mind. He actually had called the police. But the earlier screams had told him there was no time to wait. With a firm grip on Carla he called out, "Who's down there?"

A light suddenly switched on from below. A man was standing at the base of the stairs, the same attacker from Meredith's house. "We are."

Blechman, Gus presumed, the handsome young leader Meredith had told him about. He was using Morgan the same way Gus was using Carla, as a human shield with a gun to her head. Morgan would have been too small to protect his whole body, except that she was standing on the higher step and he was kneeling behind her on the lower one.

"Morgan!" Gus cried.

"Don't waste your breath," said Blechman. "She can't hear or see you."

A set of headphones filled her ears with music. Duct tape covered her eyes. *A blessing,* thought Gus. He noticed her hands and feet were tied as well. He pressed the gun more firmly to Carla's head. "Let go of my daughter, or Carla's dead."

"And where does that leave you?" Blechman said coolly.

"Let her go!"

"You can't win this, Gus. Isn't it obvious? I'm holding someone you would die for. You're holding someone who would die for *me.* Tell him, Rosa."

"Rosa?" said Gus, confused.

"The woman who used to be your sister," said Carla.

Blechman smiled. "Tell him you'd die for me."

"I would gladly die for you."

"See, Gus? Now hand over the gun and save your daughter."

"You think I'm an idiot?"

"We don't like to kill children," said Blechman. "Give us your gun, and we kill only you. Morgan goes free. Keep your gun, I blow your daughter's brains out right before your eyes."

Gus trembled. "You'll kill us both anyway!"

"Your daughter doesn't know anything. No need to kill her."

Carla said, "I won't kill my own niece, Gus."

"Oh, but you'll kill your brother?"

"You made us do it. I tried to warn you. You wouldn't listen."

Blechman shouted, "That's enough, Rosa."

Gus could barely think. "Just let Morgan go. The police are on their way. I wasn't bluffing. I called them."

"Is that true, Rosa?"

"Yes. He called again from the bedroom after he got my gun."

His eyes blazed. He tightened his grip on Morgan. "You shouldn't have done that. And you," he said to Carla, "shouldn't have let that happen."

"Take your hands off my daughter. I'll pull the trigger, I swear."

"That's Rosa's gun," said Blechman. "It isn't even loaded. Is it, Rosa?"

She struggled nervously. "That's right. It's not even loaded."

Blechman said, "Go ahead. Pull the trigger."

Gus could see Morgan was beginning to lose consciousness. Blechman had been restraining her with his right arm around her torso, but the hand was now up around her throat. "Let go of my daughter!"

Blechman's eyes locked on Carla, as if they controlled her. "Tell him. Tell him to go ahead and squeeze the trigger."

Her voice shook, but she didn't dare disobey him. "Go right ahead, Gus. The gun isn't loaded."

He could tell she was lying. If he didn't somehow keep them talking, he'd have to shoot his own sister. "What did you do with my wife?" Gus shouted.

"She's been a grave disappointment to me," said Blechman. "I put up with her disobedience for a very long time. She had a special look. She could have gone far. But Morgan looks an awful lot like her. In due time, she may go further."

His perverse intentions were suddenly laid bare. On impulse, Gus shoved Carla down the stairs, just far enough to force Blechman to drop his guard in self-defense. It was only for an instant, and it would call upon every bit of experience he'd ever had with guns, but Gus had an opening. He fired a shot that snapped Blechman's head back in a crimson explosion.

He fell into the darkness, taking Morgan with him.

"Morgan!" Gus leaped down the stairs. Blechman hadn't moved. Morgan was squirming on the cement floor, her hands and feet bound, her eyes and ears still covered. Gus ripped the headphones off and held her close.

"It's Daddy! It's okay, sweetheart. Everything's okay."

At the foot of the stairs, Carla was on her knees at Blechman's side, weeping softly. Gus grabbed Blechman's gun and shoved it in his belt. He took Morgan in his arms and stepped past his sister, leaving the duct tape over his daughter's eyes so she wouldn't see the carnage. Carla never moved as he and Morgan climbed the stairs.

At the top step he stopped and looked down into the basement. Carla leaned forward and kissed Blechman's bloody lips, then glanced up at Gus.

"You murdered my husband," she said in a voice that cracked.

Gus looked at her with both contempt and pity. She'd gone from bad to worse, from an abusive old boyfriend who used to beat her into submission to a psychopathic cult leader who controlled her very mind. From that depth, sadly, there could be no return.

Gus closed the basement door and locked it. Sirens blared in the driveway as the police arrived. With Morgan cradled tightly in his arms, he simply waited.

Sixty-eight

More than a dozen dead.

That daunting tally confronted Andie when she returned to the office in Seattle just before sunrise the following morning. Two men and three women had been brutally murdered—two more if you counted Shirley and Meredith Borge. The cult had lost another eleven members, including Blechman, Felicia, and Tom. Some had died in the fire before the FBI could evacuate them. Some had hanged themselves in the frenzy.

Andie hadn't slept all night, but her adrenaline was still pumping. Peering through the one-way glass outside the FBI's interrogation room, she finally had an opportunity to see Victoria Santos operate in top form. Isaac had called her in late last night to interrogate Gus's sister after several other agents had elicited only blank stares. Carla had never asked for an attorney, so further interrogation was legally proper. It was just a matter of finding someone with the skill and expertise to break through to a devoted follower who had just lost her beloved leader, her cult husband. Isaac thought of Victoria. And he was absolutely correct.

Andie watched for nearly a half hour, catching the tail end. Victoria seemed rejuvenated and in old form. Andie would have liked to believe what Isaac had told her earlier—that Andie had been the catalyst for the rediscovered energy, that Victoria had seen her old self in Andie and pushed through the burnout. It probably wasn't true, she figured, but it had been nice of Isaac to say it.

Just after eight, Victoria finally emerged. Andie, she, and Isaac met in a conference room across the hall. Victoria looked tired but was still running in high gear, like the winner of a dance marathon. It reminded Andie that she herself hadn't snagged a discerning look at her own face since entering the mirrorless cult. The prospects were frightening.

"How did it go?" asked Isaac.

"Good enough for the state attorney to bring murder charges against her."

"For which killings?"

"Not any of the five you're thinking of. Seems the string of murders goes back further than those two men who resembled Tom the lieutenant and the three women who resembled Beth Wheatley."

Isaac nearly groaned. "Don't tell me everyone in that damn cult has killed this way."

"No. It was intended as a rite of passage to Blechman's inner circle only. But it was an evolving concept."

"Evolving from what?"

"From what I was able to gather, Carla was the first member to reach this higher level. Originally, Blechman's thinking was that to truly rise above the level of human, you not only had to separate yourself from the people who held you back, but you had to eliminate the things—the person—who was syphoning your energy. In Carla's case, that was her abusive ex-boyfriend."

"That doesn't fit with the echo killings," said Isaac. "The victims resembled the cult member and didn't even know them. None were old boyfriends or the like."

"That's right," said Victoria. "The way Carla explained it, Blechman realized right away that it was too dangerous for his followers to try to kill the actual person who was holding them back. He would eventually end up with a group of followers whose mothers or boyfriends or husbands or wives had all been murdered. That would be a red flag for police. So he changed his initiation rites. He decided to use symbolic victims."

"Symbolic of what?" asked Isaac.

"The victim represents your old self," said Andie.

"I see," said Isaac. "The way those two men resembled Tom. And the way the three women resembled Beth Wheatley."

"Except Beth wasn't a willing participant," said Andie.

Isaac stroked his chin, thinking. "Unwilling . . . maybe. You're assuming everything she told you in your debriefing was true."

Andie said, "As traumatized as Beth was, I don't think she could possibly have kept her composure to stick to anything close to a lie."

Isaac looked skeptical. "She's still here in the building, right?"

"She and Gus are in the west conference room. They're willing to cooperate, but they'd love for me to tell them it's time to go home."

"Do you think Mrs. Wheatley would agree to talk to Victoria?" asked Isaac.

Andie started to answer, but Victoria beat her to it. "I don't see the need. I trust Andie's take on the situation."

Andie swelled inside. "Really?"

"Yeah, really. You did truly excellent work here."

"Well, I . . ." She stopped the *aw-shucks* routine, recalling Victoria's remark the first time she'd praised her—how compliments were scarce in the bureau, so just shut up and take one. "Thank you."

Victoria glanced at Isaac. "I'm bushed. If you need me anytime over the next two hours, I'll be sacked out in the infirmary downstairs. If anyone else needs me, I'm in Milwaukee."

"I'd say you've earned some shut-eye."

She shook Andie's hand. "Not that I sit around praying for more serial killers, but I do hope we'll have the chance to work together again."

"So do I."

Victoria headed for the elevator. Andie and Isaac exchanged glances. He didn't say it, perhaps because he thought it would pale in comparison to a pat on the back from Victoria Santos. But she could feel how proud he was of her.

Andie said, "Let's go see the Wheatleys, shall we?"

They walked in silence down the hall to the west conference room and stopped outside the door. The venetian blinds on the rectangular window on the door were opened just enough to see inside. Gus and his wife were seated side by side, their backs to the door. He had his arm around her. Her head lay on his shoulder.

Andie smiled with her eyes. Watching too, Isaac said, "You really do believe her, don't you?"

"Are you still undecided?"

"Just one thing bugs me. Her explanation of how her fingerprints ended up on that pay phone in Oregon. The whole idea that Blechman forced her to handle a mouthpiece while she was captive in Yakima, only so he could screw it onto the payphone in Oregon and make it look like she was there."

"Makes sense to me. After all, Beth's prints were found only on the mouthpiece and not on the buttons that had been used to punch out the 'Mary Had a Little Lamb' message on Morgan's phone. Planted evidence like that would make it look like she was involved in the cult, make it impossible for her to return to her old life."

"You're satisfied, then?"

"If you're asking whether I think she's innocent, the answer is yes."

"Completely innocent?" he pressed. "As in, everything she told you was the truth?"

"I don't think I could possibly know her well enough to know if everything she told me was the truth. But *he* does," she said, pointing with a nod toward Gus.

They watched through the window as Gus and Beth embraced. It seemed genuine, not staged in the least. They were alone inside, completely unaware of Isaac and Andie watching from the outside.

"All right," said Isaac. He sounded as if he were just then making up his mind. "Tell the Wheatleys they can go home."

"Good instincts, boss." Andie stepped toward the door.

"Hey," said Isaac, stopping her. She looked back. He seemed confused, as if there were something he wanted to say.

"Take the rest of the day off," he said.

"Thanks." She reached for the doorknob.

"Hey," he said again.

She stopped again, met his eyes.

He blinked twice, then asked, "You free for dinner?"

It was the expression on his face that had confused her—a certain nervousness that made it seem as though he was actually asking her out, not just buddies after work. "Tonight?"

"I was thinking maybe . . . Saturday night."

She smiled wryly. "I know a great little place that makes awesome camas cakes."

"What cakes?"

"Never mind. You pick the place. Just be sure the reservation is for two. Kira and Willow are staying home."

"Two it is, then," he said, smiling.

She gave a wink, then turned and entered the conference room.

"**W**heatley and Partners," the receptionist said into the phone.

Gus had a spring in his step as he passed her desk in the main lobby. Over the past eight months he'd probably heard his receptionist answer a thousand calls the same way, and the sound of it still tickled him. His own firm.

With eighteen lawyers, it wasn't Preston & Coolidge. That was the good news. They were big enough to do the same quality work, small enough to run their own lives and actually have a life beyond time sheets. Most had come over with Gus from P&C. A few were old friends of Gus's, talented lawyers who could never have gotten hired by the old firm, like Jack Shode, the bankruptcy guru who spent weekends on lead guitar in one of the hottest local bands. Maybe he didn't fit the old P&C mold, but who could have possibly known more about debt than a guy surrounded by rock-star wannabes?

"Nice earring, Jack."

"Nice wing tips, chief."

It was their standard tongue-in-cheek greeting every afternoon as they passed in the hall on their way to the coffeemaker. For Gus, it was a pleasure just to have time in the day to get off the phone and get his own cup.

It hadn't been all smiles, of course. The end of the "Echo

Killings" had been an enduring media event in Seattle. Everyone from Isaac Underwood to Steven Blechman's fifth-grade teacher had been on television. It was like the silly season, till the losses were tallied. So many innocent people had been hurt, from the murder victims themselves to the mortified families of misguided cult members. The prosecutor was determined to put the cult permanently out of business, having brought first-degree murder charges against Carla. She'd spent the last eight months in jail awaiting trial.

Neither Gus nor Beth had done much talking to the media. Just a short statement from Gus that they were sorry for the victims and were moving forward with their lives. It had taken months for the press to leave them alone, but life finally had started to take on some semblance of normality.

Their lives were changed forever, but that wasn't a bad thing. They had more time together, more dinners as a family, longer talks that reached well beyond the obligatory "how was your day?" They'd even moved to a smaller house—one with no echoes. Progress had come more quickly than expected, and not just because Gus had heard it both from Carla and Blechman that Beth had never actually joined the cult. The truth was, they had fallen out of love, but they had never stopped loving each other. Getting back the spark would just take time, and it was perhaps right around the corner. He'd noticed that Beth had recently taken to wearing those little diamond-chip earrings again, the ones he'd given to her on her twenty-first birthday. They were practically worthless, but the way Beth used to wear them on important occasions—birthdays, anniversaries—had always served as a reminder of what was good about their marriage.

It was nice to know she was sending him little reminders again.

"Excuse me, Gus?" It was his secretary poking her head into his office. Gus looked up from his desk.

"Yes?"

"Your wife's on line one. She's calling from the shop."

The shop was a fine-linen boutique in Bel Square that Beth had patronized for years. She was now the assistant manager and thinking about buying it from the seventy-year-old owner, who was about to retire. Getting into business was a good way to rebuild her confidence and focus on the future. Gus was all for it.

He picked up the phone. "Hi. What's up?"

"I'm sorry, but things are completely crazy here this afternoon. I'm tied up with the accountant for at least another hour. I know it's my turn to pick up Morgan today, but you think you can pinch-hit?"

"Sure."

"She gets out at two-thirty."

"Actually, on Tuesdays she gets out at three."

She paused on the line, as if both pleased he'd remembered and embarrassed she hadn't. "I guess I forgot."

"Nobody's perfect."

"Are you sure you can get away?"

"Well, the boss is a real tyrant over here, but maybe just this once I'll look the other way while I'm sneaking out the door."

He could sense she was smiling. She said, "I'll be home around six-thirty."

"See you then."

He hung up and got his coat. He had plenty of time to pick up Morgan, but it was best to duck out early. If he was late, she would blame Beth, and he didn't want that. He was packing his briefcase when the phone rang. He signaled to his secretary that he'd "already left," but she overruled him.

"It's Ben Albergo," she said in the tone reserved for the pope. "He's calling from Washington."

It wasn't often Gus talked to Ben, one of the true friends he had left in high places. Ben was a power broker in the new administration, a golfing buddy to the president's chief of staff.

He closed the office door and answered, "Hey, Ben. To what do I owe this honor?"

"Believe it or not, I'm calling about Martha Goldstein."

The excitement drained from his voice. "I think you dialed the wrong number."

"No, listen. She's on the president's short list for appointment to undersecretary of Treasury."

"Martha? That's a bit over her head, isn't it?"

"Your old firm is pushing her very hard."

"I'm surprised. I heard they can't stand her over there."

"That's putting it mildly. She's driving them all nuts. But from what I hear, a couple of dopes on the management committee exchanged some unbelievable e-mails about her. The 'B' word all over the place. The upshot is, they can't fire her without being sued for discrimination."

"So there's only one way to dump her," said Gus.

"Exactly. Call in all their political markers and get her appointed to a plum position here in Washington."

"What does it have to do with me?"

"You're obviously aware the president ran his campaign on a platform of moral integrity."

"Yeah, the 'I-only-sleep-with-my-wife' president."

"It works for him. But his standards have bitten a few of his appointees in the butt. We just can't take the embarrassment of another crash-and-burn nominee who hasn't exactly followed the president's fine example."

"Is this headed where I think it's headed?"

"I've heard scuttlebutt that Martha can't withstand scrutiny."

"Are you asking if she and I had an affair?"

"This is completely confidential, Gus. Personally, I don't even think she's qualified for the appointment. She's not worth fighting over. If there's dirt out there, tell me. I'll put a bug in the president's ear, we'll cross her off the short list, and move on to the next candidate. I don't intend to make this a public spectacle for you."

"So, you're saying that if I confirm to you right now that Martha has a skeleton in her closet, she loses the appointment?"

"Yes."

"Which means that my old friends over at Preston and Coolidge will be stuck with her as managing partner for life."

"That's about the size of it."

"That's *really* interesting." Gus knew his old buddy was serving him a lob, a chance to confess in confidence and settle an old score with Martha and the others at P&C. The truth was, however, he had never slept with Martha. But he still had an angle.

"This is a delicate matter," said Gus. "I'm not in a position to say that Martha Goldstein slept with a married man. Namely me."

"I understand."

"But I can tell you she sent a letter in her own handwriting to my wife saying that a certain married man had given himself to her."

"No kidding?"

"I swear, I read it myself just a few months ago."

"The president will have very strong feelings about that."

"I would expect nothing less from a divinity-school grad."

"Thanks for the help, Gus."

"No, thank you."

"You doing okay with the new firm?"

"Terrific."

"Business is good?"

"Couldn't be better." His secretary flashed him a message on the digital display phone. Morgan would be waiting for him. "Hate to cut you off, buddy, but I'm afraid I gotta run."

"Busy, busy. Still the same old Gus, I see."

He went to the closet to get the present he had bought for Morgan over lunch. "Yup," he said with a thin smile. "Same old Gus."

Acknowledgments

With each book my debt of gratitude only grows deeper. Again, my thanks to Carolyn Marino, Robin Stamm, and Joan Sanger for their editorial expertise, and to Artie and Richard Pine for being experts in pretty much everything else. Thanks also to the critics at large who endured the early drafts, Carlos Sires, Eleanor Rayner, Nancy Lehner, Jennifer Stearns, Terri Gavulic, and Roberta Hall.

Certain scenes could not have been done right without the help of James Hall, Yakima County Sheriff's Department, and Patricia Wachtel, Legal and Media Relations Liason, Washington Corrections Center for Women.

And, as always, nothing could have been done right without Tiffany. Thanks for making it all so easy.